Dear Reader,

I don't know about you, but I'm fascinated by those reality TV shows where people are in public dating contests to win the rich guy or gal. I always wonder about the men and women who are drawn to do that sort of thing. Naturally, as a writer, once you start wondering about people you begin to create characters who might find themselves in a certain situation. What if the "prize catch" was unwilling and had been manipulated into being a celebrity bachelor?

A theme that I explore a lot in my books is appearance versus reality. Most of us create images of ourselves that we project to the world. Sometimes these are very close to the "real" us and sometimes quite different. What if my celebrity bachelor ran away from his unwanted fame and chose a disguise that was a lot truer to who he really is? What if he ended up falling for a woman completely different to the woman he thought he wanted? And what if this one didn't fall at his feet?

Darren and Kate were a lot of fun to write about. I hope you enjoy their story.

For info on my upcoming releases, contests and to join my e-mail fan group, come visit me at www.nancywarren.net.

Happy reading,

Nancy Warren

This book is dedicated to Robin Taylor:
a voracious reader, supportive fan, thoughtful reviewer
and all-around nice person.
Thanks for everything, Robin.

NANCY WARREN

UNDERNEATH IT ALL

DID YOU PURCHASE THIS BOOK WITHOUT A COVER?
If you did, you should be aware it is **stolen property** as it was
reported 'unsold and destroyed' by a retailer.
Neither the author nor the publisher has received any payment
for this book.

First Published 2004
First Australian Paperback Edition 2004
ISBN 0 733 55557 8

UNDERNEATH IT ALL © 2004 by Nancy Warren
Philippine Copyright 2004
Australian Copyright 2004
New Zealand Copyright 2004
Except for use in any review, the reproduction or utilisation of this work in
whole or in part in any form by any electronic, mechanical or other means,
now known or hereafter invented, including xerography, photocopying and
recording, or in any information storage or retrieval system, is forbidden
without the permission of the publisher, Harlequin Mills & Boon, Locked Bag
7002, Chatswood D.C. N.S.W., Australia 2067.

All the characters in this book have no existence outside the imagination of
the author, and have no relation whatsoever to anyone bearing the same
name or names. They are not even distantly inspired by any individual
known or unknown to the author, and all the incidents are pure invention.

This book is sold subject to the condition that it shall not, by way of trade or
otherwise, be lent, resold, hired out or otherwise circulated without the prior
consent of the publisher in any form of binding or cover other than that in
which it is published and without a similar condition including this condition
being imposed on the subsequent purchaser.

All rights reserved including the right of reproduction in whole or in part in
any form. This edition is published by arrangement with Harlequin
Enterprises II B.V.

Published by
Harlequin Mills & Boon
3 Gibbes Street
CHATSWOOD NSW 2067
AUSTRALIA

HARLEQUIN MILLS & BOON TEMPTATION and the Rose Device are
trademarks used under license and registered in Australia, New Zealand,
Philippines, United States Patent & Trademark Office and in other countries.

Printed and bound in Australia by
McPherson's Printing Group

1

DARREN KAISER was literally on top of the world. He was chatting to one of the hottest-looking women—and there was stiff competition—at a rooftop cocktail reception in Manhattan.

"I'll call you," Darren Kaiser's new friend, Serena, said, her shoulder-length blond hair swinging against athletically sculpted shoulders perfectly displayed in a clingy black halter dress. She leaned forward to give Darren a kiss that promised a lot more than phone conversation.

"You do that," he said, giving her a kiss back that let her know he could keep up his end of whatever she had in mind. From the rooftop deck, all of New York City was laid out in noisy, sparkling splendor, far beneath the well-heeled feet of upwardly mobile twenty- and thirty-somethings.

He nodded to a couple of acquaintances, then decided he'd stayed long enough. He pulled out his cell phone to call his car service for a pickup, then slowed to redrape a sexy young woman's shawl over her shoulder from whence it had dropped. She rewarded him with a blindingly white smile and an air kiss.

Not being much of an air-kisser himself, he winked at her and kept going.

Darren Kaiser loved being a single man in Manhattan. There were so many beautiful, smart, sexy women. He was crazy about the new female power-babes who were totally up-front about what they wanted, when they wanted it and with whom.

Especially when they wanted it with him.

He whistled as he left Studio 450, where the benefit for fibromyalgia was still in full swing. The benefit was a thinly veiled excuse for singles to check one another out. Darren was here on a corporate ticket paid for by Kaiser Image Makers, and he still felt as if he was working, since he was expected to hand out a few business cards and schmooze.

So, he'd schmoozed a beautiful woman. Or, more accurately, she'd schmoozed him. These days, a man didn't even need to take a pen and paper with him to the dating-and-mating hunting grounds. If a woman was interested, she'd do what Serena had done—pull out her Palm Pilot and enter him into her database.

Thoughts of the sexy Serena almost made Darren contemplate blowing off work tonight. But he was anxious to get a few hours in—before his pseudo work in the morning. He'd found a glitch in the educational software program he was designing and he'd suddenly had an idea for how to fix it right about the time he sipped his first martini and chomped his first hors d'oeuvres.

He'd have bolted home right then, except that Serena had appeared with a toss of blond hair, an it's-your-lucky-night smile and her hand extended.

He'd enjoyed chatting with her and exchanging speculative eye contact, enjoyed the first few steps of a dance he never tired of: the dance of seduction. Unlike the bulk of Manhattanites, old and young, she hadn't wanted to talk exclusively about herself. Serena Ashcroft had seemed genuinely interested in him. His politics, his tastes in fashion, music, movies, clothes and women. Not being stupid, he'd described his ideal woman as someone a lot like Serena. He'd looked into her cool, patrician blue eyes and said, "My ideal woman is blonde, articulate, slim and sexy, and isn't afraid to go after what she wants." He leaned closer so he could smell her expensive scent. "Especially when what she wants is me." She'd looked so enthralled with his answers he almost expected her to take notes.

Still whistling, he jumped into the black limo that pulled up just as he hit the pavement, wondering how long it would take Serena to call.

Serena was pale, blonde and patrician—the sort of woman whose ancestors had traveled over on the *Mayflower*. His forbears had come over steerage-class—if they hadn't stowed away—on some overcrowded European steamer. Their first taste of America hadn't been Plymouth Rock, but Ellis Island.

He felt his blood quicken as he challenged himself to prove to this sexy blonde that he was worthy. He loved a challenge.

As he'd expected, Serena called, not the next day, but the day after, and suggested they meet for a drink after work. And for the next couple of months, they got together sporadically. They never seemed able to coordinate their schedules for serious dating, but he was busy, anyway.

She was in publishing, she told him, and he imagined

her editing the memoirs of famous men and women of letters. It was an occupation that would suit her.

A couple of times they were photographed by one or other of the paparazzi that hopped around the social scene like fleas. As a VP and son of the CEO of one of the hottest ad agencies in town, Darren was used to the attention, but usually tried to blow it off. Serena seemed to enjoy having her photo taken when they were together, however, so he put up and shut up, knowing that his father would get a thrill seeing the company name mentioned in print and his son's picture in the paper.

Then, one warm late spring day, Darren discovered Serena had set him up.

The day started as it usually did. Tired from working too late the night before at his computer, he grabbed a java from the corner coffee shop he frequented on Madison Avenue half a block from his office.

He gulped the dark, liquid caffeine, hoping it would jump-start his sleep-deprived brain, as he tried to concentrate on today's tasks. He was expecting focus-group results on a campaign for a new soda; he was increasing the TV buy for a sportswear manufacturer; and he was booked to have lunch with a prospective client.

The crowded elevator rose and let him out on his floor, the upper of the three levels that housed Kaiser Image Makers, which most people referred to simply as KIM.

"Congratulations, Darren," said Angie, the receptionist, before answering a ringing phone.

He sent her a wave, wondering why she was offering kudos. Had he done something good? He tried to recall what it was. Hopefully it would be enough to please the old man.

Sure enough, when he got to his office, his father was standing in front of Darren's gleaming white desk, his smile as glossy as the magazine in his hands. Was it *Advertising Age?* Positive industry buzz always excited his publicity hound of a father. But no, the magazine was a regular-size one with a young, dark-haired man on the cover. Must be some successful ad campaign that had his dad licking his chops.

"Hey, Dad. How's it going?"

"Congratulations, son. I knew you didn't turn out good-looking like your mother for nothing." And his father, president, CEO and founder of KIM closed the magazine and thrust it toward Darren.

Darren stared at the cover, and the bottom of his stomach went into free fall. "What the..." His words felt sucked dry as though a vacuum hose had attacked his mouth, taking the breath out of his body.

The mug grinning up at him from the front cover of *Matchmaker* magazine—nationwide circulation in the millions—was his. And the headline over the top read, "Manhattan Match of the Year, Advertising Executive, Darren Kaiser."

Darren flopped onto the black Bauhaus couch as his legs gave out on him.

"What..." He tried to pull air into his lungs, but they felt flattened. He tried again. "How did they..." Finally he reached out a hand. "Let me see that."

His father chuckled as though he were Santa Claus and this was Christmas Eve. He was smoking a cigar, which his cardiologist had forbade him, and his laughter shook the seventy or so plus pounds he was supposed to shed.

"I wasn't certain they'd pick you. But I was very persuasive." His dad chuckled again, happier than Darren had seen him in months.

"Pick me for what?" Darren asked, knowing he didn't want to hear the answer.

"Where have you been, boy? I keep telling you you've got to stay on top of popular media if you're going to make it in advertising. This Match of the Year thing is huge. It's like *People*'s Sexiest Man on Earth—which reminds me, we'll have to send them some hints to look your way now you're going to be so famous."

The thought of conducting his love life in public made him nauseous.

"Darren, your mother and I want nothing more than to see you settle down and marry a nice girl. Now that the magazine has decided you're a great catch, there'll be all kinds of publicity. You could date royalty, movie stars. Anybody!"

"No."

"I want grandchildren."

"You'll have to wait."

"You don't have to marry any of them if you don't want to. You just play the game. You'll be famous, KIM will be famous. Clients will pour out of the woodwork."

"I am not putting my love life on display so you can make a few more million. No."

"Think of the publicity. You'll be photographed everywhere, you'll get pretty girls proposing, all of America will be part of your courtship." The old man's eyes twinkled with excitement. "Think what the reality TV show did for that tire fellow."

"They broke up." A shudder shook Darren as he imagined his love life as a reality TV show. At least the magazine thing wasn't that bad. Swiftly, his media-savvy brain assessed the damage as he tried to convince himself this Match of the Year pick wasn't a total, life-altering disaster.

All at once the most obvious objection sprang to mind. "This is a nightmare. I can't believe the media group that owns *Matchmaker* magazine would choose me without my knowledge or consent. I mean, this is an invasion of privacy right here. Where did they even get this picture?" He jabbed a finger at the photograph. "That was taken at our company's annual general meeting last year." He flipped a page angrily and saw an even worse sight. "And where the hell did they get my baby picture?" he yelled.

His father chuckled, sending out a puff of cigar smoke.

And in that moment he knew. "Dad."

He and his father rarely saw eye to eye, but he'd never wanted to deck dear old dad until now. "You gave that photo to them. Didn't you?"

"Of course I did. We wanted this to be a surprise. You weren't the only possible candidate, you know. Men all over America would kill to be in your shoes."

"Who's 'we'?"

"That pleasant young woman who's the special-assignment editor for *Matchmaker* magazine. Serena Ashcroft. There's a picture of the two of you together in the four-page spread." Darren Kaiser Sr. jabbed his cigar toward the magazine. "You can't buy that kind of publicity."

Darren flipped none too gently through the pages until he saw even more photos of him at various events, with an assortment of women, including Serena of the big blue eyes and the "Oh, let's talk about you," conniving personality.

He'd talked, and she'd either recorded their conversations or she had a damn good memory. There he was, revealed in photographs and print in all his glory. His tastes in everything from music to restaurants laid out for all the world to dine on.

My ideal woman, jumped out at him. They'd displayed this little gem of wisdom in a text box with a larger type size.

My ideal woman is a blonde. She's a professional woman who knows what she wants from life and isn't afraid to go after it. Even if that something is me. She's educated, intelligent, classy, but also very sexy.

Sweat was starting to dampen his brow and he felt like he might puke. He didn't doubt he'd spouted that nonsense, but he'd never intended it for any ears but Serena's.

A quick skim told him that there was a Web site where women could write in about themselves and why they would love to date Darren. Since the magazine pledged to do its best to fix him up with eligible women throughout the year, there would be updates about his dating habits, his preferences and his experiences with the opposite sex.

He was having trouble turning the pages and he realized even his fingertips had started to sweat.

"Darren," his assistant, Jeanie, called breathlessly from his doorway. "I'm sorry to interrupt, but I've got *The Tonight Show* people on line one and *Entertainment Tonight* holding on line two."

"Wonderful. Wonderful," said his father. "I'll let you go, then."

"Dad, what have you done?" Darren asked hoarsely.

"What our company does best, son. I've given you an image as the most eligible bachelor in America."

KATE MONAHAN'S FEET ACHED, which wasn't surprising since she'd been on them all day. She was halfway through her third twelve-hour shift at New Image, the salon where she worked, in as many days. But her younger brother, Huey, needed braces and she had her eye on a DKNY skirt and jacket that her bargain-hunter nose told her was headed for another markdown, so she tried to think about her bank balance and not her feet.

Graduation season was always a busy, and lucrative, time of year.

"So," she said to her fourth high-school senior that day, "what are we doing?"

"I want it layered, you know, like Rachel in *Friends*."

"Sure."

"But with the fluttery bangs like Cameron Diaz in *Charlie's Angels*. Not the first movie but the second one."

"Aha." She shifted feet, trying to get the ache out of her lower back. Her friend and co-worker, Ruby, breezed by and they exchanged a glance, but at least her friend didn't say anything to make her laugh. With Ruby, you could never tell.

"And the same color as Julianne Moore, only more like Julia Roberts in *Pretty Woman*."

"You're going to dye your hair for grad?"

It never failed to amaze Kate what these girls' mothers let them get away with.

"Yep. Well, like your hair. What color is that?" the teenager with perfectly attractive brown hair asked her with a squint that was assessing. "Mocha berry or copper glitz?"

Kate grabbed a fistful of the mass of curls that no styling product, blow dryer or curling iron could ever entirely tame. "It's red, and it's the color God gave me."

"Well, God gave me this boring brown and I want to look as hot as you when I graduate."

Kate sent soon-to-graduate Bethany off to be shampooed and quickly phoned the girl's mother to make sure it was okay about the color. *Anything she wants*, was the answer.

At eighteen. Imagine.

Ruby stopped her and said, "Tell that girl that Ashton Kutcher has cuter bangs. And no haircut or dye job is going to make her look like Julia Roberts."

She stifled a giggle, but Ruby was right. Still, it didn't hurt to put a little magic in a young woman's life. She'd do what she could.

Once she had Bethany settled under the dryer, she passed her a sheaf of current magazines, and the brunette, soon-to-be-redhead immediately chose a well-thumbed copy of *Matchmaker* magazine.

"If I could marry him," the girl said, pointing a freshly manicured index finger at the photo on the cover, "I'd be set for life."

Kate gazed at the man's picture. "Darren Kaiser, *Matchmaker*'s Match of the Year," she read, staring at the man deemed so eligible women would go to humiliating lengths to marry him.

Darren Kaiser had *playboy* written all over him. He had Brad Pitt blond hair, a little long and with just a hint of a curl at the ends. It looked as though each strand had been individually groomed to provide that tousled disorder. He had the sensual face of a man who likes women and usually gets whatever he wants from them. His lips tilted in a smile that was only going through the motions—there was no genuine warmth. Beautiful eyes, she thought, but cynical. He wore a suit, and even though only the shoulders were visible in the picture, she was certain the clothes on his back cost more than her mother spent to feed her family for a year.

Yes, she thought, he was good-looking in a smooth, slick sort of way, but she didn't see a real man in the photo. More like a perfect image of one.

"He's a hottie," sighed her client.

"He looks altogether too full of himself. And those rich men—" Kate shook her head "—what would they want with the likes of us? We'd end up picking up their socks and propping up their egos. Bethany, take my advice and find yourself a decent man who cares about you. Leave the boy millionaires to marry girl millionaires."

She glanced at the photo of Brian she'd taped to her station. He was so different from the glossy fellow with the perfect smile. Things had been a bit weird lately between her and her boyfriend, but she thought it was because they were both so busy right now. Brian would never be a magazine cover's idea of the ideal bachelor, but he was a down-to-earth man with a steady job in banking who shared her basic values.

He was ambitious, too, which was good. Having grown up with a widowed mother and four brothers and sisters, lack of money was all too familiar. Kate appreciated an ambitious man with a steady job. Besides, with all his training and knowledge, Brian was investing her money for her so she could achieve her dreams more quickly.

She glanced at the about-to-graduate teen glued to the story of a fantasy man and shook her head. No glossy hunk on a magazine cover was going to drop into their lives and provide the happily-ever-after.

2

"I QUIT!" Darren yelled, almost as red-faced as his father. "I can't take this anymore. Women are waiting outside my co-op when I leave in the morning. Women are hanging around outside the office with signs written in lipstick reading, "Choose me!"

"You're exag—"

"I've been propositioned, stalked, proposed to about three thousand times. This morning the doorman handed me a woman's bra with a phone number on it."

"It's the excitement of the magazine, son." His father tried to sound sympathetic, but he was as gleeful as a boy with a new Hot Wheels set. "A few months from now they'll have forgotten all about you."

"Not if you can help it," he mumbled.

"We'll hire you a bodyguard," his dad replied.

"I don't want a bodyguard. I want my life back."

In fact, what he wanted was his life. His own life. Forget the family business, he wanted to succeed or fail on his own terms. Doing something he loved a lot more than creating artificial "need" in the marketplace for products anyone could live without.

"Our business has gone way up in the past week. Think of what this could mean."

"No. Dad. I'm thinking about me. I love programming, it's what I want to do with my life. Face it, I'm a computer geek and I don't belong in advertising. I'm quitting. As of now."

Their voices were rising, but Darren didn't care. He'd inherited his temper from his father, if nothing else.

Just as angry, his father shouted, "You walk out that door, young man, and you can't change your mind."

"I won't." Darren strode across the room but hesitated at the doorway of his dad's plush office, feeling not so much fear for his own future, but worry that his father couldn't cope without him. He was about to speak when he heard some sort of commotion down the hall in the direction of his own office.

He turned and swallowed an expletive. There was a camera crew in front of his office, and damned if they weren't filming some woman, some complete and utter stranger, leaving a dozen red roses outside his door. She was talking all the time, her face toward the camera so the flowers almost got knocked to the floor.

Oh, no. This had gone far enough. His dad had turned his life and his job into a joke. He'd become, not an ad exec, but a product to be marketed. The hell with it. Kaiser Image Makers would survive without Darren.

And Darren was going to be fine without Kaiser.

But before he left, he was going to give that woman and the cameraman a piece of his mind. Angrily, he made his way toward them. Instead of looking guilty and hurrying away, the woman with the roses, beamed a thousand-watt smile his way, then shouted into the camera, "There he is!"

She picked up the roses, yelled, "These are for you, Darren Kaiser. I love you," and headed his way, hampered by her red stilettos and body-hugging red dress.

She was followed by a skinny guy in a Knicks shirt balancing a TV camera on his shoulder.

In a moment of horror, Darren realized that unless he disappeared fast, whatever happened next would be filmed. He abandoned his plans to dress down the camera guy and the misguided woman. He abandoned any thoughts of standing his ground.

He turned on his heel and ran.

KIM employees stood in the hallway, mesmerized, until Darren yelled, "Out of my way," and set a world sprinting record racing for the stairwell.

He was out of here.

Running on instinct, he tore down several flights of stairs, spurred by the sounds of pursuit far above. Then he abruptly stopped and, as quietly as possible, opened the door to the twelfth floor and the law offices of Stoat, Remington, Bryce, where his buddy Bart worked. Since the receptionist knew him, she motioned him to go on through.

"You never saw me," he panted, and, ignoring her startled expression, kept going, racing through the hallowed halls of the law offices to seek temporary shelter with his old friend.

Stumbling into Bart's office without knocking, he shut the door, put his sunglasses on and borrowed the Yankees baseball cap Bart kept hanging on his wall along with a signed pennant. Then he slouched low in the leather club chair Bart kept for office visitors.

"Drop in anytime," Bart said as he watched Darren.

"I'm in trouble."

"Hey," Bart complained, as Darren tugged on the cap. "You can't wear that! You're a Giants fan."

"I'm in serious trouble, Bart." Darren panted, expecting any second to hear the sounds of that crazy female after him like a baying hound after a juicy fox.

"You have to help me."

As well as being a good friend, Bart was a dedicated lawyer. He immediately assumed an air of concern. "You did the right thing coming here. What's up?"

"I quit my job just now and I have to get out of town. Go far away where no one has ever heard of *Matchmaker*."

Bart's expression of concern was replaced with one of hastily suppressed amusement. "Is that what your trouble is?"

"Yes! It's that magazine."

"I don't want to make your day any worse, old buddy, but you're everywhere. It's not just the magazine. It's the Internet, chat groups, newspapers and on the TV. You, my friend, are news."

"I need to stop being news. Damn it, I never agreed to be Match of the Year. I want to sue Matchmaker Enterprises or whatever they call themselves, Bart."

"What for?"

"You're my lawyer. Aren't you supposed to advise me? How about defamation of character? Harassment? Libel?"

"Buddy, they aren't defaming you when they call you God's gift to women. It's supposed to be a compliment."

"I can't even live in peace in my own home. I'm being mobbed, stalked. Women I don't know give me their bras. Mary Jane Lancer proposed." He'd known Mary Jane for years. Their fathers belonged to the same club.

She was part of his social circle, but there never had been a hint of attraction between them until the bachelor thing.

A rich chuckle answered him. "Harassment. Hmm. There are men all over America who would kill to be in your shoes. You'd only make a fool of yourself."

There was a long pause. Darren waited while Bart drummed his fingers on his blotter, obviously deep in thought.

"But libel, now you've got something. Let's see, I just happen to have a copy of the magazine." He twirled his chair and found the hated magazine in a stack of papers and flipped it open. "Ah, here it is. They called you rich, good-looking and intelligent. Man, we can sue for millions."

Darren's heart sank. "Okay, very funny. So what do I do?"

"My best advice is to go with the flow. Have fun with it. Make your father's company a few more millions. Enjoy your fifteen minutes of fame and kiss a bunch of gorgeous women. Seriously, have you seen the babes who go for stuff like this? Be the rich boy all the girls want to marry. It'll be over in a year and long before that somebody else will be news."

"You don't get it. It's not just me being a minor celebrity and that's it. A week ago I was a happy single man living a wonderful single life. I was a New York bachelor. One of millions. Now I'm some freakin' great catch and no one but no one thinks I should remain a happy bachelor."

He paused to take a breath and a quick check outside Bart's office. So far he seemed safe.

"In the past week, I have been proposed to by girls with braces, women old enough to be my mother, loonies, the lonely, the desperate, and even women I thought were my friends, Like Mary Jane Lancer." That, he thought, had been the worst. "It's like they're trying to snap me up before any other woman gets a chance."

Bart started to chuckle. "Let me get this straight. Are you telling me you don't want women all over the country throwing themselves at you? Is that what I'm hearing?"

"Yes! I told Serena Ashcroft I won't cooperate. They should admit they made a mistake and find someone else. She told me to think about it. No hurry. I told her I won't change my mind and she laughed."

"I'm sure they would stop writing about you if you won't cooperate. They have the right to choose you as the most eligible bachelor, though. You can't stop them loving you."

"I don't know. She's a devious woman. Who knows what she's planning? I can't stand it anymore."

Bart shrugged. "Do what movie stars do when they want some privacy. Hide. Lay low somewhere until this blows over."

"Hide?"

"Sure. If you insist on trying to avoid publicity, why don't you pretend you're in the Witness Protection Program? Find a new locale, a new identity. Maybe a disguise."

Bart had enjoyed a brief spell of fame in college as an actor. Particularly memorable had been his Falstaff. Truly a method actor, he'd become roaring drunk every night for weeks before the performance in order to prepare for the role. He'd been good, too. Except that his brain had been so alcohol-saturated and his hangover so severe, that he'd forgotten half his lines on opening night.

What Bart was suggesting was that Darren run away. He'd never been the type to run from his problems, but suddenly it seemed as though he were being offered freedom, the likes of which he'd never known.

He sat up, slipping his sunglasses down his nose so he could regard his friend more clearly. "If I hide out somewhere, I can take some time to work on my own stuff." Not having to sneak in his real work at night would be incredible. He had some money saved up, and if he sold his BMW he would have some decent cash quickly, enough to live on for a while. He could probably finish his line of software programs in less than a year.

"Right. You're the next Bill Gates. I forgot."

Darren didn't bother to correct him. He had one line of educational software he was developing to help kids read. His younger brother Eric had a symbol-retrieval problem and he'd found a way to help him by writing a simple program. Eric was now studying engineering at college—and the fact that he'd made the difference in his younger bro's life gave him a lot more pride and satisfaction than his most successful day at the family firm. Now he wanted to see if he could create a more elaborate program that might help other kids like his brother.

Maybe his program wouldn't cure cancer, but helping kids overcome learning hurdles felt more useful to him than getting some KIM client's brand of deodorant up two percentage points in the marketplace.

"Okay. But you've got to help me."

Bart grinned. "You have come to the right place," he said, almost rubbing his hands with glee. "You're one of the most famous faces in America. But, my man, we're about to change all that." Bart, the sometime actor, rose majestically from behind his desk and gestured. "Follow me," he said. After a surreptitious glance up and down the hallway, they surmised the coast was clear, then took the elevator to the main floor.

After hiding in the back seat while Bart drove them out of the building's car park, Darren wondered how famous people handled celebrity. He felt hunted, and the baseball cap and dark glasses, not to mention the Brooks Brothers suit, weren't helping him blend in with the crowd.

They ended up in a drugstore, where Bart pondered a row of Miss Clairol boxes. "You want to blend in with the locals, but look completely different from how you look now. Where are you going, anyway?"

Maybe it was the throwaway comment about Bill Gates, but it made up Darren's mind. "Seattle."

"That's a long way away."

"Exactly. I don't know anyone there, I've no reason to go. Hell, I was only there once for a weekend. No one will think to look for me in Seattle."

Bart picked up a box of dark brown hair dye.

"What are we doing in the girl aisle?"

"Women's hair dye doesn't last as long as the men's stuff," Bart explained, reading the instructions on the box as though he might actually need them.

"I'm not dying my hair."

"Do you want to disappear or don't you?"

"Yes. But..." He stared at the box. "If I wear Miss Clairol, I might as well pierce my ears and wear pink golf shirts."

Bart snapped his fingers. "Now, that's a great—"

"Forget it."

"Listen, here's some advice from a once potentially great actor. If you want to become a character, you step into his shoes and into his skin."

"And into their hair dye. Yeah. I've got it."

"It's not just his hair. It's the whole persona. What we're doing is building a character. Who is this man who's going to appear in Seattle? We'll start with the hair and see where it goes."

A woman glanced at them curiously and then picked up a box with a picture of a blonde on it.

Darren stood there surrounded by women's hair-styling products, wondering how his life had ever come to this. Finally, he pulled out his wallet and handed Bart a twenty.

"You're buying it."

Two hours later, they were at Bart's place and his damp hair was now brown. Darren couldn't believe how it changed his appearance. His skin tone seemed lighter, his eyes darker.

"I've been thinking," said Bart, who was getting right into this dye-your-hair and dress-up thing. "You really are a computer geek, and you'll be living in Silicon Valley north, so why not dress like one? It's the perfect disguise."

"What, you mean wear plastic pocket protectors and plaid weenie shirts?"

"Too much?"

"Definitely."

"Okay. The trick is to keep people's attention off your face. I've got some black thick-framed glasses from when I played Willy Loman. They'd be perfect. The hair, baseball caps, those will help. But I'm thinking wild shirts like boarders wear. Loud, casual and cheap." His buddy laughed and then clapped him on the back.

"Geek chic."

Darren snorted. But he kind of liked the idea. Who'd look for him under a loud shirt? He'd never owned such a thing in his life.

"Okay," he said, knowing he couldn't pass up this opportunity to escape being marriage bait and at the same time follow his private dream. "I'll do it."

"Great." Bart dug in a drawer for a pair of kitchen shears. "Now, hold still," he said, and picked up a lump of Darren's still-damp hair.

"I paid two hundred bucks to have my hair cut two weeks ago," Darren informed his old buddy.

"Welcome to the world of—hey, what are you going to call yourself?" Bart asked as he started cutting.

KATE MONAHAN SAT AT HER kitchen table with her calculator and her monthly budget. She had the pleasant feeling of being ahead of her target.

She'd worked a lot of extra shifts to get here, but knowing her investment account with Brian's bank was growing, and that soon she'd be able to follow her lifelong dream and enroll in teacher's college, had her beaming.

She heard the broken cement at the end of the duplex's driveway rattle as a car rolled in. The landlord was too cheap to fix the drive, or much else, but the rent was reasonable so she didn't complain. She wondered if this could be the new tenant moving in upstairs, and got up to look out the window.

She hoped it would be someone as friendly as the last tenant, Annie.

Kate went to the kitchen window and peeked out. Well, it was a guy moving in. Annie had been a fun-loving flight attendant—a girl after Kate's heart—and the house had been more like a single home than a duplex. But Annie had been transferred to Denver. Somehow, Kate didn't think this guy and she were going to be watching old movies together and sharing bowls of popcorn, or borrowing shoes and jackets.

He got out of a nondescript beige compact that had seen better days and glanced around as though suspecting he might have been followed.

The guy was tall, and he stretched his back as though he'd been driving a long time, pulled off the baseball cap he wore low over his eyes and scratched his scalp. He had dark brown hair in a cut his barber ought to be ashamed of, glasses with thick black frames on a pleasant, strong-boned face. He looked sort of familiar, though she was certain they'd never met. But it was hard to concentrate on his face when he was wearing such a wild shirt. Bright red, with big white flowers. The shirt was open to expose a white T-shirt that was soft from many washings. He wore creased cargo shorts and navy flip flops.

Shoving the cap back on his head, he popped open the trunk and pulled out a computer keyboard and a cardboard box with computer-type stuff sticking out and started toward the outside stairs that led up to his suite. Suddenly, he stopped, his gaze focusing on her kitchen window.

Her hair. It must be her wretched hair that had caught his attention. She'd thought she was hiding behind her curtains, but obviously he'd caught sight of her.

Well, she'd have to introduce herself now.

She opened the kitchen door and stepped out. "Hi," she said, with a friendly smile.

He nodded. Not smiling. Not speaking. Looking at her as though she might be an assassin sent to kill him. Oh, great. He looked like a cross between a California surfer boy and a computer nerd, and was paranoid to boot.

He stepped past her and kept going toward the stairs. "I'm Kate," she said. "I live downstairs. If you need anything—"

The upstairs door opened and then slammed shut.

3

OH, NO. Kate groaned when she saw the note taped to the washing machine. *Now what?*

"Occupant of Apartment B," the note was headed.

Plunking her overflowing laundry basket on the floor, Kate ripped the scrap of paper from under the tape. The sight of the cramped black scrawl annoyed her even before she read the note.

Occupant of Apartment B,
   Please don't leave your clothes in the washer.
   Thank you.
            D. Edgar. (Occupant of Apartment A)

"Now, what's his problem?" Kate grumbled, her words echoing off the gray cement walls of the duplex's laundry room.

Glancing around, she quickly spotted the problem and uttered a cry of distress. On top of the dryer was a tangled, limp mess of pink and white. She recognized the remains of her brand new satin camisole, which had started life a sexy deep red. The camisole snaked around a pair of formerly white men's briefs that blushed furiously at the intimacy.

Just before breakfast she had carefully put the camisole on to wash in cold water and mild soap. Occupant

A had obviously thrown in his clothes without checking that the washer was empty and cranked up the hot water.

And goodbye to last month's clothing treat.

Kate held the limp, twisted fabric up to her body and sighed. The pitiful remains of the camisole hardly covered her full breasts. It had shrunk as well as run, ruined beyond hope.

Screwing the camisole into a ball, she hurled it at the trash. "Jerk," she muttered. Tossing back her hair, she poked her tongue at the ceiling, in the general direction of her brand-new upstairs neighbor.

Furiously she stuffed her laundry—bright reds, greens, blues, purples and dramatic blacks—into the washer and cranked the water setting back to cold. Should she stand here in the laundry room until her load was done? Computer brain might blow a circuit if he came in and discovered she'd started washing laundry and left it again.

Kate had known in her heart she wouldn't be lucky enough to get another Annie for a neighbor, but she had hoped for someone compatible.

What she'd got was the biggest jerk on the planet.

Now he was messing with her clothes. And, instead of apologizing, he was blaming her for his own mistake.

Picking up his blotchy pink briefs, she shook them at the ceiling.

"If you think I'm taking this, you need to learn a thing or two about Occupant of Apartment B."

She had to live here, but she didn't have to put up with a rude and unpleasant neighbor. Since he'd ignored her initial greeting, they hadn't seen each other again. She was working more hours than not, and he never seemed to leave his apartment.

The slammed door was bad enough, but no way she was putting up with snarky correspondence in the laundry room. But how should she send the man a message that she wasn't to be messed with?

A cold note like his wasn't going to have enough impact. Kate paused, still holding the formerly white discount-store briefs, and an idea hit her. She knew how to send him the message. A glance at her watch told her she had just enough time.

She was still smiling when she pushed through the doors of the department store and sailed toward Men's Wear. Shirts, ties, T-shirts, socks—her gaze roamed the aisles until she spotted what she was searching for.

As she entered the department, she felt uncomfortable. Did nice girls buy underwear for men they'd never met?

"Can I help you?" The young male voice stopped her in her tracks. Lunging toward a pile of woolen socks, Kate grabbed a pair of scratchy gray knee-highs and turned, pinning a bright smile on her face.

"No thanks, just looking around."

The clerk was a pimply faced boy, likely not out of his teens, and his eyes bulged when she faced him. His protuberant gaze reminded her how tight her fuchsia tank was—maybe she should have bought the large, after all—and how short her black skirt.

"Well." The word came out like a squeak. He flushed and tried again. "If you want anything, let me know. I'll be, like, you know...here."

Her own embarrassment evaporated in a smile.

"Thanks," she said casually, sifting through the socks until he moved away.

She slunk around, feeling as guilty as though she were planning to rob the place, until there was no sign of customer or clerk, then sidled into the racks of briefs, where she lost her embarrassment in the joy of the hunt.

Scanning the rows of possibilities, she was drawn first to a pair with a deep blue background dotted with perky sunshine-yellow happy faces.

No, she decided, too happy.

Then she almost succumbed to a pair of designer bikinis emblazoned with red-and-white hearts—one prominent red heart centered in the front—but heaven forbid the jerk should think she was coming on to him.

At last, she spotted them—a pair of deep burgundy bikinis adorned with ivory-colored Rubenesque cherubs. She chuckled aloud. They were more expensive than anything with so little fabric should be, but the delicious sense of revenge was worth it.

Disguising the briefs under a pair of the gray socks, Kate wandered surreptitiously out of Men's Wear and kept walking until she found a pay station with a female cashier.

She was running late for her shift by the time she returned home from the mall so she ran into the laundry room, propped the designer briefs on the dryer and penned a quick note:

Dear Occupant of Apartment A,

Tell your mother this is what men wear nowadays.

These are on me. (Crossed out).

These are for you.

Please look in washer before you add clothes next time.

    K. Monahan (Occupant of Apartment B)

CURIOSITY TUGGED HER to the laundry room the next morning. A basket of clean towels was her cover, in case Occupant A happened to be there. She was dying to see whether or not he had picked up his new briefs.

They were gone. In their place on top of the dryer was a gold-and-white box embossed with the name of Seattle's most expensive lingerie shop.

Intrigued, Kate walked over to it. She didn't see a note. Putting down the basket of towels, she removed the cover from the box. Inside, even the gold-and-white tissue was printed with the store's name. Very classy. She breathed in the scent of roses emitted by the rustling tissue as she dug into the box.

A gleam of palest cream-colored silk peeked out. She stroked it softly before withdrawing an exquisite camisole embroidered with dainty peach rosettes. The tag told her what she had already guessed, the garment was pure silk. Even without a price sticker, Kate knew this camisole was far more costly than the red polyester satin it was replacing. The garment tag also told her it was the correct size.

How could Occupant A have guessed? She stood for a moment, horrified to think he'd checked out her body while blowing her off.

She stood frowning, caressing the soft silk thoughtfully until she remembered the discarded camisole in the trash can. Sure enough, when she picked it up she saw the size label had been neatly snipped off. He'd thought of everything. Maybe he was trying to say he was sorry? She rubbed the soft fabric against her cheek and then noticed the note in the box.

Dear Occupant of Apartment B,
This is what women of taste have always worn.
D. Edgar (Occupant of Apartment A)

Kate felt a sharp pang of hurt. *Women of taste.* How classy that sounded.

Women of taste didn't grow up in her neighborhood fighting with four other siblings for a few minutes in the bathroom in the morning. Women of taste had hours to bathe and scent themselves before stepping into their silk lingerie. Kate was probably the only one in her family who owned lingerie—even if it was only polyester.

And what did Occupant A know about women of taste? Him with his too-bright shirts and horrendous hair? In the week since he'd moved in, the only company he'd had was that computer of his.

Who did he think he was to insult her like this?

Kate had an Irish temper to match her auburn hair and green eyes, and it blazed into life in a sudden rage. A veil of red shimmered before her gaze as she snatched up the camisole and marched up the outside stairs.

She was banging on the door of Apartment A in no time, ready to explode. She could hardly stand still;

phrases she would say to him bubbled madly in her boiling anger.

The door opened.

Before Occupant A could say a word, Kate threw the silk camisole in his face.

It snagged on his glasses, hanging like a tassel on a life-size loser lamp.

"Who the hell do you think you are?" she shouted.

His eyes widened.

"How dare you..." she spluttered, looking at the badly dressed, slouching, bespectacled figure in front of her.

"How dare you—*you* suggest *I* don't have taste. When I need tips on how to dress from a surfer boy comic strip I'll ask you!"

He opened his mouth to speak but she kept on shouting.

"I happen to work in a beauty salon. It contains the word *beauty*, which is something you don't know the first thing about. I have plenty of taste and not...not...computer chips for brains."

"I—"

Kate drew a shuddering breath and raised her hand to shake her forefinger in his face. "Furthermore, I hate your attitude and your rude behavior and your stupid notes and I think you owe me an apology because—"

"You're right." The words were quiet and calm.

She'd expected a shouting match and the quiet words caught her off guard.

Occupant A had taken off his glasses in order to unsnag the camisole, which seemed to be caught in the hinge. He looked down, fiddling.

"What?" she shrieked.

A pair of clear gray eyes met hers ruefully. "I said, 'You're right.' I was out of line." He sighed, his face wrinkling as though in pain. "I apologize."

All Kate could think was what a shame it was that such beautiful eyes were wasted on a jerk who covered them up with glasses and stared at a computer monitor all day.

With a nod that sent her dangling earrings swinging, she said, "Well, okay. No more nasty notes."

"It was a stupid thing to do," he agreed.

His voice was a surprise. Deep and rich, with an upper-crust East Coast accent.

Kate drew a long breath. She'd expected a battle. Adrenaline pumped through her body. She'd been ready to rant and rave and throw things.

His unexpected apology took the wind out of her sails, leaving her stalled on his doorstep, with no anger to push her on. Her rages were always over as suddenly as they began, and in the calm aftermath she felt a little foolish. She backed up a couple of steps and, taking another shaky breath, suddenly smiled.

"I'm sorry, too, if my temper led me to say anything I shouldn't have."

When she smiled at him she noticed his eyes widen in shock and he shoved the now-freed glasses back on his face.

She turned to leave.

"Wait."

She glanced back.

He was holding out the camisole. "Please keep this."

"Oh, I couldn't. It's much too expensive." It occurred

to her that this man didn't know you could buy inexpensive camisoles at any department store, as she had. He must think you had to go to a lingerie store, or one of those fancy catalogs. "You could return it."

He straightened from his careless slouch and looked down at her. He was surprisingly tall when he stood upright, over six feet. "I'm not going to take it back. If you accept it I'll know you're not still mad at me."

Something in his voice, a trace of command, made her reach out to take the wisp of silk from him. "All right," she agreed softly. "It's beautiful. Thanks."

Feeling even more foolish, she turned once again to leave.

"Maybe we should set up a schedule?"

Puzzled, she turned back. "A schedule?"

"For the laundry. If each of us has assigned laundry days, we won't have a problem in future."

Kate thought of Annie and her in the laundry room together chatting, throwing their jeans and socks together to make up a load. It used to be so much fun. She sighed. "Sure."

"I'll put something together on my computer. Do you have a preference?"

"I don't know anything about computers."

He grinned. She was amazed to see he *could* grin. "I meant days of the week."

"Oh, of course. Well, I work different shifts. I'm busiest on the weekends and usually not so busy midweek."

"I can work with that." He cleared his throat. "Um." He seemed to be struggling. Finally he held out his hand. "My name's Dean Edgar."

"Kate Monahan." She grasped the outstretched hand, which clasped hers with warm strength. She glanced up in surprise.

He pulled his hand back as though she'd given him an electric shock. Then suddenly he was gone, back into his apartment like a gopher diving down into its burrow.

She shook her head as she walked slowly down the steps. He was a strange one, all right. But she didn't think she'd have any more trouble with him, now she'd let him know she was not to be messed with.

He was even kind of cute when you got past the hair and the wardrobe.

And there was that odd tug of familiarity. It was surprising, but she worked on a lot of men in the salon. He probably looked like one of her clients.

Not that any of her clients would ever leave her chair with their hair like that.

4

DARREN KNEW he'd been a fool the minute he opened the door and his sexy new neighbor started yelling at him.

He'd played his part so well, careful to make sure she wouldn't want anything to do with him—and doing it with notes had been a master stroke—because then she never got close enough to see him clearly.

He had to act like a jerk. He needed to keep his distance from everyone in his new life. Especially hot, sexy redheads who lived at the same address. Why couldn't he have had the luck to land in a building where his fellow tenant was another guy, or a married couple with kids? Anyone but a woman who made him remember how much he liked women.

When he'd received her sassy note and a pair of bikinis, he'd been furious. The part of him that was still Darren Edgar Kaiser Jr. had taken over his actions. The women Darren Kaiser knew didn't treat him like this. So he'd bought the most elegant camisole he could find and penned a note as insulting as hers had been.

The minute she'd launched the camisole at him, he knew he'd gone too far.

It was the look of angry hurt in her eyes that made him apologize. In wanting to be certain she left him alone he had never intended to hurt her feelings. Make her think he was a jerk? Yes. Make her question her own attractiveness? No.

He'd glimpsed her through the window a few times. The way she strutted in her flamboyant clothing, she certainly didn't look like a woman who was insecure about her appearance.

So he'd acted out of character. The Dean Edgar character he and Bart had invented would never have apologized.

Of course, Dean Edgar would never buy a camisole like that in the first place. Then he certainly wouldn't have stood there while his gorgeous neighbor yelled at him—picturing the soft silk against Kate's creamy skin and auburn hair, imagining those pink cheeks flushed, not with anger, but with passion....

He'd been a fool, all right.

Darren stomped back to his computer, stretching his cramped shoulders. He removed the heavy glasses, rubbing absently at the indentation they left on the bridge of his nose, and sat down to get back to work. One thing he'd proved was that his disguise was working. Kate hadn't treated him as though he were America's most eligible bachelor; she'd looked as if she felt sorry for him.

The one good thing about the magazine disaster was that it had allowed him to leave the family firm and try to make his own career. This was the silver lining inside the black cloud of notoriety. All he needed to finish his software program was a few months with no distractions.

His mind wandered to the scene at his front door.

Kate.

Under the general heading *Distractions*, Kate would top the list.

She'd been so angry with him she couldn't get the words out fast enough. Even her hair got angry, bouncing and swinging as she shouted at him, shooting fire every time the sun hit it. That hair curled all the way down her back.

It was amazing.

The stuff of fantasies.

Still, he reasoned, if she worked at a beauty salon it could be fake.

Yeah. That should stop any fantasies before they started. Every time he thought about that hair, he would imagine her taking it off before she went to bed. And he would do the same thing with the camisole.

No!

He just wouldn't think about the camisole at all.

The blinking cursor on his screen reminded him that he'd been daydreaming again. He swore. He wondered how Kate would have reacted if she'd known who he really was. A reluctant grin pulled at his mouth. He had a strong feeling she wouldn't care a bit whom she was yelling at once she lost her temper.

Darren dragged his concentration back to the computer once more, but words and images danced meaninglessly on the screen.

He started typing.

He stopped.

He breathed deeply.

Kate was taking off her hair before she went to bed.

Underneath it—let's see—she'd gone prematurely gray and had her own hair in a crew cut.

And he was not thinking about the camisole at all.

"Smells fantastic," Kate's co-worker and best friend, Ruby, was over for dinner, a tradition they'd started that allowed them to visit inexpensively outside of salon hours.

She affected a bad imitation of a broad Irish brogue. "And you'll be makin' some lucky man a fine little wife."

"Thank you, Ma," Kate replied in a more authentic brogue. "But don't be marryin' me off now, till you've tasted it."

"Here's to mothers." Ruby raised her glass in a toast. "How is your mom, anyway?"

"Oh, I don't know. The same. They're all the same."

"Susan and her crew moved out yet?"

She shook her head. Susan, the eldest of the five children, was the only married one, and the only child apart from Kate who'd left home. She'd been married four years and had two children, but when her husband lost his job the four of them had moved back in with her mother and her other siblings. The small two-bedroom bungalow Kate grew up in now housed eight of her family.

"And I thought I'd lived in tenements." Ruby shook her head.

"You did live in tenements. You're just not Irish."

The aromatic scent of lasagna filled the air as she scooped hefty portions onto two plates. A basket of crusty garlic bread and a big bowl of salad lay between the two women.

"Oh, I wish I could cook," wailed Ruby as she did every time she came to Kate's for dinner. "Will you marry me?"

Kate shook her head. "I'm looking for somebody with enough money to get me out of hairdressing."

"Well, that lets me out. What about that escaped bachelor fellow I keep hearing about on the news? Maybe you could find him and pick up the reward."

Kate snorted. "I never even find my lost earrings." She vaguely recalled the blond man on the front of Bethany's magazine. "I'm not sure I'm the type rich men go for."

"I hear you. Why do people with money always look for people with more money? You'd think they'd try and spread the wealth a little. It's more democratic."

"I don't know. But I do know that you have to rely on yourself. Dreaming of rich guys doesn't help."

"What about your bank man? He looks like a guy with money to spend."

"You mean Brian."

"Yeah, right. How's it going?"

Kate sipped wine, thinking. "He's been working really hard lately and so have I, so we haven't seen each other that much."

"Looked to me last time I saw him like he was getting set to propose. You going to marry him?"

Kate broke apart a piece of garlic bread, the crust crunching in the silence. "No. I can't explain it. Sure, he's good-looking and has a great job, but I'm pretty sure he wants kids right away." Suddenly a bubble of despair welled up inside her. "Oh, Ruby, I'm just so tired of looking after people."

Across the table Ruby's chocolate eyes were soft with sympathy. "Don't I know it."

When the two had met at the beauty salon, they'd become instant friends. As they got to know each other, it was uncanny how similar their backgrounds were. Both came from big families headed by single women: Ruby's through divorce, Kate's through her father's death. She'd quit high school to help her mother out financially, and to look after the younger kids since her mom had to get a job long before her grief had healed. A big chunk of both her and Ruby's paychecks still went straight home to their mothers even though they had moved out on their own.

Both were willing to make extra sacrifices not to live at home ever again. Living alone meant working extra shifts, skipping breaks to squeeze a few more customers into each day, eating a lot of macaroni and being very creative with little clothing. They both agreed their freedom and the luxury of privacy was worth any sacrifice.

"He doesn't know about your family, does he?" Ruby asked.

"No." Brian certainly didn't know that her mother relied on Kate's financial support. And he didn't strike Kate as the kind of man who would ever take on that burden himself once they were married. If she did marry him, how could she give her mother money and keep it a secret?

"Well, don't rush into anything," was Ruby's advice, which was pretty much what Kate had already decided.

"Yes. We're sort of taking a break from each other for

a little while. It's easier than both of us having to cancel plans because we're working overtime." She rose to clear the table and paused. "Plus, I think the spark's gone. You know?"

After dinner, they moved to sit on the couch. Ruby unscrewed the cap on the bottle and topped up their glasses. "So, heard anything more from Angel-Butt?" she asked. Having heard the whole story, she'd now christened Kate's upstairs neighbor with that nickname.

Nodding mysteriously, Kate rose from the table and crossed to the adjacent bedroom, returning with the gold-and-white box. Ruby let out a low whistle when she saw the name of the shop. Her jaw dropped when she removed the camisole, touching it reverently. "Oh, honey! This is to die for. Was there a note?" she asked.

Kate recited it.

Ruby laughed. "Revenge of the Nerd?"

She told her friend about storming up to his apartment, and his apology, while Ruby continued fondling the silk camisole.

"And he can afford this?"

"I guess so. I told him to take it back, but he insisted I keep it, just to show there's no hard feelings."

"He's got good taste for a nerd." Ruby let out a lusty chuckle. "Why, you should model this for him some night." Ruby thrust out her impressive chest and held the camisole against it. "Give that angel a workout."

THE QUIET TAP OF THE computer keys was the only sound in the room, but Darren was having trouble concentrating. He was hungry, and he was spending so many hours alone he was starting to worry about his mental health.

Sure, he wanted to work on his project, and yes, if the media got hold of him there'd be hell to pay, but still he needed to get out more.

Little noises from downstairs told him his neighbor was home. And that was his biggest problem. The person in Seattle he most wanted to socialize with—the only one he knew—was the one he most needed to stay away from.

He told himself it was simply loneliness and not his frustrated libido that had him thinking about her when he ought to be working. Thinking about her reminded him of the schedule that anal-retentive Dean Edgar had promised to draft.

He worked out a very Dean Edgarish schedule, coded in blocks, that gave him exclusive use of the laundry facilities Saturday, Sunday and Wednesday, while Kate got Monday, Tuesday, Thursday and Friday. He printed the schedule and was just about to take it to her when he heard shrieks of laughter coming from the downstairs apartment. He smiled, enjoying the sound. Kate must have a friend over, and something had struck them pretty funny.

The laughter downstairs emphasized how quiet it was in his apartment. His first Saturday night in Seattle and he was sitting here all alone, not knowing a soul in the city and dressed like a goof. He shook his head.

Was he crazy?

He thought back to what he would be doing back home on a Saturday night. He almost groaned at the thought of all he'd left behind—the restaurants, the parties, the clubs, the women.

He glanced out the window. The stars were out tonight. Maybe he'd take a walk by himself and go find something to eat in a restaurant where there were other people. He gazed down at the quiet tree-lined street.

A young black woman emerged from the downstairs apartment, throwing a laughing comment over her shoulder. He heard Kate's voice calling out in reply. Great, the friend was gone, he could drop the schedule off on his way out.

He donned the glasses and an old jeans jacket Bart and he had found in a thrift store, shoved a Mariners cap on his head and let himself out of his apartment, the computer printout in his hand. He ran lightly down the stairs and knocked on Kate's door.

"Honestly, Ruby, you always forget something." Kate was laughing as she opened the door. The smile turned to an O of surprise when she saw Darren standing there. For some reason she blushed when she saw him.

"Hi," he said.

"Hi," she answered, an embarrassed smile playing around her lips. She had bright yellow rubber gloves on, drops of soapy water clinging to them. They looked like clown hands, Darren thought, incongruous against the cherry-red sleeveless cotton sweater and jeans. Instead of shoes she wore oversize gray wool socks.

He cleared his throat. "I brought you the schedule," he said, trying to hand it to her, but she backed away, laughing and flapping her wet yellow gloves.

"My hands are all wet. You'd better come in."

Stepping into her apartment, he was assailed by delicious aromas: garlic and cheese, spicy tomato sauce. He breathed in rapturously. "Smells like a little Italian restaurant I used to love on..." He stopped himself before he mentioned East Seventy-third street. What was the matter with him? His cover was slipping again. "I can't remember where it was," he finished lamely. She didn't look too surprised. She already thought he was a lame sort of guy.

"Lasagna." She smiled. "You probably haven't had time to get organized, do you want some?"

"No thanks," he said, before his stomach and every other part of him could make him say yes.

She was even prettier when she wasn't yelling. Her eyes were big and green with flecks of gold. Her lips were full and kissable. And that hair—if it was real—would be glorious to touch.

She peeled off the gloves and took the schedule from him. "Sure, this looks fine," she said, casually perusing the page, then she focused intently. "You remembered my first and last name. And spelled it right, too." She looked at him curiously. "Are you Irish?"

He chuckled, unable to resist. "No, I've got computer chips for brains, remember?" He leaned against the doorjamb, casually, watching one particular ringlet brush her temple. He could have watched it for hours. He'd never seen anyone with such sexy hair.

She put her hand to her cheek. She had the kind of fair skin that blushed easily. "Did I say that to you?"

"Among other things." The urge to indulge in a little light banter, initiate the game, was strong. It took an effort of will to prevent himself, to move away from the wall and stoop as he backed outside.

"I'll post that schedule in the laundry room, then. If there's anything else we should schedule, like lawn mowing, or garbage duty or whatever, just let me know." His glasses were sliding down his nose; he jabbed them irritably back up with a forefinger.

"Okay," she said, a hint of humor in her voice. "'Night."

"'Night."

A long walk would do him good. He needed something to get his mind off the first attractive female he'd met in Seattle.

It was a clear night. From the duplex on Queen Anne Hill, Darren sauntered downhill in the general direction of the harbor. The smell of summer was in the air, assorted flowers, freshly mown grass and dogwood trees in full bloom.

After a good long walk, he'd worked up quite an appetite. He passed through Pioneer Square, his feet stumbling over the restored cobbled roads. He liked this area of town. Many of the late nineteenth-century buildings had been preserved and the old shells housed new life: coffee bars, offices, shops and restaurants.

He saw bright light spilling out of a corner pub and his stomach grumbled audibly. He read the name lettered on the door—O'Malley's. He smiled to himself. It was a night for the Irish.

Inside, the atmosphere was warm. Wood paneling and a massive bar that must have been as old as the building gave an antique charm to the place. Taking a seat near the end of the long bar, Darren ordered a Redhook ale, brewed locally he was assured, and a burger. Remembering to slouch was no problem as he tried to perch his tall frame on a bar stool.

A couple of attractive women came in and looked around for somewhere to sit. They looked him over and then sat at the other end of the bar. He'd never thought of himself as attractive to women, because he'd just never thought about it. But being evaluated and found lacking was a new and unpleasant experience.

As the bar filled up, no one but the bartender came near him.

He was just finishing his second beer and thinking about heading home when a slight, balding man entered O'Malley's. His cheap suit hung awkwardly on his bony frame. The light seemed to bother him, or maybe it was a tic that caused him to blink rapidly as he looked around the room. Darren chuckled silently when the man chose the stool next to him. It seemed the man saw in him a kindred spirit. If he had to strike up a conversation with a stranger, he wished it had been the pretty girls.

The man ordered a cheeseburger and a light beer. He took a sip of his drink and turned to Darren. "Nice evening," he said.

"Yeah."

The man squinted and blinked a few times. "I wish I had my glasses on. Darn contact lenses are driving me crazy. I only wear them when I see clients."

"What kind of work do you do?" Darren asked politely, waiting to be bored.

"Computer programming."

His boredom disappeared. "No kidding, that's my line of work."

The two were soon deep in conversation, engaged in the instant bonding of two people who share the same passion. Finally, the man introduced himself as Harvey Shield. He said, "I'm surprised we haven't met before. Who do you work for?"

"I just moved to Seattle."

The blinking eyes surveyed him sharply for a few moments. Taking another sip of beer, he said, "You seem pretty knowledgeable, where'd you go to school?"

"MIT."

"Ever have a Professor Elliot?"

"Old Nellie? Sure. He was a mean old boot, but he sure knew operating systems."

Harvey Shield nodded. "Had a habit of failing more students than he passed." He took another drink of his beer. "How'd you do?"

Darren returned the scrutiny. The man beside him had contacts in the computer industry. Now was not the time for false modesty. He grinned. "Top of the class."

Harvey grinned back. "So was I, fifteen years ago." He sighed, as though a weight had been lifted off his shoulders. "Listen, I need another programmer on my team. We're falling behind on a big job. I don't have time for ads in the paper and interviews. How'd you like to come work for us for a while on contract?"

Darren blinked. He hadn't intended to look for a job, but one week of spending 24/7 with only a computer for company had him convinced that a longer stint of that was not healthy. Besides, with no other distractions, he thought about his downstairs neighbor far too often. A job in his industry would get him out of the house, give him other like-minded types to connect with, and the extra money meant he could stay in Seattle as long as he needed. He already had his own company set up, with a separate tax ID, so his paychecks wouldn't even have his name on them.

He was very glad he'd chosen this particular night, and this particular bar. "Harvey," he said extending his hand, "you have yourself a deal."

Darren walked back home in an entirely different mood. He had a job. Dean Edgar had snagged it all on his own without any help from the Kaiser name. And he had freedom like he'd never had in his life with months stretching ahead to work on his project. To succeed or fail on his own terms.

He was whistling softly when he got back to the duplex. He had to pass Kate's door to get to the stairway that led up to his own apartment. She had a motion-sensitive light hooked up that almost blinded him when it shone full on his glasses.

As he dropped his head in reaction, he had the unpleasant but now familiar experience of seeing his own newsprint-grainy face grinning up from the bottom of the recycling bin.

With a muttered curse he leaned down and snatched the paper up. Please, let them not have figured out he was in Seattle.

"Can't afford your own copy?" He jumped at the sound of Kate's voice from behind him. She sounded half amused, half exasperated.

Fighting the urge to hide the wretched thing behind his back, he flipped the paper inside out to hide his picture. "Sorry, I...ah...forgot to buy today's. Just wanted to check the sports scores."

The shock of seeing himself in the *Seattle-Post Intelligencer* made him unusually clumsy and suddenly a cascade of newsprint hit the ground. His grinning face mocked him from dead center. He stomped his sneaker square on his own face, and squatted, grabbing what he could and scrunching the paper back in the recycling bin.

Kate dropped down beside him. "Here's the Lifestyle section." She looked up at him and with a shake of her head thrust the section back in the bin. She picked up another bundle, and he could see she'd retrieved the fashion page. She didn't say a word, just gave a secret little smile and shoved it on top of the Lifestyle section.

"It's okay. I can manage," He sounded desperate. He *felt* desperate; pretty soon he was going to have to move his foot.

She was so close, her hair kept swinging against his shoulder, gleaming chestnut and ruby when she moved. No wonder she worked in a beauty salon, she was a walking advertisement for her profession. She even smelled like a beauty salon: like tropical fruit and exotic lotions. How was he supposed to think straight?

The best strategy he could come up with to prevent her from seeing the picture in the paper was to turn his head and kiss that smug smile off her red lips.

Desperate times call for desperate measures. He turned his head, longing quite fiercely to kiss her, even though it would earn him a well-deserved slap at the very least.

She turned her head at the same time, smiled and held up a page.

"Sports scores," she announced gaily.

Using the sports section as a shield, he quickly tossed the rest of the pages, including the one with his picture, into the blue bin.

He fled upstairs with a bunch of unwanted sports scores and an ache of longing in his chest.

He wished he'd had an excuse to kiss her.

Once he was back in his own apartment, he flipped on the television to catch some news before he went to bed. There was news, all right. Lots of news. The usual trouble in hot spots, the murders, the strikes, the endless politics. And then the soft features. After seeing his face on the front of Kate's paper, it didn't entirely surprise him to see himself on the TV, but it was still a nasty shock.

Damn it, why couldn't they leave him alone?

The story was simple. *Matchmaker* magazine's Match of the Year was missing. Yes, indeedy. His bolt from the metropolis had not gone unnoticed. He scowled at his TV. Was every news outlet in America this hard up for news or was this whole thing some cosmic joke engineered by God, or more likely Darren's father, to destroy Darren Jr.'s chance to prove himself in his own way.

Balked at finding their prey, eligible bachelor-hunting women were going public to find Darren and convince him to return home to various promised treats ranging from dirty weekends to love everlasting.

Serena Ashcroft was one damn smart operator, Darren realized with a sour smirk. He'd disappeared in order to lessen his news value. She'd turned his disappearance *into* news. Now the chase was on to find the missing Match of the Year. The magazine was posting a reward—and he couldn't help but wonder if dear old dad hadn't kicked in a few bucks—which immediately made him feel churlish.

His dad had been loudly angry, but he'd never betray his son intentionally.

Women were appealing for help in locating him. He might as well be on *America's Most Wanted*.

His only consolation was that he'd been sighted more often than Elvis recently, everywhere from Noma, Alaska, to Baton Rouge, Louisiana. People were calling in from all over who'd swear they'd seen him walking down the street, eating in a restaurant, buying gas. No one knew he was in Seattle. He was going to work in what sounded like a small, unpretentious computer firm, and when he wasn't working, he was going to be hiding out here at home working on his own projects.

So long as his sexy neighbor didn't clue in to his identity, he felt as well-hidden here as anywhere.

5

DARREN YANKED OFF his glasses and rubbed his tired eyes. He was having trouble focusing on the computer screen. He'd need real glasses soon. Two weeks at his cozy little job with SYX Systems to give him a few hours out of the house was more like a nightmare you could never wake from. Harvey hadn't been kidding when he'd said they were behind on a big job.

Darren didn't see how they were going to meet the deadline, even with all of them working eighteen-hour shifts. His dad—who'd wanted him to take over the advertising firm and not waste his time on computers—would be thrilled if he could see how much Darren was beginning to hate the sight of a computer screen.

The most frustrating part of his job at SYX was that it left him little time or energy to work on his own programs. Darren had fully intended to work eighteen-hour days once he started working for Harvey, but he'd planned on spending nine each day at work and another nine on his own project. If the pace didn't let up, he'd have to quit. Except he hated quitting a job before it was done; he liked the people he worked with; he was getting out of his apartment regularly; and, best of all, he doubted anyone here had ever heard of *Matchmaker*. Reward hunters, women with love on their minds and reporters could comb Seattle and the chances were good they'd never find him.

He heard a droning monotone that indicated Harvey was rallying the troops. As a motivator, the man was no fireball.

Harvey came weaving among the workstations toward Darren, buzzing and blinking like a fly caught in a beer bottle. He'd had to meet with the client again today, so he'd traded in his usual glasses, with lenses so thick he resembled a space creature, for the hated contact lenses.

"Tracked that bug down yet, Dean?" It had taken a while, but Darren was finally getting used to answering to Dean.

"Standing right in front of me." Darren mimicked a can of insect spray. "Pssst....pssst." He sprayed Harvey with the imaginary lethal aerosol.

His boss blinked, looking worried. "I meant the bug in the program."

The man had no sense of humor. Darren sighed and shoved his glasses back on. "Yeah, Harvey. I think I've disarmed it. I just need to test my fix."

In two weeks he'd become Harvey's right hand. They shared the obsession. Computers were more than just a job, they were magical creatures of endless fascination. If there were a Computer Addicts Anonymous, he and Harvey would be working on a twelve-step program.

"Just for today, I will not turn on my computer," Darren intoned gravely, "I will not touch it, communicate with it, worship its circuit boards." He didn't realize he was mumbling aloud until he saw Harvey's anxious face through the fog of tiredness.

"Maybe you should go home early." His boss appeared distinctly alarmed.

"But the night is young. It can't be more than nine or nine-thirty." In two weeks Darren hadn't once left before midnight.

Joseph Goode's voice joined the discussion. "It's nine-forty-five, and if you guys aren't fried, the rest of us are." Joseph was the only one of the computer programmers in the unit who was married, as he rarely let them forget. He swore his wife would think he was having an affair if he had to tell her he was working late every night.

Looking at him, Darren had a hard time believing he'd found *one* woman who could love him, never mind two. Apart from his annoying personality, there was the small problem of body odor.

Harvey looked around at the group of eight programmers, all bleary eyed and morose from lack of sleep. He blinked a few times and then nodded suddenly. "We'll knock off now. Yes. Good idea, Joseph. See you all back here first thing in the morning."

Darren drove home with the windows wide open to make sure he stayed awake. He was shivering when he finally stumbled out of the car. If he could just make it up the stairs, he could fall into bed and forget about computer bugs for a few hours.

He opened the door of his apartment and for a stunned moment thought he'd been burgled. He liked to keep his things tidy, and what he saw horrified him.

Dirty laundry was strewn all over the place—every night for two weeks, he'd stripped, discarding his clothes carelessly, and dropped into bed, so tired, he found it an effort to brush his teeth.

If he didn't watch it he'd be the next Joseph Goode. Sniffing the air gingerly, he thought he caught a whiff of old Joseph.

God, he stank.

He was wearing the same shirt he'd worn yesterday, because he'd discovered this morning he was out of clean clothes.

Laundry. That was it. He'd have to do some laundry. If he wasn't a grown man he would have cried. He was too tired to do laundry.

Stumbling like a drunk, he picked up jeans, socks that made his eyes water, shirts and underwear. He stripped, adding the discarded clothing to the pile, and threw the lot into the empty computer box that was his makeshift laundry hamper.

He shuffled into his bathrobe, shoved his feet into sneakers and slipped outside. The breeze of a summer evening reminded him forcibly that he was naked under his knee-length navy robe. He forced his tired legs to move faster into the laundry room next door to Kate's suite.

Darren stuffed the washer, added detergent and started the machine. He decided to wait for the load to finish so he could put his clothes in the dryer and a second load in the washer—no sense going upstairs, he'd just fall asleep and have nothing dry to wear tomorrow.

He'd never noticed how soothing the sound of a washing machine was. Maybe if he just rested his head on it for a minute...

"Dean...*Dean!*" Something was shaking him. Must be

Harvey. "Bugs all gone. Pssst pssst." He motioned his imaginary spray can at Harvey. "All fixed. Go away."

"Dean, wake up!"

That wasn't Harvey's voice. It was sweet, and lush and feminine. He was dreaming. That redhead downstairs was getting into his dreams again.

"Don't think about her," he ordered himself. "She's taking her hair off. Anybody can see it's fake," he mumbled. "No camisole. Not thinking about the camisole." Not thinking about the camisole made him smile. He was still smiling when the shaking finally woke him.

The woman from downstairs wasn't a dream, she was real and trying to pull him off the washing machine.

Darren raised his head slowly, attempting to focus on the woman in front of him.

One look at him and her eyes narrowed. She sniffed the air suspiciously, with her hands on her glorious, curvy hips. She'd pulled some of her curls on top of her head with a kind of elastic thing and they spilled down to join the rest, like a fountain.

"Have you been partying?" she demanded.

He shook his head to clear it. Walked over to the laundry sink and doused his face with cold water. "Mmm, sorry," he answered at last. "Not partying. Working."

"I was beginning to think you'd moved out." She still looked suspicious, but there was a hint of a smile in her big green eyes. She was wearing black pants that clung where they touched and a shiny lime-green shirt. She wore big gold hoops in her ears, more bright gold at her neck and bangles on her wrists.

"No, I got a job. The company's fallen behind on a big project, and we're working around the clock to catch up."

She seemed torn between amusement and annoyance. Then he saw the laundry basket on the floor beside her.

A horrible realization dawned. He groaned. "What day is it?"

It was definitely amusement in her eyes. "Tuesday. One of us seems to have misread the computer-generated schedule. Now, let's see..." She made a big production out of studying the schedule, running a bright red fingernail down the printout taped to the wall. "Why, I believe Tuesday is *my* day."

"I'm really sorry." He felt like a jackass. "It's just that I haven't had any time off in the last two weeks. I don't even know what day it is."

"That's okay, I hate schedules, anyway." Kate smiled widely, enjoying her triumph.

He just stood there, feeling too stupid from sleep deprivation to reply.

She looked at him for a long moment, and the amusement he read on her face changed to sympathy. "You look awfully tired, why don't you go to bed? I'll put your stuff in the dryer."

"Are you sure you don't mind?" He would argue if he wasn't so damned tired, but the idea of going to bed was too sweet to resist. And if he didn't go soon, he'd make a complete fool of himself by inviting her to go with him.

"Not at all. I usually do laundry on Tuesdays, anyway," she said sweetly.

He gave a tired chuckle. "Thanks, I owe you."

"Oh, and Dean?"

"Mmm?"

"You have nice legs, for a guy."

He'd forgotten he was wearing his robe. Exhausted or not, he left the laundry room at a trot, the bathrobe flapping with each hurried step.

Her bubbling laughter followed him all the way to his front door.

AS SHE FOLDED DEAN'S clothes, Kate shook her head over some of his choices. She couldn't make him out. He was so garish about his wardrobe and yet so reticent about normal friendliness. He was a mass of contradictions.

He must be awfully smart, though, to do all that complicated computer stuff. And when she'd caught him asleep on the washer, with his face unguarded, she'd felt an odd instinct to touch him. Nothing too drastic—she'd merely wanted to cup his cheek in her hand, or stroke his hair, the way you would with someone you felt affection for, which was a little crazy. She would never be attracted to someone like Dean. She was probably a little overtired, too.

Still, she stayed up longer than she'd intended to make sure his washing, as well as hers, was all done.

IT SEEMED ONLY MOMENTS LATER that the blaring alarm clock told Darren it was six-thirty. Stumbling out of bed, he made straight for the shower. It was only as he was toweling himself dry that he realized every piece of clothing Dean Edgar owned was in the laundry room. It took all his courage to don the bathrobe and prepare to walk past Kate's apartment to retrieve his clothes.

He never got past his front door.

On the landing outside, neatly folded, was his washing. She had even ironed his shirts. And she hadn't done it for Darren Kaiser Jr., heir to Kaiser Image Makers, or because some stupid magazine thought he was the Match of the Year, she'd done it for Dean Edgar, the geek with computer chips for brains.

He whistled as he dressed.

And was still whistling when he arrived at work in a freshly ironed shirt. As soon as the stores were open for the day, he called a florist and ordered a dozen long-stemmed pink roses to be delivered to Kate.

"Certainly, sir," the perky female voice said. "May I have your credit card number?"

His teeth ground audibly. *Fool.* Why did Kate Monahan make him act like he was Darren Kaiser again? All he needed was for some florist's clerk to tip off the media that Darren Edgar Kaiser Jr.'s credit card had just been used in Seattle. No. He was a cash only man these days.

"I'm sorry," he managed to say, coughing to disguise his voice. "I've changed my mind."

He put down the phone, resisting the urge to bang himself senseless with the receiver. Dean Edgar didn't send women long-stemmed roses by the dozen.

Okay, so what *did* Dean Edgar do? He decided on a little research. His colleagues were all versions of Dean Edgar. They would guide him.

He wandered back to his workstation. "Gord," he

called to a gangly young man with pale red hair and freckles who was probably the closest to himself in age.

"Whah?" Gord turned eyes so pale a blue they were almost colorless toward Darren.

"Gord, if a woman did you a favor and you wanted to thank her, what would you do?"

Gord scratched his neck. "You mean like give you a ride to work? Or make you dinner, something like that?"

"Yeah."

Gord looked up at the ceiling as though for inspiration. "I don't know, send her a thank-you e-mail, I guess," he finally answered.

There was no such thing as a private conversation among the programmers, they were jammed too tightly. Joseph Goode piped up. "You can't just send an e-mail, Gord. If a woman did something nice for me—I'm speaking hypothetically, of course, being a married man—I would buy her a small bottle of perfume. Ladies love perfume, you know," he announced in his smug way.

"Yeah, to drown out the smell of you, Sir Stinkalot," another programmer, Steve Adams, muttered.

Steve was less of an ubergeek than most of Harvey's hires, so Darren asked him, next.

"I'll tell you what you do, Dean." He leaned back as though contemplating the origins of the universe. "You want one of those big boxes of candy, in a red box—you know the ones? In the shape of a heart? You'll be in there before you know it." He made an obscene gesture in case Darren had any doubt what he meant by "in there."

"Great, thanks," Darren managed to say.

His other consultants suggested a fish fresh from Pike Place Market, a computer game, more candy and a gift certificate to a computer store.

Harvey suggested he stop wasting everybody's time since neither he nor anybody else had time for the ladies until the project was completed.

Darren decided he could please his two selves by going to Pike Place and buying fresh flowers. Ignoring Harvey's protests, he left the office.

He'd almost forgotten what daylight looked like.

He strolled down to the market, enjoying simply being out in the fresh air. He paused to enjoy the lively banter at the fish stall. He smelled all the smells—the seaweedy scent of the harbor, just-baked breads and pastries, coffee, spices and cheeses. His senses seemed starved after so many hours in front of a computer, and he let them all feast.

At the flower stall he hesitated over the colorful bouquets. None seemed quite right. Then a shelf of potted plants caught his eye. He remembered the jungle in Kate's living room, the pots of herbs growing on her window sill. He settled on a small hot pepper tree, then reluctantly he returned to work.

It was just after 1:00 a.m. when Darren got home. Taking the carefully wrapped plant out of the car, he stopped to scrawl a note that simply read *Thanks, Dean*, and set the plant by her front door before he dragged himself up to his apartment.

He didn't see Kate again until Sunday, when Harvey finally allowed the programmers a day off. Darren slept until early afternoon and woke feeling like his old self.

After cooking an omelet and tidying his apartment, he felt desperate for some fresh air and exercise. Digging out a pair of shorts and decent athletic shoes, he grabbed a faded blue T-shirt, made sure he had dark glasses and a ball cap pulled low over his face, and headed out for a run.

He fell into a blissful pounding rhythm, enjoying the warm air filling his lungs and the stretching and bunching of muscles that hadn't been exercised in weeks. He was streaming with sweat as he rounded the corner to his own street. He slowed to a walk, hunching his shoulders as soon as he saw Kate unloading groceries from her tiny hatchback.

She wore short shorts and a top that showed a lot of lightly tanned back. And the contours as she bent forward made his hands twitch. If anything, he was panting harder than during his run. Even after cursing himself for a pervert, he stood watching her bend over, digging around in the back of her car for something.

She was so different from any woman he'd known. Full of life in a sassy kind of way. He was used to cool elegance—they seemed to teach it in high school back where he came from. But what Kate had was a zesty flamboyance.

That and a body engineered for high performance.

He watched her pull up, a rogue apple in her hands, which she stuffed back into a grocery sack. She'd turn and spot him lusting after her body any minute.

"Need a hand?" he called out, stepping nearer.

She looked up and made a face. "No, thanks, you might drip on something."

He waved and carried on up to his place.

She raised her voice behind him. "Hey, I'm making a chicken stir-fry for dinner so I can try out my new hot peppers. Want to come down and eat with me?"

"Love to," he called back before he could stop himself. "I'll bring the wine."

The pleasure of an evening in with a beautiful sexy woman was one he hadn't enjoyed in a while. And this particular sexy, beautiful woman was someone he needed to keep his distance from if he wanted the Match of the Year's whereabouts to remain a mystery. He really shouldn't tempt himself—or fate.

He also knew he'd spend the rest of the day counting the minutes until he could see her again.

6

KATE WAS JUST putting the second earring in her ear when the knock came. They were flea-market earrings of brass and iridescent beads that livened up her short denim skirt and white sleeveless blouse.

She opened the door to her upstairs neighbor and was vaguely disappointed to see him in the thick glasses. Twice now she'd seen him without them and she liked his eyes. They were honest, direct eyes. It was harder to see them through the thick lenses.

He'd obviously dressed for the occasion in one of the more flamboyant of his shirts. And that was saying something. It was green and had some sort of jungle-vine motif and she thought those splashes of color might be representative of tropical birds. Or the designer's drug-induced hallucination. Hard to tell, really.

Kate flashed Dean a friendly smile as she took the proffered bottle inside its brown bag and put it on the kitchen counter.

"Thanks. Come on in." She led him through the living room and out to the back patio.

"This is nice," he said, glancing around at the potted geraniums and the plastic Adirondack chairs and patio table she'd picked up on sale at the end of summer last year.

"Thanks. Your place is a lot bigger than mine, but I really like the patio. Look around. I'll finish dinner."

She walked back into the kitchen and found Dean had followed her. "What can I do to help?" he asked.

The rice was done, the chicken was perfect, the colorful array of vegetables just about crisp tender. Pulling out her all-purpose pasta bowl ready to receive the meal, she noticed the wine still on the counter.

"You can open the wine."

"No problem." He pulled the bottle out of the bag, and her eyes widened at the elegant label.

"Oh—oh," she said. "On my budget I only drink screw-top wines. I don't even own a corkscrew." She bit her lip. "Do you have one upstairs?"

"Even better." With a flourish he produced from his pocket the biggest Swiss Army knife she'd ever seen. He pulled out a pair of scissors, tweezers, and a knife that looked sharp enough for brain surgery before he found the corkscrew. He must have interpreted her look correctly for he nodded. "I was a model Boy Scout."

"Why am I not surprised?"

She took everything outside and he followed with the wine and a couple of glasses, then waited until she was seated before sitting down himself. Such manners...

She had wondered if he would be a difficult guest, but he had picked up some social graces somewhere, and conversation was surprisingly easy.

"Mmm," he said, munching happily. "You would not believe how happy I am to be eating real food. I've lived off takeout and fast food for the last three weeks."

"I'm glad you like it," Kate answered. "To be honest

with you, I love to cook, and I don't have much opportunity living alone."

"No boyfriend?" he asked in surprise, then shook his head sharply. "Sorry. None of my business."

She wrinkled her nose. There was something about Dean that made it easy for her to confide in him. For one thing, he didn't know any of her friends. Well, he didn't know a soul in Seattle, so even if he blabbed all her secrets, they wouldn't get around. And he didn't seem like the type to blab, anyway. Plus, he was—she didn't know exactly. Comfortable, somehow.

"We're sort of taking a break," she said.

Her companion just nodded, leaving it up to her whether she wanted to continue the conversation.

"I'm..." She sighed and twisted the stem of her glass around in her fingers.

"What?"

"Have you ever felt you were getting pushed in a certain direction and you weren't sure you wanted to go there?"

"Oh, have I ever," he said with such feeling she blinked. "But this is about you. Go on."

"It's hard to explain. He works for a bank, has a good steady job with a great future. He's nice, good-looking, fun to be with." When she listed Brian's good qualities, she wondered why they were taking a break. Then she remembered. "But I think he wants to get serious, and I'm not sure."

"Serious. You mean move-in-together serious?"

She laughed. "I'm Irish Catholic, Dean. My mother would kill me before she'd see me live in sin. No. I mean marriage serious."

"Wow."

"Yes. I feel like it's all moving too fast. I think he wants kids right away."

Dean blinked at her. "Kids right away? Is he in some kind of a race?"

She laughed. "No. He's just...ambitious, I suppose." But hearing a stranger's take on this made her wonder. Brian did seem to be in a big hurry to get to a place most people took years to reach. Her instincts were telling her to take things easy. And the longer she and Brian were apart, the less likely it seemed they'd ever end up together. Soon, she was going to have to make a decision.

"And you don't want kids?"

"I do." She glanced up, surprised she was telling him all this, and yet feeling instinctively she could trust him. "I do. But not right away." She bit her lip, then decided to tell him the whole truth. "I help my family out. It's the only way my mom can manage. Brian doesn't know. Well, it's none of his business at the moment, of course, but my finances would be if we got married."

Dean was nodding across from her, his gray eyes serious behind the thick lenses. "And he wouldn't like you helping your mom?"

"I haven't asked him, but I don't think so." Brian was in such a hurry to build a nest egg and get established—as though he could fast-track his way to wealth and social position. Of course, he'd been delighted to help her with her own nest egg, and took almost as much pride as she did in watching it grow.

In fact, she realized she was overdue for a bank statement. She'd have to call and check on it. She sighed.

"He's probably not going to be very supportive of the idea of helping my family." She smiled. "I can't believe I'm telling you this stuff, things I haven't shared with Brian. You're a good listener."

"Your family is your family," Dean said. "Any man who loves you ought to see that you're a better person for helping them out."

"Oh, I—"

"No. I mean it. I'd think a lot less of someone who didn't help out their loved ones." He chuckled suddenly and she was startled at the change.

He really did have beautiful eyes, especially when they were smiling.

"What's so funny?" she asked, feeling herself smile back at him.

"Just that here I am spouting family values and I had a huge fight with my father. That's why I'm out here."

"Do you want to talk about it?" she asked, realizing the least she could do was lend him a sympathetic ear when he'd just done the same for her.

Dean shook his head as though he had something stuck in his ear. "No. I can't believe I said that. It's a stupid thing. My father and I..." He leaned back and appeared to be thinking deeply. "We want different things, I guess, but we are so much alike we butt heads. I needed to get out and do something all on my own."

She nodded enthusiastically. "I completely understand. I love my family, but I'd go crazy if I had to move back there."

"You'd rather put up with a rude neighbor?" he teased.

"You're not so bad once you stop slamming doors in my face."

"Ouch. Can't believe I ever did that. Thanks for giving me another chance."

The wine bottle was empty and the night advanced when Kate realized they had talked for hours over the dinner table. And oddly, they had talked mostly about her life, not his. What a difference from a date with Brian. Not that this was a date, of course, but still it was nice to know there were men who occasionally thought of something besides themselves.

The ringing phone jarred the cozy atmosphere, and Kate jumped up.

"Oh, hi, Brian," Kate said, wondering if he had telepathically read her mind. "How was the game tonight?" She didn't get a chance to say anything more than "Uh-huh" and "Good for you" for several minutes. She could hear the background noises of a busy bar.

Brian's voice was slightly thick, presumably from post game celebrating. He said, "Look, I've been thinking...well, I want to talk to you. I thought I'd come over."

Kate glanced at the clock on the stove. "But, Brian, it's after eleven. I've got the early shift tomorrow."

"Need to talk to you," he said. At least she thought that's what he said. The words were difficult to make out.

So much for taking a break from each other, she thought in irritation. So much for giving her some space and time to think things through.

There was no point explaining that to him in his current state. She tapped the counter, then said, "Why don't you call me tomorrow? We can talk then."

When she finished the call, Dean was stacking dishes in the kitchen.

Kate felt another jolt of shock. Brian would have walked away from the table and put the TV on to the stock market update until she'd finished clearing up.

Dean glanced up as she came into the kitchen rolling up her sleeves. "Everything okay?" he asked casually.

Kate shrugged as she slipped her rubber gloves on. "Sure. I think so."

They stood companionably side by side while Kate washed the dishes and Dean dried them. Mostly they were silent. The steamy water was causing her hair to frizz around her face. Irritably, she pushed at it with a rubber wrist.

Dean watched this gesture attentively, as though trying to see to her roots. Did he think she dyed it? She turned to face him. "It's natural, you know."

"What?" He appeared shocked.

"The color—nobody ever *asks* for red hair."

"It's not *red*, Ms. Beauty Consultant. Even I know that. It's auburn, or maybe chestnut. It reminds me of an antique mahogany table of my mom's that has this incredible rich color when candlelight hits it." He reached out and twirled a corkscrew around his finger, holding it under the light so it glowed. "That's what your hair looks like."

"Oh." Talkative Kate found herself at a loss for words. The dishes done, she stripped off the rubber gloves and began putting the dried dishes away.

Dean leaned against the counter fooling with the dish towel.

"Would you like coffee?" she asked politely.

He smiled at her. "I happen to know you've got the early shift. I'll take a rain check."

Still he didn't leave. Finally he said, "I know it's none of my business, but don't get pushed into anything by Brian, okay?"

Quick anger flared within Kate. "What do you take me for?" she snapped, turning toward him, hands firmly planted on her hips. "A complete idiot?"

He was smiling down at her, a warm light in his gray eyes. "No," he said softly. "I take you for a beautiful woman with a kind heart." He kissed her speechless lips quickly and left.

Kate stared at the closed door for long moments, her fingers touching her tingling lips.

7

THE CHAMPAGNE CORK popped and a ragged cheer went up.

"We did it, gentlemen, with hours to spare." Harvey Shield was smiling, the champagne bottle wobbling in his bony hand as he splashed foaming liquid into eight hastily wiped coffee mugs.

Darren took his mug with a nod of thanks. The effervescent fizz was loud in his ears as he idly watched the little bubbles race to the surface of the liquid popping and spurting to freedom.

He glanced around at the other programmers, God, what a pathetic bunch they were, all suffering from too much work and fast food and not enough sleep or fresh air. But they had beaten their deadline.

Darren, the newest member of the team, took as much pride in that fact as any of them. More in fact. He had already proved a few things to himself about making it on his own.

Now he had two weeks to devote entirely to his own project. Every one on the team had been offered an overtime bonus or time off. Darren hadn't hesitated. He was badly behind on his self-imposed work schedule for his educational software and he intended to spend the next two weeks catching up.

"If any of you would care to accompany me to Vincenzo's, the pizza's on me," Harvey announced, well into his third mug of champagne. There was stunned silence for a moment. Harvey's tightfistedness was a standing joke among the team.

"Great, I'll come!"

"Count me in!" called Gord and Steve in unison.

"It's all right for you single fellows, but I'm afraid the little woman will be expecting me," said Joseph Goode with his usual superior smirk. "In fact, I'd better be on my way. I thought I'd stop and pick up a little bottle of something on my way home."

"Scope or Listerine?" muttered Steve.

"Dean, you coming?" asked Gord.

"No, thanks. I'm heading straight home to bed."

"Got some hot babe warming it up for you?" Steve asked with a wink.

"Don't I wish," Darren replied. Unbidden, his imagination conjured a vision of Kate in his bed, her full curves accentuated by the silk camisole. He wished he'd never bought the damned thing. It was playing way too many tricks on his mind.

It was two weeks since he'd had dinner at her place. Two weeks of long working days and zombie sleep. Too many nights of Kate intruding on his thoughts and dreams. She was like the proverbial oasis in the middle of the desert.

And Darren was one thirsty guy.

It was odd, because he'd hardly seen her since that night, but he would hear snatches of sound from downstairs and wonder what she was doing; then lay restless in his bed thinking X-rated thoughts.

The awful truth was he wanted her. At first he'd assumed it was the combination of being away from his usual lifestyle and sharing the premises with a sexy redhead. Now that he'd come to know her better, he knew it was Kate he wanted—not a willing body at the same address, but Kate Monahan with her big green eyes, crazy hair, colorful wardrobe and sweet disposition.

Unfortunately, he had made himself as undesirable as possible, to keep women away.

What an arrogant ass.

How was he now supposed to get Kate interested in him without giving himself away? Could such a beautiful, sexy woman ever be interested in a geek?

Driving home along the darkening rain-slick streets, he pondered the problem. It was only in appearance that he'd changed. If Kate was so shallow she couldn't look deeper than appearances and appreciate the man he was inside, did he really want her, anyway?

His body answered that question for him. *Yes. God, yes.*

His beige clunkmobile screeched when he braked at a red light, then sat there rattling like an old steam engine. Not for the first time, Darren wished he was back in his BMW with a top-of-the-line CD player.

He wondered when it had rained, then thought it might have been raining on and off for a couple of days. Since he worked all the time, he tended to lose track of the weather. Though he had managed to notice that it rained a lot more out here in the Pacific Northwest than it did at home, even in the summer.

He supposed the rain was needed to water the honking great cedars and firs that grew out here. *Rain forest* was an apt description, he thought as the wipers made another desultory swipe across his windshield.

Fingers tapping on the plastic steering wheel, he surveyed the cars idling on either side of him. There was a silver Taurus station wagon on the left. Inside its respectable interior, a pair of grunge teens snuggled. The guy must have borrowed his parents' car, Darren thought with a smile, watching the black-clad, rainbow-haired teens necking with such enthusiasm they'd steamed up the windows.

Giving the kids some privacy, he shifted his attention to his right and saw a middle-aged couple chatting in a Lexus. They were less passionate than the teens, but still gave off the definite aura of two people who belonged together. They were dressed for an evening out, theater, maybe, or dinner.

With a sour pang, Darren realized it was Friday night. Date night, it seemed, for everyone but him. He glanced at the empty beige vinyl seat beside him, and knew who he wished was sitting in it, her hair a wild cloud, her green eyes sparkling. If Kate were here he'd try to act sophisticated like the Lexus couple, all the time wishing he was wrapped around her like the teen in the Taurus.

The light changed and he sputtered along behind the other cars. Up ahead he glimpsed a row of neon signs advertising every fast food known to man. On impulse, he decided to stop at a Chinese place and order takeout for two. After all, he was hungry, alone, and it was Friday night. He'd invite Kate up for dinner and start getting to know her better.

He had to admit his plan to hide in Seattle from all

womankind was working far too well. Instead of being mobbed by women who wanted to marry him, he was a lonely guy without a date on a Friday night.

He hadn't been able to stop thinking about Kate since she'd cooked him dinner. He must have wanted a woman more in his life, but he simply couldn't remember when. Probably he was close to fixated on this one because of the odd circumstances of him being forced into voluntary exile and her living at the same address.

Whatever the reason, he wanted her, and badly.

An impromptu shared take-out meal was a start. Maybe once she got to know him....

He stopped at a take-out place he'd discovered was pretty good and went for a standard combo for two.

The brown paper bag containing the stacked cardboard containers oozed steamy fragrance—and more— Darren discovered when he arrived home. As he removed the bag from the car, something wet and sticky dribbled down his pant leg.

"Aw, yuck," he cried, opening the bag and grabbing one of the paper napkins. He leaned over, dabbing at the wet mess on his pants, which made his glasses slide down his nose.

As he reached to push the damn things back up, the bottom of the soggy bag gave way. He lunged to catch the tumbling cardboard cartons and his feet hit something wet and slipped out from under him. With a thump he fell into a big, splashy, Seattle puddle.

He was so stunned he sat there for a moment in a scramble of egg foo young and chicken chow mein.

He hadn't even had time to straighten the glasses

hanging sideways down his face when the door of Kate's apartment opened and she emerged.

With a man.

Her eyes widened when she spotted Darren. Then she was running forward. "Are you all right?"

The fellow behind her was not so polite. He didn't even try to stow his grin.

Darren nodded in answer to Kate's question and glared up at the other guy. Kate's date was about Darren's own age, maybe a little younger. He looked like an ad for the rising young executive. In fact, Darren, who knew advertising, could almost believe this guy had copied everything from his medium-brown stylish hair to his shiny shoes from a layout Darren himself might have approved. He wore an expensive summer-weight jacket over a designer T-shirt. His khakis were pressed. He looked like a man who was projecting an image that wasn't natural to him—and Darren was in a position to know.

"Brian, this is Dean," Kate said.

"Hi," said Brian, having looked at Darren and his loser car and obviously decided he didn't rate a handshake. Fine by him.

"Hi."

Brian.

Of course. It was date night after all; he should have figured Kate would be going out. She'd said she was taking a break from the guy, but maybe the break was over. His night took another turn downhill.

He struggled to his feet, raining food and vegetation onto the driveway. A plump shrimp plopped onto his shoe.

Kate ran forward and squatted amongst the ruin of his evening, picking up the unopened cartons.

He grabbed the stuff from her with a curt thanks.

She was wearing a sexy little sundress and her hair was bundled on top of her head, but little corkscrews slipped out here and there, making him long to pull the whole mass of curls free.

What was she doing with a guy like Brian who showed off an expensive watch when he checked the time twice in as many minutes. If he had the money for a fancy time piece, couldn't Brian find a way to ease the life of the woman he supposedly loved? Kate worked too hard, and if he were the man in her life, Darren would try to make her life easier.

Kate smiled at him, a compassionate, friendly smile. "Have a nice evening," she said and turned away.

"Sure. You, too."

Brian slipped a possessive arm over her shoulder and walked her to the silver BMW at the curb. Sure, it was the least expensive model, but still, Brian's expensive tastes annoyed Darren when any fool could see Kate was pinching pennies to help her family and get the life she wanted.

Darren's hands squeezed into fists and another carton tumbled to the ground. His god-awful trousers clung in damp patches to his skin as he trudged slowly up to his apartment, alone and no longer hungry.

Not for Chinese food, anyway.

WOULD YOU LIKE another drink before dinner?" Brian asked Kate as he waggled his empty martini glass at the waitress behind the bar.

"No, thanks," she said, and took another sip of a margarita she wasn't enjoying. Lunch had been a granola bar snatched between a perm and streaks and as nice as the piano bar was, she wanted to get their table and eat dinner. A headache was starting to form behind her eyeballs. She wanted to enjoy the nice restaurant, but she was a little uneasy. Brian was avoiding eye contact and was fidgety. Did he want to break up permanently? If so, she wished he'd get it over with.

When she considered the idea, her heart didn't hurt at all. She didn't even hear the ding of a dent. When had her feelings changed?

Suddenly, she wanted to get this evening over with. When the waitress returned with his drink, Kate said, "Do you think we could move to our table, Brian? I'm starving."

"Oh, right," he said, taking a quick gulp and putting down the drink. "Whatever the lady wants."

It was better when they were sitting at a quiet table and her food was in front of her. Brian had ordered wine and was already well into it, but she was more interested in her salmon done with local berries and wild rice cakes. With her stomach no longer gnawing at her for attention, she could relax a bit.

Brian picked at his food, and she doubted he even knew what he was eating. Well, if she was going to get dumped, she'd like to get on with it, she decided.

"Brian, is there something on your mind?"

He opened his mouth. Closed it. Picked up his wineglass and drank. Then, with an air of casualness that she didn't buy at all, he said, "I'll tell you about it after dinner."

But she didn't want to wait in suspense. She put down her knife and fork and gave him an encouraging smile. It was better to get this over with, she decided. Maybe then they could continue as friends. "I'd rather hear whatever it is, now. Really. You'll feel better when it's out in the open."

"You sound as if you know what I have to tell you."

"I've got some ideas," she said. They'd been taking a break from each other, and now, out of the blue, he wanted a date? Sure, she had some ideas.

He reached over and took her hand. His felt surprisingly hot and a little clammy. He pulled back, shifted in his seat and said, "There's a bit of a problem with your account at the bank. It's no big deal, but I wanted to tell you about it myself."

"What kind of problem?" She kept her voice calm, but Brian looked very red in the face for something that was no big deal. Her head throbbed louder like a warning drum.

"It's down a little bit, that's all."

"Down a little bit?" The words came out high and sharp. "Brian, it's invested in certificates of deposit. That's the safest investment there is. How could it be down?"

"CDs are for chumps. I played the market for you a little bit. I didn't tell you because I didn't want you to worry. We'll be fine. We'll come back. It's just down a little right now. Temporarily." His tone was jaunty, but his expression was guilty.

There was no point reminding him that money was for her future. She'd been saving up for college. He knew that. And she'd always been clear that she wasn't interested in gambling or quick returns. She worked darned hard for her money and she'd take a low interest rate any day before she'd risk losing her principal.

Facts, she told herself. She needed facts before she went off the deep end.

"How much is my account down?"

"About nine Gs."

Her heart thumped uncomfortably against her ribs. "Nine thousand dollars?" That was more than a third of her money and it had taken her a long time to save it.

"Look, I'll put it back, I promise."

"Put it back?" She stared at him as the light began to dawn. She'd signed some kind of papers that he'd said would make it easier for him to reinvest her money without her having to come into the bank every time a CD came due. She hadn't paid a lot of attention to the wording because she'd trusted Brian. Now she realized how badly she'd misjudged him.

"You didn't gamble with the money in my account, did you? You took it out. You must have."

"Sure. But I did it for you, babe. For us. For our future," he said, sounding desperately eager to be believed, which made her certain he was lying.

"Where did you put my money?"

"The stock market. I had some good tips and I was already overextended in my own accounts. I borrowed some cash from you, that's all."

"No," she said, rising and placing her napkin carefully on the table beside her half-finished dinner. "You didn't. You took money that didn't belong to you. You stole my money, Brian. And you need to decide what you're going to do about it."

She turned and started walking.

"Wait! Don't go."

She ignored him, walking around a table where a couple was holding hands and gazing at each other, obviously having a more successful evening than she. Kate walked carefully toward the door feeling as though the floor had tilted beneath her feet. Funny, she was a woman of hot temper usually, but right now she felt cold. Maybe nine thousand dollars wasn't a lot of money to some people, but it was a hell of a lot to her.

Soon she'd be angry, she knew she would, but right now she was too stunned to feel much of anything, except the need to get home.

"Kate. Where are you going? Kate!"

Fortunately, there was a cab just arriving at the curb. She hurried over to it, and as a couple of laughing young women left, she got in and slammed the door. She heard Brian shout something, but again she ignored him.

By the time the cab pulled up in front of her apartment she was feeling again. And as angry as she was with Brian, she heaped a load of hot fury onto her own head. How could she have been such a fool?

She hadn't even got the door of her suite open when she heard the squeal of tires in her drive and knew without bothering to turn that Brian was there. On top of stealing, he was drinking and driving. What a prince.

"Kate, you have to listen."

She turned and regarded him levelly. "I don't have to do anything."

"I know you're mad. Go ahead. Yell at me. But this is

only a temporary setback. I'll get that money back. I promise I will."

She was amazed at how cool she was. He'd be only too pleased if she started yelling, she thought. He knew she had a quick temper. But shouting wasn't going to get her anywhere, and she found she didn't want a fight with Brian. She didn't want anything with him. "I'll be changing banks," she informed him.

"Please, please listen to me." He sounded desperate. "You can't tell anyone at the bank. I'll lose my job if you do. Please." He followed her inside, leaving the door open, and that was the final straw.

Now she yelled at him, good and loud.

"I did not invite you in. Get out!"

Ignoring her arm pointing toward the door, he came forward. His face was as pale as it had been red earlier, and his hands were shaking as he reached for her. "Please. Give me some time."

"I said, get out."

"Not until you promise—"

"I believe you were asked to leave," said a welcome voice. Her shouting must have brought him downstairs at a run, for he was panting slightly, taking in the scene at a glance.

Brian turned slowly. "Why don't you mind your own business?" he said, swaying slightly. The three martinis and all that wine must be catching up with him.

Dean held the door open with all the politeness of a maître d' at a five-star restaurant. "Do us all a favor. Go home and sleep it off."

Brian grabbed the door and pushed hard, obviously trying to shut Dean out. "I am having a conversation with the woman I'm going to marry," he said through gritted teeth as he pushed against the door that wasn't budging.

Dean's gaze lifted swiftly to hers, and she shook her head, a little pity seeping in under her anger. "No, you're not going to marry me, Brian. It's over."

The minute she voiced the words, Dean said, "Do you want me to turf him for you?"

She was about to say no when Brian let go of the door and jumped back so Dean was propelled inside. "I'll do the turfing, got it? Everything was fine until you moved in, and it was 'Dean this,' and 'Dean that.' I'm sick of hearing about you. You pencil-necked geek." And then Brian, who ought to be groveling at her feet, suddenly rushed forward and aimed a fist at her neighbor.

Dean dodged the drunken blow and moved away from the door, then glanced at her. "Go on up to my place, Kate. The door's open."

Brian took advantage of his momentary lapse in attention to run at him.

Kate clapped her hand over her mouth to stop herself screeching. She had seen her brothers in enough fights in her time to know that the best thing she could do was to keep quiet and stay out of the way. But she had no intention of running up to Dean's apartment and leaving him alone with Brian.

Her ex was an athletic guy who played a lot of sports. She couldn't bear it if Dean, whose only contact sport seemed to be tapping his fingers against his keyboard, got hurt. She crept toward the phone.

She was watching a classic scene of the intellectual nice guy standing up to the schoolyard bully.

Dean had jumped clear of Brian once again, but he'd obviously given up trying to get him out of her apartment without a fight. The two men started circling each other, like dogs fighting over a bone.

And she was the bone.

Her eyes stung. She wasn't about to watch a gentle man she liked get beaten to a pulp for trying to stand up for her.

Brian lunged again, and suddenly fists were flying, furniture crashing. She heard the sickening grunts as fists swung into soft flesh. She picked up the telephone receiver, hoping the police would get there fast.

Her hand was shaking. She punched 91—and then the receiver went flying as a body banged into her. She bit back a yelp and made a run for the kitchen. Dean needed help. If she couldn't get the cops, then she could grab her rolling pin and pitch in herself.

"Go upstairs, Kate!" Dean's voice was stronger, more commanding than she'd ever heard it.

She gaped at him, and suddenly noticed that it wasn't her neighbor who was getting the worst of the fight, but Brian. He was sweating and breathing in short, ragged gasps while Dean's breathing seemed closer to normal than when he'd first burst in on the scene.

She forgot about the rolling pin and tried to take in the amazing spectacle.

Dean didn't attack, she noticed, but waited for Brian to come at him, and then defended himself with an aggressiveness that left his assailant winded and bruised. One of Brian's eyes was rapidly closing and his nose was bleeding in a steady dribble. He seemed stunned, unable to believe the fight would not go his way.

A flicker of amusement crossed Dean's strong, reliable face, "Had enough?"

"Go to hell.".Brian's eyes narrowed. He lowered his head and charged. With swinging fists, Dean sent the grunting, panting Brian stumbling toward the door and with a mighty push sent him sprawling. She thought he'd aimed Brian toward the still-open door, but the other man's foot connected with an overturned chair and he hit the window. She heard the crack of glass. As Brian tried to right himself, his elbow connected with the crack and the window ended up with a gaping hole in it.

Dean grabbed his opponent by the front of his shirt, pulled him back from the window and this time when he shoved, Brian landed outside.

Right on his ass.

Then Dean slammed the door behind him and locked it. Still he stayed there alert until they both heard the roar of the car's engine and the sound of Brian driving away.

Now that it was over, the adrenaline and anger that had fueled her seemed to drain. Dean's feet and legs moved into her line of vision, white blurs on the green background. She watched them move purposely toward her and then hesitate a few feet away. He spoke to her quietly.

"Come upstairs. I'll make you some tea."

It was an effort to look up.

He stood with his hand held out, a comforting smile on his face.

She hesitated for a moment and then clasped his hand.

He held on to her all the way up the stairs and into his apartment, not letting go until she was seated on the couch. Then he went into the kitchenette and made tea. The opening of cupboards, the whistling of the kettle—the sounds of a person moving around a kitchen—were normal, everyday sounds that made her so glad he was here.

Soon she held a steaming mug in her hands. Not anemic herbal tea, thank God, but thick dark tea like her ma would make. When she sipped the scalding liquid, she felt the burn all the way down into her stomach. "What is in here?" she spluttered.

"Brandy. You looked like you needed it."

She sipped the doctored tea, letting the brandy burn its way down. Finally she looked up to find him regarding her with compassion. He'd taken off the awful glasses, leaving two red dents on either side of his nose. There weren't any other marks on his face, no bruises or cuts. Apart from some redness on his knuckles, he looked normal.

"Where did you learn to fight?" she had to ask.

There was a pause. She thought he wasn't going to answer her.

His voice was so low she could hardly hear the words. "Boxing team. University," he mumbled to the floor, as though he were ashamed.

If she hadn't seen him in action she never would have believed it. "I thought boxers needed good eyesight?"

He squirmed in his chair. "I don't need glasses all the time." His hair flopped forward, hiding his expression.

"Lucky for me you took boxing," she said. "You're a good neighbor." She thought for a moment of Annie, her much mourned former upstairs tenant. Maybe Dean wasn't as much fun on wash day, but she couldn't imagine Annie decking Brian quite so effectively.

His gaze caught hers. "I hope we're more than neighbors."

"Of course. We're friends." Impulsively, she crossed to him and kissed his cheek. There was a pleasant scrape of whiskers against her cheek and he smelled good. Like soap and clean male, with an overtone of the healthy sweat of a workout. Boxing, huh? "Thanks."

She placed the empty cup down on the cheap wooden coffee table that came with the place. "I'd better get back downstairs."

He rose as well, shaking his head firmly. "You can't sleep down there with a broken window. Tonight you'll sleep up here. I'll take the couch."

"But..." The protest stopped before it started. She read the concern on his face and knew that it wasn't cold he was worried about. He thought Brian might return.

Would he? Who knew. The man had gone from apologetic to belligerent awfully quickly. Maybe he'd come back to try again to convince her not to pull her money or go to the bank administration and tell her story.

No. She didn't want to face Brian again tonight, and she certainly didn't want Dean to have to act as her bouncer a second time.

"I'm going down now to put some cardboard in the window. Do you want to get your things?"

She nodded.

She was going to cry. She knew it as surely as she knew rain would follow a violent storm.

Holding the tears at bay, she followed Dean down the stairs and into her apartment. She grabbed her night things, then stopped to swallow a couple of pain killers for the headache still pounding behind her eyeballs.

She didn't cry when she went around her apartment righting furniture, clearing up the broken glass and crushed flowers, and inspecting the damage to her plants. Dean was there, cutting up a cardboard box and patching the window, and she had her pride.

She didn't cry when she washed and changed in his bathroom and emerged to find him bundling a pile of sheets out of his bedroom. He had changed the bedsheets for her, she realized, and that small courtesy was almost her undoing. She bit her lip hard.

At last she lay in bed in Dean's spartan room, in his double bed with a plaid bedcover that looked as though it had come from a discount store. A box with some extra computer equipment sat on his dresser. On his bedside table was a lamp, a box of tissues, a cheap clock radio and a pair of socks. That was it. There was nothing personal in the room. No pictures of family, no posters on the walls. It was as impersonal as a hotel room.

How bizarre.

Even more bizarre, the room felt comforting, she realized. There was something about Dean that made her relax. Not relaxed enough to forget she'd had a good chunk of her savings stolen, though, but a hell of a lot more relaxed than she'd be downstairs with nothing but a broken window and misery for company.

She waited until it was dark and quiet and she could hold her tears back no longer, then they came. She put the pillow over her head to muffle the little snuffling sobs that shook her—clenching her fingers against the pillow in impotent rage and grief.

She hadn't only lost her money, but her dreams, and her faith in a man she'd trusted.

She didn't hear the door open, she only knew Dean was in the room when she felt the tentative comforting touch on her shoulder. He pulled the pillow gently away and stroked her hair in long, soothing motions.

She sat up, pushing the tangle of hair out of her eyes. "I'm s-so s-sorry," she sobbed as he drew her gently into his arms. "I can't h-help it."

"It's okay," he said. "Shove over." So she did, and he sat on top of the bed and put an arm around her shoulders.

She resisted for a moment, but the broad shoulder was there beside her cheek, warm and comforting. She lay her head against it and sobbed her heart out while he held her and stroked her hair and murmured soothingly.

The storm of weeping passed and she lay quiet in his arms, noticing that she had thrown her arms around him and was clinging to him as though she were drowning in stormy seas and he were a lifeboat.

She relaxed her hold and felt the swelling and receding of his chest as he breathed. She again smelled the soap and clean male skin. Against her cheek his bathrobe was warm and soft. Where it gaped in a vee in the middle, she glimpsed a muscled chest sprinkled with dark hair. Out of nowhere came an insane urge to slip her hand inside the robe and touch him.

What was wrong with her?

One man had betrayed her and she was throwing

herself at her neighbor just because he was being nice to her? She really needed to get a grip.

She pulled away, sniffing. "Thanks, Dean." She felt suddenly shy as she dropped her gaze from the lean, muscular chest, only to see his lean, muscular legs emerging from the bottom of his robe. She shoved her hands over her eyes and rubbed away the wetness. "I'm better now."

He reached behind him and handed her the box of tissues she'd noted earlier.

While she blew her nose and wiped her eyes, he said, "Do you want to talk about it?"

Did she? There was something so easy about Dean. He was trustworthy and decent, and she knew she'd feel better if she unloaded some of her anger, so she told him.

"I gave Brian power of attorney over my investment account at his bank." She stopped and blew her nose again. "It was a convenience thing so I wouldn't have to go in every time I had a CD come due. It's all I bought in that account. I wanted safe investments."

She bit her lip and wondered if she could say the next part without bawling again.

The house was so silent she could hear the rustle of bedclothes as Dean shifted slightly, hear his breathing and the sounds of the duplex settling for the night.

"I'm listening."

"Brian took some of the money out."

"He did what?" Dean sounded as outraged as she felt. Whatever he'd suspected, it clearly hadn't been that.

"He said he invested it for me for a higher return, but

that's not true. He took the money right out of the account for his own use." She swallowed hard to prevent another outbreak of tears.

"What was he doing with it?"

"Playing the stock market. He was always trying to get rich quick."

"I bet he sucks at stock picking. Those kinds of guys usually do."

She laughed weakly. "I'm guessing you're right. I feel so *stupid*."

Dean hugged her hard. "Brian's the one who stole. Don't get down on yourself. This is his fault. Let's work on getting that money back."

"He's promised he'll return what he took—stole—but he's already lied and cheated. I find it hard to believe him, you know?"

Dean seemed to hesitate, then asked, "Was it a lot of money?"

"A third of my life savings. I know it could be worse, but I have plans, dreams. He knew that."

He played with her hair absently and she found the gesture amazingly soothing. "He sounds to me like a sneaky bastard. He made sure he had a legal right to invest your money in stocks. Of course, it was totally unethical since he went against your specific wishes. I think it's worth filing an official complaint against him, though."

"I know I was gullible. But he stole my dreams."

"If you let me, I'm going to help you get them back."

She leaned into him, letting herself take the comfort that she needed.

"It helps knowing I can talk to you."

"Well, that's something." He sounded a little sad, but she figured it was on her account.

"'Night, Kate."

"'Night." She looked at him. There was so little light in the room she could only barely see him, but even so she found she couldn't look away.

Dean tilted her chin up and she shivered slightly. Then he leaned forward and kissed her. Not enough for passion, but a little more than friendship.

She didn't move, couldn't, suddenly wondering where this was going. Where she wanted it to go.

Then he was gone. Before she quite realized he'd stopped kissing her, he was out the door.

8

KATE EASED OPEN the lid of the florist box as though a nest of snakes lay coiled inside. There were at least three dozen long-stemmed red roses crammed in the box. Her stomach constricted when she read the card.

Please forgive me. I love you. Brian.

She wished she'd been home to refuse the delivery, but she'd been at work blaming her puffy red eyes and pale cheeks on a head cold. Averting her gaze from the blood-red flowers, she marched to the garbage can, but when she opened the lid she couldn't bring herself to destroy the fresh blooms. It wasn't their fault Brian was pond scum.

Forgiveness? Was that what he really wanted? Or was he hoping a few flowers and even more flowery words would stop her reporting him to his bank's management.

Irresolute, she stood for a moment with the green plastic lid in one hand and the box of roses in the other. Finally she threw the note in the trash and drove the roses to a local seniors' home.

"A donation," she told a puzzled receptionist.

The woman glanced at her face and flashed a sympathetic smile. "From a funeral, dear?"

She smiled back, feeling her lips tremble. "Yes," she whispered. It was a funeral, all right. For all her foolish dreams. Why *had* she trusted Brian in the first place? She thought about that as she made her way home slowly. Maybe she'd bought into his plans to go places—he'd seemed to her the epitome of a confident man with a successful future, and she'd been flattered that he'd seen her as part of his future, and happy to be part of his success. Did she have so little confidence in herself?

But Brian had changed. It had been gradual, but when she'd told him they needed to take a break from each other, she'd heeded some voice inside her that recognized all was not right with him. When first they'd started seeing each other, he'd been a social drinker, but the last six months or so he'd been drinking more. She'd imagined it was the stress of his work, and maybe it was, but maybe it was also part of whatever had caused him to change from a fun-loving and kind, if self-involved guy, to a man who would borrow her savings without permission.

Her ex-boyfriend would have done better to have a new window delivered than a bunch of flowers, Kate thought, when she arrived back home. She'd been lucky to find a company that would replace the glass the same day she called, but the gleaming new pane had made another dent in her savings.

Now, on the outside, everything looked the same as it had yesterday. Including Kate. But inside she wondered how she could ever have been so blind.

There were stories in the newspapers and on TV all the time about people being conned out of their savings, and she'd always thanked her lucky stars she wasn't the kind to be taken in so easily. Now she wondered about her own judgment.

The phone was ringing when she entered her apartment. She knew who was calling and she hesitated, letting it ring, then decided to get the call over with. Her heart sank as she picked up the receiver. "Hello?"

"Oh, baby, I'm so sorry. Please forgive me." Brian's voice sounded hoarse.

"Have you stolen from all your clients? Or is it just me?" Her voice was cold and surprisingly steady since she simmered inside with hurt and anger. She hadn't decided yet what she was going to do next, but if there were other people involved, she'd have no choice but to report him.

"I didn't touch anyone else's account. I swear I didn't. And I didn't steal your money. I admit, I got in over my head. Damn market. But I bought those stocks in your name, for you. They just haven't come back up yet is all."

How typical, she thought, to blame the market for his troubles.

"So you played the market with my money, even though you knew I only wanted the safest investments."

He sighed heavily. "I screwed up. I didn't have the money to buy the stocks myself and I hated the thought of your money sitting there making a couple of measly percentage points when we could do a lot better."

"You didn't do better, though, did you. You lost the money."

"I thought I could put it back before you found out. I will get it back to you, I swear it."

She found vengeance hard to mete out to a man she'd once considered marrying. Somehow, she kept remembering the old days, when he'd been so different. "I'll give you one week."

"Please don't hang up." He was crying. She could hear the snuffling sound coming from the receiver. "I never meant to hurt you. Please, Kate, just give me another chance."

"Brian, go to AA. If you're still sober in six months, call me. In the meantime, all I want is my money back." No, she thought, that wasn't all she wanted. Some part of her knew he wasn't a bad man, but a weak and foolish one with a problem. "I'm serious. I think you need some help. If you keep going down this path you'll lose your career and all your plans for the future. Now, please don't call me again."

"Wait, Kate, I'm sorry. Please can't we—"

"If you're really sorry, you'll take my advice. You have a drinking problem. Do something about it."

She clicked the phone down. And grabbed the receiver again immediately, punching buttons rapidly. "Ruby! Can you come over tonight?"

It was her best friend's day off, so Kate hadn't been able to get her levelheaded take on the whole situation. Which, right now, was what she needed.

"Sorry, honey. I got me a hot date."

"Oh..." She tried not to sound as though she would collapse on the floor in hysterics if her friend didn't come over, even though that's how she felt. "Good for you. Have fun."

"Hey, everything okay?"

Kate put on a false cheeriness. "Yeah, sure. See you tomorrow. You can tell me all about your date then."

Hanging up, she listened to the silence. She glanced around the small apartment and knew she didn't want to be alone. She didn't want to go out and face noisy crowds, either. She just wanted a friend. Ruby was busy, and there wasn't anyone else she could talk to about this...

Dean was her friend.

The thought struck home, and she realized with a shock that it was true. After last night, they'd moved beyond neighbors. The nerdy computer guy upstairs had been there when she needed him and she knew instinctively she could trust him.

From what she'd seen, living in the same building, he didn't have much of a social life. Maybe he'd be interested in a movie? She ran to the new window and glanced out, but his car wasn't in the driveway.

She dropped the curtain back in place, fighting yet another urge to cry. It looked like she was spending the evening alone.

She padded into the kitchen and yanked open the fridge door. Yogurt, vegetables, fruit. Blah. There was a time for health food, and there was a time for junk food and wine. Tonight was made for junk food.

Trouble was, she didn't have any.

A quick survey of her cupboards revealed half a bottle of cooking sherry. She pulled the cork, sniffed and jerked her nose away. Okay, she didn't have any wine, either.

With a sigh, she slopped some yogurt into a bowl and

wandered back into the living room, where she collapsed onto the couch.

If she couldn't have junk food and wine, the next best thing would be an old black-and-white tearjerker. She turned on the TV and started flicking channels. Nature shows, sports, sitcom reruns—her spirits sank lower. She finally settled on a documentary about the disappearing rain forest. She figured it would be as depressing as any tearjerker, and at least it was educational.

The ringing doorbell made her jump, torn between dread that it was Brian and hope that Ruby had changed her mind.

A sigh of relief burst from her lips when she saw the familiar face, the glasses made huge by the distorting lens of the peephole.

She opened the door and smiled.

Dean held out a big pizza box and a bottle in a paper bag. "Could I interest you in dinner for two?" he said.

Her smile widened. "I've never been so happy to see anybody. Come on in."

The night didn't seem so lonely, or her situation so desperate, all of a sudden.

Dean was such an easy person to be around, Kate thought, as she munched the fully loaded pizza and sipped red wine. She'd expected to feel a twinge of embarrassment when she saw him again, after the way she'd cried all over him last night. But he acted so much like he always did, kind of sweet and shy, that her heart warmed to him, and the embarrassment never materialized.

"He played the market with my money."

The pizza box was empty, the wine bottle nearly so—

and Kate had a pretty good idea she'd had more than her fair share of the latter—before she brought up the subject they'd both been avoiding.

Dean didn't say a word, just nodded.

Kate looked down at the last of the red wine in the bottom of her glass, at the tiny crimson waves rolling across the surface.

"He called today and told me he'd played my money because he didn't have enough of his own that wasn't tied up. He says he'll pay it back."

"What do you think?"

"I think he's changed. I may not be the world's best judge of character, but I swear the man I met two years ago wouldn't have done something like this." She shrugged. "Or maybe I simply didn't know him. I feel so stupid. I know it's partly my fault for trusting him so blindly."

Dean was standing over her in a second. She'd never seen anyone move so fast. "Would you stop that? How the hell is it your fault? Kate, all kinds of people give their brokers power over their accounts. I do it myself. You don't expect them to play stupid games and gamble with your savings."

Dean had a broker? Somehow it was hard to imagine.

Kate laughed shakily. "Thanks. I think maybe I could have handled things differently. He didn't start out like this. When we first knew each other he was sweet. But in the last couple of months he's been different...."

"Different how?"

"It's like he was living a lie. He pretended he was one person, the banker I trusted, but all the time he was someone completely different. He was using me, using my money without telling me. It was nothing but lies. That's the worst betrayal of all."

Dean made a choking sound.

"Are you all right?"

His face was all red, and he started to cough. "Wine went down the wrong way," he gasped.

She ran into the kitchen for a glass of water, which he gulped down. "Sorry. Go on about Brian."

Too restless to resume her seat, she moved to stare at the oatmeal curtains covering the new window. She thought about Brian's grandiose plans, his loud behavior with his friends, and how often she'd seen him drink too much.

Telling him to go to AA had come out of nowhere, but Kate began to think maybe it was the drinking that had caused the change.

"You know, I don't want to talk about him anymore," she suddenly said. "He's taken up enough of my time and attention. So—" she stretched her arms above her head "—I'm free. Free of a man who didn't deserve me, free of the burden of too much money," she smiled wryly. "Free to start over."

"Free to find another man," he reminded her softly.

She wrinkled her nose. "I think I'm done with men for a while."

"Don't judge us all by one creep who didn't deserve a minute of your time. You should start over."

Kate looked back at him. He sat slumped, with his back against the sofa, knees drawn up, contemplating his sneakers.

"You're a fine one to talk. The upstairs suite hasn't exactly been rocking with passion since you moved in."

He opened his mouth, then closed it with a snap. Looking down, he twiddled with his shoelaces again, his face slowly flushing deep red.

"Oh, I'm sorry, Dean. I... Talk about out of line..."

He rose to his feet, giving her a smile that was slightly off center. "That's okay. I...I am interested in someone. I just can't have the girl I want, that's all."

"I—"

He shut the empty pizza box. "It's late. I'd better be going."

"Thanks for coming tonight. It's good to know I've got a friend in the building."

"All you have to do is call." He smiled as he opened the door.

"I hope you get your girl, Dean. You deserve her," she said to his retreating back. He gave no sign of having heard her as he shut the door softly behind him.

Kate sat down and drained the rest of her glass. Dean Edgar suffering from unrequited love? It was hard to believe. She had pictured him as having a lifelong love affair with his computer, a kind of absentminded professor who barely noticed the opposite sex. It was sad to think of him pining away for a woman who probably couldn't see past the nerd. He was such a nice guy once you got to know him.

He'd been so good to her, she wished she could help him in some way.

Suddenly she sat up straight as an idea struck, so blindingly brilliant it made her gasp.

Of course! She knew exactly what she could do to help him get his woman.

Kate smiled, a wicked, mischievous smile. She was in

the beauty business, wasn't she? She knew all about helping people look their best.

What Dean Edgar needed was a makeover!

And what better way to get her mind off her own troubles than to help her new friend out of his.

The first thing she wanted to do was throw away those glasses. Surely they made contact lenses even for people with really poor vision. Uncovering Dean's fabulous gray eyes would be a big step in the right direction.

Then there was the hair. Kate's scissor fingers itched when she was around him. She wanted to give him a shorter cut, brushed away from his face instead of hanging all over it, obscuring his features.

She couldn't figure out why any hair-care professional, even the neighborhood barber, would give him a cut like that. Perhaps his ears stuck out. She'd have to check.

Closing her eyes, she tried to picture him without glasses and with a good haircut. He had even, regular features and a really charming smile. Yes, he'd be quite passable, even attractive.

Then there were the clothes. Mentally she began undressing him. Getting rid of the horrible shirts, the baggy shorts that he seemed to buy in too big a size, and the endless supply of baseball caps. And maybe if she got him feeling more confident about his appearance, he'd stand straighter.

She thought about how he'd felt when she cried on his shoulder. She'd had her arms wrapped around him, one of his around her while he'd stroked her hair.

She sank back against the sofa cushions and remembered the sensation of warmth and safety she felt—and the strength. She felt warm again at the thought of it.

The hands that had stroked her hair, offered her a tissue, were well shaped, manly hands. All that jogging—and boxing—had given him a nice muscular build. An image of his naked chest snuck into her mind.

Yes, she thought, enthusiasm building—he could be a really nice makeover. Some decent clothes, a good haircut and contact lenses, and his mystery woman would be falling at his feet.

Kate jumped up and dashed into the bedroom, straight to the bookcase where she kept her trade journals and albums. She piled a few on her nightstand, and when she was ready for bed, she curled up, flipping pages, looking for a new hairstyle for Dean. She fell asleep on top of a Brad Pitt look-alike who wore his hair cropped close above his ears and brushed back.

She smiled in her dreams.

"WHAT DO YOU MEAN YOU won't do it?" Kate wailed.

Darren watched the excited flush fade from her pink cheeks.

On his living room table an oversize professional album of men's hairstyles lay open to a picture of a *GQ*-model kind of guy in crisp short hair. "This would look great on you," Kate insisted.

Darren knew exactly how it would look. He'd worn his hair that way a year ago, before he grew it long enough to annoy his father, but not long enough to annoy himself.

Kate had an eye for her business, that was for sure. And too sharp an eye for Darren's taste.

"Thanks, but I don't think so," he said, closing the album on a picture that reminded him uncomfortably that he was the second man Kate had trusted who was living a lie.

Darren was glad he still had more than a week before he was due back at SYX Systems. He was at the duplex most of the time, which allowed him to keep an eye on Kate. In his Neanderthal heart he hoped Brian would come back, so he could have the pleasure of pounding him into the ground. In the meantime he pounded computer keys and watched Kate try to regain her confidence.

Since the night of the pizza, Darren had discovered he had a firm friend. And when Kate was your friend, it wasn't a passive "Hi, how are you doing, let's get together sometime" kind of friend; it was an active "What can I do to fix your life" kind of friend.

Now here she was, leaning forward, green eyes aglow, outlining a program to improve his image so he could get the girl of his dreams.

He almost laughed aloud.

He lived inside a disguise while the woman he wanted was eager to redo his image for a woman she didn't realize was herself. What a mess. And Kate was nothing if not tenacious.

"Look, I'm not suggesting dyeing your hair or anything."

If she only knew. He religiously touched up his roots every couple of weeks so his sharp-eyed beauty consultant neighbor would think it was God who'd given him hair the color of mud.

"I only want to update your image a bit. Maybe this

woman you like would notice you if you looked more...um...contemporary." She sounded tentative. Maybe she thought she might hurt his feelings. He would play that up.

"I don't want a new image, Kate," he said as petulantly as he could.

"Well, of course not. Not a new image—a more flattering look. Trust me, I know what women like. I am a beauty consultant, remember?"

"No."

"Just let me cut your hair," she wheedled.

He hiked the glasses back up and leaned forward, speaking earnestly the truth he felt in his heart. "Kate, however much I care about this woman, I want her to appreciate me for who I am. A fancy haircut, expensive clothes, the right car, the right toys won't make me a better person."

"Haven't you ever heard of hiding your light under a bushel?" she shot back.

"I'm not pretending to be anything except a simple guy who works on computers." He looked directly into Kate's eyes. "A woman who can't look beyond the surface to the man I am inside is of no interest to me," he said with finality. "So, no. I won't have a makeover."

He held her gaze and her green eyes widened slightly. Her breath caught. He felt for the first time as though she was looking at him as a man instead of a nerd. He opened his mouth, but what he would have said remained a mystery.

Kate drained the last of the coffee from her mug and stood. She looked thoughtful, even a little hurt, but not beaten. "I'll leave the book. Have another look at it, maybe you'll change your mind."

As she straightened, Darren enjoyed the way the sleeveless sweater she was wearing moved with her. It complemented her rosy cheeks and the tangled glory of her hair.

"I like your sweater," he said.

She tossed her hair back, giving him her sassiest look. "Hmm. You should like me for what's underneath."

He watched in amusement as the fiery color swept her cheeks. She must have realized how he could interpret her words.

"I meant what's inside..." Her blush intensified as she waded in deeper. "*Me* I mean, not the sweater."

"I like both," he said quietly.

Her eyes flew to his and a gasp escaped her lips.

She was an intriguing combination of sexy and shy. It amazed him that the same woman who wore those wild outfits could blush like a schoolgirl and get her tongue all tied up.

"My mother made it," she said, and rushed on. "She loves knitting and crocheting."

"I'd like to meet your family some day. They sound fascinating," he said.

"You would?" She looked frankly stunned. "Go to the zoo and look in the monkey cage, then you've seen my family. Too many primates shrieking and plucking at one another in too small a space. That's my family." She smiled. "They're a good lot, though."

"My family would never shriek. Or pluck. My mother has a rule against raised voices." He shrugged. That other life seemed so far away. It was amazing he could be so content with so relatively little. A crummy apartment, no social life, looks that had gone from metrosexual to asexual. But he had work that he loved, and an intriguing project—trying to score with the woman downstairs with none of his usual arsenal.

"I guess your life back east seems a long way away," she said.

He swung on her, sharp suspicion jabbing at him. "How did you know I'm from back east?"

She blinked at him, clearly confused by his reaction. "Aren't you? Your accent is. You sound like one of the Kennedys, so I assumed..."

"Right. Sorry." He rubbed a hand over his face. What was he thinking? If Kate had figured out he was the guy in the magazine, she'd ask him about it. She wouldn't sneak around behind his back, she wasn't that kind of woman. "I think I'm working too hard."

"Oh, right. You're working. I shouldn't have interrupted. I'll let you get back to it."

He turned to face her, realizing how churlish he'd sounded. "I wasn't trying to get rid of you. Stay."

She'd paused in the doorway, so gloriously tempting he wanted to shout *Yes. Make me over. Uncover the Match of the Year. Win the prize.*

But he knew he wouldn't.

Not because he gave a damn about the bachelor thing anymore, but because he had meant what he said.

He wanted Kate to fall for him, not because they belonged to the same clubs and had the same friends, or because her father's bank wanted his father's business, or because some magazine said he was desirable. He wanted Kate to want Dean Edgar. A man who was just as real, if not more so, than Darren Edgar Kaiser Jr.

"I've got some things to do before going to work, anyway." She glanced at the computer humming quietly on the Formica kitchen table. "How's your educational software coming?"

He made a face. "Not that well. I'm working on a game to teach kids about computers in a fun way. But everything I've come up with is too technical. No fun."

"Well, I never finished high school. So if you want to experiment on me..." She snapped her mouth closed. Darren got the feeling she wished she hadn't spoken.

"I'd appreciate your comments a lot," he said. In fact, he'd appreciate anything that allowed them to spend more time together.

She walked over to the computer and ran one pointed nail over the keyboard. "Educational software...I always wanted to be a teacher." Her voice was low and he was certain he heard pain.

He shouldn't ask. It was none of his business, but he couldn't stop himself. "Why aren't you?"

"My dad died." Her hair bounced up and down once as she shrugged her shoulders. She stared at that keyboard as if she was trying to memorize it. "No money for college."

"And no money to finish high school?" he asked gently.

She shook her head. "I was lucky to get a job in a beauty salon. Turns out I have a flair for hair." She turned to him with a big smile, and said with false heartiness, "Everybody knows beauty and brains don't go together. So I stick to beauty."

He moved toward her without thought and took her stubborn chin in his hand. He yanked his glasses off to gaze down into her troubled eyes without a chunk of glass between them. "Sometimes they do. You, for instance, are both beautiful and smart."

For a moment she gazed back, a tiny frown between her brows, as though trying to find a reason to believe him. Her skin was soft and warm, and where his baby finger rested on her neck he felt her pulse leap.

Then she pulled away with a little snort of laughter. "This from a guy who takes Bart Simpson as his fashion icon."

"You can be anything you want to be, Kate," he said, ignoring her attempt to throw his compliment back at him.

She was staring at him, the frown still lodged between her brows.

"What?"

"Sometimes you remind me of someone. I just can't get it. Is there a movie star you look like?"

Damn. His picture had been in the Seattle paper yesterday. Someone claimed to have seen him in San Francisco, and the reward for finding him had gone up. He pushed the glasses back on and hunched his shoulders. "I don't have much time for the movies."

She shook her head. "I can't place it, but you remind me of someone. Anyway, let me know if you change your mind about the haircut. I can do you in thirty minutes and it won't cost you a penny." With a wink she was gone.

Darren sat back down to the computer, but he couldn't seem to concentrate. *I can do you in thirty minutes,* she'd said. Oh no, she couldn't. The things he had in mind would take all night.

He'd never wanted anything so badly as he wanted Kate Monahan. There'd been a moment there when he could have sworn she looked at him the way a woman looks at a man. But then it had passed, and she'd gone back to acting like his helpful friend and neighbor.

What would she have done if he'd come right out and told her she was the one he was interested in? Not some mystery babe, but Kate Monahan?

With a scowl, he thumped the screen back to life. If he had to guess, he imagined she'd have got all flustered and backed away as fast as her shapely legs could carry her.

Friends was better than nothing.

All Kate's talk about her family got him to thinking about his family and their quiet, well-regulated house. A pang of guilt struck. He'd been so busy with work he hadn't written home for weeks.

He was so paranoid about being tracked that he'd stopped phoning his folks. He sent letters—minus any address or phone number—to Bart, who forwarded them to his family.

Because of his paranoia about detection, he didn't even have an e-mail address. He'd never been so out of touch with his world. The strange thing was how little he missed what was back home, and how much he'd come to care for what was here in Seattle, literally right under his nose.

His family wrote to him through Bart, who mailed their letters to an obscure post office box where Darren picked up his mail. It was as slow and antiquated as the pony express, but so far, he remained undetected.

He found paper and pen and sat down again at the kitchen table, pushing the keyboard out of the way. It was halting at first, but soon words were racing across the page as he told his family about his job and his few friends.

He tried to tell them something about Kate, but he didn't know how to describe her without giving them the wrong impression. He shouldn't care what his family made of his downstairs neighbor, but he did. He cared very much. In the end he gave up and said nothing about Kate.

He was whistling, a weight of guilt eased as he pounded down the stairs for his run, with letter in hand. The whistle died in his throat, cut off by a huge grin when he saw Kate struggling with a white latticework trellis. She was balancing a nail between perfectly polished long fingernails and holding the hammer delicately while trying to steady the wobbling trellis between a knee and the palm of the hand holding the nail. Presumably she planned to attach the trellis to the side of the duplex. He lounged against the rail at the bottom of the stairs, enjoying himself.

She held the nail as though it were a delicate teacup, pinched between thumb and forefinger, with the last three fingers raised, presumably to protect her manicure. The ends of her fingers shone bright pink, painted to match the cotton-candy pink top she wore over white capris.

She tapped the hammer like a true girl, and that slight movement caused the trellis to start rocking. She jiggled on one foot, trying to hold it steady with her raised knee, looking like a drunk flamingo.

"Need a hand?" he called, trying to keep the laughter out of his voice.

She jumped at the sound of his voice. "I'm not the handy type."

She held out the hammer. He took it and said kindly, "This is really a job for two people. You hold it steady."

He'd meant to save her pride, and then realized his mistake. When she stood so close to him he could smell her hair and count the nutmeg-over-cream sprinkle of freckles, he was lost.

As though she felt the intensity of his gaze, she turned to glance at him, and if he'd thought he was lost before, he was now tossed out of the universe.

Her eyes sparkled with laughter and fun, but as his gaze caught hers and held on, the laughter died and a moment of keen awareness took its place. A bird was chirping somewhere close by, and the scent of summer roses was heavy in the air. He wanted to touch her, kiss her, tell her everything. With a hiccuppy breath, she turned her head.

"The roses are so gorgeous. They're climbing roses, you know. Well, you wouldn't, because they're lying there in a heap, so this year I decided to rescue them." She was babbling he realized, and felt hope. That attraction between them had been fierce. It had also been mutual.

Maybe it was time to show her that he wanted more than friendship.

"My hero," she gushed.

He laughed back at her, noticing that she didn't pull

her hand back when their fingers inadvertently touched. Darren felt a small electric storm; she seemed to be obsessed by the side of his head.

"What? Do I have something in my hair?"

"Do your ears stick out?" she finally asked.

"I don't think so." He pulled a hunk of hair up at the side so she could see his ear.

She looked closely and then nodded as though she'd won an argument. "Just as I thought. Nice ears." She must have read the puzzlement in his face, for she laughed. "Sorry, professional curiosity." Then she looked closer. "Do you dye your hair?"

Damn it. He'd been so good about touching up his roots. He must have missed a spot.

"Yes. I went prematurely gray." He tried to smile. "We all have our vanity."

He jammed the hair back in place. He didn't want to hear anything more about haircuts, or ears, or dye or makeovers.

He knelt down and reached for one of the rose stems. The bottom was thick and gnarly with age, but lots of twiny, narrower green stems snaked around, laden with fragrant butter-colored blossoms.

The stems were also covered in thorns. He dropped his painful burden and was about to suggest they find some leather gloves when she obviously discovered the thorns herself.

"Ouch," she said, shaking her index finger as though a bee had stung it. Then held it out. "Do you see blood?"

On the pretext of bad eyesight, he took her hand in his. Her skin was so soft and smooth. He lifted her finger and could see the tiny red dot of the puncture. No blood. Lifting his gaze to hers, he pressed his lips against her fingertip. "All better," he said, unable to keep the huskiness from his tone.

She blinked, and for a second they crouched there among the roses, the sun beating down, her hand in his, the pulse in her wrist jumping beneath his fingertips. She licked her lips, and with his eyes still on hers, he leaned slowly forward.

A little gasp stopped him, and she pulled her hand away, then said, "I need gardening gloves. Twine. Shears."

"Want me to help?" he said, wondering what would have happened if she'd let him kiss her. Wondering if he was the biggest fool in the world.

"No. Thanks." She rose. "No. I'm fine." She glanced down at herself. "I should change, anyway. I'm not dressed for gardening. I saw the trellis and had to have it and then was too impulsive to wait five minutes before putting it up." She was babbling again. He decided he liked the fact that she was starting to feel flustered around him. He wasn't Dean the hopeless geek in need of a makeover. He was Darren, the hopeless geek who wanted this woman in his bed. Sure he could dress better and ditch the glasses and go back to his normal hair. But he was still the same man inside. And that's who he wanted Kate to fall for.

"Okay," he said. "I was on my way for a run anyway." And he retrieved his letter and set off, pounding the pavement with a light heart. He had a job, a life, time to work on his own programs and the challenge of wooing a beautiful woman. If the beautiful woman looked on him as anything but the "before picture" in one of those magazine makeovers, his life would be perfect.

Warm air heated his lungs as he increased his pace. He jogged past a woman in a pale blue cardigan and a plaid skirt walking a tiny black poodle. The poodle told him off sharply, in yappy little barks. The owner looked reprovingly at Darren's bare legs pumping down the quiet street. "Nice day!" he greeted the woman as he bounced past. "Humph" and "Yap, yap, yap" were the only replies.

It was a beautiful day, and not a grumpy dog or its grumpy owner were going to stop him enjoying it.

A makeover.

He grinned. One day soon he was going to let Kate make him over, but not until she saw him for the man he was inside. He wanted his princess to kiss the frog before she knew there was a prince inside.

It was a challenge. The biggest of his life.

9

SMILING AND CHATTING, blow-drying, snipping, perming and streaking, Kate made it through another long day.

They were just closing up, when the owner of the New Image salon took Ruby and Kate aside in the little storage room and slipped envelopes into their hands. "I wanted to give you a little something for your birthday, Kate, but really these are bonuses, so you get one, too, Ruby.

"We've done so well this year and you two worked harder than anyone. This is a little thank-you for all your hard work." Mona Warkentin wasn't a woman who gave compliments, or gifts, readily, so Ruby and Kate were in shock as they hugged the woman with the upswept platinum-blond hair and stumbled out of the salon.

They piled in Ruby's car and hastily tore into the envelopes. "How much did you get?" Ruby asked.

"Five hundred bucks." Kate felt the shock of the windfall. "You?"

"Same." Ruby looked as surprised as Kate.

"Wow, what are you going to do with yours?"

"The same as you." Ruby's white teeth gleamed. "Girl, we are going shopping."

And so Kate found herself at the mall, being bullied

and pushed from clothing store to clothing store and shoved into one eye-popping dress after another.

"But, Ruby, I can't afford this," she argued staring at the reflection of herself in a skimpy little skirt and tube top that left little to the imagination. She ought to put the five hundred bucks into her decimated savings account, but right now, her dreams seemed hopelessly unattainable.

"Oh, I wish I had your body," Ruby groaned. "This morning you couldn't afford it. Now you have five hundred bucks and you're not doing anything sensible with it. You are buying yourself a birthday present. A great dress." She glared at Kate before adding, "And shoes!"

"Oh, all right," Kate said, unable to resist the temptation. Maybe a shopping spree would cheer her. "This one's a little flashy, let's see what else there is." Combing through the rack, she pulled out a simple green cocktail dress. She knew the minute she tried it on it was the one. A greeny-blue silk sheath with a gauzy shawl that floated a little when she hooked it over her elbows. The dress fit where it touched, flattering her figure and allowing her hair to rule uncontested. "You like it?" she asked Ruby.

A low wolf whistle was the answer.

She turned around once more in the mirror, admiring the way the light caught the silk and turned it iridescent.

She felt good in this dress. A line echoed through her head: *Women of taste*. That's what Dean had written in the note with the silk camisole: it was what women of taste wore. So was this dress. Wearing it made Kate feel classy. It was the kind of dress you could wear with real silk lingerie and not feel like the wrong part of the outfit was on the outside.

Of course, this one classy little dress cost as much as she spent on clothing in a whole year, but Ruby was right. The money was an unexpected bonus, and what had all her scrimping and saving got her, anyway?

She took a deep breath. "I'll take it," she said to the salesclerk.

While Kate was trying not to think about how much money she was forking over, Ruby disappeared into the change room with a kaleidoscope of dresses.

Soon her friend emerged in gold lamé that appeared to be a size too small for her. "Wow!" said Kate.

An earthy chuckle escaped her friend as she strutted in front of the triple mirror. "I look like a chocolate toffee, just waiting for some lucky man to unwrap the gold foil."

"Or an expensive hooker on a Saturday night."

Another lusty chuckle. "Just see if I don't get Marvin to notice me in this." Marvin was the latest object of Ruby's lust. He worked in a music store across the street from the salon.

"And just how are you going to get Marvin to see you in this dress? Wear it to work?"

"Uh-uh. I'm asking him to a concert. One of those bands he's always yammering about is coming to town." Her smile was wide and white. "He won't be able to resist."

Kate had a superstition about clothes. An outfit was lucky or unlucky. And the trouble was you could never tell which until you'd worn the thing. Usually, if you wore a dress and had a great time, you would ever after have a great time every time you wore that particular outfit.

Unfortunately, the reverse was also true. No matter how great the clothing, if you had a lousy time the first time you wore it, it was jinxed. If she paid a lot of money for something and really wanted it to be a lucky dress, she tried to manipulate fate by wearing it to something she was almost guaranteed would be fun.

Like her birthday party. All her friends along with their significant others would be there. She lifted her chin. If she didn't have Brian hanging on her arm, she was bound to have a good time.

She and Ruby grabbed a quick dinner in the food court, giggling like kids over their new purchases. Especially over how Marvin was going to react when he saw Ruby in the gold lamé.

A pang of loneliness struck, and Kate wondered if she should wait and wear her new dress another time. Or manipulate fate a little herself.

"Who are you bringing to your birthday party?" Ruby asked her, following her thoughts nicely.

"I'm thinking of asking my upstairs neighbor."

Ruby blinked. "You haven't been getting up close and personal with those cherubs, have you?"

"No! He's a friend, that's all." But for some reason, she couldn't meet Ruby's gaze. Instead she looked for something else to snag her friend's attention and quickly found it in a coat shop off the food court. "Oh, that leather jacket would look great on you...look, the red one."

KATE WOKE TO FIND HER birthday had fallen on a gloriously sunny day. She stretched and got out of bed and padded into the kitchen to start coffee. Then she showered while it was brewing. Halfway through her first cup, the phone rang.

She lifted the receiver and held it a few inches from her ear, having an idea what was coming. "Happy birthday to you, happy birthday to you!" bellowed in her ear as her tuneless but enthusiastic younger siblings and her mother sang their greeting.

"Thanks for deafening me on my twenty-fourth birthday," she said, laughing, after they'd finished.

"Twenty-four. I can't believe you've grown so fast," sighed her mother, immediately making her feel half her age.

"And what are you planning for the big day?"

"I have to work and then I've got my party tonight. We're going out to a restaurant."

"Oh, that's grand, love. And you'll come here for your birthday dinner on Sunday."

"Yes, of course. I can't wait."

"Well, I know you've got to get off to work, so happy birthday again, darling."

"Thanks, Mom. See you then."

She hung up, smiling, and then paused as she heard someone knocking on her front door. Her bathrobe wasn't elegant, but at eight in the morning, she didn't imagine that mattered. She peeked through the door, wondering who it could be, and saw Dean.

"Hi," she said, surprised. She'd thought about inviting him tonight, but had decided against it on the grounds she didn't know him all that well and didn't want him thinking she was after a present when he found out it was her birthday.

"Happy birthday," he said, and she blinked in surprise.

"How did you know?"

"When I picked up the mail I noticed a few of those special-occasion envelopes. I held one up to the light and it was a birthday card."

She crossed her arms over her chest. "It wouldn't have said which day unless you steamed open the envelope."

"You have no faith in my powers of detection," he said with mock hurt. Then he dropped the pose and grinned down at her. "I called the salon and asked your friend Ruby."

"You called Ruby?"

"Sure, why not?"

"You don't even know her."

"I'd like to. I've heard you talk about her, and she sounds like a nice woman." He held out a brown paper bag. "Can I come in?"

"Is that what I think it is?"

"Fresh bagels. Still warm."

She opened the door wide.

"Pour coffee," she said over her shoulder as she strode for her bedroom. "I'll get dressed."

"Don't bother on my account," he said, and she laughed. Already it was turning out to be a good day.

When she got back he'd poured coffee, there were fresh bagels on a plate and cream cheese. He'd even picked up fresh-squeezed orange juice.

"You are turning out to be the best neighbor a girl ever had," she said, saluting him with her orange juice.

He didn't say anything to that, merely presented her with a small rectangular box wrapped in floral birthday paper and with a tiny mauve bow on top. With it was a card.

"Oh, Dean," she said.

He smiled and motioned her to open it.

When he'd caught sight of the topaz-and-gold earrings in the jeweler's window, Darren had immediately pictured them against her hair. He must be some kind of masochist. Now he had a new prop for his night fantasies. Kate, smiling at him, topaz glinting from her ears, swinging against that fabulous hair, while her breasts begged to be released from the silk camisole.

Her cry of delight brought him back to the present. Carefully, she removed the earrings from the small box, swinging them to and fro to watch them catch the light.

"Oh, Dean, they're beautiful." In her impetuous way, she yanked out the gold hoops she was wearing and put the new earrings on. Then she dashed to the mirror hanging in the hallway to admire them.

"I can't believe it. I love them." She danced over to him, tossing her head to make the little jewels swing. She leaned down to give him a kiss. He could tell she was aiming for his cheek, but as he moved left, she moved right, so instead of a kiss on the cheek, they ended up mouth to mouth.

He heard her sharp intake of breath when she found herself kissing him. Her lips were soft and full and tremulous against his, and the touch of that tender flesh against his mouth sparked right through him. Something lit up deep in his vitals and he had to fight all his instincts not to drag her hard against him.

With a nervous giggle, she pulled away, her color heightened and her eyes searching his with a startled expression in their depths. He gazed back into her eyes. The tiny flecks of gold sparkling in the green iris made the winking topaz seem dull.

He refused to break eye contact first. Let her see all the things he couldn't tell her. She turned to busy herself with bagels and cream cheese, while they chatted about the latest book she was reading, a runner-up for the Pulitzer, which he'd read when it first came out. In the background, the news played softly. After a bit, she said, "How'd you like to pretend to be my boyfriend at my birthday party tonight?"

"I don't know if I could ever stop," he replied. His tone was bantering, but he turned his head as he spoke and caught a gleam of interest in Kate's eyes that made his heart jump. The moment stretched as awareness flickered between them.

He smiled to let her off the hook from answering and then rose. "I'd better let you get ready for work. I'll see you later."

"Yes. Sure," she answered, still staring at him with a look of complete surprise on her face.

He was almost at the door when she said, "Dean?"

"Uh-huh?"

He watched her lick her lips, still staring at him. "Did you feel something just then?" she asked in a hushed tone.

Oh, yeah. "When?"

"When I... When you..."

"When we kissed?" he said, finishing the sentence for her.

"Yes." Her color was heightened, but her tone of stunned shock cut right through him. He'd chinked her armor, and he wasn't a man not to go after what he wanted when he sensed an opening.

"I felt this," he said, walking back toward her. He put his hands on her shoulders, gave her a moment to evade and, when she didn't, lowered his mouth to hers.

This time there was no accidental brushing of lips. He kissed her with everything he had. She was sweet and special and making him lose sleep, and he let her know it, taking her mouth with gentle persuasion and making it his.

Oh, she tasted good. Like orange juice and fresh, sweet woman. Her hair was a tangle of wet curls clinging to her back, her body slim and supple as he ran his hands down her spine.

He kissed her until she swayed against him, and he felt her hands climb his chest and link behind his neck. He kissed her until they were both breathless, and he knew he had to stop soon or neither of them were going to make it to work today.

"Happy birthday, Kate," he said at last, pulling away.

Her lips were parted and her eyes glazed. He'd like to think it was all from passion, but with an inner chuckle, he suspected it was partly shock.

"I'll see you tonight," he said, and left. She still hadn't managed to articulate a word.

"Why didn't you tell me Dean called here?" Kate demanded later that morning when she ran into the back with Ruby to grab a quick coffee between clients.

"Why didn't you tell me Angel-Butt had such a sexy voice?"

"You'd better not call him Angel-Butt at dinner tonight."

Ruby turned to her, the stir stick stopping in mid-stir. "You invited him to your party?"

She blushed. It was ridiculous. One kiss. One major steamy kiss didn't mean anything. It was her birthday, she could indulge in steamy kisses with her male friends if she wanted. "Yes. He's a nice guy, and he doesn't know many people, so be nice to him."

"The word *angel* will not pass my lips," Ruby promised with an evil smirk.

"Are you bringing Marvin?"

The evil smirk intensified. "Oh, yeah."

Kate arrived home with just enough time to shower and change. As she got out of her car, Dean came out his door and jogged down the steps with a courier envelope.

"For you," he said.

"Thanks." She looked at the envelope and not at Dean. She felt ridiculously shy after their passionate embrace in her kitchen earlier.

"Have a good day at work?"

"Yes. It was great." She glanced up at him and she could have sworn he knew damn well she was feeling shy and confused. There was an extra twinkle behind his glasses that looked suspiciously like humor.

"Can you be ready in half an hour?"

"Of course."

She took her envelope into her own suite. Who would send something to her by courier? She glanced at the shipping slip and felt sickness in the pit of her stomach.

It was from Brian.

If she were smart, she'd toss the envelope in the trash unopened, or at least leave it until tomorrow to open. She sighed. If she were smart, she never would have trusted the man in the first place. Her curiosity overcoming her common sense, and not for the first time, she opened the envelope.

Inside was a birthday card. She tapped it against her hand, then slit it open. Nothing mushy, thank goodness. It was the sort of card you'd send to an acquaintance. Or a client she thought, as she read the generic greeting on the front. She opened the card and blinked. There was a check inside. For five hundred bucks. There was also a folded, typewritten note.

Dear Kate,
I'm so sorry. What I did was wrong. I'm trying to make amends. I can't give you the money back all at once, but I'm going to send you a minimum of five hundred dollars a month, and more if I can. I'm paying you the same interest you would have got on your CD.
I got into a bad place and what I did was wrong.
I hope some day you'll be able to forgive me.

There was no closing salutation, just his name scrawled in black ink. Brian.

Well, she thought cynically, if he kept his word it would take him eighteen months to pay her back. Still, it was a start. She hoped he did keep his word, for his own sake as much as hers.

She'd closed her account with Brian's bank the Monday morning after she found out what he'd done and moved her money to a rival institution where no one but no one was getting her power of attorney.

The five hundred was a hint Brian hadn't been completely amoral. That was a start.

She showered, did her hair and makeup with a pleasant sense of anticipation. She loved parties, and when they were for her, they were extra special. She tried to tell herself, as she slipped her new earrings back into her lobes, that the exciting kiss this morning, from a most surprising source, had nothing to do with the bubbles of excitement racing through her system.

But she couldn't stop the thoughts that had teased her all day. Dean didn't kiss like an amateur, or a nerd, or a geek who loved computers more than women.

He kissed like a man who'd been put on earth to please women. She bit back a smile. A man who could kiss like that left a girl wondering what else he was good at.

When she opened her underwear drawer, she paused, and then, with a delicious thrill of excitement, walked to her closet and reached for the gift box Dean had left for her in the laundry room that day. She eased open the camisole she'd never yet worn and decided the time had come to christen the silk garment.

It felt smooth as, well, silk as she slipped it over her head and found it fit perfectly. Unable to resist a peek in the mirror, she thought Dean couldn't have chosen better. The color brought out the creaminess of her skin and didn't clash with the reddish-brown of her hair.

And it was so darned elegant, she felt like a princess. One day, she thought, she'd buy herself some panties to match. In the meantime, she slipped into a pair of beige satin-and-lace ones that sort of went with the camisole—the way a street urchin went with royalty.

With a shrug, she slipped into her new dress and heels, happy at least that her expensive new outfit didn't let down the camisole, and prepared to let the evening take its course. After all, a birthday was made for surprises.

When Dean knocked on her door right on time, she was vaguely disappointed not to be more surprised. Why, since her feelings for him seemed to have undergone a change, did she suddenly expect his appearance to alter?

It hadn't.

He looked the same. His glasses still shielded his beautiful eyes, the baseball cap still hung low, and his shoulders slouched. His shirt would make a Hawaiian sit up and take notice, but it wasn't the worst of his collection, at least. And he wore a pair of nice khaki colored slacks and decent loafers, at least.

He looked her up and down, long and slow, before saying, "Wow" in a tone that made her new dress worth every penny. "You look more beautiful than I've ever seen you."

She smiled back at him. "I thought you said you don't need those glasses all the time."

"I need them for driving," he said. Then shot her a

look that had her stomach jumping. "I'll take them off later. I promise."

Later? She didn't know about later. She'd just have to see where the evening went.

As they drove to the restaurant, she filled Dean in on everyone who'd be there and he listened intently.

"I think I've got it." He fished into his pocket when they pulled into the parking lot and out came a small black box with buttons.

"Let me just program all this into my pocket notebook. I can run into the bathroom and study if I get lost."

"You're kidding, right?" She jerked her head in the direction of the little box. "You can store notes there?"

He glanced at her in surprise. "Haven't you ever used a PDA?"

"No. Beauty consulting is pretty low tech. You don't have to go to MIT to mix perm solutions." She hated it when people made her feel stupid. For such a smart guy, Dean didn't usually make her feel ignorant.

"I don't know. You might find this useful. You could program all your appointments, track your billing, even write little memos about your clients. Like what products they like, or personal stuff about them that would make them think you really listen to them when they yack away in the chair."

"I *do* listen to them. I don't need a machine so I can pretend I'm interested in my customers. So keep your fancy gadget and your magic machine that takes the place of being a real human being. I'm perfectly happy being an ignorant hairdresser."

Even though she wouldn't look at him, she felt his eyes staring at her.

When his hand reached out to touch hers she wanted to smack it away. "I'm sorry," he said softly. "I didn't mean that the way it came out." Even through her annoyance, she felt the warmth from his hand.

She huffed out a breath. "I'm sorry. I get a little touchy sometimes when I think people are talking down to me."

"That's quite a big chip you have on your shoulder about your lack of education, isn't it?"

He was her friend and friends were honest. "Yes. I guess."

"There are different kinds of education, Kate. You've got a kind of wisdom about you that all the schooling in the world won't teach."

The way he said it she could tell he meant the words and was flattered to her toes. "Thanks."

When they arrived at the restaurant, there was a long table already set up and about half of her friends were seated. A chair with a bright pink Happy Birthday balloon floating on its own helium high, paired with a matching silver Princess balloon, made her chuckle. Her friends weren't into understatement.

She received kisses and hugs, felt herself pushed into the Happy Birthday chair and only then did she turn to introduce her date for the evening. It took her a second to find him. Dean had wedged himself into the last seat, which put him in a dimly lit corner.

As she watched, he glanced around the crowded restaurant as though searching for people he knew. Then, to her immense relief, he pulled off his baseball cap.

She introduced him around the table and he shook hands with everyone. Ruby, dragging Marvin with her, sat beside him, for which Kate was grateful. No one could be shy when Ruby was around.

10

"Did you have a good time?" Kate asked Dean as he drove them home.

"Yeah. I did. Your friends are a lot like you."

"Is that a good thing?"

He laughed. "It's a very good thing." He glanced over at her. "Fun, upbeat, the kind of people who make the best of things."

"Oh. That's nice."

They pulled into the driveway and the jumpiness in her stomach returned. All night they'd been exchanging glances across the table, and when they'd gone back to Ruby's place for cake he'd suddenly lost the shyness he'd exhibited at the restaurant and become easy and talkative. But the glances that were for her alone had continued.

Now that they were home, she didn't know what to do. They got out of his car and she turned to him, wishing she could see behind the lenses to his eyes, wishing he'd do something, say something. But, she realized, he was leaving the next move to her.

"Would you like to come in for coffee?" she asked, as though they hadn't already had plenty of caffeine at Ruby's place.

He put his hands on her shoulders and she experienced the same startled thrill she had this morning. "If I come in for coffee," he said, "it will be breakfast coffee."

Her breath kind of whooshed in and out fast. "I know," she said, finally committing herself.

"Kate..." The harsh urgency of the voice spoke to her woman's heart. He pulled her to him and kissed her, hard and possessively.

"Yes. Oh, yes," she murmured back. She wrapped her arms around him and leaned in, kissing him back. After a while, her eyelids drifted open and she was staring into luminous gray eyes that told her of need and love and urgency.

She felt as though he had always been waiting for her and she for him. Her eyes locked on his, answering all the questions that had plagued her throughout the day with the inevitable answer.

"Yes," she whispered again, throwing herself back into kissing him, wanting him so badly she was rubbing her body against his in a very unsubtle invitation.

"We'd better get inside," he said on a shaky laugh, "before we break some kind of law."

She laughed back, amazed that now she'd made her decision, the butterflies had fled her stomach. No nerves now, only anticipation.

There was something about the way this man kissed her that made her think tonight would be special. Taking his hand, she led him inside her apartment and straight to her bedroom where she flipped on the bedside lamp. A pool of soft light cast a romantic glow as he turned her to him and took her mouth once again.

Excitement was beginning to build insistently. He traced his fingertips up the sides of her thighs, raising the hem of her dress as he did so, and the caress went straight through her.

Feeling cocky and in control—it was her birthday, after all—she pushed him to her bed and he obligingly fell onto his back and toed his shoes off so they plopped quietly to the carpet.

Enjoying herself, and this last present she'd be unwrapping, she climbed over top, so her knees were on either side of his thighs.

The first thing she did was carefully remove his glasses and lay them on her night table. Then she leaned forward, always watching those eyes. Her hair fell around them and he made a sound of pleasure, but obligingly didn't move. When their lips met, it was as surprising a jolt as the first kiss. She wondered if he'd always surprise her.

He lay still beneath her, following her lead as she deepened the kiss slowly, tentatively letting her tongue trace his full bottom lip from tilted corner to tilted corner before dipping inside. He groaned as her tongue touched his. She could feel the power of his restraint, as he lay quiescent, moving only his lips and tongue against hers.

Then as though unable to stop himself he raised his hands and dug them deep into her hair.

"I love your hair," he said.

Her own hands ached with the need to touch him. She reached under his shirt, dragging it upward to rub her palms over the rough hair on his chest, seeking and finding his nipples which hardened instantly. Her breasts came to taut attention in response. Dean traced the curls that framed her face. She trembled, and where she'd felt so in control a moment ago she now felt the opposite.

He caressed her slowly, his touch soft as a whisper, letting his hands roam her body, through the silk of the dress until she was so turned on she was panting, and even the thin layers of silk felt like armor.

"Sit up," he said at last, his voice gravelly with lust. She did and raised her hands, so he could ease the dress over her head.

She heard him make a tiny sound. It sounded like the word *yes*, but it was so soft it could have been a sigh. She was glad she'd chosen to wear the silk camisole she'd once thrown at him.

His eyes seemed to burn through the silk and her breasts caught the flame.

She moved to strip the camisole away but he stopped her hands.

"Leave it on," he whispered hoarsely. One of his hands came forward to touch her through the silk. His hand was not quite steady. "Do you have any idea how many times I've dreamed of seeing that camisole on you?"

While he stroked her through the silk and then slipped his hands underneath to caress her flesh, she unbuttoned his shirt, taking as much time as he had.

She opened one button, then leaned forward to touch her tongue to the part of his chest she'd exposed. She could feel the torment she was causing, and smiled at her power. When she got to the bottom of the shirt, she zipped open his slacks and began easing them off his hips.

Cherub after cherub smiled cheekily at her. She

looked up to catch the reflection of her laughter in his eyes.

"I never imagined I'd see you in these," she whispered as she removed his pants completely, leaving him naked but for the cherub bikinis.

"I couldn't stop fantasizing about you in this." He touched the camisole as he spoke, then pulled her into his arms for a kiss that left her breathless.

Still they moved slowly, treasuring each touch, each whisper. His hands were on her back, one hand sliding up the silk while the other clung to her hair.

His hungry eyes burned over her face, and when he brought his lips down on hers they were no longer gentle. His mouth plundered, demanded and received her response. He kissed every bit of her he could reach without taking off the camisole, licking and nibbling the swells of her breasts, her shoulders and her belly where the silk and her panties had parted ways, leaving a gap of flesh.

"Oh," he groaned, "I want to make love to you in this, but I want to see you." He sounded so desperate to have her, so eager that she grew hotter, enflamed by his lust which sparked her own.

His hands moved restlessly, lifting the camisole so his mouth could follow up her belly until she raised her torso once again and he slipped the garment over her head, laying it carefully aside before reaching for the aching breasts that strained toward him.

Kate gasped when he touched her, watching with a mixture of shyness and delight as his eyes devoured her. With just a fingertip he traced the contours of her breasts. Did he know he was tormenting her? Her nipples were on fire, but he ignored them and brought his mouth back to hers.

She was trembling with excitement and desire, her body a mass of needy nerve endings, each yelling to be appeased. Dean didn't kiss like a computer geek; he kissed like a seasoned professional. And she had a sneaking suspicion it was deliberate provocation on his part to have abandoned her breasts before he even got to the good part.

At last his lips left her mouth and trailed a slow wet path to her chest. He licked her breasts from the bottom up, as though they were ice-cream sundaes and he was leaving the cherry on top for last.

She was panting helplessly when he finally popped a nipple in his mouth. She grabbed the back of his head and cried out, holding him against her while his tongue did delicious things to her tender flesh. She felt a trembling begin deep inside her body and realized she was about to lose control completely.

Restless, her hands clutched at his fine-muscled back, and down over the hard round buttocks. She pulled them toward her, reveling in the hard shaft straining against the fabric of his cherub bikinis. She yanked at the waistband, dragging them down over his hips, and he pulled them the rest of the way.

He whispered, in a voice soft with reverence. "You are the most beautiful thing I have ever seen."

"So are you," she whispered back. The odd thing was that it was true. What that guy had been hiding under his geek-boarder wardrobe was a crime. His habitual slouch hid the nicest pair of shoulders she'd ever seen. Underneath those tacky shirts he'd stashed a chest fit and bronzed, abs that would have a sculptor running for marble and a chisel, while the too-big boarder shorts hung on lean hips that currently bracketed a breathtakingly impressive erection.

He took a deep breath, let his trembling finger trace the line of her temple. "Are you sure about this?" he asked, seeking the truth in her eyes.

She smiled, amazed at how right this felt. "Yes."

He nodded, and she knew the grateful relief in the smile that lit up his face. Digging into the pocket of his pants for protection, he sheathed himself in record time. So, she thought, he'd been thinking they'd end the evening the same way she had.

He slipped off her panties and lay beside her then, kissing her with passion and patience while his hands learned her body. He trailed his hands down her belly and gently opened her thighs. She cried out when he touched her.

"Now," she cried out. "Come to me now."

With fierce concentration he fitted himself against the brink of her passage, which was already beginning to throb, and grasped her hips in his hands. Then with one long thrust he entered her as she rose to meet him.

He filled her completely. She wrapped arms and legs around him, kissing him with wild abandon as they rocked together. He pushed deep inside her with each thrust, causing a timeless gasping pleasure she wanted to last forever. When she could sustain the peak no longer, she rocketed over the edge in a rainbow of light. In the echo of her own cry she heard him cry out as he thrust home one final time.

A SHAFT OF SUNSHINE poked Kate in the eye, and she realized she'd forgotten to close her bedroom curtains last night. Turning her head, she found her cheek was resting against the warm skin of Dean's chest, his heartbeat pulsing against her jaw. If she raised her head just a fraction, her lips would brush the jut of his chin.

She thought she might wake him starting with a kiss on that rather nice jaw, and fell asleep on the thought.

A lazy smile touched Kate's lips as she stretched, waking slowly. She opened her eyes to find Dean regarding her with an amused expression in his eyes.

"Hi," he said. He leaned over and kissed her briefly on the lips.

"Wow," she answered. "That was some night."

He grinned wolfishly, "Lady, you ain't seen nothing yet." He traced his hand over the outline of her breast, and of its own accord the flesh puckered and rose to meet his knowing fingers.

His touch on her body was like nothing she had ever known. She throbbed to instant life under his hands and mouth, and abandoned herself to the sensation.

It was midmorning by his watch when they finally got around to dragging themselves out of bed.

"I seem to recall you inviting me in for coffee," he reminded her.

"I did. But I didn't say I'd make it," she countered. She shook her tangled hair back, feeling well loved. "I need to shower first," she said on a yawn.

"I'd offer to wash your back, but I don't think I've got any strength left in my legs."

She laughed. "Make coffee and I am your slave."

"Done."

She stood under the rushing water, humming as she lathered her body with soap.

She emerged from the bathroom in a cloud of steam, damp curls tickling her cheeks and neck. She smiled as she watched Dean moving around the kitchen in last night's shirt—looking a whole lot better for being unbuttoned—and his pants. He was a puzzle. In some ways she felt she knew him well, and in others he was a total stranger.

He was such a good friend, she wasn't sure she was ready for them to be lovers. To trust a man so soon after the Brian horror story was probably a bad idea. And what did they have in common, anyway, a genius like him with a girl who never finished high school.

Wordlessly, she got out eggs and her frying pan.

Dean was whistling behind her as he prepared coffee, finding endless excuses to pass close enough to brush her body, each soft touch like a comforting whisper. *It will be okay.*

And she needed the reassurance. She beat the eggs until they were fluffy and lemon-colored in an effort to still her disquieting thoughts.

What was the matter with her? What had she done? She'd slept with a man she didn't know all that well, who lived right in her building, for heaven's sake. What if this thing didn't work out?

What was he thinking?

Suddenly she turned and faced him. "Dean..." Her voice came out too high. She swallowed and tried again, her eyes fixed on the Tyrolean painted bread board behind him. "Dean," she said again, more firmly this time. "I...I don't do this."

"I know," he said, a smile in his voice.

"I mean..." Suddenly things she hadn't considered last night came back to haunt her. Conversations they'd had. "I'm not casual about sex. It's not in my genetic makeup."

"I know that, too," he said, putting a hand around the back of her neck.

She tried to take comfort from him, and suddenly remembered the last time he'd comforted her, when he'd brought pizza and wine the night after Brian admitted he'd taken her money. He'd been sweet then, as well, but even as she swayed against him, certain she'd made a better choice in men this time, one comment he'd made that night stabbed at her.

He was interested in someone else. He'd told her as much. This mystery woman that he was so crazy about. Why hadn't Kate remembered her existence before throwing herself at the man?

Oh, God. She couldn't take another man lying to her. But that's what he's done, and she wouldn't hang around to be treated like a fool a second time.

She shook her head, pulling away, all the warm fuzzy feelings of a few minutes ago gone. "You lied to me," she wailed. How could she have been so stupid a second time?

Before he could say a word, she rushed out of the kitchen and went to sit on the back patio, hoping she could get herself under control before she started bawling. It was becoming too much of a habit when Dean was around.

Darren stood there for a long time feeling his euphoria drain. The smell of coffee filled the air, pungent and rich. He poured two mugs, remembered she liked hers with cream only, and carried the drinks out to where she sat gazing moodily at the fence. At least, that's what she seemed to be staring at. She certainly wasn't looking at him.

He put her coffee down with a careful click on the patio table beside her and sank to the chair he'd occupied when they ate dinner together that first time.

Her profile was set, her jaw rigid. What had happened between her getting in the shower and getting out of it? She'd called him a liar, which rankled uncomfortably. He didn't want that to be true, but had to admit it was. And yet, how could she possibly know? And what did she know? He'd been so careful.

Something didn't make sense.

He scratched his head, trying to puzzle out the sudden change in Kate. If she already knew who he was, then she must have known before they made love. So why was she looking like she was close to crying now?

Darren was a rational guy. He liked things that made sense. Mathematics, computers—he was a whiz at finding the logical answer, but women and emotions always confused him.

She picked up her coffee with a murmured word of thanks, no smile.

Bad sign.

He took a large swallow of coffee and tried to take strength from the caffeine jolt, then leaned toward her. He might as well face the music and get it over with.

"What is it, Kate?" he asked.

"Friends don't lie to each other." Her low words quavered slightly and pierced him to the heart.

"What have I lied about?" He'd see how much she knew and take it from there. That was logical. God, he was a jerk.

"Everything," she announced with a dramatic fling of her arms. "You manipulated me into falling into bed with you."

He jerked forward so fast she slopped her coffee onto her shorts, then rubbed at the spill with her finger, refusing to look at him. He took her chin in his hand and forced her head up until she was staring straight into his eyes.

He was suddenly furious. "Don't do this. You know exactly what happened last night. And you wanted it just as much as I did."

He wanted to shake some sense into the woman, but he controlled that impulse. He couldn't control his voice, however, which was getting louder as hurt and anger fueled it. "It was not a mistake," he almost shouted. "We made love last night and it was fantastic."

She wrenched her chin out of his hand, her cheeks flamed. "Oh, sure last night was wonderful, but it wasn't me you really wanted, was it?"

In corny old movies he'd often heard the hero say, "You're beautiful when you're angry," and he'd scoffed. But looking at Kate he realized it could be true. Her hair seemed to take on a life of its own when she got mad, spitting rays of molten copper and gold, and the way her cheeks flushed and her eyes sparkled—

well, the only time she'd been more gorgeous was in bed last night.

And if he didn't figure out what the hell her problem was, he had a pretty good idea he wouldn't be seeing her in bed again anytime soon.

"What the hell are you talking about?" he demanded.

"What about the mystery woman, the one you worshipped from afar? The one the makeover was for?" Her voice had risen too— She leaned toward him, her jaw at a belligerent angle. "Or did you conveniently forget about her while I was in your bed?"

A slow grin began deep inside his belly. He could feel it hit his face and he couldn't do a thing to stop it.

Kate was jealous.

She did care about him. He watched her eyes narrow until he expected her to hiss. He leaned back in his chair, enjoying the moment. He rubbed the new growth of stubble on his chin, watching her.

"Do you think it's funny?"

"I'm enjoying the moment. You see, I told you I could get her without a makeover," he said at last, not even trying to keep the smugness out of his voice.

Darren watched the emotions cross her face as his words sank in: confusion, realization and finally embarrassment. "You mean...?" Her voice was soft, tentative.

He couldn't help himself, he chuckled out loud. "That's right. *You* were the mystery woman. *You* were the one I worshipped from afar." He leaned back and stretched his arms over his head. "Ever since the moment you threw your underwear in my face I've wanted you."

Her face was flushed, her lips parted to reveal a glimpse of white teeth.

"And the more I've come to know you, the more I've wanted you," he added softly.

"Oh, Dean." He could hear the hint of tears back in her voice and he reached for her, holding her close when she threw herself into his arms. He dug his fingers into her hair, twirled a fiery ringlet on his index finger.

"I am such an idiot," she said.

"You're a darling," he corrected.

She raised her face to his. "I might make you breakfast, after all."

He kissed her slowly, savoring the soft lips that tasted of coffee.

He had to tell Kate the truth about himself. Now they'd slept together, it seemed wrong to share his naked body with her, know her in the most intimate way possible, and yet come to her with a false name and a bogus identity.

Oh, it had been fun all right to get her to fall for the geek, but he needed to share all of himself with her. He wasn't entirely sure why, except that he was pretty sure his feelings ran deeper than he was prepared to admit.

He'd tell Kate that he was really Darren Kaiser, escaped millionaire bachelor. He'd tell her soon.

But not the very first morning after they'd very first made love. Nothing was going to spoil today.

11

"I THOUGHT I was going crazy," she said after they'd had breakfast and were sitting on her couch with a last cup of coffee. Neither of them wanted to part, so they didn't.

"I mean, we're so different. You're so smart and I'm so—" She squeaked as his hand closed over her mouth.

"I hate it when you put yourself down," he said. "As well as being beautiful and kind and fun you are as intelligent as anyone I know."

She pulled his hand away and bit it softly. "Come on. I bet everyone you know has a fancy college degree," she whispered.

A lot of things were starting to make sense. The way she got all stressed out if a day went by and she didn't get a chance to read the newspaper, the way she watched educational TV and only read serious books.

He stroked her hair, took a sip of coffee. He remembered fighting with his father about which Ivy League college he'd go to—while Kate had had her chance at college taken away. The coffee tasted like ashes in his mouth.

He thought for a moment. "Why don't you go back to school? I bet you've got enough money saved to go part-time."

"It's my dream. But with a chunk of my savings gone, I'm not sure I can manage it quite yet."

"Tell me about your dream," he said, loving the sound of her voice and the contentment that filled him after enjoying the best sex of his life.

She shifted against him, snuggling her body closer to his. "I always wanted to be a teacher. Always. When we were kids I always wanted to play school." She laughed, miles away in her memories. "I had plenty of siblings to practice on, and if they got too lippy I had a couple of dolls—the perfect students."

His hands had moved around her and were comfortably settled under her breasts. She traced his hands with one of her fingers. "When the kids would learn, oh, I don't know, a new word, maybe, or get the alphabet right the first time, I'd get this feeling right here, like my heart was swelling." She touched her chest for emphasis.

He felt his own heart swelling.

She shifted uncomfortably. "I've thought about going back, but I don't know. I'd feel so stupid going to high school at twenty-four."

He grinned into her hair. "I could help you in and out of class in your walker and adjust your hearing aid."

She jabbed him in the ribs with a sharp elbow and they wrestled for a few minutes until he'd trapped her beneath him. He looked down at her, pink-cheeked, her hair spilling around her. She was laughing breathlessly.

"You'd better say yes," he warned, "before I have to resort to tickling you."

"No!" she shrieked.

"Don't say you weren't warned," he said, and, pulling up her top, began tickling her belly while she screamed with laughter wiggling crazily beneath him. Just watching her naked abdomen twist and turn beneath him was giving him ideas. He wanted her so much. Each time they made love he wanted her more.

"I mean yes," she shouted at last.

She was so beautiful, with her hair flowing out around her head, her cheeks flushed, eyes bright.

He stopped tickling but held his hands at the ready. "You mean you'll finish high school?"

"Yes." She poked her tongue at him. "And not because you are tickling me, but because it's something I have to do."

"All right."

"Is this my reward?" she asked in a breathless voice a few minutes later. One hand had sneaked up her abdomen and under her bra, where it cupped a breast. His mouth was busily trailing kisses down her throat. When she spoke he could feel the words vibrate against his lips.

With a conscious effort he raised himself off her. She'd think he was a sex maniac if he didn't turn his thoughts to something else. Trouble was, his thoughts had turned stubborn—and they were sending constant messages to another stubborn member of his anatomy with a mind all its own.

"Nope." He rose reluctantly to his feet, pulling her with him. In the distance a lawn mower buzzed, and nearby he heard birds chirping. "Your reward is that I will personally cook you dinner tonight, in the penthouse suite," he said, pointing at the ceiling.

"You cook?"

"I am a man of many surprises." More than she'd bargained for, as she'd find out as soon as they were comfortable enough with each other that he could tell her the truth.

How could he tell her now he was Darren Edgar Kaiser Jr.? She'd just started an affair with Dean Edgar, the dork who dressed like a Hawaiian Ken doll and drove the clunkmobile. If she was stressed out about the differences in their education, what would she do when she found out their socioeconomic brackets weren't quite the same, either?

She'd freak. And if he knew Kate, she'd dump him first and worry about listening to him later. Or never.

He had to move slowly, gain her wobbly confidence.

He wanted to tell Kate the truth—almost had this morning—but what she'd said about lying scared him silly. Every day he hid his true identity from her made his crime worse.

She was a woman he wanted to spend a lot more time with. She was feisty and smart and loyal and so sexy he couldn't keep his hands off her, yet underneath she was vulnerable and sweet and he found himself wanting to make life easier for her. She'd had it so damn tough all her life, and she'd made the best of things.

When he compared her life with his, he felt ashamed of himself. A thumb-sucking whiner, that's what he was. And this stupid child's prank he'd pulled could cost him the woman he was crazy about.

If he told her the truth about his identity now, she'd tell him to get lost. He knew it after what she'd said about hating lies and liars. Maybe if he just gave it a bit more time until she knew him better, then he could find a way to tell her about himself.

He felt like scum continuing with the deception, but the thought of losing Kate now, just when they'd found each other, was unthinkable. And even if she did end up telling him to take a hike, he could help her take her own life where she wanted it to go. He was beginning to see she lacked confidence in herself. She needed him to help her see how great she was.

He wanted to give her back her dreams. Whatever happened, she deserved her dreams.

THAT AFTERNOON he shopped for a meal that he knew how to cook well, and that he thought she'd enjoy. When he saw live lobsters at the market, flown in from Maine, he felt a pang of homesickness for the East Coast. His family had summered in Maine for years. Maybe it was a sly way of beginning to let her know who he really was, but he'd begin by hints and work his way up to a full-blown admission of the truth.

Nobody looked at him twice with his cap pulled low, his dark sunglasses, brown hair and the slouch that was starting to give him a permanent backache. Bart had been right. If people did look at him, it was usually one of his preposterous shirts that had snagged their attention.

Bart was smarter than he looked.

He arrived home and noticed her car was in the drive, so Kate was probably home. However, he suppressed his instinctive desire to go haul her away from whatever she was doing and make love to her.

They lived in the same building. He'd never slept

with a woman before who was geographically so very close. In fact, in his old life, he'd have automatically crossed Kate off the list of possible lovers because he wouldn't want to feel hemmed in by a woman.

Boy, had he changed. Still, he was going to have to be careful to respect her space and her privacy. They lived in the same building. It didn't mean they lived together.

So he went up to his place and started preparing dinner, forcing himself not to wonder what Kate was doing one floor below. Obviously, she was either practicing the same restraint, or not feeling the same pull to him, for he heard nothing from her until she knocked on his door at five o'clock, the appointed time for their date.

He headed for the door and noticed his glasses sitting on the table. He hesitated, then resolutely pushed them back into the plastic case and tucked them in a drawer. Maybe he could take off his disguise a little at a time, let her do her makeover.

When he answered the door, his jaw dropped. He felt the damn thing actually fall away, dragging his chin down to his navel.

He'd always thought Kate was gorgeous, but she absolutely knocked his socks off in a skimpy little halter dress that loved her body so much it clung to every curve.

"If I were a piece of clothing, I would want to be that dress," he said when he got his voice back.

"You don't think it's too short?" She glanced down. They both did, at her long, slim legs, miles of which showed beneath the short hem.

"That dress is far too short to wear anywhere else. For here, it's perfect."

She'd done her hair up on her head, with a few escapee curls around her face, and she was wearing the earrings he'd given her. He couldn't take his eyes off her. In her hand she held a bunch of summer daisies.

She was smiling at him in a way that told him she knew she'd knocked him out. She handed him the flowers. "I wasn't sure what to bring. But men never think of flowers."

He chuckled. She was right. He'd planned food, wine, even picked up a couple of new CDs he thought Kate might like. Hadn't given a thought to flowers for the table. "Thanks."

"You look pretty good yourself," she said, running her hands over his chest. "This is a new shirt."

In fact, it was a Darren shirt. One of the few items of clothing that were predisguise. Little by little he'd peel off the layers of his disguise. Ease her into the truth. It was the best idea he'd been able to come up with.

"Lady, if you want to eat, you'd better get your hands off me now," he ordered.

She pulled her hands back in mock surrender, holding them high. "Okay, I'm starving." She sniffed the air appreciatively.

"Sit down and I'll bring you some champagne."

He eased the cork out until the bottle opened with just a sigh and poured out two glasses. He'd bought antipasto at the market and bread at a trendy bakery. It had a crunchy crust and was baked with olive oil and rosemary.

He lifted his glass in a toast. "To us," he said.

She tasted the dancing liquid and her eyes widened in surprise. "Is this the real thing?" she asked.

"A lady like you deserves the best." he said.

She reached for the bottle. "Dom Pérignon. I've never even tasted it before. Oh, Dean. You mustn't waste all your money on me."

He lifted his glass at her. "It's all right, Kate. I have lots of money." Another hint dropped. The way he was going, she was going to know he was Darren Edgar Kaiser Jr. within the hour.

"Well, you won't have any money if you keep buying real French champagne."

"Isn't it great?"

"Mmm."

Soft jazz played in the background while they drank champagne, munched antipasto and talked with the easy familiarity of friends and the intimacy of lovers.

Since he had an idea Kate wasn't the type to relish boiling live lobsters—truth to tell it wasn't his favorite skill, either—he'd already done the deed and they sat, bright pink and succulent, ready to eat.

"I saw live lobsters at the market today and couldn't resist," he told her.

"Now, that's another thing I've never tried."

"Well, it's a messy business. At home my family used to summer in Maine. The best way to eat a lobster is on the beach in front of a fire. But, the second best way is right here in my apartment with lots of melted butter and a stack of napkins," he told her as he ushered her to the dinette table that looked marginally better with the blue tablecloth he had remembered to buy. Her flowers sat in the middle—a bouquet of cheerful bright yellow.

They sat, and he brought out the salad, the lobster crackers, lemon wedges and the melted butter.

Suddenly, and for the first time since he'd moved to Seattle, he missed the amenities of seduction that were a big feature of his Manhattan apartment. The killer sound system—he was making do with a ghetto blaster, the German cutlery, the Swedish wineglasses so thin and delicate he was constantly replacing them. The designer dishes a former girlfriend had picked out.

He missed his nice things, not even for himself, he decided, as he eased the cork out of a Sancerre, but for Kate, a woman he wanted to shower with the best life had to offer.

He poured wine into plebian glasses and decided it would taste just as good.

Maybe the setting left something to be desired, but the company certainly didn't. Kate was like those daisies she'd brought—colorful, cheerful and natural. For a man who'd spent his life around hothouse roses, the difference was startling and welcome.

He eased into his seat across from Kate and she looked at the perfectly cooked lobster on her plate, glanced at him and said, "Help. I have no idea how to eat this."

"Right," he said, and prepared to give his first lesson in lobster cracking. "The first thing we have to do is shield you from the mess we are about to make."

He went to the bathroom and emerged with two bath towels. "Sorry, there's no color choice. I only have blue," he said as he wrapped a towel around her neck.

"You need a safety pin to fasten it."

"Do I look like a man who has safety pins?"

She laughed. "I've got some downstairs."

"No. We'll improvise." A skill he'd enjoyed developing over the last few weeks. "Paper clips." And he dug through his stuff until he found some.

"Lobster is an aphrodisiac, you know?" he said, once she'd got the hang of digging the meat out of the claws. He watched her lick white meat from her fingers.

Her eyes gleamed with both humor and the same lust that was sparking through his body. "Are you sure it's the lobster?"

Kate laughed as Dean very deliberately pushed a plump and buttery piece of lobster between her lips, then swooped in for a quick kiss. "Oh, yeah. I'm sure."

"I thought that oysters were aphrodisiacs," she replied around the seafood. It was so delicious she wanted to moan with pleasure.

"We'll have oysters tomorrow night."

"Oh, Dean. You spoil me."

"I could spend the rest of my life spoiling you," he promised. And when she looked into his eyes, startled, she had the momentary feeling that he meant it.

They talked of nothing much. His job, her job, her friends from the party. But every time her eyes met Dean's or their hands brushed in passing, her belly would constrict with excitement. They both knew how the night would end.

Each prolonging moment was a painful teasing of the senses. Kate felt alive in every cell of her body. Her taste seemed sharper, her sense of smell more intense as she savored each different texture and flavor. Everything about the night was magical.

"I've got something special planned for dessert," he said.

"What is it?"

"You."

Her heart skipped a beat as she watched him rise and advance around the table. He leaned forward to kiss her, then, before she realized what he planned, he'd hoisted her into his arms and carried her to his bedroom.

He made short work of her dress and then laid her out on his bed.

It was the second time she'd been in his bed, she realized, and this time she was having a lot more fun.

He kissed her, dazed her with his hands and mouth and whispered promises. He kissed her everywhere, taking her up and up until she felt as plump and buttery as the lobster.

She cried out the first time when he touched her with his tongue.

She cried out again when he entered her body and took them both over the edge.

12

"How was your weekend?" Ruby asked.

"Fine." Kate reached under her work counter for a curling iron, letting her hair swing forward to hide her face. The women were preparing their stations before opening, sharing a hurried few minutes before customers began arriving.

Ruby perched on her chair in front of her mirror, rapidly applying makeup. "Fine," she snorted. "Angel-Butt has the worst case of unrequited love I have ever seen. And you have to live in the same building with the man. If he was Denzel Washington, well okay—but Angel-Butt?"

"Don't you think he's nice?"

"Well, sure I do. He's terrific. But what would the two of you do for fun? One of those fancy crossword puzzles? Discuss nuclear physics? Play the Mensa lovers' board game?" Ruby was enjoying her own jokes so much her lipstick was going on crooked.

"Well we could do what we did this weekend. Let's see, we ate lobster, drank champagne and... there was something else. Oh, I know. We made love endlessly," Kate told her in a husky undertone, drawing out each word, especially the last three.

"Whaah!" Ruby shrieked, jerking the lipstick in a thick crimson streak in the direction of her nose.

It was Kate's turn for unholy amusement, as she handed her friend a tissue. "Wipe your mouth, you look like the Joker from *Batman*."

"You're kidding me, right?" Ruby ignored the tissue, eyes round as saucers. She gave Kate a searching look. "Oh, my God, you're serious."

"Oh, Ruby, I'm crazy about him. He's not like I thought he was at all. He's sweet and kind and... well...I've never known anyone like him."

Seeing her friend's knowing leer, she felt her cheeks warm.

"It's not just the sex. It's him, and me...the way he makes me feel. It was just incredible."

"Honey, I have got to know, what'd he look like in nothing but angels?"

Kate thought back to the moment she'd peeled away his jeans and left him in nothing but the cherub bikinis bursting with his arousal. "He looked fantastic," she purred.

"Well, get that smile off your face, girl. Here comes your first customer." And in a louder voice Ruby called out, "Good morning, Mrs. Hodgkins. You ask about Kate's weekend, it's quite a story." And with a quick wink at Kate, who scowled at her furiously, she turned to welcome her own first customer.

While Kate cut and streaked, permed and colored, she thought about how Brian, who had seemed so right, had been so completely wrong for her. And that Dean, who'd seemed so completely wrong, could turn out to be so perfect.

Well, it was early days yet, of course, but she felt as though she were entering territory she'd never trod before. She wasn't a promiscuous woman. She gave her body only when she cared deeply. How had she come to care so deeply for Dean in a matter of weeks?

And how deeply did she care? She had the disturbing feeling that she was falling in love with the man. This time, she decided she wasn't going to be fooled by a slick appearance and ambition like Brian's. She was going to accept Dean as he was and love him for the man he was inside.

It didn't matter that his hair was awful or his clothing taste questionable, she decided. Only the man inside mattered. He was the one she was falling for. And she was falling hard and fast. She could barely wait for her shift to be over so she could get back to Dean.

However, she decided, they were going to wear themselves out if they didn't take a break from the constant sex. She shivered inside, thinking that she'd gone to sleep last night with her body still pulsing with aftershocks.

This morning, not her alarm, but Dean's tongue had woken her. She sighed. She could get used to beginning her days in such a fashion.

He'd shown her one of his favorite traditions with the lobster. Maybe she'd surprise him with one of her favorite summertime activities. A picnic.

With that in mind, she called him at home, where she knew he was still working. Soon he'd be back at his regular job and she was sort of dreading losing him so many hours to his work.

"Hi," she said when he answered.

"Hi," he said, his voice perking up when he recognized hers. "My bed felt empty when you left this morning. Do you know you make the craziest sounds right before you—"

"I think I must have the wrong number," she interrupted in the primmest tone she could manage while her body melted with heat.

He chuckled. "Don't think so. What's up?"

"I'm asking you for a date."

"Wonderful. I accept."

"You don't know what it is. Or when. You might be busy."

"I am never too busy for you."

"Also, you don't know anyone in Seattle, aren't working right now and I'm practically your only friend."

"And then there's that," he said, laughter still in his tone.

She loved how they could be so silly together, but always, underneath it was a cord that pulled them closer. It was strange, and scary and exhilarating.

"I get off work at three today. Would four be too early for dinner?"

"Right now would not be too early for dinner if it involves you."

"It involves you, me and a picnic basket."

There was a short pause. "Oh. A picnic." He didn't sound thrilled.

"What is it? You're not allergic to grass or something, are you?"

"No. I hate crowds, that's all."

Now she thought about it, apart from going to his job and out to run or shop for groceries, he barely left the house. She hadn't thought much about it, but now she wondered if he maybe had some kind of phobia.

Even when they'd been out for dinner with her friends he'd acted a little weird.

"You're not agoraphobic, are you?"

"No. No. It's fine. I'll be ready at four."

She stopped at the deli and got all the best picnic foods. Fried chicken, potato salad, some gourmet olives, crunchy bread rolls and cheese. She thought about dessert, blushed at the direction of her own thoughts, remembered they'd be out in public when they ate dinner this time, and bought some oatmeal-raisin cookies and some fruit.

She got home with enough time for a quick shower, a change into white shorts and a blue halter top, since the weather continued hot and sunny, packed her wicker basket and dug out her picnic blanket. She made lemonade and poured it in a jug. She added that to her basket along with a couple of pretty plastic glasses and some napkins. The plates and cutlery were already strapped in to the lid of the basket.

Dean looked dorkier than usual, she thought when he descended the stairs as she was packing the picnic stuff in her hatchback. She was surprised until she realized that he wasn't looking dorkier now, he'd simply made more of an effort during their weekend together. He'd barely worn his glasses once since Saturday night, and if he'd slouched she hadn't noticed. Of course, his wardrobe hadn't been much of an issue since they'd mostly been naked.

Oh, well. She remembered her self-administered lecture of earlier. He'd turned down her offer of a makeover. Obviously his appearance was a touchy subject and she'd fallen for who he was. If his outer appearance was less prepossessing, that was okay. It was the man himself who appealed to her. Not his looks.

Although, she did like his looks. She loved his serious, sexy gray eyes and the strong angles of his face. She loved his body and his smile.

He was currently wearing a ball cap for a hockey team, big dark glasses and a shirt that made her dizzy to look at. He also wore his usual too-big board shorts and clunky sandals. But he was cute in his own way.

He kissed her hello and she decided he was more than cute. He was also sexy and adorable.

"What are you smiling at?" he asked her, kissing her again so her answer was delayed.

"You. You're a true original."

She thought his grin stiffened, but as he turned away just then it was hard to be certain.

He got in the passenger side and they started off. "I know you don't like crowds, so I'm taking you to an out-of-the-way waterfront park that shouldn't be too crowded."

They ate their picnic on a grassy patch overlooking the water. After the first few minutes when Dean seemed to shrink into himself and cast wary glances around the park, he finally relaxed. Perhaps he was a shade agoraphobic and didn't realize it. She wondered if she could help him overcome his fear of crowds and open spaces. Maybe outings like this were the best thing for him.

Soon he relaxed and they ate the food, drank their

lemonade and watched the water and the other couples and the families that were enjoying a sunny evening.

She pulled out the cookies and grinned at him. "I'm sorry my dessert isn't as exciting as yours was."

When he returned her meaningful glance with interest, her shorts almost melted. Well, maybe they couldn't indulge in anything too sexual in a public park, but foreplay could take all sorts of forms.

Instead of reaching for a cookie, she plucked a bunch of red grapes from the basket and pulled off a particularly plump one.

She leaned over and slipped the grape between his lips, making sure her fingers made contact with his mouth. "When we get home," she told him in a soft, sultry voice, "you will get your real dessert."

"WHAT'S THIS?" KATE EYED the flat box, with its bright gift wrapping and gold bow, eagerly. "Another camisole?"

"Considering the last one I gave you is almost in rags, I guess it should be," Dean said, giving her a look that made her cheeks warm. "But no, guess again."

"A picture?"

He shook his head, grinning, and pushed the box toward her.

She pulled off the bow and tore at the wrapping. She'd always loved surprises, and the familiar fluttery feeling inside her stomach told her she wasn't too old to get excited about presents. She expected something intimate and sexy, and felt a warm glow deep inside as she tried to imagine what she'd find under the wrapping. Something black and lacy? Would it be transparent?

She pulled open the lid and the warm glow died. Confusion took its place. Inside the box was a flat sheaf of papers. She picked up the first one and read it over quickly.

Her heart bounded against her ribs as panic set in. "I can't believe you did this," she cried. She flicked rapidly through the rest of the papers. When she could finally speak, her voice was a husky whisper. "You registered me for school?"

"It's a special class for adults to finish high school. You start next Thursday night, but you can change it. It's up to you."

She licked dry lips, still flipping through the pages. "I was going to do it, you know. I was just kind of thinking nothing would start until the fall."

"I know." His voice was soft, full of understanding.

"Next Thursday, huh?"

"Yep. There's a summer session. If you work hard enough, you could finish high school in time to go to college next year."

"If Brian stops paying me back, I won't be able to afford it."

"You wouldn't accept my help before and I understood. But we're lovers now, Kate. Lovers help each other out. I'd lend you the money if you needed it."

She felt she could hardly breathe. Already she was nervous. One thing at a time, she told herself. First high school. Then she'd think about college. "You'll help me with my homework?"

Her dream. Maybe it didn't have to be a dream anymore. Maybe it could be reality. Maybe she'd end up continuing as a beauty consultant because she enjoyed her work and was good at it. The important thing was she'd have more options if she finished school.

"Yep."

She smiled broadly, suddenly excited. She threw her arms around Dean and kissed him. Then a sudden qualm hit her.

"What do adults wear to high school?"

KATE WAS SO NERVOUS she thought she was going to lose her supper. She crept into the classroom, hoping no one would notice her, and headed immediately for the back of the room. She sat down, her stack of new books on her lap, and glanced around. The classroom contained what looked like ordinary plastic stacking chairs, but some of the dozen or so students already there had a sort of tray thing in front of them.

Kate peered down beside her chair, and sure enough, there was her hinged desktop, hanging down the side. She reached down and tried to pull the thing up. A terrible screeching sound of metal resisting metal tore through the air. Every eye turned her way as she struggled and yanked at the tray. She got the stupid thing halfway up when it stuck, jerking Kate—and all her new books—out of the seat. The books tumbled to the floor in a series of thumps and crashes, and she followed, landing on her butt with her skirt flipped over her hips and her legs thrust in the air like a demented synchronized swimmer.

She heard a snicker from somewhere in front and felt herself grow crimson with humiliation as she scrambled to her feet. What was she doing here anyway at high school for dummies? If she couldn't figure out how to put her desk together, what hope did she have to graduate? She scrambled to her feet and was just about ready to storm out of the class forever when a quiet older man's voice at her elbow said, "They stick sometimes. Here, let me help."

Her savior was a balding man she guessed to be in his fifties. He wore blue slacks and a matching shirt with his name, Eddie, embroidered on the pocket. With two sharp tugs he had the tabletop in place and Kate sat back down with her hastily collected books.

"Thanks," she whispered to the man, who took the seat beside her.

"You're welcome," he whispered back. "My name's Eddie."

"I know," Kate smiled, pointing to his shirt pocket.

Eddie grimaced. "I got no time to change after work."

"Me, neither," she whispered back. If she'd had time to change, she would have worn jeans and borrowed an old Harvard sweatshirt she'd seen in Dean's closet, just for good luck. "I'm Kate...and I'm scared."

The older man smiled his understanding. "So was I, my first day, but it's no sweat. Just do your homework and you'll be fine."

There was a blackboard at the front of the room, and the smell of chalk dust took her back to childhood.

Then the teacher entered the room and she forgot to be scared anymore. What she felt was a stab of pure envy. The woman was probably Kate's own age, a petite blonde with a surprisingly large voice. And she was a teacher.

Kate's determination to succeed solidified as she scribbled frantically while the night school teacher outlined the curriculum and what would be expected of each student.

By the end of the two-hour class, she understood what Eddie had meant. Her progress would be entirely up to her. If she wanted to finish the year of high school she lacked in six months, she'd be doing a lot of homework. All she had to do was challenge herself a little bit and work hard.

Well, she was used to working hard, wasn't she? And this was the first step to a better education.

A bubble of excitement tickled its way through her body. She'd be grappling with subjects she hadn't thought about in years. Algebra, English composition, biology and Spanish. She could hardly wait to get started.

13

"What's another word for *ameliorate?*" Kate asked, turning her head so her hair swung dizzily behind her. She was seated at Darren's computer, working on an essay while he prepared dinner.

Darren loved to watch her work. He loved to see her getting such a charge out of writing essays and working out algebra equations.

He stepped behind her and fed her a marinated olive, one of the spicy ones he kept in stock especially because she loved them. "Improve?"

She nodded, the crease of concentration disappearing from between her brows. "Thanks," she said, chewing.

Her eyes were glossy and full of fun and the joy of life rarely seen in anyone over the age of ten. And yet, she wasn't childlike in any way. It was more a sense that her life was an adventure.

"What?" she asked as he continued to stare at her. "Do you need the computer?"

He shook his head. He'd risen early this morning so he could get some extra hours in and worked the whole time she was at the salon. "I just like looking at you. I love this whole schoolgirl thing you've got going on. It turns me on."

She smiled and turned her head back to the screen.

"Kate?"

"Mmm?" she answered absently.

"What's another word for *turgid*?"

For answer, her right hand left the keyboard and reached behind her, where she patted the bulge in his pants as though he were an eager puppy. "*Hard*. And forget it. You'll have to wait until I finish my homework."

He loved her seriousness and her playfulness. He loved that she never complained about the fact that she was working at her regular job and then putting in hours and hours to fast-track herself to her high school diploma.

He loved her hair and her wild fashion sense, her body and the sleepy way she always licked her lips when she woke, as though she were already savoring the day.

He loved her.

With a sound halfway between a moan and a quiet sigh of acceptance, he knew that the truth had hit him and hit him hard.

He loved Kate.

He, Darren Edgar Kaiser Jr., the man who'd bolted to the other side of the country rather than face anything more serious than casual dating, had fallen in love.

With a woman who didn't know his damned name.

Love. Phew. He opened a bottle of dry white wine and poured two glasses. He set one by the side of those industriously tapping fingers, the nails flying around the keyboard like ten speeding red Corvettes as she wrote her essay.

"Thanks," she mumbled, her fingers never slowing.

He sipped his wine. Sipped again and went back to

preparing pasta and fresh seafood. All right. He was in love with the woman. It wasn't a huge surprise, it had been coming on for a while. Love. Wow.

He'd flirted with the idea of being in love once or twice before, but the feelings had passed and he remembered both those women with fondness, but no regrets. What he felt for Kate was as different as, well, as the man he was now was different from Darren Kaiser Jr.

He chopped fresh ginger and glanced at the woman who'd slipped into his heart so effortlessly.

Somehow, the give-and-take worked out. He should have totally freaked about practically living with this woman, but in fact the domestic aspect suited him perfectly. They were great together. He and Kate were a team.

Breath seemed to hesitate before entering his lungs as he faced the obvious. He couldn't love this woman and not be completely open and honest. He had to tell her the truth.

Tonight. He'd tell her tonight.

As they often did, they carried their food down to her outside patio. The sun had disappeared behind a cloud, but it was still warm enough to sit outside.

"You are such a great cook," she gushed as she bit into the halibut.

"I love cooking for you." Okay. He thought. That was a great start. He'd managed to get *I, love,* and *you* all into the same sentence. Now he simply had to get the extra words out of the way and say it again.

She blushed in that totally adorable redheaded fashion and shifted, crossing her legs. The movement had his mouth going dry. Her legs were amazing, curvy but long, and all he could think about was how they felt wrapped tight around him.

"Well, you can cook for me anytime. Tomorrow, for instance." She glanced up at him a gleam of mischief deep in her eyes.

"I would, except that tomorrow is your day off, and I have to go to SYX. Therefore, you should cook."

"Well, it won't be fancy," she said. "I need to do some studying tomorrow."

"We could go out for dinner and both have a break," he said, feeling foolishly reckless because he was in love and wanted to show off this woman to the world.

Of course, one of the best things about their current relationship was they had lots of reasons *not* to go out. Since there'd been no sightings of him recently, the media had cooled off a lot, so he felt he could go out with the woman he loved and not be spotted.

By then, she'd know the truth, anyway, if he told her tonight. He shifted on the hard plastic deck chair. He was *going* to tell her tonight.

"How about a walk after dinner?" he suggested, thinking it might be easier to talk to her if they were doing something companionable like strolling along on a summer evening. Where even if she was shocked and initially irate, he'd have time to explain.

"All right. I need to throw on a load of laundry first," she said. "Do you have anything?"

They'd taken to combining stuff to make up a load. It was a new experience to Darren to think about things like washer-load efficiency, but Kate was big on conserving water, conserving energy, conserving money.

He respected her enough to cooperate. Besides, there was something downright erotic about thinking of their intimate garments twisting and spinning together. "Sure," he said. "I've got some things."

After they'd done the dinner dishes, he ran upstairs and grabbed his laundry, thinking he'd started falling in love with her over laundry.

When he got downstairs, she was already in the laundry room, bending down and stuffing things in the washer. Lust spiked through him as the shorts hiked up showing a lot of slim, lightly tanned thigh, and her nicely-rounded ass.

"Do you have anything?" she asked, her voice echoing oddly around the steel drum in the front-loading washer.

"Oh, yeah. I've got something."

"I'm doing lights," she informed him as he advanced on her from behind.

"There's a smudge on your white shorts," he lied. "You should throw them in while you're washing lights."

"There is?" she tilted her head around to look up at him, and he said, "It's right here," gently squeezing the middle of a firm cheek. "Best put it in the wash now," he continued, and while her eyes twinkled with devilry, he slipped the shorts down her hips.

"While we're at it..." he said, then took the white panties down as well. She gasped and a tremor ran over her body as she stepped out of the garments and rose.

He'd give Kate credit. She wasn't slow about catching up in the lust department. Her arms went around his neck and she kissed him as though they'd been denied each other for months instead of hours.

"Your boarders are smudged, also," she said, looking into his eyes and nowhere near his fictitiously dirty shorts.

"They're kind of a gray color. Can they go in with the lights?" He was teasing, but sort of not. He never could figure out where the defining line was between darks and lights. Luckily for him, Kate never had any laundry angst. Especially not now.

She didn't even answer, merely reached for the fly and unbuttoned him. Off came his shorts and white briefs.

"T-shirt," she demanded, and he stripped it off and handed it to her rather than stuffing it in the washer himself. He wanted to watch her turn and bend over once more.

When she'd added his shirt, she said, "Anything else?"

"Your own shirt is very grubby."

With a grin she stripped it off, and didn't even wait for him to critique her snowy-white bra, merely removed it with gratifying haste and shoved it into the washer.

While his brain was too lust-soaked to function, she managed to figure out soap and turn the thing on so it chugged and vibrated quietly against the cement floor.

He kissed her, ran his hands down her back and over her hips, then hoisted her so she was sitting on the rocking washer.

"Aah," she gasped. "It's cold."

"I'll warm you," he promised, and parted her thighs.

The gentle vibration went all through her, he noted. Her hair trembled, catching light and glowing red and chestnut and amber. Her breasts didn't bounce so much as shudder, intriguing him until he reached forward and tasted the coral tips.

His hand slipped lower, to where she was wet and open, and already quivering in time with the washer. He helped her along with his fingers until she was doing a lot more shaking than the machine, and certainly being a lot louder about it.

With his lips still glued to a breast, he thrust two fingers inside her and that was enough to send her over the edge.

She slid bonelessly down into his arms. He caught her hips and her legs went around him to clasp tight around his waist as he eased her open body right onto his straining erection.

"Mmm," she said as he entered all that hot sweetness, which clasped him tightly.

His reply was even less coherent.

Her eyes were dazed with passion, little tremors still chasing up and down her flesh. She kissed him deep and hard, her arms wrapped around his neck, her hair floating around them both.

His climax had him staggering, holding tight to his precious burden so they didn't both fall to the ground.

Once they had their breath back, she laughed softly.

"What's so funny?"

"Unless you want to shock the neighbors, we're trapped in here until the dryer cycle's done."

"Can't have that," he said, kissing her again. "I wonder what we can find to do?"

She returned the kiss. He got the feeling they had the same idea.

Of course, by the time the washing was dry, it was too late to go for a walk.

Tomorrow, he decided, would be better, anyway.

Kate knelt in the freshly dug flower beds, admiring her work as she put chrysanthemums and dahlias in the small front garden so they'd have lots of color through fall. A disturbed worm twisted over on itself and began to burrow slowly back into the sun-warmed earth.

Summer was aging, she realized as she put in the flowers that would liven up her garden right through November if the weather stayed mild. What was with her and this domestic streak suddenly? She'd heard of pregnant women getting the nesting instinct—with her, falling in love seemed to bring out a domestic mania. Okay, so she wanted a permanent home with a permanent garden and a permanent man. A place where the flowers would bloom from year to year, the plants growing mature along with her love.

She and Dean hadn't declared their love for each other aloud, but it was there every time they touched, when she'd catch his gaze on her, when they fought over which DVD to rent or who was cooking dinner.

She pushed a warm curl back up off her forehead with her gloved wrist, stretching out her back at the same time in the late afternoon sunshine.

Pulling back the cuff of one red gardening glove, she glanced at her watch. If she hurried, Kate just had time to get the rest of the plants in, shower and change to get to school on time.

She smiled to herself, picturing her essay, neatly typed on Darren's computer, all ready to hand in: *Tom Sawyer and Huck Finn: A Stylistic Comparison*. She was proud of her essay, proud of her work at school and the budding certainty that she could make it into college. By then she'd have her high school diploma and enough money from what she could save and the regular payments from Brian. His second check had been for two thousand. He'd included a note telling her he was working on his problems, so that was good.

She picked up a small plastic pot and dug out a purple mum, placing it carefully into the prepared hole. The soft breeze carried the scent of the roses that had rewarded her new trellis by blooming all over the place. A low, contented buzzing told her a fat bumblebee was already checking out the mums. A feeling of pure bliss stole over her as she pressed the plant into the crumbly black earth. Everything in Kate's life seemed to be blooming.

She was in love with a man who seemed to be flowering beneath her eyes. She no longer thought of him as a computer geek. He still wore a lot of questionable clothes and insisted on keeping his terrible glasses for work, but now he was the man she loved. And whatever he looked like to the outside world, he looked wonderful to his lover.

For the first time in a long time, Kate believed she could do anything she put her mind to. When she'd brought home her first A from school, she'd walked on air.

Dean had been as excited as she was, and opened champagne to celebrate. Each step forward was easier, she discovered, because she had more confidence in herself, and because someone else believed in her. Dean was a pretty smart guy. If he thought she could fulfill her dream, it was easier to believe she could.

She was debating whether to put a red dahlia beside the purple one, or a yellow one, when she heard the car draw up. She glanced up to see a dark blue sedan purring slowly along the street, and would have turned back to her planting had the car not stopped in front of the duplex.

A heavyset man in a sports jacket stepped out of the car, squinted at the house number and back at a piece of paper in his hand, then started toward her. She didn't know why, but at the sight of him approaching, the hairs on the back of her neck began to prickle. She fought the urge to run into her suite and slam the door.

The man stopped a pace away from where she had risen to stand facing him. "Excuse me, ma'am. I'm looking for a Dean Edgar, does he live here?"

"Who are you?" Her words came out sharper than Kate intended, but something about this man filled her with dread. She didn't plan to show her worry to a strange man in an ill-fitting suit.

He pulled out his wallet. *Oh, my God, it's the police* was her first thought. *What's Dean done?*

"I'm a private investigator, ma'am," the man said.

She took the proffered card in a nerveless hand. Hank Sweeney, Private Investigator, and then some letters and addresses and more phone numbers than she'd ever seen on one small business card.

"What's this about?"

She felt like her head was full of cobwebs; nothing made sense.

"A man calling himself Dean Edgar does live here?"

"What do you mean 'calling himself Dean Edgar'?" she challenged sharply. "He *is* Dean Edgar, and yes, he lives upstairs."

"I'd like to show you a picture. Would you please identify the man as the Dean Edgar who lives at this address?"

He reached one meaty hand into an inside pocket of his blazer and Kate could see a wet patch of perspiration on the crumpled underarm of his shirt.

She took the picture in hands that shook slightly as dread settled more firmly in her stomach. She glanced down at a studio portrait of a handsome young man smiling confidently into the camera. "No," she said, almost sighing with relief. "That's not him."

"Take another look, ma'am. He could be in disguise."

Even as she opened her mouth to say the man she knew and loved would never sneak around in a disguise, the similarities between the guy in the picture and Dean began to sink in. She stared at the photo more carefully.

All at once everything fell into a pattern, like a kaleidoscope turned a certain way. Now she knew who Dean had reminded her of. Not a movie star at all. "Isn't this that missing bachelor? The one from *Matchmaker* magazine?"

"Yep."

Her eyes widened as the horrible truth began to sink in.

The hair was professionally styled, and Kate knew

the signs of a top groomer when she saw them. The style was similar to the one she'd wanted to give Dean—and which he'd refused. Somewhere inside her she registered a small note of professional pride. She'd been right, the style looked great on him.

And he was blond. Not a gray hair on his lying, cheating head. The man had dyed his hair brown to cover up its true color.

In the picture, he exuded an air of confidence. Gone was the stooping, shuffling stance she was used to; this guy knew his worth. "Cocksure," she would have called him.

Even though she could only see the upper body, it was obvious his clothes were the best. No cheap, loud shirts and oversize shorts for him. She still might have insisted the man in the picture was a stranger, had it not been for the eyes. They were Dean's gray eyes, smiling so surely back at her. The ones she loved so much.

And surprise, surprise. He wasn't wearing glasses.

"Why is he here?" she finally managed to whisper through a dry throat.

"You do recognize him?"

She nodded, unable to speak.

The man misinterpreted her reaction, for he said in a fatherly way, "Don't worry, he's not dangerous. He's just some rich young playboy from the East who left home without leaving a forwarding address. His father's had a heart attack and the family needs him to come home."

He studied her face for a moment and then moved forward to take her arm. "Honest, honey. He's not a criminal or anything. Just a cocky young fellow who thought he'd like to hide out for a while. Sit down. Can I get you a glass of water?"

She shook her head and plopped down on the stone pathway, hoping her head would clear soon.

"I thought the missing bachelor's name was Kaiser." Her voice sounded dull and tinny in her ears.

"Darren Kaiser—uh, Edgar's his middle name." She heard the satisfaction in Hank Sweeney's voice. He was obviously pleased with himself for cracking the case.

"I—I didn't really pay attention to the news stories about him, but isn't he from a wealthy family?"

The detective nodded back, winking conspiratorially. He looked the duplex over. "Guess the young lord went slumming." He scratched his ample belly. "Who can figure rich folks?"

Kate sat there staring stupidly at the brightly colored chrysanthemums still waiting to be planted.

The investigator's gaze followed hers. "They should go in before they wilt," he commented.

She was going to lose it any second. She could feel emotions welling up inside like a volcano and she knew she was going to explode any darned minute. But she certainly wasn't about to do it in front of a private investigator.

She struggled to her feet. "You'll...you'll have to excuse me, I...um...have to go out for a while."

"Sure," said her companion. "Mind if I wait? I can put the rest of the plants in for you."

"Thanks." She was already racing up the path to her door. She didn't want to be here when *Darren* returned. Didn't want to see him—not now, not ever.

Don't think about it now! she warned herself. *Just grab your car keys and go.*

Car keys.

They weren't on the little red key holder where they belonged—but then they never were. She glanced frantically round the kitchen, no sign of the keys.

She had to get out, and fast. Starting to panic now, she tore around the small apartment, willing the keys to appear.

Not in the bathroom, not in her sweater pocket.

She dumped her big leather purse upside down and a jingling cascade of items hit the floor. She hunted through loose change, rolling lipsticks, scruffy tissues, hair clips and old sales receipts. No car keys.

Her body was beginning to tremble. Where the hell were they? Without her keys she was trapped. She dashed out to the car, sneaking out the back way to avoid the detective. Not in the ignition, not on the seat or the floor...

"Excuse me, ma'am." The voice grated on her so she wanted to scream. *Don't shoot the messenger*, she reminded herself.

"Yes?" she called back.

"Are these your keys?" He was on his knees, his jacket off. In one hand he held a small trowel and in the other a dangling silver bundle.

"Oh, thank goodness."

"You left them in the dahlias."

She ran forward with a murmured thanks. When she reached him, he held out the keys and closed his fingers over her hand when she reached for them. She glanced down and saw the kindness in his eyes.

"Don't you worry, little lady," he said gently. "Everything will work out. He's probably got a good explanation."

His ugly-kind face blurred before her eyes. "How did you know?" she whispered.

He chuckled softly. "I'm a detective, remember? Figuring things out is what I do. And if I couldn't figure out you're in love with this fellow after all the clues you've been throwing my way, well, I wouldn't be much of a detective, would I?"

She gave a shaky laugh. "I guess not. It's such a shock. I've just got to get out of here before he gets back. I...I can't see him right now."

"Sure." He hesitated, still holding her hand. "You okay to drive?"

"Uh-huh."

He appeared doubtful, so she forced a smile. "I'm not going far."

"My guess is you're too good for him, anyway." He squeezed her hand before letting it go.

"Right again, Detective," she said, and, turning with a wave, ran lightly back to her car.

Not until she was sitting in Ruby's living room did she finally let the lava overflow. And when it did, she thought it would never stop—burning molten liquid scorched twin paths down her cheeks. Her eyes were burning, her head, her stomach.

"I thought he loved me," she wailed into a damp tissue, one of about two hundred little wet balls that surrounded her. On her lap sat an empty box of tissues, and an unopened one sat ready at her side.

"Hey, now. You don't know he doesn't," Ruby said, her face wrinkled with worry.

"But he lied to me, Ruby. His whole life with me was n-nothing but a l-lie."

"All I know is I'd like to shove those damn fake glasses of his down his pencil neck." Ruby said savagely, making a jabbing motion with her hand. She refilled their empty wineglasses and drank deeply.

Kate pulled another tissue from the pack. Her cheeks were beginning to chap, she'd been crying so long.

"And as for that computer—well, I know where I'd shove that."

It was after midnight when Kate pulled into the driveway of the duplex. She heaved a sigh of relief. The place looked deserted.

It wasn't until she was almost at her door that she spotted him, sitting on the dark step, waiting.

"You've got no business here, Mr. Kaiser," she said coldly.

He rose stiffly, as though he'd been sitting on the outside step a long time. He had a key to her place, but he hadn't let himself in. Perversely, that annoyed Kate as much as if he'd assumed the right to wait inside.

"I have to talk to you."

She thought she'd cried every tear out, but the naked appeal in his voice brought another lump to her throat. Her swollen eyes ached with emotion.

"More lies? I don't think so."

"Look, I was afraid to tell you the truth. Afraid to lose you. I love you, Kate."

He finally said those words she'd longed to hear, and

now she wanted to throw them back in his face. "How do I know that's not another lie?"

Her eyes were becoming used to the dim light, and she could see he was wearing different clothes, which hung perfectly on his tall, straight physique. Already he was a stranger.

She wanted to cry for the sweet, kind of hopeless nerd she'd come to love. The one who didn't really exist. She hated this perfectly turned-out celebrity-on-the run for robbing her of Dean.

"Please, Kate. I have to go back home. My dad's sick. I couldn't leave without seeing you."

"So you've seen me. Now, if you ever felt anything for me, leave me alone." The quiver in her voice infuriated her so much she shoved the key into the lock, yanked the door open and walked in without a backward glance.

"Kate, please...I tried so many times to give you hints, and every time I got close to telling you, I guess I chickened out. Nothing in my life has ever meant as much to me as the time I've spent out here with you. I didn't mean to get close to you, I never meant to hurt you and I sure never meant to fall in love with you, but it happened."

She turned on him, fury almost choking her.

"You've had your fun hanging around with poor people and losers, now get the hell back to where you belong and stay away from me. How could you do this? I feel like the dupe in one of those reality shows. Only I never signed on for a TV show. I only wanted to live my life." She sniffed and stared into the face she'd believed she could trust. Once again she'd been made a fool of, but this, she knew, was going to hurt so much more than the Brian fiasco. "All I've ever wanted is honesty."

She didn't slam the door, she simply closed it quietly in his face, shutting him out of her life forever.

14

DARREN'S FOOTSTEPS echoed eerily down the endless maze of hospital corridors until he entered the intensive care unit; there the floors were carpeted. It reminded him of a library, everybody trying so hard to be quiet.

His steps slowed as he approached the nurses' station.

He suddenly felt he wasn't ready to see his father. His collar was choking him—how long had it been since he'd worn a tie? He did so now out of respect, but it felt as foreign to him as those stupid glasses had a few months ago.

A smiling nurse gave him directions and warned him not to stay long. And then suddenly he was there in the doorway looking down at his father.

A lump formed in his throat. It was all wrong to see his powerful father lying there looking so vulnerable in a pale blue hospital gown, tubes snaking everywhere from his body to countless blinking, burbling machines.

He was the only patient in the room, but it seemed to be walled completely in glass, so privacy was an illusion at best. Darren knew the nurses were monitoring his father constantly, but still, the lack of privacy irked him.

His father regarded him with eyes that were restless and alert in the gray, slack skin of his face.

"Hello, Dad," Darren said at last.

"So, I almost have to kick the bucket to see my own son."

"Aw, Dad, I'm sorry." His voice sounded husky. He cleared his throat and tried again. "How are you feeling?"

"How do you think I feel? I've got goddamn tubes up every orifice, and they punched in a few new holes just to put in some extra wiring."

Darren smiled slightly. This was more like his dad. He sat in the plastic chair angled near the bed.

His father turned his head to face him. "Even that useless lawyer of yours, Bart, couldn't find you quickly. Your mother's been going crazy."

"I never thought you'd need me." Darren looked down at his hands clenched together in his lap. "I just had to get away and see if I could do something on my own."

"Hmm. And did you?"

Darren nodded, glancing warily up at his father.

"Well, what is it? Tell me quick before I have another heart attack."

"Computers. I've almost finished the special education software program I was working on."

"Goddamn computers," the older man muttered.

Darren shrugged. "This is what I spent all my spare time on in Seattle. The program needs testing, of course, but I think it could have a significant impact on teaching struggling readers."

His father regarded him through narrowed eyes. "So

you did something useful, then? I suppose this means you're not coming back to KIM?"

Darren was watching his father carefully. His Dad was quiet but for the buzz and whir of machinery. He breathed in the antiseptic smell and waited.

He did not want to be having this conversation right now. Darren was terrified his father would fly into one of his anti-computer rages and set off all the machines clanging and banging and flashing all over the ICU.

"I had to make my own path, Dad."

To his surprise, a slow grin spread across his father's face. "Me, I went to New York."

"What?" Darren felt his eyes widen. He'd expected a tongue-lashing and he was getting smiles.

"I was younger than you, and I guess I thought my old man was as much of a stick-in-the-mud as you think I am. So I left our home in Pittsburgh. Your grandfather had a deli business he wanted me to inherit, but I wanted to wear a suit and drive a fancy car. I moved to New York, started on the bottom rung as an ad copywriter. Well," he said with a wheezy chuckle. "You know the story from there."

He turned a fierce eye on Darren and picked up a hand to shake a finger at him, flapping the intravenous tubes like skipping ropes. "But I respected my father and the things he talked to me about, like working hard and giving good value to the customer, even though I thought he was an old stick and he thought I was a cocky young know-it-all."

Darren shifted uncomfortably in the hard chair, which seemed designed to encourage visitors to keep their visiting to a minimum. "Point taken."

There was a pause that magnified the blips and gurgles of the monitors. "Mary Jane Lancer got engaged to Larry Norbert."

Darren couldn't believe it. He snorted with laughter. "She's going to marry Larry? The tennis pro?"

"He's a junior banker now in her father's firm." His father's voice crackled with disapproval.

"Huh, what do you know?" He breathed deeply, wondering if his father could take any more. "I, um...I have something else to tell you, Dad."

"From the look on your face I'd say it's going to cost me big."

"No! No! It's just that I met a woman in Seattle." He dropped his head into his hands. "Oh, God, Dad, I made a mess of everything."

"Some little gold digger get her claws into you?"

"No!" Darren felt anger rising. "She doesn't know who I am. I mean, she didn't. Now she knows, she threw me over."

It was his father's turn to be outraged. "What do you mean she threw over a Kaiser of Kaiser Image Makers? Does she have any idea of your net worth?"

Darren chuckled softly. "I doubt it. She loved me when I was a struggling computer nerd, now she knows I'm the Match of the Year, she thinks I'm a jerk."

His father looked suspicious, eyes narrowed. "She's not touched in the head, is she, son?"

"No, Dad." He thought for a moment. "You know, you'd like her. She's straight-talking, she has a hot temper, and she's so pretty it hurts to look at her."

"And you let her get away?"

"I told you, she dumped me when she found out I'm a rich guy."

Darren Kaiser Sr. sighed loudly, raising his gaze to the ceiling. "Women!"

A smiling nurse appeared, a small tray in her hands. "Time for your medicine, Mr. Kaiser, and I think this young man has taken up enough of your time for today." Her smile was still wide but her tone was clear. It was time to go.

He and his father exchanged a glance, which said, as clearly as his father just had, "Women!"

Darren moved to the bed and held out his hand. His father shook it. The clasp wasn't as firm as usual, but it was there.

"I'll be back tomorrow, Dad. Take it easy."

"You, too, son." His father was smiling as Darren left.

KATE KNEW DARREN WAS GONE the minute she returned home to the duplex after work. She felt his absence. It was like a physical ache, knowing he had betrayed her and then left.

She glanced around, half expecting to see a letter addressed to her, which her fingers itched to tear up, unread—but there wasn't one. She found her key, though, in the middle of the dining table. He hadn't even taken it off the silly plastic key ring she'd given him. Just seeing the white plastic computer shape with the red printing, Computer Programmers Do It with Bytes brought an ache of longing.

She waited for flowers with a "let's make up" note, but none were delivered. Too bad, the old folks home was probably ready for some new blooms.

She had expected the first night after he left to be the worst, and it was. She worked doggedly on her homework, determined to make up for the class she'd missed while she was crying her heart out at Ruby's. She was just as determined to put Darren Edgar Kaiser Jr. out of her mind. But he kept coming back, like the twin specters of Dr. Jekyll and Mr. Hyde she was writing about for her next essay.

Dean Edgar was gone. Had never, in fact, existed. But his loss was like the death of a loved one. For she had loved him, and he would never come back.

Darren Kaiser was the kind of uptown guy who looked down his nose at girls like Kate. All his girlfriends probably had hyphenated last names, and a different purse and shoes to match each designer outfit.

Kate swore as she scratched out yet another wrong answer to a simple math problem.

So he'd come to Seattle slumming. He was probably having a few martinis down at some absurdly exclusive rich boys' club with his friends about now, laughing about his adventures in Seattle. And the girl he'd made a fool of.

Her teeth ground together; the pencil snapped in her hand. With a cry of frustration she threw the pencil pieces across the room and took herself out for a punishing walk. She had to keep busy or she'd drive herself crazy.

She took on extra shifts at work, and every spare minute she had, Kate worked on her high school diploma. She was more determined than ever to succeed. And if, at the end of working a double shift and spending several hours plodding through algebra problems, or writing compound complex sentences, she went to bed only to lie wide eyed and aching with a pain that wouldn't ease, then no one had to know about it.

Ruby did her best to be a great friend, forcing her out to a movie one night, but unfortunately it turned out to be a bittersweet love story that left Kate sobbing.

She refused to answer her phone, and a couple of times she stood over the ringing telephone, knowing with some sixth sense that it was Darren at the other end. She turned on her heel and left the apartment before she weakened, the phone still echoing in her ears as she reached the road.

After several weeks the pain hadn't lessened. If anything, it was getting worse.

"You look terrible," Ruby said to her over a cappuccino at Starbucks.

"Thanks." Kate stirred the coffee vigorously until the foam looked like whitewater rapids.

"What are you trying to prove, girl? Working your tail off, pulling in straight A's at that foolish school of yours, and for what? To pretend Angel-Butt didn't break your heart?"

Kate had spilled some sugar on the table; now she was engrossed in drawing patterns in it. But at this she looked up into the accusing eyes of her friend.

"Well, he did break your heart. So get over it. Get a life!"

"I'm trying, Ruby. It's just so hard," she said, choking on the words.

"No, you are not trying. You are wallowing in self-pity. How many letters have you got from him?"

"None." Kate jabbed the air with her index finger.

"What! You telling me you dumped a guy and he doesn't even have the decency to grovel?"

"Well, he sent me eight letters so far, but I tore them all up before I read them," Kate admitted.

"Well, all right. That's better.... Phone calls?"

Kate flicked her hair back over her shoulders. "I don't answer my phone, and I unplugged my answering machine."

"Ooh, you've got it bad." Ruby sat back and crossed her arms. "You're going to have to move."

"Move?" Kate was stunned.

"Sure. That place is full of memories. Every time the phone rings you think it's him. Every time the mail arrives you check to see if there's a letter or a card from Angel-Butt just so you can tear it up. You gotta get out of there before you end up as Mrs. Butt."

"Not hardly. Didn't you see *Darren* on *Entertainment Tonight?*"

"Damn, I was hoping you'd missed it. I never would have recognized him."

There'd been a short feature about the return of the Match of the Year, but the report had focused on Darren's father and his brush with death, how his devoted son had rushed back to his father's side. When pressed as to what he'd been doing all this time, Darren had merely said, "I was pursuing some personal interests."

Kate had almost broken her television remote control when she jabbed the off button. He'd found time for a haircut and his color was back to golden-boy blond. He'd worn casual clothes, but not the garish shirts and board shorts she'd grown to like. No. He could play a round of golf in Beverly Hills in these casual clothes.

Unlike Ruby, she'd have recognized him anywhere.

She had to get him out of her mind, out of her heart and out of her dreams. Moving was so logical, Kate couldn't believe she hadn't thought of it herself.

"You're right. A new start, that's what I need. I should find a cheaper place, anyway. Maybe I can get something closer to the university." Since she'd be cutting back on her hours at the salon to attend classes in the fall, it made perfect sense.

"And far from bad memories."

"Ruby, you are a genius." She raised her cappuccino cup in a mock toast, forcing cheer into her voice. "To a new beginning."

Once she'd decided on her course of action, Kate wasted no time. She gave notice on her apartment and started concentrating on her new life while she tried to put the old one behind her.

When the telegram arrived, Kate had her head under the kitchen sink packing up the cleaning supplies. She answered the door, debating whether to keep the bug spray or, since she was too much of a softy ever to spray bugs, anyway, to throw the stuff out.

"Is your phone out of order, miss?" the uniformed messenger asked. "We've been trying to get you."

The phone had been ringing every hour, spurring Kate's cleaning and packing efforts. She blushed. "Oh, I've been busy, sorry."

Telegrams delivered at the door always reminded her of war movies when the little square of paper said somebody wasn't coming home from battle. Maybe that's why she just signed the receipt book before checking who it was from. She shut the door and tore open the telegram with anxious hands.

Kate:
   Arrive Seattle tonight. Must see you.

   Darren.

"Damn you, Darren Edgar Kaiser," she shouted at the paper in her hands, then tore it into pieces over and over again until it looked like confetti all over the floor.

She uncapped the lethal bug destroyer and sprayed the little pieces of paper with a vicious hissing until she was coughing in a cloud of noxious fumes.

She grabbed the phone and dialed. "Ruby, Darren's coming back tonight. Can I stay at your place for a couple of days?"

"Don't you think you should at least see him?"

The bug spray was on the kitchen counter, pictures of scaly lifeless corpses on a satisfyingly bloodthirsty red background. "If I see him I'll end up arrested for murder. You've got to help me out."

"Sure, honey. Come on over. We'll have a Friday night pizza and rent a movie. Sound good?"

THE SALON WAS BUSY with the usual Saturday rush.

Kate and Ruby worked side by side perming, coloring, curling, snipping, exchanging a few brief words in passing.

In defiance of her low spirits, Kate was brightly dressed in an electric-blue cotton miniskirt and a blue-and-fluorescent-green floral sleeveless top.

It was about midday and she was between clients when she noticed a run in her panty hose and dashed into the supply room to change into a fresh pair. She had the old pair off and the new one pulled up to her knees when the receptionist ran in.

"Oh, there you are, Kate. You've got a new customer and he's a hottie. I put him in your chair already." The girl tried to leave but Kate grabbed her by the arm.

"Wait," she squeaked, dragging the girl back into the small room. She dove behind the door and peeked out through the crack.

Just as she'd suspected. It was Darren. Sitting there, in her chair, just like he had a right to be there.

"Ow, you're hurting my arm! What's going on?" the girl cried out from behind her.

"Get Ruby. Send her in here."

"But she's just going off on her lunch break."

"Do it!" Kate turned savagely on the young receptionist, who stepped back hastily when she saw Kate's face.

"All right. Be cool."

The girl sped out of the room.

Kate remained crouched behind the door, eyes narrowed to slits, glaring out at Darren.

He was sitting at ease in her chair, looking around with interest at the salon.

She wanted to use her hot curling iron like a cattle prod and eject him out of her chair. The nerve of him, coming into her salon and sitting in her chair, just as though he hadn't lied to her and broken her heart.

How dare he?

She didn't see Ruby coming until the door flew open.

She squealed with pain and fell back onto the floor, holding her throbbing nose.

"What is going on?" Ruby hissed. "Sally thinks you're having a fit of some kind."

"It's hib." Kate gestured with one hand, the other still clapped to her nose. "Id by chair."

Ruby stared out the door, a slow smile warming her face. "Angel-Butt went and got himself gorgeous."

"He's evil." Her nose felt like it was swollen. "I think I broke by dose."

Ruby peered down at her, still crouched on the floor. "No, you didn't," she said kindly. "If you'd broken it you'd be bleeding all over the place like a stuck pig."

"You have to do him, Ruby. I'll sneak out the back."

Her friend glanced out the door again and then back. She shook her head. "He's your customer, and that's your chair."

"I can't, Ruby, I can't." Surely the tears that welled in her eyes were due to her injured nose. She sniffed loudly, prodding gingerly to see how badly swollen it was.

"Honey, it's time to stop running and hiding. You're a big girl. If you don't want him, tell him to his handsome face." She put her hands on her hips. "And then put him in my chair."

Kate's chest felt like an elephant was standing on it. "I'm scared," she whispered.

"Look, you're on your turf, with your friends and customers all around you. What can he do? Be a grown-up and get it over with." She held out a hand to help Kate up.

She struggled to her feet and pushed her hair back

over her shoulders. "You're right. I can't wait to take my scissors to him." She reached for the doorknob.

"Honey?"

She turned back to Ruby, her brows lifted.

"You'll make a better impression if you pull up your panty hose first."

THEIR EYES MET IN THE mirror. She saw emotion blaze in his and then it was gone.

"Hello, Kate." That deep rich voice that had once whispered endearments and promises to her was steady.

She licked dry lips, willing her heart to slow down. "What do you want?"

I want you back his eyes said. "A haircut," he said out loud. He'd already had at least one since she'd last seen him. He wore a burgundy golf shirt with an insignia on the pocket and perfectly pressed taupe pants. He resembled the man in the picture the private detective had shown her.

"Last time I offered you a haircut you turned me down."

"I changed my mind."

She was determined to hang on to her professional demeanor in spite of the hurt and anger that threatened to overwhelm her. She picked up a comb and ran it through his hair. The thick strands brushed her fingers and brought back memories of all the times she had run her fingers through his hair in play and passion. Of course, it had been brown in those days. Just part of the false veneer.

Their eyes met again in the mirror.

He felt it, too, she could tell. Then, as he scanned her face, a frown appeared between his lying, 20/20 eyes.

"What happened to your nose?" he asked.

She flushed uncomfortably. "I banged into a door," she said stiffly.

"How are you?"

"I'm fine. Never been better." Lies, lies, lies.

She wasn't going to tell him about her own life. She'd chatter all that inconsequential stuff she managed all day long. Except she couldn't think of a single inane thing to say.

Instead, she babbled the first thing that came to mind.

"Brian has a new girlfriend. A woman he met at AA. He came by the salon last week to apologize to me. I guess he's getting himself straightened out."

"Did he give you the rest of your money back?"

She nodded. "He sold his car."

"It's one of those steps they have to take in the program. Right old wrongs and stuff. His girlfriend was with him. She'll be good for him; she's tough, she'll keep him in line."

Darren settled back in his seat. "Good."

"Come on," she said. "Let's get you shampooed."

Of course, the shampoo girl already had one wet head in her sink and another customer waiting. If she stuck Darren in the line, he'd be in the salon that much longer. She just wanted him out of her chair and out of her life as soon as possible, which meant shampooing him herself.

She sat him down, stuck his head in the sink and tried to remember which shampoo smelled the worst.

She worked the lather through his hair, massaging

his scalp just as she would with any customer. Never had a simple shampoo been so difficult. She was forced to bend over him, knowing her breasts were just inches from his face. She felt herself responding to his nearness, while she felt him looking at her, breathing beneath her, and she wanted to hurt him. And she wanted to kiss him.

She rinsed the shampoo out of his hair and wrapped a clean towel round his head, giving it a brisk rub, then led him back to her station.

She combed his wet hair and made a production of preparing her scissors and combs on the tray in front of her. Then she took a deep breath and picked up a comb and scissors, and began trimming his hair.

"Kate, I started to tell you who I was about twenty times, but I always got scared. I thought I'd lose you." His voice was low and intense. She forced herself to concentrate on his hair so she wouldn't weaken and gaze longingly into the gray eyes reflected in the mirror.

His hair grated against the sharp blades of the scissors as she cut through it. "You were right," she said coldly.

"You thought I was lying, but I wasn't. That guy you knew is me as well."

Snip, snip.

"God, I don't even know who I am anymore. The time I spent in Seattle was more real to me than my other life. It's so easy to get trapped into what other people think we should be. How we should act, how we should look, who we should be with. It takes courage to change."

"Or some hair dye and a handy discount store."

"I was a coward, I ran away because I was turning into something I didn't want to be. Can you see that? I was always That Darren Kaiser, who was only a vice president of Kaiser Image Makers because his father built the company. I wanted to know if I could do anything else but be That Darren Kaiser. The *Matchmaker* magazine was the kick in the ass I needed. It gave me the perfect excuse to follow my own path, and I found out I could be the real me."

He raised his head to search her face in the mirror. "And I found you."

"Stop moving your head, please." She meant it to sound sharp and professional, but her voice wavered. He'd be served right if she gave him a buzz cut that would take months to grow out.

"I was so busy thinking about myself, I never thought about what this might do to you. Right from the beginning I tried to stay miles away from you, make sure you didn't want to know me. But I was lost from the minute I saw you."

"Bend forward." She moved behind him, pushing his head forward with unnecessary force. She heard his chin strike his chest.

"I'm not asking you to take me back." His voice was muffled against his chest. "I just want you to give this new guy a try. Get to know me. I'm miserable without you. And you look pretty miserable, too."

"Well, I'm not. I'm tired from studying." She paused. "I start college in the fall."

His head flew up, almost knocking the scissors out of her hand. "Kate, that's great." He beamed at her.

"Come on. Let me take you out to dinner tonight, to celebrate. As friends, no more."

She bit on her lower lip, considering.

She couldn't keep tearing up letters, dodging telegrams and moving. Maybe she should just have dinner with him, make it clear it could never work between them. Say goodbye with class. He didn't deserve it, but *she* did.

Tapping a comb against one palm, she said slowly, "I'm staying at Ruby's. You'll have to pick me up there."

He grinned at her. "Deal."

15

KATE PACED up and down Ruby's small apartment. "Do you think this dress is too short?" she asked anxiously.

"You've already changed three times," Ruby answered in exasperation. "The man knows you've got legs, forget about it."

She had settled on the green dress she'd worn to her birthday dinner. It brought back painful memories, but it was the best thing she owned to wear to a fancy restaurant.

"Does my nose still look swollen?" She touched the tender spot where she'd applied an extra coat of foundation to cover the redness.

"You look gorgeous."

They heard a car approaching. He was right on time. Kate turned to her friend in panic. "Oh, God, Ruby, I'm going to throw up."

"No you're not. You are not going to the best restaurant in town smelling like vomit. Breathe." Ruby stood up and demonstrated, waving her arm theatrically: "In—one, two, three. Out—one, two, three. In—one, two, three…" The doorbell pealed and she moved to answer the door. "Out—one, two, three."

"In—one, two, three," Kate gasped. "Out—one, two, three."

She was panting like a thirsty dog on a hot day.

She heard Ruby and Darren at the door making wary chitchat.

In—onetwothree. Gasp.

She stumbled forward.

And forgot to breathe at all.

Darren was standing there—and so was Dean. His lightweight navy suit was superbly cut. That was definitely Kaiser, as were the rest of the clothes, shoes and posture. But the face belonged to her Dean, and his hair was her creation.

When she looked into his eyes, she knew him. The expression was warm as those gray eyes looked back at her, but he treated her like an old friend. No kiss or touch, just a "Hi" and then they were off.

"Where's your car?" Kate asked, looking for the old clunkmobile.

"Here," he said, gesturing to a late-model Ford. "It's a rental. I flew in last night."

Of course he wouldn't drive the beater anymore. He'd gone back to his old life. She had to remember that. But then why was he here with her? What part could she possibly play in the life of Darren Kaiser of Kaiser Image Makers?

Her feeling of disorientation continued as they walked through the crowded restaurant to a window table. She could see women's heads turning to look at Darren. It had never happened before when she'd been with him and she didn't like the twinge of possessiveness she felt.

Finally they were seated and she was sipping a glass of wine while Darren swirled a Scotch on the rocks.

"How is your father?" she asked politely.

"He's home now and out of danger." He put the drink down with a dull thud on the white tablecloth, causing amber liquid to splash out of the glass. "I was a jackass to go like that and make it so hard for them to find me. He could be dead now."

Of all the feelings she'd expected to experience in his company, this sudden surge of empathy and remembered pain were a surprise. She nodded, knowing exactly what he was going through.

"You always feel guilty—and angry—when they die." She drew a little pattern on the white cloth with her fingernail. "My dad promised me he'd dance with me at my high school prom. He promised me I could be anything I wanted to be when I grew up."

Her voice was growing husky. She paused, swallowing. She remembered the rage she'd felt after her father's death. It had shocked her, and made her feel guilty.

She remembered the bitter reality. Prom season was a busy time at the beauty salon, and every year it came around, Kate felt like Cinderella dressing her stepsisters for the ball she couldn't attend.

"He lied to me," she whispered at last. "He didn't mean to, but he lied. It seems a habit with the men in my life."

She dipped her head to her glass, blinking the sudden moisture away.

"Kate, I never lied to you."

"Your whole life here was a lie."

"No! You saw the real me. Oh, not the phony glasses and those insane shirts, but the guy who shoots straight to the moon every time he gets his hands on a computer. That's more me than a desk in an advertising agency."

She gave a noncommittal grunt.

"I'm also the guy who loves you. All the time we spent together, all the hours we made love...damn it, didn't that tell you anything?"

"Dea—Darren, please..."

"Okay, so I look a little more presentable and have a few bucks, is that so terrible?" He waved a hovering waiter away with a quick gesture, holding Kate's eyes with his own.

"I don't see why you didn't just go off and do a computer thing as the real you." She leaned forward.

"It was knowing that if I did I could always run to my dad if I got in trouble. That if I tried to get a loan, I wouldn't know if I got it on my own merits or because my dad plays golf every week with the bank manager. Coming out here gave me a clean start, and whatever I did I would do on my own. It probably sounds nuts to you. It sounds nuts to me now, but at the time, I had to do it. That's all."

"You should have told me." Her voice vibrated with pain.

"And have you run away even sooner? Everything's a risk, Kate. And love's the biggest risk of all—I love you, and I'm willing to do whatever it takes to give us a another try. How about you? Are you too scared to take a chance?"

All through dinner, when she ate delicacy after delicacy, which all tasted like sawdust, and drank expensive wine that could have been tap water, she tried to avoid answering his question. Darren must have realized he'd given her enough to think about, for he backed off and asked about school, her family and her plans for the future.

Just as he'd promised, he drove her back to Ruby's apartment before midnight. He didn't even suggest taking her back to his hotel room.

She was relieved. Of course, she was relieved.

Darren turned to her. In the glow of the streetlight his face was vague, so she had to rely on his voice and eyes, both so very familiar to her.

"Kate, I have to go back East in a few days. Dad needs me at KIM for a while. I can't let him down again."

Her heart sank. So he thought she didn't need him? "I understand."

"Come with me," he said.

"Are you crazy?"

"You could go to university in the East. There are some great schools."

"And you or your Dad would pull some strings?" She couldn't keep the scorn out of her voice.

He chuckled softly. "Now you know how I felt. No, you have the marks to get into a good school all by yourself."

"You're asking me to leave everything I know and move to the other side of the country for you. To do that, I'd have to trust you, and I can't."

"You know, one advantage to being That Darren Kaiser is that I can afford to make things easier for you and your family. You could come home and visit whenever you want, in time we could help your mother find a better place to—"

"How dare you?" she lashed out in blind fury. "We've never had to turn to charity yet, Darren, and I sure as hell won't take it from you."

He reached for her hand, forcing the connection between them she didn't want to feel. "Forget about all the surface stuff. Trust your heart. In your heart you know me."

She felt as fluttery as a trapped moth. "I don't know you...I don't."

"Trust this," he said, and, leaning forward, cupped her face in his hands and kissed her. She made a little moaning sound of despair in the back of her throat as her body leaned in closer to his embrace. She could feel his life force flowing through her, and her answering response flow back to him.

He pulled away at last, and she felt bereft without his warmth.

He got out of the car and walked around to Kate's side to open her car door. He walked her up the path to Ruby's door. "Sleep on it," he said. "I'll call you tomorrow."

The door opened to reveal Ruby in a crimson bathrobe, a towel wound into a turban around her head. Before Kate could reply, he had waved to both women and was walking back to his car.

Sleep on it, he'd said. Hah. Sleep was farther than it had ever been. How could she trust him, how could she be sure he wouldn't desert her when she needed him?

Ruby's old pullout was about as comfortable as a bed of nails. She lay staring at the ceiling, more frightened and confused than she'd ever been.

She imagined going off with him to some cold marble

mansion in the East, far away from her mother and Ruby and Mona, far away from everything and everyone she knew. God, she'd miss them all. Even Mrs. Hodgkins seemed like a surrogate grandmother when Kate thought about leaving her.

Her life wasn't perfect, not by a mile, but at least it was familiar and predictable and safe.

Suddenly she couldn't stand lying there in pain and misery any longer. She hauled herself out of the pullout, which groaned and squeaked before disgorging her from its lumpy depths with the painful poke of a popped spring.

Kate rubbed her bruised backside and silently dressed.

She arrived back at the duplex just after 3:00 a.m. It seemed forlorn and cheerless with moving boxes scattered around, most of the ornaments and books already packed away.

She walked into the bedroom and flopped on the bed

"What am I going to do?" she whispered to the ceiling. She curled up in a ball on the bare mattress, staring into the dark.

WELL, AS REUNIONS WENT, last night hadn't been a complete fiasco, Darren thought as he drove the quiet Sunday streets. The night hadn't ended the way his body had ached for it to end, but she hadn't slammed the door on his hopes, either.

If he knew anything for certain anymore, it was that he and Kate belonged together. When she'd told him about her father's death, quite a few things had begun to make sense.

"He lied to me," she'd said.

A big searchlight went on in his head when she'd said those words. It was like the moment when you discovered the source of a computer bug—that wonderful eureka moment that was the first step to solving the problem.

Not that Kate was like a computer—God, she was a lot more complex than that—but he had the key to her fear now, and her thing about lies. When it was just him and the computer, he always felt he had logic on his side. With Kate, he had to contend with emotions and feelings. He'd have a better chance winning at chess with Deep Blue than convincing the most stubborn, hot-tempered woman he'd ever known that she loved him.

He couldn't make her trust him. He hammered his hands against the wheel in frustration.

He drove aimlessly, thinking. He was willing to take a risk, couldn't she see that? What if, instead of asking her to trust him, he could show her how much *he* trusted *her?*

His heart began to pound. Why couldn't he show her he trusted her with his life?

He checked his mirrors and then jerked the wheel around for a U-turn. His blood hummed with anticipation as he headed the car in the direction of the duplex. She'd be home now, he was sure, now she didn't have to hide from him at her friend's place.

The car slowed as he entered the street where she lived. He felt suddenly dry-mouthed and hollow-bellied. What if he couldn't convince her?

Parking across the street, he marshaled his arguments. His palms were damp as he counted off on his fingers all the reasons why she should take a chance and trust him with her happiness.

In the end, he knew there was only one reason that counted. Did she love him? The answer to that question terrified him.

ACTION, THAT'S WHAT SHE needed. It was a lesson Kate had learned from her mother. "There are few problems that can't be solved with a scrub brush in your hand" her mother loved to say. Well, there was plenty of scrubbing and cleaning to be done before she moved at the end of the month. Kate scrutinized the small apartment. Sunshine streamed through dusty windows. That was a good place to start—with the windows.

Dragging one of the dining chairs over to the living room window, she climbed up, unhooking the drapes. She sneezed twice as dust tickled her nose. She pulled out the drapery hooks and piled the dirty drapes into her wicker laundry basket. She'd put the drapes on to wash now, then come back and wash the windows. She'd have the curtains washed and ironed and hanging over sparkling clean windows by nightfall.

Hiking the curtains into the laundry room, she crammed them into the washer and checked her watch. The washer would take about thirty minutes.

Back in her apartment, she tied her hair back out of the way and changed into old sweats and a T-shirt that had a hole in it. She put soap and vinegar into the bucket, added hot water and dug through the storage closet for her window washer.

She dipped the squeegee into the hot soapy water and began washing the windows. Up and down, then a swipe with the rubber end and the glass pane was clear. If only her fears could be cleared away as easily. She fell into a soothing rhythm, which allowed her thoughts free rein. They were anything but soothing.

She knew one thing now for certain.

She loved Darren. Whatever and whoever he was, she loved him.

And he'd come back for her.

But how could she trust him?

She remembered Ruby's words. "Be a grown-up, Kate" she'd said. Kate wasn't the girl she'd been half a year ago, when she'd seriously thought about spending her life with someone like Brian. She had grown up since then. It was Darren who'd helped her see who she really was, who'd encouraged her to take a risk and go back to school.

So what if she went with him and it didn't work? So what?

Swish up, swish down, squeak of rubber and on to the next strip.

She could always come back to Seattle, get another job. She'd be all right.

But if he broke her heart again, she didn't know if she could survive.

Back and forth her thoughts chased one another like the rubber swiper chasing drips down the window. He was going to phone today, and she had no idea what she was going to say to him.

She finished the last of the inside windows, emptied the bucket and dried her hands. She checked her watch. It was time to put the curtains in the dryer, then she could start on the outside of the windows. She stretched her arms over her head, rotating her shoulders, then headed back to the laundry room.

She stopped dead. Her heart lurched to her throat. There was a note taped to the washer. The cramped black sprawl as familiar as her own heartbeat.

> Occupant of Apartment B,
> Will you marry me?
> Darren Edgar Kaiser

There was only one answer. It was time to trust her heart.

She looked around for a pen or pencil, anything to write with. The closest she could find to a writing implement was a dust-covered sliver of yellow soap lying in a corner.

Digging shaking hands in her sweatpants she pulled out an old lipstick and uncapped it. It was bright red. Perfect. She walked slowly over to the washer and wrote *Yes!* across the note in huge crooked letters, framing her answer in a thick, gooey red heart.

She felt his presence even before she turned around. "I hope you can read that far without your glasses," she teased, her voice husky through her tears.

"I have perfect vision. That's how I found you," he said softly.

"Kiss me, husband to be." She held her arms out, smiling through misty eyes.

He was quick to comply.

From *Matchmaker* magazine's October issue
   Kaiser Meets His Match
Runaway Match of the Year, Darren Edgar Kaiser Jr., heir to the Kaiser Image Makers empire, is no longer missing. Sadly for this magazine and hopeful single women across the country, he's no longer a bachelor, either.

Darren Kaiser met his match, Kate Monahan Kaiser, on a recent trip to the West Coast.

The couple currently reside in Boston, where Kate attends university and Darren is working with a charitable education foundation to improve reading skills with a software program he developed.

Dear Reader,

Trey Marbury and Libby Parrish are caught in both a meteorological heat wave and a heat wave of their own making in the fictional town of Belfort, South Carolina. Those of you familiar with the Low Country might recognise the real town that Belfort is based upon, although I'm not sure that a real Southern town would have quite so many charming and eccentric characters living within its limits. Or maybe it would. Maybe that's exactly what I love so much about the South.

In any case, I hope you enjoy the ideas Trey and Libby come up with to beat the heat....

Happy reading,

Kate Hoffmann

KATE HOFFMANN

HOT & BOTHERED

Harlequin Mills & Boon

Temptation

DID YOU PURCHASE THIS BOOK WITHOUT A COVER?
If you did, you should be aware it is **stolen property** as it was
reported 'unsold and destroyed' by a retailer.
Neither the author nor the publisher has received any payment
for this book.

First Published 2004
First Australian Paperback Edition 2004
ISBN 0 733 55557 8

HOT & BOTHERED © 2004 by Peggy A. Hoffmann
Philippine Copyright 2004
Australian Copyright 2004
New Zealand Copyright 2004
Except for use in any review, the reproduction or utilisation of this work in
whole or in part in any form by any electronic, mechanical or other means,
now known or hereafter invented, including xerography, photocopying and
recording, or in any information storage or retrieval system, is forbidden
without the permission of the publisher, Harlequin Mills & Boon, Locked Bag
7002, Chatswood D.C. N.S.W., Australia 2067.

All the characters in this book have no existence outside the imagination of
the author, and have no relation whatsoever to anyone bearing the same
name or names. They are not even distantly inspired by any individual
known or unknown to the author, and all the incidents are pure invention.

This book is sold subject to the condition that it shall not, by way of trade or
otherwise, be lent, resold, hired out or otherwise circulated without the prior
consent of the publisher in any form of binding or cover other than that in
which it is published and without a similar condition including this condition
being imposed on the subsequent purchaser.

All rights reserved including the right of reproduction in whole or in part in
any form. This edition is published by arrangement with Harlequin
Enterprises II B.V.

Published by
Harlequin Mills & Boon
3 Gibbes Street
CHATSWOOD NSW 2067
AUSTRALIA

HARLEQUIN MILLS & BOON TEMPTATION and the Rose Device are
trademarks used under license and registered in Australia, New Zealand,
Philippines, United States Patent & Trademark Office and in other countries.

Printed and bound in Australia by
McPherson's Printing Group

Prologue

A BUMBLEBEE BUZZED in lazy circles around a potted jasmine, the sound breaking the silence of the oppressive midday heat. A few steps away on the wide veranda of the house on Charles Street, the Throckmorton sisters stirred the heavy afternoon air with rice-paper fans. A silver tray rested on the table between their two wicker chairs, holding a pitcher of iced tea and two sweaty glasses.

"We're doomed," Eulalie Throckmorton said, her fan fluttering like the wings of a hummingbird.

Eudora Throckmorton took in the morose expression on her twin sister's face and sighed. "It's just the heat, Lalie. When I'm drenched in perspiration, I don't feel like chatting. Neither do the rest of the ladies of the Thursday Ladies' Bridge and Luncheon Club."

"But it was as quiet as a Quaker wake."

Eudora shifted in her chair. "If you'd just agree to install air-conditionin' in the house, then we wouldn't have this problem. Grace Rose Alston just had air-conditionin' put in her house and she says it's been a godsend with this mid-summer heat."

"We don't need air-conditionin', Dora. We have this lovely veranda. Mama and Papa lived here for over fifty years and they never had air-conditionin'.

Besides, we'd just shut ourselves up in the house and never see our neighbors strolling by. Out here, we're part of the world. Good gracious, if I wanted to live in the cool and dark, I'd run down to Wilbur Varner's funeral home, buy myself a nice coffin and move in next to Mama and Papa at the cemetery."

"There's no need to get all dramatic about it," Eudora replied. "I swear, you've always had a way of pilin' on the agony. You should have taken up a career on the stage. You could have given that *Driving Miss Daisy* lady a run for her money."

"And you should be sellin' gadgets on the Home Shopping Network, with your fondness for new-fangled inventions. Need I remind you that we have an electric juicer sittin' in our kitchen that you've never even used?"

"Air-conditionin' is not a new-fangled invention," Eudora countered. "Some would argue it's a necessity in the heat of a South Carolina summer. And we are approachin' an age where personal comfort is all we can look forward to on a good day."

"Let's be honest, Dora. It isn't our lack of a temperature-controlled environment that will spell the end of our beloved bridge club. It's the shortage of decent gossip. There's just nothin' left to talk about in this backwater town!"

The Thursday Ladies' Bridge and Luncheon Club was nearly a century old. Founded by Eulalie and Eudora's grandmother and a group of her friends, members were all prominent socialites in the town of Belfort, South Carolina. The club was a Belfort institution that had weathered two World Wars, Prohibition, the Great Depression and an attempted seditious coup by several members who wanted to replace the bridge games with gin rummy. But through it all, the ladies had always shared lively conversation among the sixteen members. Eulalie might call it gossip, but Eudora preferred to think of it as...illuminating discourse.

"Maybe we should consider bringin' in some new members," Eudora suggested. "Some ladies who might have some interestin' topics to share. I met a lovely widow at the Winn-Dixie who just moved from New York City."

"The ladies would never tolerate a Yankee." Eulalie shook her head. "Besides, we've always had sixteen members and until one of our ladies goes to her great reward, we can't bring in a new member. It's in our bylaws, and you should know our bylaws since you've served as president twice!"

"According to Charlotte Villiers, she herself is circlin' the drain as we speak," Eudora muttered. "If I have to listen to one more recitation of her medical woes, I do believe I might just get great-granddaddy's dueling pistol from the gun cabinet and kill her myself."

Eulalie chuckled, her mood lifting at her sister's audacious remarks. Still, this was serious business. If the bridge club struggled under her watch as president, the ladies might find some way to put the blame on her. "It wouldn't have to be anything major," she murmured. "Just somethin' juicy. Perhaps a nice political scandal would spice things up. Bribery, blackmail, corruption. Or even better, a scandal of the—" she lowered her voice to a whisper "—*private* kind, if you catch my meanin'. You know, I always believed Desmond Whitley was a homosexual. Maybe we could convince him that this would be a nice time to come out of the woodshed."

"That's closet, sister. Come out of the closet."

"Closet, woodshed. Now that would be something worth talking about."

"I like Desmond," Eudora said. "And to tell the honest truth, I don't much care if he is a homosexual. He does lovely flower arrangements for the fall bazaar at the church and he embroidered that tablecloth for the Friends of the Library auction. And he's a very fine dancer."

"All right," Eulalie grumbled. "Forget Desmond. Besides, he's sixty-two. We need to find someone younger. All the better, someone who has a spotless reputation, someone who is a stranger to scandal." She paused. "Someone who actually might participate in passionate...unbridled...slightly kinky..." She paused again, this time fanning herself frantically. "Well, I'm sure you understand what I'm gettin' at."

"Sex," Eudora said plainly. "You're speakin' of sex, sister. Good gracious, I may be eighty-three years old, but I'm a modern woman and I'm not afraid to talk about these matters out loud. Even though we're both considered maiden ladies, you and I have some experience with men. It's no use pretendin' we've never even seen the one-eyed monster."

Eulalie nearly choked on her iced tea and a fierce blush warmed her cheeks. She snatched up a linen napkin and pressed it to her lips, then cleared her throat. "There is no need for such plain speakin', Eudora."

Her sister shrugged. "You blush when I use proper

medical terminology and you blush when I choose a euphemism."

"The point I'm makin' is that despite our experience, we're still innocent to the ways of the modern world. Things have changed a bit since we were young women. Back then, a boy couldn't lay a hand on a girl's bosom without a proposal of marriage. It takes a lot more to get folks talkin' these days."

"This is silly, Lalie. We can't *make* a scandal happen. They just do."

A slow smile broke across Eulalie's face. "But we can help it along a bit."

"And how will you accomplish that?"

"Rumor, innuendo, baseless accusations. I'll think of somethin'."

"And just who will you get to participate in your little scandal?"

Eulalie slowly fanned herself. "I don't know. Someone with an upstandin' reputation." She stared at the house across the street, its wide verandas lined with hanging baskets of fuchsias. "That will take careful consideration. But one thing I can guarantee you, sister. There'll be a lot more to talk about in Belfort after I'm done stirrin' the pot. And our precious bridge club will be safe for another hundred years."

1

EVERYTHING IN BELFORT moved a little slower in the heat of summer. Dogs didn't pull at their leashes; birds retreated to the cooling shade of the live oak trees. Even the sunset took a lazy route to the horizon. Trey Marbury wiped a trickle of sweat from his neck as he waited at one of Belfort's three stoplights, grateful that night had finally fallen on a stiflingly hot day.

He peered out the windshield of his Jeep at storefronts that had once been so familiar. Sam Harrington's hardware store had a new neon sign in the front window and Royal Farley had added fancy new pumps at the filling station. But beyond that, everything was pretty much as he'd left it that day he'd driven out of Belfort, South Carolina, for the last time.

"No parade, no Welcome Home banners, no marching band," Trey muttered, turning onto Center Street. So far, the return of Belfort's former favorite son had caused little notice.

Twelve years ago, Trey had been an all-conference quarterback, homecoming king, an honor student, and had won a football scholarship to Georgia Tech—all in one year. Belfort had expected great things from Clayton Marbury III, but not nearly what his father had demanded from his only child. Clayton Marbury II wanted nothing short of perfection—and unquestioning obedience.

Trey had been relieved when he tore up his shoulder in his junior year at Tech. The pressure was off, the expectations gone. He and his father had nothing more to fight about, except the surgery that Trey refused to have and the disinterest he had shown in the family business.

In the end, that's what had brought him back to Belfort, back to his past—unfinished business. Home was no longer this sleepy little town in the Carolina low country, but a high-rise condo on the Gold Coast of Chicago. He'd lived in the north for so long he'd grown accustomed to the cold winters and the fast pace. The deep drawl that had marked his speech when he had arrived in the Windy City was nearly gone, along with his tolerance for summer weather so hot it made a man's fingernails sweat.

Trey swung the Jeep onto River Street and pulled into the parking lot of Garland Van Pelt's convenience store. He ignored the curious stares from the small group of men gathered around a television set as he walked inside. He pulled a six-pack from the cooler, then he grabbed a package of pretzels and headed to the counter.

"Trey Marbury?"

Trey glanced up from his wallet to find the storeowner staring at him. "Hey there, Garland. How's it going?" He frowned inwardly. His drawl had suddenly reappeared, each word of his greeting sliding into the next.

"Well, well," Garland crowed, clapping his hands. "Look who we have here, boys. It's Trey Marbury. We were just talkin' about you last week. About that game against Marshall. You remember that? You dropped back, Bobby Ray Talbert threw that block and you hurled the ball down the field. It bounced off the defender's back and into Lanny Freemann's arms. Belfort wins by three." The group of men erupted in a cheer, giving each other high fives.

"That was a great game," Trey said as he tossed a twenty on the counter.

"What are you doin' back in town?"

"I'm taking care of a few things for my father's estate."

The men dropped silent and Garland nodded soberly. "I heard about your dad. I'm real sorry, Trey. He was a good man."

Trey forced a smile. To most people in town, Clayton Marbury *was* a good guy, the picture of an upstanding citizen and model family man. He just hadn't been a loving father to his son. In truth, Trey couldn't remember his father ever showing an ounce of affection toward him. "Thanks," he murmured. Trey pushed the money closer to Garland, hoping to make a quick exit.

"He weren't no cheapwad, either. I never met a more generous guy. Told the funniest stories down at the lodge and could make a mean barbecue. Always threw that big shindig every year on his birthday. Yep, he looked out for his friends, he did."

"And made life miserable for his enemies," Trey added.

Garland chuckled. "You're right about that, son. Though there hasn't been much to the feud since Wade Parrish and his wife moved out of town three years ago. I think that took all the fight out of your dad. He and your ma left for their place in Arkansas a few months later." Garland totaled the price of the beer and pretzels, then dropped them both in a bag. "So how long you plannin' on stayin' here in Belfort?"

"My mother asked if I'd liquidate the last of the real estate around here and in Charleston. I've got to meet with Realtors, get some repairs made to some of the properties. I guess I'll be here for a few months at least. Just until everything closes. Then I'm headed back home. I mean, back to Chicago."

Garland nodded. "You got a place here in town?"

"The motor lodge out on Highway 32, though it took a bit of sweet-talking since I have my dog with me. I'm thinking of buying a place and renovating it in my free time. You guys know of any properties I could pick up quick?"

Garland chuckled. "Boy, the apple don't fall far from the tree. You're just like your daddy, boy! Clay Marbury was always on the lookout for a good buy. He had the Midas touch, he did."

Trey had heard just about enough about the great Clayton Marbury II. He grabbed the bag and nodded, a tight smile pasted on his face. "Thanks, Garland. Be seeing you boys."

The storekeeper scratched his chin. "Now that I think of it, the old Sawyer place is goin' up for sale. They moved Mrs. Sawyer to an old folks' home up in Florence, where her daughter lives. The house is fallin' down, so I reckon you could get a good price for it. My daughter's a real estate agent. I'll have her give you a call."

Trey waved at Garland as he counted out his change. "Keep it," he said. "Buy the boys a beer on me."

As Trey backed the Jeep out of the parking lot, he knew it would be a matter of minutes before all the town gossips knew that he was back in Belfort. No doubt, there'd be all kinds of speculation about where he'd been and what he'd been doing these past twelve years. "I should have taken a place in Charleston." He sighed. "Maybe it's true—you can't go home again."

Trey swung the Jeep back onto Center Street and headed for the old residential section of town. Belfort sat at the junction of two rivers, rivers that emptied into the Atlantic about fifteen miles downstream. Most of the huge white clapboard homes were located on the wide peninsula of land that split the rivers in two, set on streets shaded by centuries-old live oaks and boasting huge lots that backed up on the water.

Trey knew where the Sawyer house was located and headed down Charles Street. As he pulled up in front of it, his gaze drifted to the house next door. This had always been considered Parrish territory, the east side of the historic district. Since the War Between the States, Parrish supporters had lived east of Hamilton Street and Marbury supporters lived west of the dividing line. A person declared their allegiance by where they chose to buy their home. Trey chuckled softly. Buying in enemy territory would have sent his father into an apoplectic fit.

Trey reached over and grabbed a beer, then popped it open and took a long sip. Even if there were still Parrishes living in the house next door, the feud was over now. As the only Marbury heir, he had no intention of continuing the hostilities. And to his recollection, there was only one Parrish heir left and that was Lisbeth Parrish; she'd probably taken off for parts unknown at her first available opportunity.

He hopped out of the Jeep and strolled up to the Sawyer house, the facade looming darkly among the overgrown bushes and trees. Like the house next door, it boasted wide verandas that circled all four sides on both stories, shading the house from the relentless summer sun. He could see the place was badly in need of paint, and the verandas were sagging in spots. But even if it were falling apart inside, a guy didn't come across a house like this every day. The craftsmanship was incredible, the detailing probably untouched since it had been built in the mid-1800s.

Trey wiped his hand over a dusty window and tried to see inside, making out an old carved mantel and furniture covered with sheets. Suddenly, he'd found a reason to set up housekeeping in Belfort. Smiling, Trey turned back to the street. Hell, he didn't care what they wanted for the house—he'd pay it. After eight years designing everything from shopping centers to condo complexes, it would be fun to wield a hammer and saw again.

Halfway to his Jeep, Trey turned around. There had always been a secret path around the back of the old Sawyer house, a path that he and his buddies had taken numerous times on a hot summer night. It led through a dense thicket of trees and kudzu to a tiny inlet in the river, a deep pool with a sandy bottom. The high school had built a swimming pool the year after he'd graduated and the spot probably had been long forgotten. A swim might be nice before he headed back to the motel.

He retrieved the rest of the six-pack from the Jeep and then walked past the empty house into the deep backyard. Crickets chirped and unseen night animals rustled as he searched for the entrance to the path. Though the inlet required trespassing on Parrish property, that had never stopped Trey and his friends. If they didn't get too loud and cleaned up after themselves, they usually went undetected.

As he pushed through the brush, Trey recalled one time when he had been caught, and not by old man Parrish. His memories of that night, just a few days before his eighteenth birthday, were still strangely vivid, for they had represented a turning point in his life. Maybe it had been the setting or the events leading up to the encounter. Or maybe it had been his unbidden reaction that had burned the memory so deeply into his mind.

It had been his last night in Belfort before leaving for summer football practice at Tech. He'd started the evening embroiled in an argument with his father, who had insisted he'd pay nothing for Trey's education. Though Clayton Marbury II had been born into wealth, he had somehow gotten the idea that his son would benefit from working his way through college. At the time, Trey wasn't sure how he'd be able to juggle football, architecture courses and a job, but he'd seen the advantage of being completely free of his father's control.

He'd stormed out, ready to find a cold six-pack and some buddies to drink it with. But in the end, he had decided to spend his last night alone, away from all the big talk about athletic accomplishments and his bright future in college football. In a few days, he'd be considered a man. It was time to start acting like one.

He'd found himself at the inlet, angry and overwhelmed, confused about the direction his life was taking and scared that he might not be able to cope. She'd appeared sometime between his third and fourth beer and, at first, Trey had thought he might be hallucinating. But once he'd realized she wasn't just a by-product of a drunken buzz, Trey had been glad for the company.

Libby Parrish hadn't run with the in crowd at Belfort High School. Shy and bookish, she'd never stood out in the midst of prettier, more popular girls. She was also just a junior. And she was a Parrish, the only flaw that made any difference in his world. But that night, in the moonlight, she became something more to him.

The moment he saw her, he almost bolted. But then she spoke, telling him he didn't have to leave, that she wouldn't tell her father. Trey still remembered the look in her eyes, the curiosity mixed with a little bit of fear. Hell, he hadn't wanted to go home anyway, so why not? Besides, spending time with Libby Parrish was as good as thumbing his nose at his father.

Trey let the memories drift through his mind as he stepped around the last clump of bushes and walked into a small clearing. Moonlight sparkled on the river, and in the distance, a duck took flight, its wings flapping in the dark. Trey found an old log near the spot where they used to build a fire to fend off the mosquitoes. He sat down on the ground and leaned back against it, taking another long sip of his beer. For the first time since he'd driven into Belfort, he felt like he'd found a memory worth reliving.

But a moment after he settled in, Trey heard rustling in the bushes behind him. With a soft curse, he crawled behind the log and lay flat on his stomach, then reached over to grab the rest of the beer. Though he hadn't minded breaking the law as a kid, Trey was pretty much a stranger in town now and he wasn't sure how the owner would feel about his presence on private property.

He waited, holding his breath, half expecting a group of kids to appear. But a single figure stepped through the bushes, a woman, her slender body outlined by a loose cotton sundress, her pale hair shining in the moonlight. She reached for the hem of her dress and in one easy motion, pulled it over her head, then kicked off her sandals and walked to the edge of the water.

Trey sucked in a sharp breath, nearly choking as he did. She wore nothing beneath the dress and the shock of seeing a naked woman just a few feet away made his pulse suddenly quicken. He wanted to look away, but he couldn't. She was just about the most beautiful thing he'd ever seen.

Her body was perfect, her limbs long and delicate, her backside perfectly shaped. The light played over her skin and he found himself caught by the graceful curve of her shoulders and the gentle indentation at the small of her back. She lifted her arms and slipped her hands beneath her hair, holding the wavy mass off her neck. Trey shifted slightly as he felt himself grow hard, a crease in his jeans making the reaction a little painful.

But as he moved, his foot slipped and a stick cracked beneath him. She froze and then glanced over her shoulder, like a wild animal deciding whether to stay or flee. Her profile, illuminated by the moonlight, was instantly recognizable and Trey sank down behind the log.

"Libby Parrish," he said, her name touching his lips without a sound. Trey smiled. Such an odd symmetry to find her here on his first night back in town, when she'd been here on his last night.

As she walked into the water, Trey searched for a moment to make his escape. This was definitely not the time for a reunion, with her stark naked and him so obviously aroused.

The bushes directly behind him were thick and impossible to crawl through without making a noise. He'd have to get back to the path on his belly or just make a dash for it. But in the end, Trey decided not to leave. He rolled over on his back and stared up at the stars as he listened to Libby splash in the water.

She'd changed so much since the last time he'd seen her. She'd become a woman, more lovely than he could ever have imagined. But he still remembered the girl he'd known and with that memory came every detail of that night so long ago.

They'd talked for hours—Trey pouring out all his anger and frustration, giving voice to the insecurities that had plagued him, and Libby listening raptly, as if what he was saying were the most important thing in the world.

No one had ever taken the time to listen to what

he wanted out of life. Everyone had an image of who he was and what he was supposed to become. Trey had expended so much energy trying to please his parents, his teachers, his coaches and his friends, that he had wondered whether any part of his life truly belonged to him.

The night had closed in around them and Trey had felt almost desperate to stay with her for just a little longer, certain that talking with her would solve all his problems. He hadn't meant to kiss her, but it had seemed like such a natural thing. And when she'd returned the kiss, he'd felt as if the weight of the world had been lifted off his shoulders.

After that, everything had moved so quickly. She'd unbuttoned his shirt and then skimmed her fingers over his naked chest. And though the night had been hot and humid, Trey remembered shivering, all the heat in his body leaving his limbs to pool in his lap. Until then, he'd considered himself a ladies' man by high school standards, smooth and confident in the rather limited experience he'd had with willing partners.

Trey had wanted to stop, but he couldn't deny the need he'd felt with Libby. He'd longed for something more intimate, something to give him the courage to face his future. He'd found it that night in her body, in her soft touch and in the sweet taste of her mouth—in the way she'd moved beneath him.

It had been twelve years and he'd made love to plenty of women since Libby. But he still searched for that unexplainable connection they'd found, still sought a woman who combined guileless innocence with unrestrained passion, a woman who could capture his body and his soul. Though Libby had been a virgin that night, she'd been the one with the power to seduce, daring him to make love to her, soothing his doubts with her lips and her fingers.

And when it had been over and they'd dressed, he'd walked her to the path, her delicate hand tucked in his. She'd smiled at him, as if they'd shared a special secret that they'd both relive again and again after he was gone. And then he'd made her memorize his address at school and told her to write to him; he promised that he'd come home again. And that had been the last he'd seen or heard of Libby—until tonight.

Trey rolled back onto his stomach and looked over the log. Libby slowly walked to the shore, the soft moonlight gleaming on her wet skin. If he thought she was beautiful from the back, he was unprepared for the view from the front. He remembered a famous painting he'd seen on a vacation to Italy—Venus rising naked from a river. He couldn't remember the artist or where he'd seen it, but he was living it right now.

Water dripped from her hair, sluicing over her body, her skin slick. His fingers clenched involuntarily as he imagined what it would be like to touch her again. God, she was beautiful—not skinny and gawky as she'd been all those years ago. Libby Parrish had grown into a woman who could steal the breath from his lungs and make him ache with desire.

She picked up the dress and slipped it back over her naked body, then stepped into her sandals. Drawing a deep breath, she took one last look at the river before heading back to the path. Trey fought the urge to call out to her, to make the moment last longer. There were so many questions he needed answered— why hadn't she written to him, why hadn't she responded to his letters, had she come to regret the night they'd spent together? He watched as she disappeared from view, then groaned softly.

Great. Now he'd have this image swimming around in his head for the rest of the night! Especially since he was going to spend the night alone, with only his dog for company, trapped in a motel room on the edge of town. A motel room where the only distraction was an old television. An old television that got only one channel—the church channel.

Not even twenty-four-hour religion would banish his sinful thoughts or erase the image of a naked Libby Parrish from his mind. There was only one thing to do, besides leaving town at sunrise and never setting foot in Belfort again.

He'd just have to buy the house next door and find out exactly what kind of woman Libby Parrish had become.

"Would you please get away from that window?" Libby Parrish grabbed a handful of biscuit dough, took aim and hit the back of Sarah Cantrell's head.

The dough plopped onto the floor and Sarah turned around, rubbing her head. "Aren't you in the least bit curious? He's lived over there for a week. Don't tell me you haven't done a little spying of your own."

Libby sighed as she dumped the biscuit dough onto the floured counter. Sarah had been her best friend since the seventh grade, but there were times when she was an outright pain in the ass. And now that they worked together, that fact was made apparent on a daily basis. "Of course I'm not interested. Why would I have the slightest interest in what that man is doing?" She tried to add a good dose of disdain to "that man," but she only came out sounding like a prissy old woman. "Now, let's get back to this biscuit recipe. I'm concerned about the directions for working with the dough. Kneading is the wrong word to use here, especially if my readers take it in the context of bread. Kneading will make the dough too tough and—"

"He's mowing his lawn," Sarah said in her lazy drawl. "In a pair of baggy cargo shorts that are just barely hanging on to those nice slender hips of his. Oh, my, how I do wish he'd bend over and—"

"Stop it!" Libby cried, her heart skipping a beat. She drew a deep breath and tried to quash the fluttery feelings in her stomach.

"He's also neglected to put on his shirt, naughty boy." Sarah turned and grinned at her friend. "Now, I consider myself a connoisseur when it comes to the male form and I wouldn't mind taking a taste of what Trey Marbury has to offer. There was talk back in the day about how he was quite…confident with the ladies."

"Enough!" Libby shouted. She hurried to the window and grabbed the lace curtain from Sarah's fingers, dragging it back into place over the kitchen window. The very last thing Libby needed rattling around her head was talk about Trey Marbury's sexual prowess. She'd experienced that firsthand.

Her friend arched her eyebrow at Libby. "You're blushing. Why, after all these years, does Trey Marbury still have the power to get you all hot and bothered?"

"I'm not hot," Libby muttered. "Just bothered. And you know exactly why."

"Because he had the high nerve to move in next door to you? You and the Throckmorton sisters have been complaining about the falling-down condition of that house for three years now. You should be happy someone has moved in and started fixing it up."

"You know that's not why I'm bothered," Libby said.

Sarah's eyes rolled up and she groaned. "Oh, please, must we talk about that silly feud again? It's over. His daddy's passed on, your daddy's moved to Palm Beach and the rest of us in this sleepy little town have all but forgotten why the feud ever started in the first place."

"I'm not talking about the feud." Libby paused. "I can't believe you don't remember. It was only the most humiliating experience in my young life."

"Oh, the kiss heard 'round the world." Sarah grinned. "The kiss that changed your life. The kiss that—"

"I am holding a rolling pin," Libby warned. "And in my experienced hands, it could be considered a lethal weapon."

"You threw yourself at him and he couldn't resist your charms. Then he left town, never to be heard from again."

"And then, I was stupid enough to write him a letter and profess my adoration for him. Not just a few pages of 'Hi, how are you?', but a ten-page dissertation on my feelings. I actually thought we were the modern-day equivalent of Romeo and Juliet." Libby moaned. "Oh, God, I quoted Shakespeare and Elizabeth Barrett Browning."

"You never told me about the letter," Sarah said.

"He never wrote back. And he never came back to Belfort. I hear he spent his vacations working construction in Atlanta. He was probably too terrified to set foot in the town where I was living."

"It was just a kiss. A high school kiss. How good could it have been?"

Libby felt her cheeks warm. She'd been carrying the secret around for so long. Maybe it was time to tell Sarah. "It was more than a kiss. I lost my virginity to Trey Marbury that night."

Sarah gasped. "What? You and Trey Marbury—wait a second. How come you never told me this?"

"I wanted to. But after it happened I needed to think about it for a while. And then, when he didn't write back, I was embarrassed. I never was very confident with the boys and that certainly didn't help."

"And now you blame Trey Marbury for your lack of a social life?"

"No," Libby said. "I blame my busy career and living in a small town and the lack of eligible men in Belfort."

"Your career? Honey, you're every man's wet dream. You're beautiful, you make a lot of money *and* you cook. All that's missing is a short career as a stripper."

"Oh, right. Just the other day I saw a bunch of handsome single guys hanging out watching Julia Child. They were all saying how she was really hot and they wished they could see her naked." She slowly shook her head and sighed. "Sometimes I wonder how I ended up with this life. Why didn't I ever get out of this town? I'm living in my parents' old house, I spend my days stirring and slicing and sautéing. My idea of an exciting evening is writing grocery lists and reading old cookbooks. When did I turn into my mother?"

"Why *didn't* you get out of town?" Sarah asked.

Libby shrugged. "This is going to sound pathetic but I guess I always hoped he'd come back someday. At least that's what kept me here during college. And now, I have this house and I feel safe here." She sighed. "Maybe I should move. I could buy a place in Charleston and get out of Belfort for good."

Sarah watched Libby from across the kitchen, her expression filled with concern. "Or maybe you ought to just face him and put the past in the past. Bake some cookies, wander over into his yard and reintroduce yourself to your new neighbor." Sarah crossed the kitchen and grabbed Libby's hand, dragging her to the window. "Look at that," she ordered. "If you still want that man, you'd better make a move, because every other single woman in town is eyeing him up. Including me."

Suddenly, Libby didn't care about her biscuit recipe. She pushed the curtain aside and searched the yard for the subject of their discussion. "Why did he have to buy the house next door? It's like he just wanted to get under my skin."

"He probably doesn't even remember you live here," Sarah said.

"Believe me, he knows I live here. And I think that's why he bought the house. I—" Suddenly, Trey

Marbury came back into view and her words died in her throat. Libby held her breath as she watched him walk the length of the side lawn. Sweat glistened on his bare chest and his finely muscled arms strained against the push mower. As he passed, her gaze didn't waver. His dark hair clung damply to the nape of his neck and Libby's eyes dropped lower, to the small of his back, revealed by the low-riding shorts. Sarah had been right. If his shorts dropped any lower, she'd enjoy a full appreciation of his backside.

He turned and started back in the opposite direction, Libby's gaze now taking in a deeply tanned torso, marked by paler skin above the waist of his shorts and a line of hair that ran from his belly to beneath the faded fabric. She lingered over the view for a moment longer, then realized she'd forgotten to breathe. "He's changed," she murmured.

"It's been twelve years," Sarah said as she began to gather up her papers from the table. "We've all changed."

Libby looked over her shoulder with a rueful expression. "I guess we have." But Trey Marbury had become a man in those years, a man who seemed to exude power and strength, even in the simple act of mowing his lawn. Libby swallowed hard, memories of their night together flooding her brain.

A girl's first experience was supposed to be awkward and painful. But that wasn't how Libby remembered it. He'd been so gentle and sweet to her, taking her places she'd never been before. Libby couldn't help but wonder what twelve years had done to his abilities in the bedroom.

"I wonder why he came back," Libby murmured.

"He's not really back," Sarah replied. "Wanda Van Pelt sold him the house and she says that he's taking care of his daddy's business concerns in the area and just renovating the house as an investment. He's been living in Chicago and has some big career up there." Sarah turned away from the window and wandered over to the recipes they had spread across the table, finally resigned to getting back to the job at hand.

"He probably doesn't even remember the letter you sent him," Sarah murmured. "And you could use a few more male prospects besides Carlisle Whitby, Bobby Ray Talbert and Wiley Boone."

"Carlisle is my mailman," Libby said. "And Bobby Ray is our police chief. And I barely know Wiley Boone."

"He's the city building inspector and Flora down at the drugstore says that Wiley was inquiring about you the other day. I think he plans to ask you out. And Carlisle always gives you the extra coupon flyers and he hangs around on your porch after he delivers your mail, just hoping you'll come outside. And Bobby Ray asks you out every New Year's Eve and every Fourth of July, regular as clockwork. So which would you prefer—one of those three besotted fools or Trey Marbury?" She raised her eyebrow. "Or maybe you want to end up like the Throckmorton sisters?"

"I'm not going to be a spinster!" Libby said. "I could have a man in my life—if I wanted one. I just haven't found the right one."

"Now you've got four to pick from."

"That's some choice," she murmured.

"Well, I'm off," Sarah said, gathering up her things. "Like panties on prom night."

Libby chuckled softly. "I'll try the biscuit recipe tonight and see how the cheese variation turns out."

"You could try bits of sausage or bacon as a variation, too."

Libby turned back to the window. "Fine. Bacon sounds good." She heard the front door close; her gaze was firmly fixed on the man who lived next door. Clayton Marbury the third. He'd been Trey for as along as Libby could remember, the only son of Clayton and Helene Marbury. At one time, the Marburys had owned the bank, the general store, a string of gas stations, two car dealerships, the newspaper and half the commercial properties on Center Street. The Parrish family had owned the other half, a fact that only added fuel to the conflict over which family was the most powerful in Belfort.

Had any other single, handsome man moved in next door, Libby might have been happy. After all, it had been five years since the humiliation of her last boyfriend's infidelity, five years since she'd had a serious relationship with a man. But Trey Marbury? Every instinct told her to stay away.

Libby closed her eyes, then slipped her hands beneath her hair and lifted the pale blond strands off her neck. This heat wave was setting her nerves on edge. And the fact that she was almost a month late with her newest cookbook wasn't helping matters. In another week, she'd begin taping the next season of *Southern Comforts*, the PBS cooking show she'd been doing for the past two years. The book had to be printed and ready to ship when the first show aired in January, or she'd lose sales and viewers.

"So get to work," Libby muttered, letting her hair

drop back onto her shoulders. "And stop thinking about the past. You were a silly lovesick girl living out a fantasy that was never supposed to be real. And he was nothing more than a one-night stand." She took a last look out the window and then froze, her fingers clutching the lace of the curtain.

Trey Marbury was no longer cutting the grass. He now stood in the side yard chatting with Sarah Cantrell! Libby's mouth dropped open as she watched her best friend flirt with the enemy. They seemed to be caught up in a lively exchange, laughing and joking with each other. When Sarah reached out and brushed her hand along Trey's biceps, Libby ground her teeth. "Traitor," she muttered beneath her breath.

Libby's fingers twitched as she tried to imagine the sensation of touching him...smooth skin, slicked with sweat, hard muscle rippling beneath. She hadn't touched a man in so long that she'd nearly forgotten what it felt like to run her palms over long limbs, to sink against a male body and to be enveloped in a strong embrace. He was tall, well over six feet, with wide shoulders and a narrow waist—not a trace of the boy was left in him.

Why had he always fascinated her so? From the time she'd first known who Trey Marbury was, her parents had warned her against him. There'd be no socializing with the enemy. It wasn't difficult, considering she and Trey ran with different crowds—Trey with the popular kids, and Libby with those who preferred the library to football games and Saturday night dances.

It wasn't until she began noticing the opposite sex that Libby realized how dangerous Trey really was.

Just looking at him made her think of things that her mother had warned her about—meeting boys beneath the bleachers before school, kissing in the balcony at the movie theater, doing unspeakable things in the back seats of cars. Whenever Libby had thought about these things, the boy in her head had always been Trey and the girl he'd chosen to seduce had been her.

As she peered through the window, an unbidden rush of jealousy and a warm flood of desire collided deep inside of her. Desperate to know what Sarah and Trey were talking about, Libby tried to read their lips. But the attempt brought only frustration. She'd need to get closer. If she just wandered out to the veranda to water her hanging baskets, she might be able to overhear their conversation.

Libby grabbed her watering can from beside the back door and tiptoed to the side veranda, but all she could hear was the indistinct murmur of voices—and laughter, lots of laughter. Sarah had always been more comfortable around men, but this was ridiculous! This wasn't just a friendly conversation anymore—Sarah was flirting!

She'd have to get closer. Drawing a deep breath, she headed toward the steps and then crept along the line of azalea bushes that created a hedge between the two properties. The voices got louder and when she finally settled between two rose bushes, she could hear everything Sarah was saying.

"I'm sure she'll stop by soon," Sarah said. "She's been very busy, what with the book and the show. She starts taping the new season in the next few weeks. Have you ever seen her show?"

"I can't say that I have," Trey replied. "I've been living in Chicago."

"Oh, we're on the PBS station in Chicago."

"You're on the show, too?" Trey asked.

"No, I produce the show. And I help Libby edit her cookbooks and test her recipes."

A rustling in the azaleas drew Libby's attention away from the conversation. She nearly screamed when a wet nose poked through a hole in the bushes. Libby gave the golden retriever a gentle shove and wriggled back a few inches.

"Is that your dog?" Sarah asked. "You better not let him in Libby's yard. She is pathological about her roses. Her grandma planted those roses years ago and Libby treats them like her children."

Trey whistled softly. "Come here, Beau. Come on, boy. He's been chasing squirrels all day. You can take the dog out of the city, but you can't take the city out of the dog."

"Go," Libby whispered, waving her hand in the dog's face. "Get out of here, you mangy mutt!" But Beau took her frantic movements as encouragement and he leapt through the bushes and knocked Libby flat on her back. Libby flailed her arms as the dog stood above her and licked her face with his cold tongue, his muddy paws planted firmly on her chest. Libby closed her eyes and covered her face with her hands.

When the dog finally stopped, she risked a look up to find both Trey and Sarah staring down at her. An amused grin quirked Trey's lips.

He chuckled softly. "Well, well, well. If it isn't Lisbeth Parrish."

"I—I have to go now," Sarah said, forcing a smile.

"I've got recipes to type. I'll call you later, Lib. Nice seeing you again, Trey. Y'all take care now."

"Oh, we will be talking," Libby muttered, pushing up on her elbows and brushing her hair out of her eyes.

Trey grinned, his arms crossed over his bare chest. "I was wondering when you were going to stop by and welcome me to the neighborhood." He held out his hand to her, but Libby slapped it away, humiliated that she'd been caught spying on him.

"Is that any way to welcome me to the neighborhood? Where's my chicken casserole and my pineapple upside-down cake?"

Libby struggled to get to her feet, the roses scratching at her arms and face. He found this all so amusing. Probably as amusing as he'd found her letter, full of flowery prose and professions of love. "I only bake casseroles for people I'm happy to see."

"Lisbeth, I expected a much more hospitable welcome."

Biting back a curse, Libby brushed the mud off her cotton sundress. "I may have to tolerate your presence next door, but I don't have to like it, *Clayton*. You're a Marbury and I'm a Parrish. What do you expect from me beyond hostility?"

Trey frowned and for a moment, Libby regretted her sharp words. This was not the way she wanted to begin, but he seemed to delight in her embarrassment. He took a step toward her and she backed away, but he managed to capture her chin.

"Stay still." He slowly turned her head, then ran his thumb along her cheek.

"What—what are you doing?"

"You're bleeding," Trey said. He reached down

and withdrew a bandanna from the pocket of his shorts. Gently, he dabbed at her cheek. "You shouldn't lurk in the roses. They have thorns."

Libby stared up at his face, unable to drag her gaze away. He was much more handsome than she remembered—but then, she remembered him as a boy, a high school football star with a disarming smile and a body worthy of a Greek god. He was a man now, and his features had a harder edge; his mouth was firmer and his jaw stronger. She felt her heartbeat quicken and suddenly, she couldn't breathe.

"I—I wasn't lurking."

His gaze met hers directly and she saw eyes so blue they sent shivers down her spine. When he licked his upper lip, Libby lapsed into contemplation of how his tongue might feel moving across her mouth, tracing a path along her neck, dipping a bit lower. She swallowed hard. Why was this happening to her? She'd had other men in her life—handsome, attentive men. But they'd never made her feel this way, all light-headed and breathless, as if she were teetering on the edge of something very dangerous.

"It doesn't look too bad," he said, leaning closer to examine her wounds. "Shouldn't leave a scar."

"I suppose I should thank you," Libby said as she drew away. "But since your dog was the cause of my accident, I don't think I will."

He stared at her for a long moment, as if he could read her mind, and then shrugged. "Just trying to be neighborly."

Libby brushed the dirt off her dress. "With a line like that, it's a good thing we're standing in my garden," she muttered. "My roses need the fertilizer."

Trey hitched his hands up on his waist and shook his head. "Maybe you ought to just lay back down with the rest of the prickly things in this garden, Lisbeth."

The insult stung. She hadn't meant to act so nasty, but Trey had a way of making her feel like a seventeen-year-old geek all over again. "So we finally see the real Trey Marbury," Libby murmured, crossing her arms beneath her breasts and straightening her spine.

"What is that supposed to mean?"

She tipped up her chin. "Tell me, of all the houses in Belfort, why did you choose to move into this one?"

"You think I bought this house because of you?" Trey chuckled. "Now don't you have a low eye for a high fence."

Libby ground her teeth. He looked so satisfied, as if he had her exactly where he wanted her! All the confidence he'd possessed as a teenager had increased tenfold and Libby knew he'd have a snappy retort for anything she might throw his way. Well, she wasn't a girl anymore. She was a woman fully capable of defending herself against his charms. "You're no better than any other Marbury, all of you crooked as a barrel of snakes."

"So that's how it's going to be?" Trey asked, taking a step toward her, his eyes glittering with amusement, goading her.

"Just stay out of my way," Libby warned. "Keep your dog out of my garden and keep your nose out of my business. I'm watching you."

"Yes, I know. I've seen you peering out from behind those starched curtains. For someone who values her privacy, you're just a little too interested in your neighbors. Or is it just me you find so fascinating?"

Libby took a step forward, standing so close to him she could feel the heat of his body. She poked him in the chest, setting him back on his heels. "Don't dare presume that I have even the slightest interest in you, Marbury."

His jaw went tight as he stared into her eyes. Then, in one quick movement, he grabbed her hand and swept it behind her back, pulling her body up against his. At first, she was too stunned to protest. And then, when she opened her mouth to speak, all she could manage was a tiny gasp.

Libby's eyes drifted down to his lips and she wondered if he had any intention of kissing her. If he did, she wasn't sure that she'd be able to do anything about it—except perhaps kiss him back. But when her eyes met his again, Libby's heart froze. It was there, in the icy blue depths. He knew exactly what she was thinking.

Trey's lips curled into a grin and he chuckled softly. "What? Can't think of anything to say?"

"What I have to say to you isn't fit for civilized ears."

He leaned closer to her, taking his own sweet time as he did. Libby waited, frantically wracking her brain for some acidic comeback or well-aimed put-down, certain he was about to kiss her and knowing she didn't want to stop him. But before his lips touched hers, he paused, hovering so close she could feel his breath on her face.

Her heart hammered in her chest and Libby felt herself losing touch with reality. All she could think about was this moment and how everything hinged on her reaction. She didn't move, barely breathed, her body trembling with anticipation.

And then, he did it. She knew it was coming, but she still wasn't prepared for the flood of desire that raced through her bloodstream. In single fleeting moment, his lips were on hers. A tiny moan slipped from her throat as she collapsed against him, and he took it as an invitation. His tongue slowly traced along her bottom lip and then invaded, taking possession of both her mouth and her ability to reason.

Every nerve in her body seemed to come alive, every thought focused on the feel of his lips on hers. She'd kissed a small number of boys in her life, but this wasn't just a kiss. It was a challenge, a dare, the first salvo in a battle that had just begun—and Libby couldn't show any weakness. They weren't kids anymore and along the way, they'd acquired some very adult weapons.

She returned the kiss in full measure, her tongue meeting his, touching and tangling until the taste of him filled her. Her hands flitted to his face and then furrowed through his hair, tempting him to surrender and declare her the victor.

When he finally drew away, Libby looked up at him, proud of her effort. She expected to see the self-satisfied grin she'd come to know, but instead he appeared to be as consumed by the kiss as she was. He gazed down at her through half-hooded eyes, and his breathing was shallow and quick.

"I think we've gotten off to a fine start," he murmured, allowing his nose to bump against hers. "In fact, I think I'm going to enjoy the neighborhood just fine."

With that, he let go of her arm. Libby stumbled back, light-headed and weak-kneed, nearly falling into the rose bushes again. But she caught herself just in time, straightening her posture and smoothing her trembling hands over the front of her dress. "Don't be so sure. Just because you managed to kiss me doesn't mean I've changed my mind about you."

"*Managed* to kiss you? Considering your response, I more than managed. Besides, if you think there was anything romantic about that kiss, you're wrong."

"Really?" Libby said. "Why did you kiss me then?"

"It was the only way to keep you from hurling another insult at me," Trey replied.

"Well, there's a much easier way to accomplish that. You could just run on down to the train tracks and take yourself a nice long nap." She glanced at her watch. "The train comes through at about three, so why don't you plan on sleeping 'til four?"

"I don't think I'll be doing that," Trey said.

"Then just stay out of my life. Keep your dog out of my garden and your face out of my line of vision and we'll get on just fine. And if you're going to do yard work, at least wear a shirt."

"My, I have missed that Southern hospitality." He slowly backed away. "Just warms a man's heart."

Libby ground her teeth. There was no winning with him, no getting the last word! Deciding it was best to cut her losses, she turned on her heel and started for the house.

"I'm looking forward to that cake, Parrish."

Libby clenched her fingers into fists. "No more than I'm looking forward to the day when you lose your testicles in a tragic lawn mower accident, Marbury," she shouted over her shoulder.

As she continued her retreat to the house, Libby smiled to herself. Maybe she had gotten the last word. It wasn't the most poetic turn of phrase, but the imagery had certainly hit the mark. Yet, there was no satisfaction in the victory. Though she might have won the battle, Libby wasn't looking forward to waging the war.

It was entirely too difficult to remember that Trey Marbury was the enemy—and that falling for him again would mean surrendering the last shreds of dignity she had left.

2

TREY SEARCHED THROUGH the darkened room for his drill bits, the heat in the second-story bedroom making it hard to breathe. Since he'd moved in, he'd been sleeping on an old sofa downstairs, the tall windows thrown open to catch even the slightest breeze.

Hell, he'd been living up north for so long that he'd forgotten what a South Carolina summer was like—the unrelenting humidity, so thick it made everything stick to the skin, including whatever clothes a person could stand to wear.

It was easier to work inside once the sun went down, and there was plenty of work to do. The old Sawyer house had been left to ruin three years ago; its elderly owner had been reluctant to sell after she'd moved to a nursing home. It had been on the market just a few days when Trey moved back to Belfort and he'd jumped at the chance to buy it, offering a cash deal to speed up the sale. He'd moved in before the deal closed, ready to begin the renovations.

He'd told himself that the work would take the place of a social life in town. But after his encounter with Libby three days ago, Trey had been forced to reexamine his motives for choosing to buy this particular house.

Over the years, he'd thought about Libby, about their night at the river. No matter how he rationalized what had happened, it all still felt unfinished to him, as if there were still words that hadn't been said, feelings that hadn't been resolved.

The moment he drove into town, it was as if he were driving into the rest of his life. As much as he wanted to deny his small-town Southern roots, he'd come home, to a place where he had history. He'd come home to a place where people knew him and cared about him. Maybe he'd come back to Belfort hoping that he'd find Libby.

Trey bent down and picked through a pile of paint scrapers he'd tossed on the floor. So their first meeting hadn't gone very well. Trey hadn't expected it to be a lovefest, considering the feud that had always stood between their families. But he hadn't expected outright hostility. They'd shared an incredible night; certainly that had to have meant something.

Obviously, it hadn't. She'd never written him, never tried to make contact, even through he'd sent five or six letters. But all that had happened a lifetime ago. Libby was no longer the pale and skinny girl he knew, her wide green eyes always watching him but never meeting his gaze, taking such care to stay out of his way. She was a woman now and he was a man. Things had changed.

Trey sucked in a sharp breath. Maybe that was the way to rationalize the kiss he'd shared with her—it was just a male response to a beautiful female, purely animal in its origins. But Trey had never acted on impulse when it came to women. Every move in his romantic life had come after careful consideration. But what he felt for Libby Parrish had nothing to do with romance.

Trey snatched up the plastic case that held his drill bits and then straightened. He'd been thinking about Libby all afternoon and evening, trying to figure out what it was that had caused him to temporarily lose his mind. Yes, he was attracted to her, but at the same time, he knew to keep a safe distance. Trey was already the subject of rampant speculation around town and the last thing he wanted was to add a woman—especially Libby Parrish—to the mix of rumor and gossip. If he wanted a sex life, he'd have to find it in Savannah or Charleston, not next door.

Crossing the room to the window, Trey vowed to put every last thought of her out of his head—to forget the sweet taste of her, the feel of her body against his. But when he pushed aside the dusty drapes to open the window, he found himself faced with something more than just a mental picture. The bedroom window looked right out on Libby's bedroom, now ablaze with light. He stepped back and let the moth-eaten curtain drop, but his curiosity got the better of him. Hell, if she could spy on him, he could certainly return the favor.

He parted the drapes again and watched. It was obvious she wasn't aware of the view he had, or maybe the house had been empty for so long that it had never been a concern. Three tall windows spanned the width of her bedroom and opened onto the second-floor veranda. She hadn't bothered to pull the lace curtains that hung on either side.

Trey watched her make the bed, shaking out freshly laundered sheets and smoothing them over the mattress of the huge four-poster. She wore a simple cotton dress, loose and flowing, like the one she'd worn that night at the river. The fabric clung to her body and outlined long slender legs and a tiny waist. The neckline was cut just low enough and gaped slightly when she bent over the bed. But Trey was left to fill in the image with memories of their kiss, his hand sliding along her back and then around to her hip, her breasts pressed against his naked chest.

She walked to the window and Trey fought the impulse to step away. He knew the room was dark and that he couldn't be seen. Libby slowly unbuttoned the front of her dress, then turned and lifted her hair from her neck, letting the meager breeze cool her. Trey gnawed on his lower lip, suddenly wondering if she knew he was there, if every move was meant to taunt him further.

With a soft curse, he turned away from the window. He'd do well to find some feminine companionship and find it fast. Fantasizing about Libby Parrish was an exercise in masochism. She'd made her feelings about him patently clear—there was no love lost between the Parrishes and the Marburys, and there'd be none to find between him and Libby.

Trey tucked the drill bits into his back pocket and headed downstairs. Beau was waiting for him, his leash in his mouth and his tail thumping on the floor. "No way," Trey murmured to the golden retriever. "We're not going for a walk now. Nighttime is work time." The dog trotted after him into the kitchen where Trey grabbed a cold beer from the refrigerator. He popped the top and then took a long drink, tipping his head back to let the ice-cold liquid slide down his throat.

The interior of the house was a wreck, the result of his enthusiastic demolition. The kitchen was the only thing he hadn't touched. A guy had to eat, though he hadn't been doing much of that lately. Chicago was known for great restaurants and he'd been spoiled, never taking the time to cook for himself. But Belfort had a much more limited selection, though the restaurants served good Southern home cooking.

"What I wouldn't do for some decent Thai food," he muttered, his stomach growling. As he took another sip of his beer, Trey's cell phone rang. He picked it up from the kitchen table. "Trey Marbury," he said.

"When the hell are you coming back to Chicago?"

He immediately recognized the voice of his business partner. The day to day stress of running a successful real estate development company seemed to result in an edgy, almost frantic tone for Mark Callahan and Trey knew that this was a phone call he wasn't anxious to take. "Hey, Mark. What's up?"

"This isn't going to work."

"It hasn't even been two weeks," Trey said. "That's barely a standard vacation. Besides, I spoke with Dave this morning. If there are any problems, he's promised to call me. I can always drive back for a day or two if necessary."

"Listen, when you said you had to leave for a couple of months, I figured you'd be gone a couple of days. You're not actually going to stay away for two months, are you?"

"I need some time," Trey said. "I've got a lot of crap to sort out. When my father died in May, I came down here for the funeral and left the same day. I'm not sure I really dealt with what was going on. I need to do that now. Besides, isn't this one of the benefits of being a partner?"

"Can't you deal with your crap up here? We've got really good psychologists in Chicago."

"No, it's got to be here. I've got to take care of some things for his estate and I bought a house that I'm renovating."

Mark gasped. "You bought a house?"

"Yeah, you ought to see this place. It was built in the mid-1800s and it's got all the original architectural detailing. It's going to be sweet when it's finished. I'm doing a lot of the work myself. I was going to flip it, but I'm thinking I might just keep it for a vacation home."

"It sounds to me like you're planning to stay a lot longer than two months," Mark said.

"Well, I'm not. Now, was there a specific problem you called to discuss, or can I get back to work?" They chatted for a few more minutes, Trey reassuring his partner that he was not abandoning the business. When he finally got off the phone, Beau was still sitting at the back door, his tail thumping. Trey tossed the phone on the table and then let the dog out. But to his dismay, Beau made a beeline for the azalea hedge. "Ah, hell," he muttered, shaking his head.

Running after the dog, he got to the bushes just as the golden retriever scampered through a hole. Trey whistled softly and called, but the dog had never been very obedient. Had it been any other backyard, Trey would have walked away and let the dog wander. But he didn't need Libby Parrish banging on his door at sunrise to complain about the condition of her roses.

The grass was cool and damp beneath his bare feet as he circled around the hedge and walked into Libby's garden. As he came around the back corner of the house, he saw Beau sitting on the back porch, his nose pressed against the screen door.

"Get over here!" Trey hissed. "Beau! Come."

The dog glanced over at his master, but refused to follow orders. Trey started toward the back door, but then a figure appeared in the doorway and he froze.

She had changed from her dress to a gauzy nightgown that left her arms and shoulders bare. Her hair had been pulled up and twisted into a knot, but damp tendrils brushed her temples and curled against her neck. At that moment, Trey was certain that he'd never seen anything quite as beautiful as Libby Parrish. The light from the kitchen outlined her slender form and created a shimmering halo around her body. She looked like an angel, pure and unapproachable.

"What are you doing here?" she asked.

For a moment, Trey thought she was talking to him, but then he realized she was speaking to Beau. He waited, unwilling to break the silence of the night, hoping that the dog would turn and run.

Libby glanced both ways, then pushed the screen door open. "Are you lost? You live over there, not here." She reached down and patted the dog on the head. Trey winced. Beau was an easy mark. The slightest show of affection turned the dog into a loyal friend. It would take ten pounds of raw steak to get Beau to leave now.

"Are you hungry?" Libby asked. Beau wagged his

tail and stood up, nuzzling her hand. "Wait here," she said. "Stay. Sit."

Libby disappeared into the house and returned a moment later with a plate of biscuits. The smell drifted through the air and Trey groaned softly. He hadn't eaten anything since lunch and the scent made his mouth water. He watched as Libby plucked a biscuit off the plate and held it up for the dog.

Beau jumped up and snatched it out of her fingers, gulping the treat down in one bite. "You like that?" she asked. "Bacon bits. Here, try this one. It's got cheddar cheese and bits of jalapeño." The dog gobbled down the second offering without even chewing. "You're hungry. Doesn't anyone feed you over there? Good dog. Try this one. It's got little bits of sausage in it. Very savory."

The light from the house shone behind her and every time she shifted, the fabric of her nightgown became virtually transparent. His image of an angel disappeared and instead, Trey saw a temptress, nearly naked to his eyes. He knew he ought to feel guilty for keeping to the shadows, yet he couldn't seem to bring himself to announce his presence.

His gaze drifted up from her bare feet, along her legs, to her belly and the dark triangle just below. She wore nothing beneath the nightgown and as his eyes moved up, he could see the soft curve of her breasts and the deeper pink of her nipples.

Trey felt himself growing hard, his body as stimulated as his mind had become. What was this instant desire he felt and why couldn't he control it? Trey took a step back, ready to make a safe escape. But the minute he moved, Beau pricked up his ears and trotted down the steps.

To Trey's dismay, Libby followed. He stepped out of the shadows and Libby jumped in surprise. "I'm sorry," he said. "I didn't mean to scare you. He ran over here before I could stop him."

Libby stared at him for a long moment, as if trying to decide whether to speak or just walk back inside. "You don't scare me," she murmured, shrugging her shoulders.

"Sorry," Trey repeated, keeping his eyes fixed on her face and hoping his shorts were baggy enough to hide the growing bulge. "It smells good out here."

"I'm testing biscuit recipes," Libby said.

Trey forced a smile, fighting an urge to cross the distance between them and kiss her again. Only this time, the kiss would be gentle and seductive. "It's been a long time since I've had a decent biscuit. Up north, they eat toast and English muffins for breakfast."

"And try to find good grits," she said. "Well, that's impossible."

Trey nodded, remembering the intoxicating taste of her mouth. "Although they make decent hash browns at this place on Division and—well, never mind." He wasn't even sure what he was talking about, only that it was keeping his mind from thoughts of running his hands over every inch of Libby's body. Trey cleared his throat. "I'll just take my dog and you can get back to your biscuits."

"Would you like some?" Libby asked. "I have extra."

The offer took him by surprise, an unexpected truce he didn't want to rebuff. It wasn't a kiss, but it was a step in the right direction. "Sure."

"I'll just go get some." She hurried back into the

house and returned a moment later with a small basket. She'd taken the time to line it with a checkered napkin before stacking the biscuits neatly inside.

Trey slowly approached her and took the basket from her outstretched arms, his fingers brushing against hers. The contact sent a frisson of heat through his arm. "Thanks. They smell great."

"Try one," she urged.

He smiled, cocking his eyebrow up. "You didn't happen to slip a little rat poison in these, did you?"

"No," she said, sending him a playful glare. "But I can whip up another batch in a few minutes if you like."

Trey grabbed a biscuit and bit into it. "Oh, God," he murmured as the biscuit melted on his tongue. The outside was golden brown and flaky, and inside, it was still warm. "This is the best biscuit I've ever eaten. You know, these are almost better than—" Trey paused and cleared his throat.

"What?" Libby asked.

"Nothing."

"No, really. Be honest."

Trey shook his head. "I was going to say they were better than…sex."

This brought a tiny smile to her lips. "Bad food and bad women. Is that the real reason you decided to leave Chicago?"

"I'm glad I'm home," Trey said, his gaze meeting hers.

They stared at each other for a long time, neither one of them moving or speaking. He fought the urge to pull her into his arms again and test the limits of their attraction. Would she welcome another kiss?

Did she even realize how much he wanted her? Crazy thoughts raced through his head, fantasies that involved more than just a kiss. Trey glanced down at Beau, looking for anything to take his mind off the woman standing in front of him. "Well, thanks for the biscuits." He held the basket out to her.

"No, take them with you. You can bring the basket back later."

"Great," Trey said. He reached down and grabbed Beau's collar, tugging him along after him. "And I'll make sure he doesn't get in your yard. High fences make good neighbors, right?"

"Right," she said. "Good night."

He glanced over his shoulder. "Good night... Libby." Using her first name seemed almost too intimate, but Trey was past caring. All this treading carefully was making him crazy. Without another thought he let go of Beau's collar and dropped the basket on the grass. In a few long strides, Trey crossed the distance between them.

Taking her face in his hands, he kissed her, his mouth covering hers, his tongue gently teasing. When he finally drew away, he looked down into her face. Her eyes were closed and a tiny smile curled her lips. "There," he murmured. "That's better."

Her eyes fluttered open and she drew a shaky breath. "Th-that thing I said about the lawn mower accident? I didn't really mean it."

Trey chuckled. "Yes, you did. But I won't hold it against you." He slowly walked back to Beau and grabbed the dog's collar again, then picked up the basket. "I'll see you around, Libby."

"See ya," she called.

THE ELECTRIC FAN whirred on Libby's bedside table but did nothing to dispel the heat in her bedroom. She lay unmoving on the bed, her arms and legs splayed, the sheets tossed aside. She thought about turning on the old air conditioner, but it made so much noise that she'd never get to sleep. And sleep would be her only relief from the thoughts that plagued her mind.

A tiny breeze fluttered at the curtains and Libby sighed softly, then rolled onto her stomach. She'd been trying to sleep for nearly three hours and was just a few minutes short of giving up completely.

"Damn him," she muttered, punching her pillow. "Damn that Trey Marbury."

Libby was loath to admit what had been keeping her awake, but that didn't stop her mind from wandering into inappropriate territory—namely Marburyland. From the moment he'd moved in next door, she'd vowed to maintain her distance. It had taken her years to get over him the first time and she wasn't going to go through that again.

She touched her lips as she remembered how it felt to kiss him. There had been times in the past when she'd thought back to the night they spent at the river, the passion they'd shared. But a simple kiss in the here and now was enough to make all those memories pale in comparison.

A shiver skittered down her spine. If only the moment had been repugnant or disgusting, then maybe she wouldn't be faced with a long night spent thinking about Trey. But the way he had pulled her into his embrace, the way he'd taken possession of her mouth and shattered her resistance...she wanted to hate him for the power he held over her, but instead, Libby was drawn to him, intrigued by desire she couldn't control.

She rolled over again and closed her eyes, but the images wouldn't go away, and this time, they didn't stop with just a kiss. Libby imagined his hands on her body, brushing aside her nightgown, searching for bare skin. He'd cup her breast, smooth his thumb over her nipple and tease it to a peak.

A tiny moan slipped from her throat as desire twisted at her core. His touch wouldn't be gentle or tentative. He'd know how to make her ache, how to make her shiver and writhe. And when his fingers weren't enough, he'd use his tongue and his lips to drive her wild.

Libby rubbed her stomach with her palm, tempted to satisfy the ache herself simply to get Trey Marbury out of her head. It wasn't him she wanted, Libby rationalized. She'd just been without a man for such a long time…it was about pure desire. It had nothing to do with how he made her feel.

With a low curse, Libby clenched her fists and pounded them into her pillow. He wasn't going to make her want him again. Tomorrow morning, she'd wake up and she'd forget he lived next door. She'd go on about her life without reliving the kisses they'd shared, without rewinding their conversations.

Libby rolled off the bed and walked out to the hall. French doors opened from the hallway onto the back veranda and she wandered over to them. From there, she could see the back part of Trey's house as well as his yard. The house was still ablaze with light and she wondered if he was having as much trouble sleeping as she was.

As she stared out into the quiet night, Libby ran her fingertip along her lower lip. "So he's a good kisser," she murmured. "He's probably had a lot of practice." But even thinking about all the women he'd had since that long-ago night didn't alleviate the desire.

Her mind flashed an image of him, naked, lying in her bed, fully aroused. She swallowed and tried to put the picture out of her head, but it was slowly burning into her brain, a spot of intense light that wouldn't disappear even when she closed her eyes.

"Stop it!" she said, clenching her fists at her side. "This is ridiculous!" There had to be a way to put an end to this fascination, to make sure neither one of them ever crossed that line again. But how could she bring up the subject in conversation, especially since she'd vowed to stay away from him?

"I'll write him a letter," Libby murmured.

She turned and hurried down the stairs to her office. Her desk was stacked with vintage Southern cookbooks and sheets of hand-written recipes. Libby reached out to turn on her computer, but decided a personal note would be best. She grabbed several sheets of her personalized stationery and then picked out her favorite fountain pen before wandering back upstairs to her bedroom.

Libby sat down in the overstuffed chintz chair near the window and fanned herself with the stationery as she considered what to write. "I should outline my expectations," she murmured. "We need to maintain a cordial, but neighborly relationship."

She gnawed on the cap of the pen for a long moment before she began writing. "Dear Mr. Marbury." She shook her head. "Dear Trey?"

Dear? "Dear" seemed far too affectionate. But what other choice was there?

"I'm writing this letter so I might address some of the...concerns I have over our recent..." She groaned. "I can't say 'kiss.' Our recent interactions. Though the enmity between our two families has been long-standing, I am hopeful that we can put the past behind us and maintain a cordial, if not friendly, relationship."

Libby reread the first part of the letter and nodded. It was clear that more kissing would not be welcomed. "To that end, I'd like to suggest we follow a prescribed set of guidelines when it comes to our future interactions."

The letter sounded so formal. This was a man whose kisses made her toes tingle, a man she had a very memorable sexual history with, a man who had caused her heart to race and her head to spin. Why would *any* unmarried woman want a man like that to stay out of her life?

"Because, I'm completely insane," Libby muttered. "The gossip around town would be unbearable. And if my parents ever found out, they'd probably kill me. And, after he goes back to Chicago, I'll be a complete wreck. Four good reasons."

Libby wrote a few more lines, then read the letter again. But suddenly, the idea of making rules to follow seemed childish. She picked up the paper and crumpled it into a ball; then she began again.

There had to be a way to put her feelings into words, to make him understand her insecurities without admitting how long it had taken to get over him the first time. Any contact between them would only be tempting fate.

By the time she finished her fifth draft of the letter, the sun was beginning to brighten the horizon. Downstairs, the mantel clock struck five and Libby signed the letter, folded it and slipped it into an envelope. It had taken nearly three hours, but she'd managed to put her thoughts into words. Now she just had to deliver the letter.

Libby crawled out of the chair, rubbing her tired eyes with her fingertips. She grabbed her robe and slipped into it, then tucked the note in her pocket. If she snuck out under cover of darkness, she could avoid the nosy neighbors and running into Trey.

The neighborhood was quiet as she stepped outside, the sound of a blue jay's call echoing from the top of an oak tree. Libby glanced up and down the street, then hurried down the front steps and across the damp grass. All the lights were off at Trey's house and she tiptoed up to the front door. Wincing, she opened the squeaky top of the brass mailbox and shoved the letter inside. For a moment, she considered snatching it back out, but then decided that a letter was the only way to handle the situation between them.

As she ran back to her house, her feet wet with the morning dew, Libby breathed a sigh of relief. She'd done it. She'd put any possibility of a relationship with Trey firmly behind her. Now, she could finally stop spending her days and nights thinking about him.

She yanked the door open and rushed inside, then slammed it shut behind her. Her heart beat hard and she gulped in a deep breath. "Everything's going to be all right now," she whispered to herself. "Everything can get back to normal." But even as she said the words, Libby didn't believe them.

As long as Trey Marbury was living next door, nothing would ever be normal again.

TREY FROWNED as he heard the soft thud of footsteps on the front porch. Grabbing his mug of coffee, he strolled to the front door and peeked out the beveled-glass window, only to see Libby Parrish racing across his front lawn. He quickly opened the door, anxious to speak to her again. But by the time he got outside, Libby had already disappeared.

He shook his head and then glanced around. If she'd come for a reason, then she'd obviously changed her mind. The fact that he didn't find a flaming bag of dog poo on the porch or eggs splattered on the windows was a good sign. At least they'd moved past open hostility.

With a shrug, he picked up the newspaper and walked back inside. For now, he wasn't going to try to figure out what was going through Libby's mind. It was enough to know she enjoyed kissing him.

He started back to the kitchen, his stomach rumbling with hunger. Trey grabbed the orange juice from the ancient refrigerator and a box of cereal from the counter. He'd just filled a bowl of Cap'n Crunch when a knock sounded on the front door. Trey jumped up and wiped his hands on his shorts, wondering if Libby had changed her mind. But when he caught sight of his visitor, Trey frowned.

"Hello," the mailman said.

"Hi," Trey replied.

"I thought I'd take the opportunity to introduce myself, Mr. Marbury. I'm Carlisle Whitby. I'm your U.S. postal carrier. I'll be responsible for delivering your mail."

"Great," Trey said, wondering why that warranted a personal introduction.

"You probably don't remember me. We attended high school together."

"Right, Carl Whitby. You were a couple of years older, weren't you?"

"That's correct, Mr. Marbury. But I go by the name Carlisle now. It's more befitting an employee of the U.S. Postal Service. Fourteen-year veteran. Joined up after I graduated from Belfort High."

Trey rubbed the back of his neck, working out a kink from spending another night on the couch. "Is there something I can do for you, Carlisle?"

"No, but there's something I can do for you." The mailman held out a stack of mail, then pointed to an envelope on the top. "I found that in your box."

"What is it?"

"It's not a piece of stamped and postmarked mail. Postal regulations prohibit the use of a designated U.S. Postal Service mailbox for anything other than the U.S. mail. Now, I'm willing to let you go this one time, but I'd appreciate it if you'd inform whoever placed this envelope in your box that it is against federal regulations."

Trey took the mail from Carlisle and then examined the envelope in question. "I'm not sure who this is from."

Carlisle snatched the envelope back and examined it. "Looks like an invitation," he said. "A-2 envelope, linen finish. This would be one of your finer grades of stationery. Many of the ladies around town use it. Tansy Miller orders it special down at the Paper Barn."

"Thanks," Trey said, grabbing the envelope and adding it to the stack of mail.

Carlisle smiled. "I know my mail. I know my zip codes, too. Ask me any city in our fine state and I can tell you the zip code."

"I'll keep that in mind if I ever need to mail a letter," Trey said. He nodded, then quickly stepped back inside the house. When he closed the door behind him, he sighed. There were some benefits to an anonymous life in the big city. In Chicago, he'd never even met his mailman.

He tossed the stack of mail on the end table and examined the plain envelope. A floral scent drifted through the air and he touched the letter to his nose. Whoever had written it had doused it with perfume before dropping it in his mailbox.

His curiosity piqued, Trey slipped his finger under the flap and pulled out a single folded page.

I dreamt about you last night. I wasn't sure I should tell you, but the dream was so vivid, I woke up believing it was real. Did you come to me in the darkness? Did we act out some forbidden fantasy? Or was the memory of your touch merely imagined? All I remember is I wasn't surprised when you appeared in my bedroom. You didn't have to tell me why you'd come, because deep inside, I knew I willed you to that exact place in time. We didn't speak.

There was nothing to say once you kissed me. I wanted you to possess me, to own me. I felt your hands on my body, touching me, making me ache for something more. I should have told you to stop, but I didn't. And when you finally brushed aside my clothes and carried me to the bed, I was beyond all reason, desperate to feel your body above mine, inside mine. Was it a dream? And if it was, will it come again tonight?

Trey stared at the letter in disbelief. What the hell was this? He flipped the paper over, but there was nothing written on the back, no indication of whom it came from, no signature, no return address on the envelope, nothing.

"This has got to be some kind of a joke," he murmured. But as he read it over a second time, he realized it wasn't obscene enough to be a joke. Whoever wrote it knew how to spell and how to put together a sentence. The handwriting looked distinctly feminine and a bit old-fashioned and the stationery was watermarked and expensive.

"Libby," he murmured, a gasp of surprise slipping out with her name. She'd been on his porch this morning. What else could she have been doing except slipping the note in his mailbox?

"Libby Parrish, you naughty girl," Trey murmured with a chuckle. She seemed so cautious around him, as if wary of his motives. He scanned the letter again.

If he were a suspicious man, he might believe she was leading him on, simply for the chance to shut him down when the time came. She was a Parrish and he was a Marbury. And she had dumped him once before. Trey could see her taking a perverse pleasure in doing it again.

Trey shook his head. Libby had lived in Belfort her whole life; and folks in town expected her to be the picture of Southern propriety and gentility. He knew all about expectations. Maybe she just wanted to cut loose every now and then, to enjoy the pleasures of the flesh with a willing partner.

But was he a willing partner? To his eyes, Libby was just about the sexiest woman he'd ever met. Since he'd first set eyes on her again, his thoughts had been filled with images of her, his mind conjuring one fantasy after another, fantasies that usually involved the two of them naked and aroused.

Though his mind had occasionally wandered into the land of sexual fantasy, Trey hadn't made a habit of lapsing into daydreams about sex—until now. What was it about Libby that intrigued him so?

He'd had a social life in Chicago but, in retrospect, the women he'd dated and bedded had always worn their sexuality on the outside, unafraid to make their wants and needs known, almost aggressive in their pursuit of pleasure. There'd been no coy glances and hidden longings, no indecision, no pretending and certainly no erotic notes left in his mailbox. Sex had been a transaction, an exchange of mutually beneficial orgasms. In short, there'd been no mystery.

At first he'd found no-strings sex to be a welcome convenience. But he'd grown up believing that women were supposed to be capricious and unpredictable, that sex was an illicit pleasure, and that made the chase and conquest even more satisfying. How could he not be intrigued by a woman who'd take the time to put her feelings of lust into a letter?

So what the hell was he going to do about it? He could throw the note out and pretend he'd never received it. Or he could march across the lawn and demand to know why she'd sent it. Trey drew a deep breath. Or he could walk through her door tonight and do exactly what she asked. He could seduce her.

A knot of desire twisted inside of him and he groaned. He'd be the first to admit that it had been too long between sexual encounters. But was he ready to throw himself into a passionate affair with Libby? And was he ready to face what would come after that? Hot, sweaty sex between the heirs to the Marbury-Parrish feud would not go unnoticed in Belfort. And then there was the whole prospect of walking away from her again. He'd done it once before and he wasn't sure he'd be able to do it again.

Trey tossed the note onto the pile of mail, determined to put thoughts of Libby out of his mind for now. He'd wait until they ran into each other again and then decide how to proceed. He'd take careful stock of her mood, determine her motives and then make a decision.

Trey strode to the kitchen and picked up the keys to the Jeep and then noticed the empty basket sitting on the counter, still lined with the checkered napkin. He had an excuse to see her again—to return the basket and thank her for the biscuits. Perhaps he should use the opportunity to figure out what was going on in Libby's head.

As he jogged down the back steps, the humidity

nearly knocked him over. The heat wave had been relentless, making him restless and on edge with the lack of sleep. How was a guy supposed to think straight in an atmosphere that seemed to melt away all his inhibitions?

Up north, he'd grown numb to his environment, to the grating sounds of traffic and smells of a busy city. But here, everything seemed to be designed to tempt the senses—the heavy scent of flowers, the lazy songs of the birds, the rustle of a fickle breeze in the live oaks and the taste of a freshly baked biscuit. He wanted to indulge in it all, to satisfy every little desire.

Trey hopped inside the Jeep, turned the ignition and opened all the windows. The air conditioner blew out hot air and he cursed softly at the merciless weather. What he wouldn't give right now for a crisp autumn day in Chicago, with the wind blowing off the lake and the clouds drifting in front of the sun. Summer in the South could really get under a guy's skin.

Everything moved slower—people, cars, even the stoplights seemed to take their time changing. Trey headed for the drugstore; Band-Aids were the first thing on his list. He pulled into a parking spot in front and jumped out of the Jeep, smiling at a little girl sitting outside the door with a drippy Popsicle.

Harley Simpson was behind the counter when Trey walked in, the bell jangling above the door. Trey gave him a wave and Harley called out his name. "I see Tech got that quarterback from Charleston. Threw for over three hundred yards in one game. That'll never beat the game you played against Carter High where you and Frankie Jackson connected on that 98-yard touchdown in the last ten seconds. Lord, that was a sight."

"That was somethin'," Trey said, forcing a smile. The townsfolk seemed caught in a time warp, still thriving on talk of his past glory at Belfort High and Georgia Tech. He hurried to the back of the store, hoping to avoid any more dissertations on how it was a damn shame he'd wrecked his arm and how he'd have been a great NFL quarterback if it hadn't been for his injury. Trey had given up that dream years ago; the folks in Belfort were still living it.

Harley's wife was minding the pharmacy and she smiled at Trey as he plucked a box of bandages off the shelf. He turned to walk back up to the front, but paused beside a display of condoms. He stared at the colorful boxes, some promising increased pleasure, others touting better lubrication. He reached for a box of twelve, knowing that he should be prepared for any eventuality.

"Those are a top seller. You can't go wrong there."

Trey jumped at the sound of Flora Simpson's voice and glanced over his shoulder to find her standing behind him. "Thanks," he murmured.

"Although these are our second-best seller." She pointed to a blue box. "See, they have these ribs. Supposed to be good for the lady." Though Libby's pleasure was of paramount importance to Trey, he wasn't about to discuss it with Flora Simpson.

The bell above the door jangled and Trey snatched up a box of three, but Flora grabbed his arm. "That's not your best buy," she said. "This twelve-pack saves you twenty-three percent. And then we have the economy pack. Harley always says you get more bang for your buck that way." She smiled up at Trey. "So, who's the lucky lady?"

"There is no lucky lady—I mean, there isn't, yet. I just—"

"Flora, I need some boric acid. I've got these ants building hills in my rose garden and..." Her voice trailed off as Libby noticed Trey standing next to Flora. Her gaze met his and Trey smiled. Lord, she was pretty. Even though the heat wilted everything in sight, she looked so...fresh. He wanted to pull her into his arms and inhale the scent of her hair, run his hands over her smooth skin. Had Flora not been standing next to them, he would have pulled her behind the condom display and kissed her.

"Hi," Trey said.

Libby glanced between Flora and Trey. Her gaze dropped down to take in the small package in his hand. "I—I'm sorry. I didn't mean to interrupt."

"You weren't," Trey said, shoving the box back onto the rack. He held up the Band-Aids. "I just stopped by for these."

Flora watched the two of them with a suspicious eye and then smiled. "Say, Libby, I have a recipe you might like. It's for my grandmother's Brunswick stew. I'd be happy to make it on your show. I know you had the governor on last season and he did his mama's Frogmore stew. Though I've never tasted the governor's stew, I'm sure my Brunswick stew is much better and I'd—"

"I could use that boric acid," Libby said.

Flora sighed. "I've got to check in the back."

"No, that's all right," Libby said, "I'll—"

"No, no," Flora insisted. "I'll fetch it straightaway." She bustled off, leaving Trey and Libby standing in front of the condom display.

She smiled wanly. "Ever since I had Governor Winston on, everyone in town is looking for a guest spot."

Trey drew a deep breath and marshaled his thoughts. The scent of her perfume, hints of citrus and flowers, filled the air. He tried to recall the scent on the letter, but couldn't place it. "I'm glad I ran into you," Trey said, reaching out to hook her hand with his little finger. He ran his thumb over the back of her wrist.

She shifted uneasily, glancing over her shoulder to see who might be watching, her pale hair falling in careless waves around her face. He searched her gaze, looking for some sign that she'd sent him the letter, afraid she was about to bolt. But what the hell was he looking for—lust, guilt, embarrassment? Or was that part of the game she was playing, this calculated indifference? He was tempted to sweep her into his arms and kiss her, simply to gauge her reaction.

"I wanted to thank you again for the biscuits," he said. "I had the last of them for breakfast."

"Great." Another long silence descended around them and she forced a smile. "Well, I should really go. I've got a lot of work to do. Tell Flora I'll stop by for the boric acid later."

He nodded. "I'll see you, Libby."

She backed away, her smile fading slightly. "Bye, Trey."

By the time Flora returned with the box of boric acid, Trey had managed to curse himself up one side and down the other. God, Libby Parrish made him feel like a bumbling kid again! Looking into those green eyes, he could hardly put a sentence together, much less express a coherent thought.

"Where did she go?" Flora asked.

Trey shrugged. "She said she'd stop back later," he murmured. He smiled as he took the box of Band-Aids to the counter. Though Libby maintained a very proper facade in public, he knew what was bubbling beneath the surface. She was a passionate woman and tonight, he'd find out how far she was willing to go for pleasure.

3

"He was buying condoms! You know what that means, don't you?"

Sarah took a long sip of her lemonade, watching Libby over the rim of her glass. "He's a sexually responsible adult who apparently doesn't buy into that whole 'saving it for marriage' concept?"

"No," Libby countered. "It means he's planning to have sex. A man doesn't buy condoms unless he has…prospects."

"You think he has the hots for someone around town?"

"I don't know…."

Sarah's eyes popped open wide. "You think he's going to make the moves on you!" she accused.

"I do not," Libby lied. "Having sex with Trey Marbury has never once crossed my mind. It would be a stupid thing to do, especially after what happened the last time."

"I thought it was good," Sarah said.

"The sex was. But the leaving part wasn't. I'm not going to put myself through that again. I don't want him." She drew a deep breath. "I don't."

"Sell that story somewhere else," Sarah countered. "I don't believe you. If Trey walked in here right now, ripped off his clothes and offered himself to me, I'd jump his bones without a second thought."

Libby glared at her friend as she folded whipped egg whites into the custard mixture for an orange-buttermilk pie, a recipe she'd found in an old church cookbook. "I should have put that letter in his mailbox."

"What letter?"

"I wrote him a letter last night explaining how I hoped we could be friends. I put it in his mailbox, but then I had second thoughts and took it out a few hours later."

"So, you're still hot for him," Sarah said. "That doesn't surprise me. Before I left the other day, I must say, I saw some sparks between the two of you."

"And you were the one waiting on the sideline with the can of gasoline. If you hadn't talked to him, I wouldn't have fallen in the rose bushes and Trey and I wouldn't have had a blistering argument. I also wouldn't have suggested a messy lawn mower accident involving his manhood."

Sarah gasped, laughter bubbling from her throat. "You didn't."

"I did. And then to make things worse, I let him kiss me. And then, later, his dog came over and then he came over and I gave him some biscuits and...I let him kiss me again."

"Trey or the dog?" she interrupted.

Libby rolled her eyes. "Very funny. Trey. And don't look at me like that. I just happened to have some biscuits fresh out of the oven."

Sarah wagged her finger. "I've known you far too long, Libby, and that's the way it always starts. You see a guy you like, you find some way to ply him with your cooking and a few bites later, he's putty in your hands."

"Well, not this time. I was just being neighborly."

"Oh, and you kiss all your new neighbors?" Sarah grinned. "I think Trey does plan on having sex with you."

Libby paused before pouring the filling into the partially baked piecrust. "Did I invite you here tonight or did you just show up to bug me? I can't recall."

"I didn't have anything better to do on a Friday night."

The clock in the front parlor began to strike eleven and Libby wiped her hands on a dishtowel. "Go home. And take that sweet potato pie recipe with you. We've got that and the orange-buttermilk pie recipe to test and then we're done with the desserts."

"Then we're done for good," Sarah said.

"We are?"

She nodded. "I've tested everything else. This is the only thing I've been waiting for."

"The cookbook is done?" Libby murmured, her voice laced with disbelief. "It can't be done."

"We've finished everything you outlined last fall. We've tested every recipe and prepared every menu. You've written all the copy and I've proofread all the recipes."

Libby set down the mixing bowl and spatula, stunned that the year's worth of work was done. The time had passed so quickly. In just a few months, she'd be thirty years old. She frowned. Her career had consumed her life, so much that the days seemed to fly by in a haze of ingredients and manuscript pages. Last year at this time, she'd had so many plans, both professional and personal. She'd resolved to take a vacation, to meet new people, to find a nice man to date, all before her thirtieth birthday.

"What's wrong?" Sarah asked.

Libby looked up, her thoughts interrupted. "Nothing. I was just thinking how fast time passes. It seems like just yesterday that we finished the last cookbook." She paused. "I thought things would be different, that's all."

"How?"

Libby shrugged. "I don't know. I guess I was hoping something exciting would happen in my life, something major."

"Your show was picked up by seven more stations. You're about to publish your second cookbook. I'd say life is definitely looking up."

Libby grabbed the pie and bent to place it in the oven. When she straightened, Sarah was watching her with a discerning gaze. "I'm happy. I am. And I'm grateful to you. The show was your idea. I just wanted to put my family recipes in a cookbook. You're the one who made it all happen."

"Good, you should be thankful," Sarah said, giving Libby a hug. "I'm a very good friend. And as your friend, I'm going to give you a little advice. If you want something exciting to happen in your life, you're going to have to take a few risks."

Libby was about to argue but then sighed and smiled wearily at her friend, too tired to protest. "You're probably right." She rubbed her temple. "This heat is really getting to me. I think I'm going to clean up here and take a nice cool bath. Why don't we start proofing the rest of the cookbook manuscript next week? We've got to go to Charleston tomorrow to check out the new set and we can go over the menus that we have planned with the graphics people. I have some ideas there that I'd like them to try."

Sarah gathered up her things and stuffed them into her tote. "I'll pick you up tomorrow morning at ten."

Libby nodded and then followed Sarah to the front door. She watched as her friend walked to her car parked at the curb, waving as Sarah drove off. Turning back to the silent house, Libby tried to shake the melancholy that had come over her in the kitchen. She did have an exciting life. Her career was taking off, speaking engagements all over the country had given her a chance to travel and she was becoming known as an expert in low-country southern cooking. What more could she want?

When she reached the kitchen, she stood in front of the counter and groaned. "This is what my life is. Pie." Bourbon pecan pie, orange-buttermilk pie, lemon meringue pie. She'd spent her entire day baking pies in ninety-five-degree weather. "But they're excellent pies."

She'd been satisfied with her life until Trey had moved in next door. Now, she spent her time thinking about him, fantasizing about what they might share, wondering if it would be as wonderful as she imagined.

She grabbed up a towel, ready to begin cleaning up the spilt flour and dirty bowls, but then immediately tossed the towel aside. Instead, she retrieved the pitcher of lemonade from the refrigerator, poured a tall glassful and walked out to the back veranda, turning off the kitchen lights as she left.

Libby stood at the screen door, pressing the cool lemonade glass against her cheek. Her knit camisole and cotton skirt clung to her damp skin, but a tiny breeze rustled the live oaks in the backyard. She pushed at the door and walked outside, sipping the tart drink as she strolled through the yard.

The scent of roses hung in the air and the musical sound of the crickets drifted through the quiet night. In the distance, thunder rumbled and lightning flickered. Above, the moon shone through a gauzy haze. She stood in the middle of the lawn and closed her eyes, drawing a deep breath and waiting for the breeze to freshen.

Just a few minutes ago, while saying goodbye to Sarah, she'd been exhausted, spent by the heat. But now, when left alone with her thoughts, she became restless, her mind filled with images of Trey.

She wanted to put him out of her head. Yet something about the man held her in this strange limbo—he was dangerous and intriguing, maddening and exciting. She wanted to hate him, to punish him for what he'd done all those years ago. Yet he represented everything she was missing in her life.

"It's just the heat," she murmured, her eyes still closed. "If it would only rain, these feelings would go away." People had been known to go stark raving mad in the midst of a heat wave. Libby was beginning to understand why.

She opened her eyes and her breath caught in her throat. He stood ten feet away, next to the hedge, his tall frame barely visible in the dark. Libby blinked, certain that it was just a trick of the moonlight. She took a step back and he moved. It was only then that Libby realized the man standing in front of her was real, flesh and blood, and not some apparition she'd fantasized.

It was late, far later than proper for a neighborly visit. And he was barely dressed—a cotton shirt open to the waist, baggy shorts and bare feet. Her heart slammed in her chest and she prayed that he'd disappear as quickly as he'd appeared. But then he began a slow approach, his gaze fixed on her face.

For every step he took toward her, she took one backwards, unsure of what to do. She needed time to think. Time to understand what this undeniable attraction really was. When she reached the steps, she hurried inside the house and then stood at the screen door and watched him. He waited there in the moonlight, unyielding, unmoving.

With a trembling hand, she reached for the latch on the door, then drew her fingers away. Common sense warned her to run, but she was tired of running. For once, she wanted to take a risk, like she had that night twelve years ago. Libby gave the screen door a shove, opening it wide, then turned and slowly walked through the darkened house.

Her feet brushed softly over the oriental carpet on the stairs, her mind acutely aware of the sensation. All her senses seemed to be suddenly keener, taking in the cool of the wooden banister, the smell of lemon furniture polish and the sound of her heart thudding in her chest.

When she reached her room, she sat on the edge of the bed and waited. Seconds ticked by, her pulse settling into an easy rhythm. Libby closed her eyes again. Had she imagined seeing him? Was this all part of a cruel trick her mind had played?

She slowly counted to one hundred and then opened her eyes. He stood in the doorway of her bedroom, watching her again, waiting. Her mind scrambled for something to say. Why had he come? What was he expecting?

She slowly rose and opened her mouth to speak, but he shook his head and touched his finger to his lips. Then, he held out his hand, giving her the choice. She could walk into his arms and be lost forever, or she could turn away and he'd disappear. It all came down to one choice—her whole life down to this single moment, a heartbeat to make a decision that might change things forever.

Libby drew a deep breath and crossed the room. Wrapping her arms around his neck, she stared up at him. His hands moved up to cup her face and he kissed her, his tongue gently testing, then invading. She should have been surprised, but she wasn't. This was exactly what she'd been waiting for, this undeniable heat. She'd just never expected to find it again with Trey.

She had thought so much about the feel of his lips on hers, about the taste of his tongue; it was as if one hunger was being satisfied, only to have another spring to life inside her. She wanted his hands on her body, his skin touching hers.

His lips moved from her mouth to her neck. Brushing aside the strap of her camisole, he kissed her shoulder, then gently grazed the skin with his teeth. A shudder raced through her and she felt her knees wobble. All the secrets that she'd kept about that night became clear in her mind. This was what she remembered—this power to possess, this helpless hunger.

He traced a line with his tongue, from her shoulder, along the curve of her neck to the base of her throat, then lower. And when her top stopped his descent, he reached down and grabbed the hem. In one motion, he pulled it up and over her head.

His mouth found hers again and he furrowed his fingers through her hair as he kissed her. The taste of Trey was intoxicating, melting the last shreds of her resistance. Libby's breasts pressed against his naked chest, her nipples hard with the contact against damp skin.

She'd formulated so many fantasies involving Trey over the past few days, but the experience of his touch was so much more than she'd ever imagined. His fingertips were electric on her body, his lips a fiery brand. She wasn't a girl and he wasn't a boy anymore. They were both adults now and they knew what they wanted.

His hand slipped down to caress her breast, his thumb teasing her nipple. Her sigh sounded loud to her ears and she realized that they hadn't said a word. The seduction was unfolding in silence. But there were no words for what she was feeling, this inexorable climb toward her release. Every touch drew her closer and closer, and Libby was suddenly afraid of the power he held over her. She'd kept such tight control over her life. Could she allow herself this vulnerability?

Libby drew back, staring up into his eyes, but she could barely see his face in the feeble moonlight that filtered through the windows. He kissed her again, deeply, then scooped her up and carried her towards the bed.

As Trey set her back on her feet, he reached around for the button of her skirt and a moment later, the thin cotton garment was pooled on the floor. His shirt followed before he gently pushed her back and they tumbled onto the bed together.

Outside, thunder rumbled and the wind shifted direction, blowing at the lace curtains and whistling through the screens. The storm inside her body raged even more violently as she lost herself in Trey's seduction. His hands and lips and tongue danced over her sweat-slicked skin. She should have wanted to stop him, but everything inside her ached for more of the same.

Trey rolled to her side and she caught sight of his face in a flash of lightning. His expression was intense, his brow furrowed. Libby reached up and smoothed her hand across his forehead and then along his beard-roughened cheek. It had been so easy to hate Trey, but the reasons didn't make sense anymore, especially when he made her feel so…alive.

His lips found her breast and Libby sank back into the mattress, arching as he teased at her nipple with his tongue. When he finished, he moved lower, kiss by kiss, trailing a damp line to her belly. She sucked in a sharp breath, her body beginning to tremble, her mind losing touch with reality.

And then he was there, first with his fingers, sending wild waves of sensation through her body. Libby cried out as he slipped a finger inside of her. She didn't need to think. Her mind automatically focused on his touch, sure and determined, yet incredibly gentle. And when his tongue found the nub of her desire, spasms rocked her body.

Libby writhed on the bed as he played out her orgasm, begging for him to stop the torment yet unable to control the shudders that raced through her. It seemed to go on forever, further evidence of his power over her. And though she felt at her most vulnerable, something inside of her sensed that she could trust him with this.

He brought her down slowly; her breath came in tiny gasps, her hands twisted through his hair. And when he moved back beside her, his lean body brushed along hers, sending a fresh wave of desire to her core.

Trey nuzzled the curve of her neck, his face still damp with her release. She closed her eyes and listened as the storm rolled through, crashing all around them. And when the rain began and Trey got up to close the windows, Libby closed her eyes, relieved that it was finally over—the heat wave, the longing inside her, the anger and regret she'd carried for so long. They all seemed to be one and the same.

She drifted off, exhaustion overwhelming her, and when Libby opened her eyes to the pale dawn, he was gone. It hadn't been a dream. Her body still tingled where he'd touched her and the scent of him still hung in the air. She was past trying to figure out what made her want him. Desire was unpredictable and sometimes undeniable.

And for now, that was explanation enough.

EUDORA THROCKMORTON SAT primly on the edge of the sofa, watching her sister sleep. It was nearly ten in the morning and Eulalie was normally up with the chickens. She also preferred to sleep in her own bed, not in their mama's favorite Chippendale chair pulled up next to the front parlor window.

"Sister!" she whispered. "Sister, wake up!"

Eulalie's eyes popped open and the field glasses she'd been holding landed on the carpet with a soft thud. "Good Lord, what time is it?"

"Ten in the morning. Did you fall asleep here? When I went up to bed, you said you'd be right along."

A tiny smiled twitched at the corners of Eulalie's mouth. "It worked. As sure as rain when there's clothes on the line, my plan has worked."

"What plan?"

"My plan to create a little scandal in Belfort. It worked. Last night, due to my efforts, Lisbeth Parrish and our new neighbor, Clayton Marbury, had a secret assignation. I do believe they might have had—" she lowered her voice "—intimate relations."

"Great day in the mornin', what are you babblin' on about? Have you gone completely 'round the bend?"

"I've come to believe that it was Providence that brought Mr. Marbury to buy the Sawyer house. Imagine Parrishes and Marburys living right next door to each other. And that Clayton is such a handsome young fellow. And Lisbeth, a lovely girl, but flirtin' with spinsterhood. It was bound to happen. I just helped it along a bit."

"Let me get you a cup of tea, sister. I believe you've become delusional. I'm going to call Dr. Lassiter."

Eulalie grabbed Eudora's hand before she had a chance to escape. "I'm in full possession of my faculties, Dora, and the picture of good health."

Eudora clutched at her sister's hand. "Then explain what this is all about."

"I placed a letter in Mr. Marbury's mailbox yesterday. A very...erotic letter suggestin' that a certain lady wanted him to pay her a visit. Of course, I didn't use names. I let Mr. Marbury believe what he would. I watched the house all day and all night and—well, let us just say, when you have a rooster, he's bound to crow."

"You told me you were watchin' birds with Papa's field glasses but I don't believe roosters are found in Mr. Audubon's *Guide to Birds*."

"Back to the point, I saw Clayton Marbury leaving the Parrish house at two in the mornin'. And he wasn't wearin' his shirt or his shoes. How do you think Belfort is going to react to that little bit of scandal?"

Eudora shook her head. "There is just no chance of a Marbury and a Parrish falling into an illicit affair. Her father would be furious and his daddy would turn over in his grave. I can't believe you'd countenance that! Libby Parrish is our second cousin twice removed, and we owe a loyalty to her. We have Parrish blood runnin' through our veins."

"Oh, please, sister, everyone is long past carin' about that feud." Eulalie snatched up the field glasses from the carpet and peered out the window. "There she is! Waterin' her fuchsias. She has a glow about her this morning." She stood up. "I'm going to go have a chat with her. See if I might be able to ascertain a bit of factual information from her."

"Don't you dare," Eudora warned, reaching out. "I won't have you stirrin' up trouble."

Eulalie slapped at her sister's restraining hand.

"I'll be able to tell exactly what happened. I have a very fine eye for these things."

Eudora had no choice but to follow her sister outside. Whatever had prompted this ridiculous behavior would have to be nipped directly in the bud. The Throckmorton sisters had a reputation to maintain in Belfort. Resorting to scandal-mongering would be unacceptable.

"You are not going to spread lies about these two young people," Eudora said. "I won't allow it."

"Hush, now," Eulalie said as she hurried across the street. "Lisbeth! Lisbeth, dear. I must speak with you."

The sisters bustled up the front walk of the Parrish home and greeted Lisbeth with cheery waves. Eudora studied their neighbor carefully and was surprised to notice a rather remarkable change in her appearance. Her complexion looked rosier, her green eyes brighter, and a tiny, self-satisfied smile touched her lips.

"We just had to come over and see how you were doin', dear," Eulalie continued. "After this unfortunate turn of events, we've had you in our prayers."

"Unfortunate?"

"The Sawyer house," Eulalie said. "The nerve of that man, buying property right next door to yours. Like a slap in the face, don't you think? Those Marburys are no better than trash."

Libby sent Eulalie an uneasy smile. "I'm sure Trey Marbury has the right to buy a house anywhere he wants."

Eudora frowned. Perhaps her sister was correct. For a Parrish to show tolerance to a Marbury was unheard of in Belfort. "Has he spoken to you?"

A tiny blush crept up Lisbeth's cheeks. "Of course. We have a very cordial and neighborly relationship. That silly feud is in the past. I think it's time it came to an end, don't you? Besides, I don't even remember what it was all about."

"Oh, I know," Eudora chirped up. "Your families have been fighting since the War Between the States. His great-great-great-grandfather accused your great-great-great-grandmother of sympathizing with the North. Your great-great-great-grandfather called him out and they had a duel right in the middle of Charles Street. Lucius Marbury shot Edmund Parrish in the back."

"More like the backside," Eulalie said. "The way Mama told it, after Edmund took a wild shot and missed, he decided that he didn't feel like dyin' on that particular day so he took off like a rabbit out of a hole."

"That's not how it went, sister."

Lisbeth held up her hand. "I'm sorry. I really have to be going now. I have to drive to Charleston today. But I'm grateful for your concern."

The sisters watched her hurry up the front steps and disappear inside the house. Eulalie turned to Eudora and smiled. "Can there be any doubt, Dora?"

Eudora clutched her sister's arm. "I don't believe there can be. Lisbeth Parrish looks like she enjoyed the company of a man last night. And I do believe that man was Clayton Marbury III."

"Come, sister," Eulalie said, pulling Eudora back across the street. "We have another letter to write. Only this time, it will be addressed to the young lady. Now, I'm concerned about the theme of this letter. It was quite simple to write the first since it contained a lady's sensibilities. But how are we to choose words that might come from the mind of man?"

"They are complex creatures," Eudora mused. "But when it comes to sex, I believe they're all pretty much the same, dear. Perhaps we might have to do some research. Harley Simpson carries some of those men's magazines down at the drugstore. They must be quite racy since he has to wrap them in brown paper before he puts them out on the shelves."

"*Playhouse,*" Eulalie said.

"*Playboy,*" Eudora corrected. "The problem is, I'm not so sure that our buyin' a men's magazine might not just stir up more gossip than the gossip we're tryin' to create."

"Then we'll just have to take a little road trip, Dora. There's a lovely adult bookstore out on the interstate. I'm sure they'll have what we're lookin' for."

"Good idea," Eudora said. "I've always wondered what would cause a man to just stop what he's doin' to visit a store like that. Now I'll know."

LIBBY STARED OUT the window as Sarah pulled the car off the highway and headed into Belfort. The sun had set over an hour ago, calling an end to an exhausting day of production planning for the next season of *Southern Comforts*. Charleston had been caught in the grip of the same heat wave, but the studio had been an air-conditioned oasis.

"You really like the set?" Sarah asked.

Libby nodded. "Sure. It's great. It's very nice."

Sarah glanced over at her, a concerned frown wrinkling her brow. "Come on, Lib. What's wrong?

You always have strong opinions on these matters. You've been walking around in a fog all day. Give me a little feedback."

"I've just got a lot to think about."

"*I'm* supposed to think about all the problems with the set and the taping schedule and the lighting. I'm the producer."

"Right," Libby said, forcing a smile. In truth, her thoughts had been firmly in the realm of her personal life, not her professional life. Though she'd managed to escape Trey's presence for an entire day, she hadn't been able to keep him out of her head.

Warmth flooded her cheeks as memories of the previous night filled her thoughts. Every instinct told her that she'd made a mistake, that making love to Trey would just draw her back into all the pain she'd experienced twelve years ago. Libby wanted to believe she'd grown past that, but had she? The desire she'd felt last night had been more powerful than anything she'd ever experienced before. It wasn't something she could just forget once Trey left town. "This heat is making me crazy," she murmured.

"I thought we'd finally get some relief last night," Sarah commented. "But it just seemed to get hotter after that storm."

"I hate the heat," Libby said, slumping down into her seat and turning the air-conditioning vents toward her. "I should just move. Go north, where the summers are at least tolerable."

"What is causing this mood of yours? And if you say Trey Marbury, I'm going to pull this car over and slap the silly out of you."

"Please do," Libby said. "It might help."

"All right, do I have to guess, or are you going to tell me?"

Libby closed her eyes and tipped her head back. "You'll never guess. Even I don't believe it."

"You kissed him again," Sarah said, her words blunt and matter-of-fact.

Libby chuckled softly. "If only I'd stopped there. But that was just the start of it."

"Oh, Lib, I was just kidding about the kiss. Don't tell me you threw yourself at him again."

"Nope. This time, he threw himself at me. He just appeared last night, right before the storm hit and one thing led to another and we…"

"Wait!" Sarah commanded. She pulled the car over to the curb and turned her full attention to Libby. "Did you have sex with him?"

Libby pressed her hands to her flaming cheeks. "We didn't actually have sex, but we did some very serious messing around. He…he satisfied me, if you will."

"Oh, this is all my fault," Sarah said, her words filled with regret.

"*Now* you've decided to take the blame?" Libby accused. "I think you're a little late."

"I was the one who encouraged you to take more risks. I shouldn't have told you that. It can only lead to heartache."

"It doesn't have to," Libby said, trying to appear indifferent to the entire situation. "What happened between us was just one night. It doesn't have to happen again. I won't let it."

Sarah steered the car back into traffic and headed to Libby's house, her expression pensive. When she pulled to a stop on Charles Street, Sarah switched off the ignition and then turned to her. "Do you want it to happen again?"

"No!" Libby grabbed her things, shoved open the car door and hurried up the sidewalk, Sarah following close on her heels. "Yes!" She groaned. "I don't know what I want," she said, stomping up the front steps. "I just don't want to get hurt again." She grabbed the mail from the mailbox, then unlocked the front door and stepped inside.

Sarah followed her in. Libby kicked off her shoes, flopped down on the sofa and then distractedly began to sort the mail, searching for anything to take her mind off the chaos that Trey had created in her life. She picked out a plain envelope that was stuck between two catalogs, turning it over in her hands.

"What is it?" Sarah asked.

Libby shrugged and handed the envelope to her friend. "It's probably from the Throckmortons. They stopped by this morning to offer their sympathies. They're concerned about riffraff moving into the neighborhood. Their grandmother was a Parrish, you know, and they've never trusted the Marburys. Go ahead, read it."

Sarah opened the envelope and took out a single sheet of stationery. "I haven't stopped thinking about you since last night," she began. "With everything I touch, I feel your skin beneath my fingertips. With—"

Libby snatched the letter from Sarah's hand.

"I don't think that's from the Throckmortons,"

Sarah muttered, "unless they've decided to make a lifestyle change at age eighty."

Libby read the note silently, her heart slamming in her chest as her gaze skimmed over the tidy penmanship.

> I haven't stopped thinking about you since last night. With everything I touch, I feel your skin beneath my fingertips. With every breeze that blows, I remember the warmth of your breath on my cheek. I taste your mouth, I smell your hair, I hear your soft cries for release. Every memory of that night is still fresh in my mind. And when I'm alone, I think about the next time and how it will be between us. You'll come to me, ready for more. And I'll wait, knowing that this time you'll please me. Why do I need you so much? Is this punishment for some long-ago sin or are we meant to take pleasure where we can find it? I'm here, close by, and this time, I'll wait for you. Don't make me wait too long.

"It's from him," Libby murmured, handing the note back to Sarah.

Sarah sat down on the sofa beside Libby and finished reading. "Wow," she murmured. "I can't believe he wrote this to you. I mean, Trey probably knows exactly how to please a woman in bed, but this..." She took a shaky breath and fanned herself with the letter. "This is so...it could make a girl... why hasn't anyone ever written a note like this to me?"

"How am I supposed to resist him?" Libby moaned, her voice thick with tightly checked tears.

"I don't think you are. No woman could resist a letter like this. It's not possible."

They both sat on the sofa for a long time, each of them taking turns rereading the note. When a knock sounded on the back door, both Sarah and Libby jumped to their feet.

"That's probably him," Sarah said.

"He said I was supposed to come to him!" Libby cried.

"Maybe he got tired of waiting." Sarah fussed with Libby's hair. "Try not to look so terrified. And call me. I want to know everything. And make sure you put on some pretty underwear. Men love that lacy black stuff."

Libby nodded, giving her friend a wan smile as Sarah hurried out the front door. She stood frozen in place, unsure of what to do next. If she ran upstairs to change her underwear, he might grow impatient and leave. And if she answered the door, then this would start all over again, this undeniable heat between the two of them. Did she really want to complicate her life like this? Even Trey wasn't aware of the power he held over her, the power to make her lose all sense of who she was and how she should behave.

Another knock echoed through the house and she cursed softly, then hurried to the kitchen. If she didn't put an end to this now, there was no telling what might happen. "He probably thinks I'm just some lonely, small-town spinster, happy to find a man—any man—willing to hop in my bed! And he wanders into town with his sexy smile and killer body, figuring he'll show me a good time before he wanders back out again."

By the time she reached the door, her indecision had been replaced by righteous resolution. She grabbed the door and swung it open, ready to send him packing. But as soon as she did, all the anger seemed to rush from inside her, like air from a pricked balloon.

He smiled, his blue eyes lighting up when he saw her. "Hey there," Trey said.

Libby held on to the door for balance as she shifted back and forth on her feet. "Hello." The word caught in her throat and she swallowed hard.

"I just thought I'd bring back your basket." He held it up. "I wanted to thank you again for the biscuits."

Libby opened the door a crack, grabbed the basket and then closed it. She knew the door was the only thing keeping her from falling into Trey's arms. "Thanks."

They stared at each other for a long moment and he smiled again. "I was wondering if you might want to go down to the river for a swim."

"The river?"

"Yeah. I know about the inlet. I used to swim there with my buddies. Your father chased us off a couple of times, but we'd always sneak back." He held up a coil of rope. "I thought we could string this up and make a swing."

"You want to go swimming?"

"Sure," Trey said. "Don't you?"

Frolicking around in the water with a barely dressed Trey would tempt any woman. He just looked so good without a shirt. Add wet hair and a little kissing and Libby would be lost. She swallowed hard. "I—I can't. I have a lot of work to do and I—well, I just can't. But thank you very much for asking. And—and feel free to go on your own."

Silence fell between them and Libby tried to think of a way to make a graceful exit. But when Trey pulled the screen door open, she realized that she'd missed her chance. She backed up as he stepped inside, retreating to the kitchen doorway.

"Libby, what's wrong?"

She forced a smile. "Nothing. I'm just not in the mood for a swim right now."

"What are you in the mood for? Because the way you're looking at me, I'm thinking you're probably in the mood for an argument. Am I wrong?"

"I don't want to argue with you, Trey." She tried to keep her tone light, but her voice cracked when he grabbed her around the waist and pulled her against his body.

Trey cupped her cheek in his hand, his gaze fixed on her mouth. "I don't want to argue either," he murmured.

He leaned forward and brushed a kiss across her lips and Libby felt her limbs go limp. How was she supposed to resist this? Every ounce of her being craved his touch, ached for the feel of his mouth on her body and longed for the release that she'd experienced with him.

"You don't regret what we did last night, do you?"

Mustering all her resolve, Libby pulled back. "No. I wish I did, but I don't. It was wonderful."

He frowned as he looked down at her. Could he see what it had cost her to admit the power he held over her? Did he know how close she was to complete and total surrender?

His hand slipped down from her face to her neck and then dropped lower, to her breast. He gently teased at her nipple through the silk blouse she wore. "I've been thinking about touching you all day long," he murmured with a teasing grin.

She thought back to that night twelve years ago, to the trust he'd broken. He'd promised to come back, promised that what they'd shared meant something to him. If she let him touch her again, then she'd be doomed to suffer that humiliation all over again.

Libby closed her eyes and tipped back her head; his hands sent frissons of desire through her body. She mustered the last shred of her resistance. "Please don't do this to me," she begged.

Her words stopped him short and he gasped softly, his hands dropping to his side. "What is this, Libby? Just because you deny the desire between us, it isn't going to go away."

She opened her eyes and found him staring down at her, his jaw tight, his eyes cold. A shiver raced through her. She didn't want it to go away. It was like an insidious, addictive drug—something she craved in spite of the danger.

"I'm willing to admit what I want. I want you, Libby, more than I've ever wanted any other woman in my life." He cursed softly, then took her face between his hands and kissed her. His tongue teased at her lips, gently forcing her to respond.

Against all her instincts, Libby opened beneath the assault, her arms slipping around his neck, her body pressing against the lean length of his. A knot of desire twisted inside of her, consuming her with need. She wanted his hands on her again, stripping away her clothes, parting her legs, making her moist and ready. It would take so little just to give up, to let him make love to her.

"Tell me I can't make you want me," he murmured against her mouth. "Tell me you don't do the same for me. I was there in your bed, Libby. I know what I made you feel."

She drew a ragged breath and backed out of his embrace, trying to keep her knees from buckling beneath her. "That was lust," Libby said, her voice thin and tight. "And a little bit of curiosity. But one night was enough."

His jaw twitched as he stared into her eyes, as if searching her soul for answers she didn't have. Libby prayed that he'd leave, that she wouldn't be faced with making a choice.

"One night every twelve years? Hell, if that's all I can hope for, then I guess I'll see you in another twelve." He turned and walked out, letting the door slam behind him.

Libby listened to his footsteps on the veranda and then on the stairs leading to the backyard. And when she was sure that he was gone for good, Libby slowly sank to the floor and buried her face in her knees.

Her life had been so simple until Trey had moved back to Belfort. And she'd cursed that simplicity, longed for someone or something to make her life exciting again. "Be careful what you wish for," she murmured, rubbing at knots of tension in her neck.

Never in a thousand years would she have wished for Trey's return. He'd touched her and she'd become seventeen again, filled with hopes and dreams, doubts and insecurities, and silly notions of romance.

She'd become infatuated with him all over again and there was nothing she could do to stop it.

Libby tipped her head back and sighed, fighting the tears that pressed at the corners of her eyes. Or maybe she'd just never stopped wanting him in the first place. Whatever it was about Trey, it didn't make any difference. If she didn't stop this irrational behavior, she'd be picking up the pieces of her heart for the rest of her life.

4

TREY SWUNG the Jeep onto Center Street and then took a sip of coffee from the mug he'd brought from home. The caffeine slowly pumped through his bloodstream, giving him a badly needed boost after another sleepless night.

For the past week, he'd spent the end of each day and the beginning of the next working on the house, conveniently avoiding the prospect of sleep. It made no sense at all, since it was impossible to sleep in the heat of the day. But he'd slipped into a routine of short catnaps whenever exhaustion overwhelmed him. Only then could he lie down without lapsing into fantasies about Libby Parrish.

He was due to travel to Savannah the next day to settle the sale of one of his father's properties. Perhaps an air-conditioned hotel room and sixty miles of space between him and Libby would result in a decent night's sleep.

Five long days and as many restless nights had passed since he'd made the mistake of returning her biscuit basket. At first, Trey had assumed he'd caught her at a bad time, maybe in the midst of a professional crisis. Then, he decided it might have been the heat. But since then, Libby had steadfastly avoided him and he'd been forced to draw the obvious conclusion—she wanted nothing more to do with him.

Trey wasn't quite sure how to take that. He'd never been a guy to doubt his abilities in the bedroom or to misread a woman's reaction to those abilities. Libby had enjoyed everything he'd done to her and he'd been certain it would lead to something more.

But now, he was faced with the realization that he'd made a mistake taking her letter seriously. She'd promised to write to him after that night they'd spent together twelve years ago and he'd never received a single piece of mail from her. Though Trey had written to her, after six letters, he'd been forced to admit that she wanted nothing more to do with him.

Why start it all up again, only to stop when things began to get interesting? Was she playing some sort of game with him? Trey shook his head. She'd accused him of playing games with her. What the hell was that letter all about if it wasn't about seduction? "Geez, I thought I understood women," he muttered. "But I don't know what the hell Libby Parrish is thinking."

He pulled the Jeep up in front of the drugstore. After he turned off the ignition, he rested his hands on the steering wheel and allowed his mind to fill with images of Libby. He'd never wanted a woman as much as he'd wanted her that night—and every night since then.

It had taken every bit of his willpower not to take their encounter to its logical resolution. When he'd begun, he'd assumed it had all been just a little fun between consenting adults. But somewhere after the first kiss and before her orgasm, his feelings had changed. And he had realized he wanted more than just sex. He wanted that connection back, that special something that they'd experienced as teenagers.

But what was that connection? It couldn't have been love, not at that age and not after just one night together. It had been much deeper than lust, though. He'd experienced only lust since then, and he knew exactly how it felt to want a woman's body but not her soul. What he'd shared with Libby, both in the past and in the present, had fallen into some strange gray area—more than lust, but not quite love.

Whatever it was, it didn't erase the fact that he still wanted her. He wanted to touch her at will, to slowly undress her and enjoy the beauty of her naked body. He wanted to draw her close and make her shudder with need. And more than anything, he wanted to possess her, to move inside of her until his control shattered and his desire was spent.

Trey could lose himself in the storm of sensations Libby made him feel. He could forget there were reasons why it would never work between them. In a few months, he'd be back in Chicago and Libby would be living her life as if he'd never touched her or kissed her or made her cry out in pleasure. Somehow, Trey was certain he'd feel the loss much more acutely than she would.

"So then stop thinking about her," he muttered as he jumped out of the Jeep. He looked both ways before jogging across the street to the drugstore. As he stepped inside the cool interior, Trey noticed a group of ladies at the cosmetics counter. They stopped their conversation to stare at him and then lowered their voices to a whisper.

He shrugged it off and headed down the center aisle in search of a bottle of aspirin. All the manual labor had taken a toll, leaving him with achy muscles and a nagging cramp in his neck. Maybe that's why he'd had trouble sleeping.

He caught sight of Harley Simpson at the far end of the aisle and waved at him. "I'm looking for the aspirin," Trey called.

Harley grabbed a bottle from the shelf as he passed and bustled up to Trey. "Here you are," he said. "That's the generic. No use payin' for the brand name."

"Thanks." Trey turned for the counter, but Harley reached out to stop him.

He bent closer to Trey and lowered his voice. "I want you to know that when it comes to the purchase of prophylactical items, you can count on Simpson's Drugstore to be discreet."

"Thank you," Trey said, taken aback by the man's comment. "I'll keep that in mind."

"Believe me, I understand how the gossips in this town work. You give them a little to chew on and they make a feast out of it."

"Are they talking about me?" Trey whispered.

"Well, I'm not one to go passin' it on, but you have been the subject of a fair amount of jawin' these last few days."

"Well, you can tell everyone if they have any questions, they can come directly to me. I'll tell them what they want to know."

"Are you sure you ought to be doin' that?" Harley asked. "The young lady in question might not want you sullyin' her reputation around town."

"The young lady?"

"Yeah. Libby Parrish. She's the one you've been keepin' company with. Now, I never believed all they said about her—that she was some ice queen or a cold fish. Still waters do tend to run deep, if you know what I mean. You look at Mrs. Simpson and she don't look it, but she's a regular hellcat in the bedroom and I—"

"People are talking about me and Libby Parrish?" Trey interrupted.

"Well, yeah. Story is you spent the night with her last week."

Trey glanced around the store to find several of the patrons staring at him. So that's what this was all about. He'd noticed people acting strangely around him, suddenly going quiet, sending curious glances his way. But how the hell had they found out about him and Libby? He hadn't said a word to anyone.

Trey turned away from Harley and headed to the door. He tossed the aspirin on the counter as he passed, not bothering to buy it. Had Libby heard the gossip? Was that what was keeping her at a distance? He shoved open the door and then stepped out onto the sidewalk, the midday heat hitting him like a wet blanket.

As he jogged across the street to his Jeep, he saw Libby leave the post office. Trey changed direction and headed her off, joining her in front of Harrington's Hardware. "I have to talk to you," he said, catching hold of her elbow and steering her around the corner. He glanced both ways and then stepped into the shade of the side entrance to the hardware store.

"What are you doing?" Libby asked, pulling out of his grasp. "Do you want the whole town gossiping about us?"

His breath suddenly died in his throat. God, she was beautiful. In just a week, he'd forgotten how pale her hair was, how it fell so softly around her face and how it smelled like flowers when he got close to her. "I'm afraid they already are," Trey said.

Libby gasped, her green eyes growing wide. "What? Why?"

"They know we spent a night together."

"Who did you tell?"

"No one," Trey replied. "I figured you'd told someone." He reached up to tuck a strand of hair behind her ear, anxious to touch her again.

She avoided his gaze, choosing to stare at his chest. "No! No one...except—no, she'd never tell anyone. Sarah's my friend."

"It doesn't really matter," Trey said, frustrated that she refused to look him in the eye. "Besides, we're both adults. Our private lives are private. Let them talk."

"You don't have to live in this town," she snapped. "You're just passing through."

Trey pushed aside his growing anger, grabbing her chin and forcing her gaze up to his. "What kind of game are you playing here, Libby?"

"What are you talking about? You're the one playing games."

"I was there that night. You act like you don't remember what it was like between us. Can you stop thinking about it? Because I can't. I touched your body," he said, smoothing his palm over her bare shoulder. "I felt you come in my arms. That was real, whether you want to admit it or not."

"Stop it!" she hissed.

"I don't think you want me to stop. I think this little game excites you. I'm forbidden fruit, a Marbury, and as long as what we share has to be hidden, you enjoy it more." Trey backed her up against the door, bracing his hands on either side of her head. "Say it, Libby. Just say you don't want me and I'll go away. I promise."

She closed her eyes for a moment and then met his gaze defiantly. He considered kissing her, trying to prove his point with actions rather than words. Trey leaned closer, searching for some sign she'd respond. "Say it," he demanded, so close he felt her breath on his lips, craved the taste of her tongue.

"All right. I do want you. Are you happy now?"

Trey reached up and brushed his thumb across her lower lip. "Yeah, I'm happy."

She turned into his touch for a moment and then shook her head. One second she was there, waiting for him to kiss her; the next, she'd ducked down and slipped out of his grasp. "Now, keep your promise and leave me alone!" Libby shouted as she hurried down the street.

Trey started after her and then thought better of it. "This isn't over, Libby. We're not done yet," he called.

When he turned back around, he saw a small crowd gathered at the door of the hardware store, peering at him through the glass. "All right, the show's over," he yelled. "Nothing more to see here."

Cursing softly, Trey started down the street to his Jeep. No wonder he'd left this damn town far behind him. He couldn't sneeze in Belfort without half the town speculating about the state of his health. Now they had something much juicier to contemplate—a steamy sexual relationship between a Parrish and Marbury.

"Let them talk," Trey muttered. "And as long as they are, I'm going to try like hell to give them something new to talk about."

He wasn't done with Libby, not by a long shot. There was something between them and he wasn't leaving town until he found out exactly what it was.

"MY MOTHER IS GOING to kill me," Libby murmured.

Sarah sighed. "You know what they say. If it's not one thing, it's your mother."

"And after she kills me, she's going to kill herself," Libby muttered. "Trey's father made my father's life miserable. They were constantly in competition, and I'm sure the stress of it took its toll. If Daddy hears that Trey is back in town, he might just move back to Belfort and start this whole feud up again."

"I think you're making an awful lot of a few rumors," Sarah commented as she picked at her chicken salad. She stabbed a grape and popped it in her mouth. "People are talking. So far, it's just speculation. Besides, I think your reputation could do with a little tarnishing."

"I'm not worried about my reputation," Libby said. "I'm sick to death of people thinking I'm something I'm not. I have needs just like any other woman." She frowned and then sat down at the kitchen table. "I just wish I knew where the rumor got started."

The front doorbell rang and Sarah glanced up at Libby. "Maybe that's Trey, ready to make some new rumors."

"I don't think so. I'm pretty sure he's going to be

staying away from me after our little encounter yesterday morning."

Libby pushed up from the table and walked through the wide entrance hall that spanned the depth of the house. Sarah joined her a few seconds later to find Carlisle Whitby standing on the other side of the screen door. She frowned. Carlisle usually made his deliveries in the morning.

"Hello, Carlisle," Libby murmured. "What can I do for you?"

"I have your mail here, Lisbeth. I thought there might be something important."

"You can just leave the mail in the box," Libby suggested as gently as she could.

"I—I wonder if we might have a word," he said. Carlisle shot a glance over to Sarah. "In private."

Libby stifled a smile as she heard Sarah giggle behind her. She stepped out onto the veranda and followed Carlisle to the steps. "What is it?"

"I've been hearing rumors around town," he said, staring at his government-issue shoes. "Rumors that have called into question your reputation."

"Carlisle, I think that—"

"No, let me finish what I've come to say. I don't know the source of these scurrilous accusations, though I do have my suspicions." Carlisle paused to send a hostile look in the direction of Trey's house. "But I'm determined to find out and once I do, I plan to make sure that the scoundrel pays."

"Scoundrel?" Libby bit her bottom lip. "I'm not sure I've ever heard that word used in conversation, Carlisle. Have you been reading a little too much *Gone with the Wind* lately?"

"I understand. You're using humor to hide your distress. But I'm here to offer my assistance."

"Are you going to call this person out?" Libby teased. "Pistols at ten paces? I appreciate the gesture, Carlisle, but I can take care of this myself."

"I only wish that dueling was still legal. But, since it isn't, I'd like to offer my services in another way. I'd like to take you out on a date. It would help to face these rumors straight on, to show everyone in Belfort that they couldn't possibly be true. And to be seen in the company of an employee of the U.S. Postal Service might restore your reputation to its former unimpeachable status."

Libby cleared her throat and forced a smile. "I appreciate the offer, Carlisle, but I'm sure the rumors will die down over time. Besides, the scoundrel, as you call him, will be leaving town in a month or two and this will all be forgotten."

"It can't be too soon for me," Carlisle said. "I found illegal mail in his box the other day. You can't trust a man like that." He nodded and then started down the steps. "Oh, I forgot to give you this." He handed Libby a slip of paper. "There's a package waiting for you at the post office with postage due. I'd be happy to pay the postage and bring it over to you after my shift."

"No, I'll take care of this myself. It's just a cookbook I ordered. Thanks for your concern, Carlisle. You'd better get back to work. I wouldn't want to put you off schedule."

Carlisle hoisted his bag onto his shoulder and hurried off down the sidewalk, his stubby legs carrying him as fast as they could. Libby sighed and then walked back inside the house.

Sarah was waiting for her in the kitchen. "Good grief," she muttered. "I think all that school paste Carlisle ate as a kid has seriously affected his brain."

"He was concerned about all the rumors."

"Or maybe it's you that's affected his brain," Sarah teased. "Remember when he jumped off the top of the monkey bars just to impress you? Poor kid broke his leg."

"He just asked me out. He thought it might help to be seen in the company of a U.S. postal carrier." Libby slid into a chair at the table and cupped her chin in her hand. "You know what the really awful thing is? For a moment, I actually considered accepting."

"Carlisle Whitby?"

"He's not so bad. He's a little short and little bald and he still lives at home with his mama, but other than that, he's all right."

"And after all, you don't have any other prospects on the horizon."

"I'm serious," Libby said. "What has my life come to?"

"A choice," Sarah said. "Taking the safe route with Carlisle or—"

"Risking it all with a guy like Trey?" Libby finished. "I thought you weren't in favor of risk."

"Well, I've been thinking about it and I know he hurt you in the past, Lib, but you're a grown-up now. If you don't figure out how you feel about him, you may never be able to move on with your life. You can control this—you can decide where it goes and when it stops. And maybe, if you dump him this time, you can balance the scales a bit."

"I suppose I could," Libby murmured. "But don't

you think that's like playing with fire? When I'm with Trey, I just forget all common sense."

"Then take control," Sarah said. "Make him want you on your terms. And if he can't handle that, then walk away."

"My terms," Libby said.

Sarah picked up her plate and took it to the sink, then wiped her hands on a dish towel. "I've got a meeting at the station tomorrow to go over the Web site design for the new season. Do you want to drive in with me and see what they have planned?"

Libby shook her head. "No, right now, I don't want to think about work. I just want to relax and think about my...options."

"Don't forget, you've got that trip to New Orleans next weekend. They've set you up in a very nice hotel and you'll be doing a book signing and a radio interview along with your seminar. I've got your itinerary all set."

"I'll look at it later." Libby grabbed a magazine from the table and slowly fanned herself. "I hear it's supposed to rain tonight. Maybe I'll finally be able to sleep."

Sarah waved as she walked out of the kitchen, leaving Libby alone with her thoughts. She'd seduced Trey once when she was seventeen. She should be able to do much better now that she was a little older.

Libby pushed back from the table and retrieved the letter from the drawer beneath the phone. She'd contemplated burning it, so that she'd never have to look at it again. But she'd nearly memorized it, along with all the feelings that the words evoked.

Passion had never been a priority in her relationships in the past. After her first experience with Trey, she'd always measured her romances against that night, a night that, over time, had become mythic in her mind.

"Closure," Libby muttered, the concept coming to her at that very moment. Perhaps that was why she couldn't put her feelings about Trey in the past. There were so many questions and very few answers. Why hadn't he ever tried to contact her after that night? How did he feel about what they'd shared? Did he remember it in the same way she did?

Libby cursed softly. She was nearly thirty years old and she was still stuck reliving an event that had happened when she was a teenager. This wasn't just about closure; it was about her inability to move her life forward!

The patterns of her life had been set early. When she was younger, she had preferred to stay at home or study at the library, rather than participate in school activities. After she'd graduated from high school, she'd chosen the same small liberal arts college in Savannah that Sarah was attending and continued to live at home. And when she couldn't find a job with her art history degree, her mother had suggested they work on a cookbook. Even the television show had been Sarah's idea, instigated after she took a job with the PBS station in Charleston.

Libby had always waited for life to happen to her, waited for that one big event that would send her future in a new and exciting direction. Now she had a chance to *make* things happen; whether they turned out good or bad in the end, at least she wouldn't be sitting around waiting.

With a sigh, she glanced down at the letter. Yes, she'd seduced him once. But he wasn't the same high school boy who'd made love to her all those years ago. Seducing a man experienced in the sexual arts was a whole different matter. She'd have to give him something totally unexpected, something he'd never be able to forget.

> And when I'm alone, I think about the next time and how it will be between us. You'll come to me, ready for more. And I'll wait, knowing that you'll please me.

Her mind wandered back to the night he'd appeared in her garden, standing in the moonlight and waiting for her to ask him in. They hadn't bothered with words then; instead, they let the heat of their passion determine the course of events.

A tremor raced through her body at the thought of what they had shared, the thought of giving Trey the same kind of pleasure that he'd given her. Libby refolded the letter and tucked it back inside the drawer.

She'd have to make her move soon. The longer she waited, the more reasons she'd find to back out. But she needed an opening line, some way to indicate her feelings had changed since the last time they'd seen each other. With a tiny smile, Libby yanked open the freezer door and pulled out a pineapple upside-down cake that she'd made a few days ago.

She'd intended to give it to Trey anyway, so why not use it now? She took the pan and popped it in the oven, then turned the heat to low. If it were warm, he'd think she'd just baked it, and maybe he'd invite her in to share a piece with him. Who knows where a little cake and conversation might lead?

While the cake was warming, Libby raced upstairs and rummaged through her clothes for a fresh cotton sundress and her sexiest underwear. Taking a shower might wash away her courage, so she splashed water on her face and ran a damp cloth over her sticky skin. Then she applied a dab of mascara and a bit of lipstick and headed back to the kitchen.

She flipped the cake onto a plate, decorated it with a few rosettes from a can of whipped cream, then headed out the back door. Drawing a deep breath and marshaling her resolve, Libby walked around the azalea bushes into Trey's backyard. It was nearly dinnertime, so he'd probably be hungry. She could offer to make him something to eat before she actually got down to the business of seduction. "After all, I'm probably better at cooking and baking than making a man crazy with desire," Libby muttered.

The back door to Trey's house was propped open and Libby stepped inside the kitchen. Unlike her home, the old Sawyer place was in a sad state. The kitchen dated back to the 1920s and everything in it was covered with a thin coating of dust. An ancient stove and icebox were the only conveniences.

"Hello!" she called.

A few seconds later, Beau ran into the room, his black nose covered with white plaster dust. He wriggled around her legs, his tail thumping on the floor. "Sorry, no biscuits today."

Beau's entrance was quickly followed by Trey's. He stopped short as he entered the kitchen. "Hi," he said.

He was dressed in his usual attire of baggy shorts and sport sandals, but this time, he was bare-chested, his skin coated with the same layer of plaster dust that coated everything else in the house. Libby's breath caught in her throat as she let her gaze drift along his body, over his wide, muscular chest to his rippled abdomen. His arms and legs were long and well muscled, and his strong hands rested on impossibly narrow hips.

She swallowed hard, her eyes watering slightly from all the dust in the house. She could feel her pulse racing and her mouth had gone dry, making it difficult to speak. Had she been bolder, she might have been able to walk directly into his arms and kiss him, but Libby couldn't be sure how he'd react.

She didn't want to deal with the preliminaries, the nervous moments and the stilted conversation. Libby wanted to begin where they'd left off the night of the storm—hot, eager, uninhibited. "I thought it was about time I brought that cake you requested."

He glanced over his shoulder, the tension evident in the set of his jaw. "And I thought you didn't want anything more to do with me. Now you bring me a cake? Kind of mixed signals, don't you think, Lib?"

"I'm sorry about yesterday. I shouldn't have taken my frustrations out on you. I know you didn't say anything."

"I've never been one to kiss and tell."

Libby smiled ruefully, wondering how she might convince him to touch her again. She glanced down at his fingers and a shiver ran through her at the memory of what he'd done to her that night in her bed. "That's a very good policy, especially in Belfort."

They stood in silence for a long moment; then Libby held out the cake. "I think you'll enjoy it. It's a really good recipe. It's from an old electric company cookbook." Damn the cake! Right now, she was ready to toss it over her shoulder and throw herself into his arms. Conversing about cake was not a good start to a seduction. "Don't you want it?" she asked.

"I think you know what I want," Trey said, his gaze never wavering.

She swallowed hard. If she was waiting for an opening, then this was it. He'd spelled it out in the letter so she could have no doubts. Libby turned around and set the cake on the counter. "I do know what you want," she murmured.

But when she turned back to him, he was staring down at a blueprint spread over the kitchen table. "Listen, I'd really like to chat, but I've got a lot of work to do. I've got the plaster guys tearing up the dining room and the plumber is working on the bathroom upstairs. You probably should get out of here before they wander in or we'll be subject to a whole new round of rumor and innuendo."

Libby felt anger flare inside of her. So this was the way it would be. A battle for control. Though he seemed so cool and distant, when Libby met his gaze, she saw the truth. He wanted her as much as she wanted him. His eyes couldn't lie.

His gaze dropped to her lips and she knew he was thinking about kissing her. Libby slowly drew her tongue along her lower lip, inviting him to give in to the urge. "We wouldn't want that," she murmured.

He frowned. Then, with a soft curse, he snatched up the blueprint. "You'd better go." With that, Trey turned and walked out of the room, leaving Libby to wonder whether she had any chance at all of controlling Trey. As long as they were using sex as a weapon, one of them was bound to lose. She just didn't want it to be her.

"Cake, bad idea," she muttered as she walked out of the house. "Timing, also very bad. And I could probably sex up the outfit a little bit."

This whole seduction was going to take much more thought and planning. Libby frowned. Trey had accomplished his objective with so much ease. Why was it so difficult for her?

"Looks like the electrician did a good job," Wiley Boone said. "I can sign off on that, but you need to call the plumber back and have him put a new shut-off valve on the main line. You can't count on those old valves on the meter anymore."

"I've got the heating and air-conditioning guy coming in next week, so I'll need you back to inspect that job."

"You sure you want to spend all that money on a house you're just gonna turn around and sell? Wasn't that your plan?"

Trey leaned back against the kitchen counter, crossing his arms over his chest. That was the question he'd been asking himself. What was his plan, not just for this house, but for Libby? After all her protests, she'd appeared at his door, cake in hand, ready to be friends again.

But he'd seen right through her platonic facade. She wanted him to kiss her again, to pull her into his arms and run his hands over her body. This dance they were doing with each other was designed to drive him mad and unless she capitulated completely, he wasn't going to give in.

"I 'spose it'll increase the value of the house," Wiley continued.

"And it will make my stay here a lot more comfortable," Trey added.

The building inspector nodded. "Yep, it does get a little warm 'round these parts." Wiley's eyes fixed on a spot next to Trey. "That looks like a mighty fine cake you got there. Pineapple upside-down is just about my most favorite. Is that one of Libby Parrish's cakes? 'Cause I heard that you and her were on cake bakin' terms."

Was this a new Belfort euphemism for sex, Trey wondered? "I'd really like to know where that rumor got started."

"No tellin'," Wiley said, still eyeing the cake. "You plannin' to eat that cake, 'cause if you let it sit there, it's just gonna dry up."

"Would you like a piece?" Trey asked.

"Don't mind if I do," Wiley said.

Trey rummaged around for a knife, cut a generous slice of the cake and put it on a paper plate for the inspector. "So you'll come back late next week?"

"That Libby Parrish sure makes a good cake. I tell ya, she's gonna make some man a fine wife. And I don't have to say, I'd sure like to be that man."

"Have you and Libby dated?" Trey asked.

"No. But I'm thinkin' on askin' her out. You think she'd go out with me?"

Trey wasn't sure what to say. He certainly was in no position to encourage Wiley, but he was also fairly sure that Libby wouldn't accept. He just shrugged, walked Wiley to the front door and shook his hand before he left. Wandering back through the house, he took stock of the work he'd accomplished so far.

The cracked plaster had been repaired, the ornate carved moldings had been restored and layers of paint had been scraped off the old mantels in the dining room and front parlor. He had to paint the walls and strip the pine floors, but after that, he could move on to the upstairs. Central heat and air would make the house as comfortable as it was beautiful.

He ran his fingers through his dusty hair, then shook his head. Right now, he needed a long swim in a cool river. Trey grabbed a beer from the refrigerator and headed out the back door, unbuttoning his shirt as he walked. But he stopped in his tracks the moment he saw Libby standing on the veranda, Beau sitting at her feet.

"Your dog's been in my rose garden again."

Trey shouldn't have been surprised to see her, but it was her appearance that took his breath away. She wore a clingy black dress, barely more than a slip, made of a fabric that seemed to mould to her body. The hem was high and the neckline low, showing off more skin that Libby normally displayed. And her blond hair, usually pulled back in a haphazard knot was a riot of loose waves that brushed her bare shoulders.

Trey opened his mouth to warn her off. He wasn't going to get sucked into this game she was playing. But Libby shook her head and pressed her finger to her lips. "Don't speak," she murmured. "If you say anything, I'll walk away."

His gaze fixed on her as she approached and he felt his heart start to pound. She carried a silk scarf that brushed along her leg as she walked, and his fingers twitched as Trey imagined drawing the dress up and over her head and revealing the naked body beneath.

When she reached the top of the steps, she slowly sauntered over to him, her hips swaying suggestively as she walked. "I warned you about the dog, didn't I?"

Trey groaned inwardly, heat already pumping through his veins. She wasn't here to scold him about Beau, or to pay another social call. From the look in Libby's eyes, she had other things on her mind.

"I've been trying to figure you out, Trey Marbury," Libby murmured, walking around him, letting her body brush up against his as she did. "I'm wondering why you came back to town and decided to buy this house. And why you were so determined to seduce me. And, most especially, why you wrote me that letter."

Trey frowned. He wasn't sure what letter she was referring to—maybe one of the six he sent all those years ago—but he didn't feel the urge to question her at the present time. Besides, talking was against the rules and now that Trey had decided to get back in the game, he didn't want to break them.

She flipped the scarf over his shoulder and then drew the fabric forward along his neck, the feel of it like a caress. "But then, I realized it doesn't really matter. You said it the other day. We're both adults. We should be able to handle a purely physical attraction." This time as she circled him, she let her hand brush up against his backside. And when she came around again, her fingers drifted over his crotch, lingering there for a few seconds before moving on.

Trey bit back a moan. If she was bent on torturing him, then she'd made a good start. He felt himself growing hard, his erection pressing against the fabric of his shorts. Though he ought to have been embarrassed by his immediate reaction, somehow, he knew Libby's actions were having the effect she desired. She hadn't come here to talk; she'd come to entice him.

"I've decided I might have overreacted earlier. I'll admit, I haven't been able to stop thinking about that night you came to my room. And given our mutual desires, I think we can both get what we want," she continued. She looked up at him, her green eyes wide. "Don't you agree?"

Trey nodded.

This time as she circled him, she dragged the scarf across his feet. She caught one of his hands as she passed, then looped the silk around his wrist. Trey laughed softly as she took his other arm and knotted his hands together behind him.

"I suppose you're wondering what I'm doing." She gently pushed him back against the railing of the veranda and then tied the loose ends of the scarf to the balustrade. "I think we should make this all about your pleasure tonight. That's what you want, isn't it?"

He couldn't think of an objection, so Trey shrugged. Sure, he'd take his pleasure, or come close. But he'd find a way to free his hands and return the favor before things got too out of hand.

Glancing down, he watched her unbutton his shirt, so slowly that the simple act of undressing him turned undeniably erotic. When Libby was finished, she pushed the shirt off his shoulders and shoved it down to his wrists, leaving his torso bare.

Her fingertips trailed over his skin, sending a current buzzing to his nerve ends. Trey tipped his head back and closed his eyes, focusing on the sensation of her hands on his body. The lazy pace of her caress piqued his desire and he found himself wanting more. But it was clear Libby wasn't going to race through this. She was going to take her time in seducing him, and he anticipated a fight to maintain control.

When her lips pressed against his skin, Trey opened his eyes again and looked down at her. He drew a deep breath, inhaling the scent of her hair, the strands brushing at his chin. He longed to taste her lips, to steal a kiss. But Libby's tongue delved lower, circling around his nipple, teasing it to a peak.

A low groan slipped from Trey's lips followed by a soft chuckle. Again, he was stunned by the sudden shift in her mood. She'd gone from insecure to wanton in a matter of hours, and he found himself captivated by the contrast.

Why had no man managed to capture her heart? Libby was sweet and sexy and smart, everything a man could want from a lover. For now, she had chosen to turn her affections toward him, and he wasn't about to question his good fortune.

As she kissed his chest, Libby's palms smoothed over his belly, her fingers dipping provocatively beneath his waistband. Then suddenly, her fingers were at the front of his shorts cupping him, the fabric providing a flimsy barrier to her touch.

"You're driving me crazy," he murmured.

"You're not supposed to speak."

"If you kiss me, I'll stop," Trey bargained. "I promise."

She looked up and smiled at him, the beauty of her face sending another wave of heat through his body. Libby slowly worked her way back across familiar territory and then covered his lips with hers, her tongue tantalizing, taking possession of his mouth. She'd become the aggressor and Trey found the new dynamic between them very stimulating.

Trey's mind spun as he lost himself in the kiss. How the hell was he supposed to last? He was lucky his hands were tied behind his back, because just the thought of touching her was bringing him right to the edge.

"Is this it?" she murmured, her lips trailing down his chest again. "Is this your fantasy?"

"This is better than any fantasy I ever had," Trey replied.

As her fingers dropped to the waistband of his shorts, Trey sucked in a sharp breath. He'd never been seduced like this before, never allowed a woman such absolute control over his desire. But Libby had taken it and he was happy to step back and see where this led.

A moment later, his shorts slid over his hips, and then she tugged on his boxers. His shaft caught in the waistband, then sprung free, completely erect and achingly sensitive. He didn't have time to contemplate what came next. When her lips closed over him, Trey lost the ability to think at all.

Slowly, she began to move, taking him in before drawing away, sending wild currents coursing through his body. He had to close his eyes because watching her was too much. She brought him close several times, but Trey yanked himself back from the edge, wanting to enjoy her just a moment longer, knowing that to come would mean an end to this sweet torture.

Her tongue teased, running from the base of his shaft, then lingering on the tip. Trey's heart slammed in his chest and his breathing came in short gasps. He murmured her name, but it wasn't enough. Trey needed his hands free, to run his fingers through her hair, to slow her pace so that it wouldn't be over too quickly. But instead, he was forced to concentrate on a single point of contact between them.

And then her fingers took over and she worked her way back up his chest. He caught her lips with his and kissed her, drinking in the taste like a man parched with thirst. As her body pressed against his and her stroke quickened, Trey plunged his tongue into her mouth, imagining what it would be like to move inside her.

A moment later, he exploded in her hand. The orgasm sent waves of pleasure washing over him. She slowed her caress, nuzzling into his neck as she took him to the very limits of his pleasure. Trey shuddered and then groaned, sensitive in the aftermath of his orgasm.

"What do you want now? Tell me," Libby murmured, smoothing her hand over his damp belly.

"I want to make love to you," he whispered in her ear. He bit back another groan. "But I don't think I can."

Libby stepped back and looked into his face. "Why not? Did I wear you out?"

A grin twitched at the corners of his mouth. "I'm

probably good to go another time or two," he said. "I just don't have any protection."

"What about the—"

"I didn't buy them. If I buy condoms here in town, everyone is going to know what you and I are up to. I figure I'm going to have to go to Charleston or Savannah to avoid the gossips."

"Then I think you'd better take a road trip," Libby suggested. "And call me when you get back." She slowly drew away, then gave him a quick kiss before sauntering to the steps. "I'll be seein' you, Trey Marbury."

"Wait a second," Trey called. "There are a lot of other things we could do that wouldn't require condoms."

"No, I think it's best to wait," she said. "We might just get carried away and...well, we'll save that for later." She gave him a little wave.

"You're just going to leave me tied up here?"

"Now we're even," she said, laughing softly.

"If you untie me, I'll invite you in for cake. I have this really great cake."

"No, I don't think so," Libby said.

Trey didn't want to her to leave. He scrambled for something, anything to keep her just a few minutes longer. "I'm going to Savannah tomorrow on business. Why don't you come with me?" Trey offered.

"I think you can pick up condoms on your own."

"We can get out of town and spend some time together, without all the gossips wondering what we're up to. We'll have lunch, take a carriage ride or maybe a walk along the harbor."

"I can't," Libby said in a teasing voice.

"You can't or you won't?"

"Does it matter?"

"We're going to have to talk about this thing between us sooner or later, Libby. It's not going to go away."

"Oh, it will go away," she murmured.

"How? When?"

"When you leave town." With that she turned on her heel and hurried across the lawn. A few seconds later, she disappeared behind the azalea bushes.

Trey closed his eyes and tipped his head back, drawing in a deep breath of the humid night air. This whole thing felt like a dream, like some heat-induced hallucination meant to drive him crazy.

It took him a few minutes to untie the knots and when he did, Trey reached down and adjusted the front of his boxers, shaking his head. He'd known a lot of women in his life, but he'd never met a woman as mercurial and mysterious as Lisbeth Parrish. He could never predict where he stood with her day to day. One moment, she was yelling at him, the next, she was running away, and the next, she was seducing him.

Trey held the scarf up to his nose, the scent of her perfume wafting off of the silk. He smiled as he walked back inside. He had a life waiting for him back in Chicago, but suddenly he'd grown very fond of Belfort. There were things in this town a man might not be able to find anywhere else in the world—a decent bowl of grits, a beautiful old house filled with great architectural details and, of course, a woman who could arouse him with a simple smile.

5

"You're going out with who?"

"Whom. And you heard me," Libby said. "I have a date with Carlisle Whitby. I called him up this morning and accepted his offer. We're having dinner at Tarrington's tonight. He's picking me up at five."

"I can't believe this," Sarah said, raking her hand through her auburn hair. "You're throwing over a guy like Trey Marbury for a dweeb like Carlisle. The man collects Civil War bullets. Little bitty pieces of lead that he finds with his metal detector. He spends his weekends running around dressed like a Confederate general. If you date him, then you might as well give up any hope of a normal guy ever asking you out."

"There are no normal guys in Belfort." Libby rose out of the wicker chair that overlooked her garden and grabbed her empty glass. "Don't you see? It's the perfect plan," she explained. "If I date Carlisle, it will deflect all the gossip. And that's all I really want to do."

She grabbed the pitcher from the small table near the back door, refilled her glass and then held the pitcher out to Sarah. Her friend shook her head. "Why are you so worried about the gossip?" she asked.

"I might as well tell you I have decided to engage

in a purely sexual relationship with Trey. And I don't want everyone in town to speculate about the details. Otherwise, I'm going to be stuck explaining what happened between us after he leaves. For the next five years, everyone is going to feel sorry for me, how poor Libby Parrish got taken in by that scoundrel, Trey Marbury. But if I can deflect some of the attention to Carlisle, then all the better for me and Trey, don't you think?"

"You know what I think? I think the heat has finally fried your brain." Sarah dipped a paper napkin in her iced tea and tried to dab at Libby's forehead, but Libby slapped away her hand. "How do you think Carlisle is going to feel when he finds out you used him? Sleeping with one guy while you're dating another is not a very nice thing to do."

Libby stared at her fingernails, studying her manicure while she came up with a decent reply. "Maybe it's not the nicest thing in the world to do. But don't you think Carlisle might get a little out of it, too?"

"What? Are you going to put out for him? Are you and Carlisle going to drive down to Walker's Point and smooch in the back of his mama's station wagon?"

"I was referring to the fact that dating me might make Carlisle look a little better in the eyes of some of the other single women in Belfort."

Sarah frowned. "Well, I suppose that might happen. I hear he's been chasing after Jenny Dalton. She's a checker down at the Winn-Dixie."

"It's only going to be a few dates. Just until everyone stops talking about Trey and me. And Carlisle is the one who volunteered to help restore my reputation, so I shouldn't have to feel guilty."

"Lib, are you sure you have this thing under control? Because it doesn't sound like you really know what you're doing. I know what a romantic you are. How can you be so nonchalant about this?"

"Because I know Trey is leaving. And I know he's not the kind of man who'd want to stay here in Belfort and marry me and raise a bunch of children. So it's simple. For once, I'm going to be practical and take this relationship for exactly what it is—an exciting, exhilarating sexual carnival ride that will come to an end."

Sarah turned her empty glass around and around in her hands as she pondered Libby's revelation. "Somehow, I don't think it's as simple as you make it sound."

Libby reached over and grabbed her best friend's hand. "You don't have to worry."

"I'm never going to stop worrying about you, Lib. We've been friends for far too long." She pushed out of her chair and set her glass down on the table. "I have to go. My folks invited me over for dinner tonight and I'm supposed to bring the dessert. You don't have a spare pie or cake in your refrigerator, do you?"

"There's a bourbon pecan pie in the freezer. Throw it in the oven when you serve dinner and it should be nice and warm when you're finished."

"Thanks," she said. "I'll see you later. And behave tonight. The last thing I want is to have to squelch rumors about you and Carlisle Whitby. Don't let him seduce you with all that mailman talk."

Libby giggled. "I won't." She sighed softly as she sat back and sipped at her iced tea, staring out at the garden, lush and green. The scent of roses hung in the air and Libby closed her eyes and smiled. An image of Trey, naked and aroused, drifted through her mind and she let it linger there. There was no doubt in her mind that they'd be together again. Now that she'd made the decision, the rest seemed to be quite simple.

"Hey there."

Libby opened her eyes to find the subject of her fantasy standing on the back steps, as if she'd summoned him merely by will. He was dressed in a starched white shirt and trousers, his tie undone and his usually mussed hair combed neatly. "You're back," she said.

"I am." He slowly climbed the steps. "I wanted to return this," Trey said, pulling her scarf out from behind his back.

Libby blushed as she took the scarf from his fingers. "I guess you managed to get free then."

"Yeah. Wiley Boone untied me this morning when he dropped off another building permit."

Libby's eyes went wide. "You spent the night—"

"No," Trey said. "But next time you decide to tie me up, it would be nice if you untied me afterward." He paused, sending her a devilish grin. "So, are you planning to tie me up again, Libby?"

She shrugged, pleased with the hint of challenge in his voice. "I'm not sure. Did you enjoy being tied up?"

"Oh, yeah," Trey said. "In fact, you can tie me up whenever you want, just as long as you make me feel like that again."

Libby's blush deepened, making her cheeks hot. "I'm glad you liked it."

Trey strolled up the steps and leaned against the railing in front of her, his long legs crossed and his hands braced beside him. There were times when Libby couldn't breathe for looking at him. He was by far the sexiest man she'd ever met. He had an easy charm about him, a way of making her feel as if she was the sexiest person in his world.

"You know, I was serious about getting out of town. Why don't we drive down to Savannah tonight? We could see a movie, go out to dinner and rent an expensive hotel room."

"You just came back from Savannah."

"Then we'll go to Charleston."

Though Libby was tempted to accept his offer, her plans with Carlisle were more important to the future of her relationship with Trey. "I can't. Not tonight."

He chuckled. "Why, do you have a date?"

Libby's smiled faded slightly. "I do have a date."

He nodded slowly, as if trying to hide his reaction behind a bland expression. "A date. Well, that's interesting. And just who would be taking you out tonight?"

"Carlisle Whitby."

Trey gasped and then laughed. "The mailman? You're going out with our mailman?"

"Yes. Are you jealous?"

Trey shrugged. "No. Hell, if Carlisle is your type, then I can't compete. He's got the mailbag and the uniform and that cute little truck with the steering wheel on the wrong side. I don't have a chance against a guy like that."

"He's not my type," Libby said. "And I'm only going out with him because I'm hoping it will put an end to all the talk around town about us. And it's just dinner at Tarrington's."

Trey grabbed her hands and pulled her to her feet. "Forget about all the talk. It's just speculation anyway." He bent his head and brushed a kiss across her lips. "Call Carlisle and tell him you have other plans. We'll get out of here and do something fun." He nuzzled her neck, nipping at it playfully. "I'll let you tie me up again. Or, if you want, I'll tie you up."

"No!" Libby said, pulling out of his embrace. She was supposed to be in control, not him! How easily he was able to take that control from her with just a little kiss or an innocent caress. He had to understand that there were limits to how far she was willing to go. "Not tonight."

He frowned, his gaze searching her expression for some clue to her reaction. "I thought we'd gotten past this. You want me, I want you. It's all pretty simple when you think about it."

"And that's the way I want to keep it," Libby said. "Simple. And very private."

"Fine," Trey said. "Great. The next time you want me, just write me another letter." With that, he turned and jogged down the steps.

Libby gasped. Another letter? Anger bubbled up inside of her. She'd done that twelve years ago and all it had brought her was regret. He'd stolen her heart back then and he was trying his damnedest to do it again. But she wasn't going to let him.

Maybe Sarah had been right. What seemed like a simple plan had suddenly turned complicated. If she knew what was good for her, she would learn to accept life as it was before Trey Marbury came back into town.

But now that she'd had a taste of excitement, it was awfully hard to go back.

TREY SLID onto a bar stool and ordered a whiskey neat from the bartender at Tarrington's. He glanced around at the other patrons, then thought about tossing some money on the bar and leaving. Getting caught up in this silly plan of Libby's was tantamount to admitting he had serious feelings for her. Here he was, ready to intrude on her date with another man, simply because the thought of sharing Libby with any other man—even Carlisle Whitby—was too much to bear.

Why the hell did she feel it necessary to put on this charade? Was his presence in her life so unthinkable that she had to go to these measures to make people believe they meant nothing to each other?

The bartender set the glass of whiskey in front of Trey and he snatched it up and took a deep swallow. He'd spent hours trying to figure out how he really felt about her, and now this. So far, the relationship had been mostly physical. But from the beginning, Trey had sensed there could be something much more to it.

All those years ago, they'd come together for one night and something had happened to him. A switch inside him had been flipped on, filling him with a sense of the man he was meant to become. And now that he was back in Belfort, with Libby so close, he felt as if he belonged here.

After he'd left for college, Trey had managed to convince himself he'd been in love with Libby. Over time, the feelings had faded. But in retrospect, Trey realized they'd never completely gone away. Was what he felt now really love, or was it the same silly infatuation he'd experienced as a teenager?

All he knew for sure was that he didn't like Libby

"dating" Carlisle Whitby. And if the gossips in Belfort were going to link one man to Libby Parrish, Trey wanted to be that man.

"I haven't seen you here before."

Trey glanced to his left to find a woman sitting on the bar stool next to him. "I haven't been here before," he replied.

"So does that mean you're new in town?"

"You could say that."

"My name's Lila. I'm not from around here."

She held out her perfectly manicured hand and Trey took it. "Nice to meet you, Lila. I'm Trey." He smiled, then picked up his drink and took a slow sip. He'd known a few women like Lila before, women who spent hours in the gym and in the salon, yet managed to look older than they really were. Her smile, her mannerisms, even her sultry drawl were trained to tease and entice. Tonight, she'd chosen to turn her charms in Trey's direction and he was glad for the distraction.

"Are you here alone?" she asked.

"Not anymore," Trey replied. He motioned to the bartender and ordered Lila a drink. After a few minutes of small talk, it was clear that Lila was looking for a lot more than just conversation. Her hand rested on his thigh and she rubbed her leg against his provocatively.

"Why don't we go somewhere a bit more private?" she suggested.

"Actually, I could use something to eat," Trey replied. Though he wanted to leave, he wasn't about to leave with Lila. And maybe being seen spending time with Lila would help with Libby's ridiculous plan to divert attention.

"We'll eat before we leave." She drained her glass of wine, then slid off the bar stool and took his arm. They walked toward the dining room, but before they reached the hostess, the door of the restaurant swung open and Libby stepped inside.

She froze, a startled expression on her face, when she saw Trey. Carlisle ran into her from behind, the door hitting him in the backside. Her gaze darted back and forth between Trey and Lila.

"What are you doing here?" she hissed.

"I heard this was a great place for dinner. Thought I'd give it a try. Libby, this is Lila. Lila, this is my neighbor, Libby Parrish." He leaned forward and held out his hand. "Hello, Carlisle. How's the mail business going?"

"Hello," said Carlisle, a suspicious glint in his eye.

Suddenly, the bar seemed to go quiet and Trey could feel the other patrons watching them all. "Now that we ran into each other, why don't we have dinner together?" Trey suggested. "Carlisle, you wouldn't mind, would you? Lila doesn't know many folks in town and I'm sure she'd enjoy meeting new people."

"Well, I—"

"Great," Trey said. "I'll get us a table." He smiled to himself as he slipped past Libby, his arm brushing against hers for a fleeting moment. He steered Lila through the dining room, his hand resting on the small of her back. The hostess showed them to a table near the windows, and Trey stepped around Lila's chair and pulled it out for her. Libby waited for Carlisle to do the same and when he didn't, Trey took the job.

But the instant she sat down, Libby jumped back up again, clutching her purse in her hands. "If you'll excuse me, I'll be right back." She hurried out of the dining room, turning back long enough to give Trey a desperate look.

"I'm just going to get another drink," Trey said. "Would you two care for anything else?" He didn't wait for an answer before heading off after Libby.

They met near the ladies' room, Libby pacing back and forth in the small hallway, her color high, her green eyes bright with anger. "What do you think you're doing?" she demanded. "And who is that woman you're with?"

"Her name is Lila. I just met her at the bar. She's real friendly, but she's not from around here."

"She's real friendly, I'm sure. You had your hand on her butt!"

"You know, you might be on to something there," Trey said, lowering his voice to a conspiratorial whisper. "If I'm seen with Lila and you're seen with Carlisle, then your plan is bound to work. By the way, how's that plan of yours going?"

"It's going just fine," Libby said. "But I really don't think it's necessary for you to participate."

"Why not? While you're enjoying yourself, I should be able to have a good time, too, don't you think?"

"A good time? Is that what you want?" She cursed beneath her breath, then spun on her heel and shoved the bathroom door open. It swung back, but Trey slipped inside before it shut.

"You're not upset, are you?"

"Get out of this bathroom. You're causing a scene!"

He glanced around. "There's no one in here but us, Libby. Who's here to see?"

"You did this on purpose. You're jealous of Carlisle and you're angry because I wouldn't cancel our date, so you came down here to spoil our evening together."

"No," Trey said, backing her up against the sink. In one effortless motion, he grabbed her around the waist and set her on the edge of the vanity. "I came down here for a drink. But now that I am here, I think I will do my best to spoil your evening." Trey hooked his finger under her chin and drew her lips to his. "Because I know you'd rather be spending the night with me."

"Don't you dare kiss me," she warned.

"I have to kiss you," Trey whispered, brushing his lips across her mouth. He slowly ran his palms up and down her thighs, pushing her skirt up higher each time. "And I think you have to kiss me, too."

Trey didn't wait for her to refuse again. His hands slipped beneath her skirt as he covered her mouth with his. She didn't resist and he tested her lips with his tongue. A tiny sigh slipped from her throat and her fingers found his nape, furrowing through his hair and pulling him closer.

Libby tipped her head back and Trey traced a line with his tongue from her mouth to her ear and then lower. He pulled her silk blouse off her shoulder and sucked gently on the skin at the base of her neck. He wanted to leave a mark, proof that he was the only one who could possess her.

His hands wandered over her body, growing more familiar with the soft curves and warm flesh. Trey tugged at her blouse and Libby followed his cue, frantically unbuttoning his shirt and yanking it from his trousers.

They touched bare skin at the very same time, their soft moans mingling. The danger of discovery was part of the thrill and in the back of Trey's mind; he wanted someone to walk in, wanted to prove that everything he'd shared with Libby was real and not just the stuff of rumors.

He pushed Libby's skirt even higher and then grabbed her thighs, pulling her against him so she could feel his need, hard and hot beneath his trousers. She locked her ankles around his waist and Trey gently leaned over her, grateful for the barrier of fabric between them. If it wasn't there, Trey would have slipped inside of her, damn the danger of discovery. But when he made love to Libby Parrish, he didn't want to do it in a public restroom. He wanted her alone, with nothing to interrupt them, nothing to keep them from exploring the real limits of their desire.

He wasn't sure how long they kissed and touched and tore at each other's clothes, but Trey was beyond caring where he was. So, when door of the bathroom swung open, neither one of them heard it. But they did hear the admonition that followed.

"Goodness gracious, this is the ladies' room, not some brothel!"

Sucking in a sharp breath, Libby pulled back and risked a glance at the door, all the while scrambling to restore order to her clothes and hair.

"Lisbeth Parrish, is that you? Who is that with you?"

Trey smiled and nodded. "Trey Marbury. Nice to meet you." He gave the elderly woman a little wave.

"If you'll give us a few seconds, we'll just get out of your way."

To his relief, the woman stepped back outside, offering them a chance to compose themselves. Trey helped Libby button her blouse and then smoothed his hands over her rumpled hair. Her face was flushed and her breath was coming in quick gasps. "I didn't hear her open the door," he murmured.

"Do you know who that was?" Libby said, stepping out of range of his grasp. "That was Charlotte Villiers. She's the biggest blabbermouth in town. Thanks to you, it's not going to be speculation anymore. By tomorrow morning, everyone in Belfort is going to know about you and me and how she found us nearly naked in the ladies' room at Tarrington's. I hope you're happy."

Trey shrugged. "I'm not happy that we had to stop. But maybe it's for the best. This really isn't the proper place for—"

"And you know of a better place? Why don't we just do it in the middle of Center Street and we'll invite the whole town? I live here, Trey, and you don't. How do you think it feels to have people whispering about me?"

"Let them whisper. I say, let's give them something to whisper about."

He tried to slip his hands around her waist, but Libby pushed him away and walked to the door. "Just go home," she ordered. "I'll talk to you later."

"What about Lila?"

"Maybe you should take her with you, if she's really what you want." She pulled the door open and walked out.

Trey turned to the mirror and stared at his reflection for a long moment. Trey should have been happy to step into the arms of a woman like Lilah—a woman so obviously interested in pleasure. But there was something about Libby he couldn't seem to resist. Since he first set eyes on her again, other women held absolutely no appeal. He flipped on the faucet and splashed cold water on his face, patiently waiting for his desire to cool.

"Maybe you should just walk away," he said as he dried his hands and face with a paper towel. But Libby was like unfinished business—or untapped potential. If he didn't stick around to explore what was possible between them, then he'd always wonder.

When Trey stepped out of the ladies' room, Charlotte Villiers was standing outside. He sent her one of his most charming grins and she couldn't help but return the smile. "I believe I might be falling in love with her," Trey whispered. "What do you think? Do you think I have a chance?"

"You could find a more appropriate place to court her than a public washroom," Charlotte suggested.

He chuckled and then strolled down the hallway. Hell, if people were going to gossip, then let them speculate about a romance between them. Because this wasn't just about sex anymore, Trey mused. He was beginning to believe that he and Libby had been meant for each other all along.

LIBBY KNEW THE PATH by heart. She could walk it with her eyes closed or in the dark of night and still find her way through the thick brush and overgrown trees. When she stepped out into the clearing, she drew a deep breath of the warm night air. Mosquitoes buzzed around her and she brushed them away as she pulled her dress over her head and kicked off her shoes.

The water was cool as she walked in and she let it lap around her body. Libby closed her eyes and sank down, then dipped her head back to wet her hair. All she wanted was to wash away every thought of Trey. She lay on her back and floated, looking up at the stars.

A few weeks ago, she'd wished for a little excitement in her life and now there seemed to be too much. Since Trey had come back to Belfort, her entire world had shifted. How could she possibly still want him after all these years?

Things between them had always been unfinished in her mind. After writing him that ridiculous letter, the ramblings of a love-struck seventeen-year-old, Libby had convinced herself that they were destined to be together. When he hadn't answered, she'd imagined him at school, surrounded by beautiful college girls with bouncy hair and perfect cheerleader figures.

Why would he have wanted to come home to a mousy high schooler who'd never been able to fill out a bra or turn a cartwheel? There had been a time when just the thought of Trey had made her feel inadequate. But now it was different.

It felt good to be pursued, to know that he wanted her now as much as she'd wanted him then. Maybe this was the way it was supposed to be. She'd make him fall in love with her, and the scales would suddenly balance and her life would make sense. Maybe then she could erase the hurt from the past.

But Libby couldn't deny she had feelings for him. The jealousy she felt when she saw him with Lila was proof of that. Just the thought of him touching another woman made her want to throttle him.

"How's the water?"

With a tiny yelp, Libby sank down in water up to her neck. She didn't have to see him to know he was standing on the shore. "Go away, Trey. Haven't you caused enough trouble tonight?"

"Not quite," Trey said. "In fact, there's a whole lot more trouble to be had now that I've found you."

She retreated to deeper water. "What happened when you and Lila left? She looked eager to please. Why aren't you seducing her tonight instead of bothering me?"

His deep voice came out of the dark, sending a shiver down her spine. "Come on, Libby, you know you're the only one I want to be with. If you need me to say it out loud, there it is." He reached for the front of his shirt and began to unbutton it. "I only have eyes for Libby Parrish."

"You're not coming in this water."

"Oh, I think I am."

"No you're not. You're trespassing. This is Parrish property and if I want you to leave, then I have every legal right to ask you."

"You can ask, sweetheart, but you don't want me to leave." He shrugged out of the shirt and started on his trousers, kicking off his shoes and socks along the way. He paused before he unzipped his fly. "We are skinny-dipping, aren't we? I'd hate to get out there and find out you're not really naked."

Libby watched as he skimmed his boxers over his

hips. She couldn't see much in the dark, but she could see enough to appreciate his broad chest and narrow hips. A soft sigh caught in her throat as he moved closer to the water. He was beautiful and so undeniably masculine. She'd seen him nearly naked on several occasions, but now, without a stitch of clothing, Libby considered him much more dangerous—and irresistible.

She felt a knot of desire twist inside of her, sending warmth snaking through her bloodstream. They'd been so close that night in her bed and even that night on his veranda. The need inside her had been building for days and she ached to touch him, to have his hands on her body, to linger over lovemaking as if they had all the time in the world.

He walked through the shallows, then dove cleanly into the water. With strong strokes, Trey crossed the short distance to where she stood. When he popped up in front of her, he shook his head. Libby covered her face and yelped in protest as he splashed water in her face.

"The water feels good," he said, swimming around her, his shoulders and backside breaking the surface.

"I should be angry with you." Libby bobbed away from him, unwilling to let him touch her. If he did, she'd find herself in the same situation as she had in the bathroom—out of control. Once Trey laid his hands on her, she couldn't seem to resist him.

"Come on, Lib. I'm sorry I messed up your evening. But you have to admit, dating Carlisle was kind of a silly idea."

"It would have worked if you hadn't shown up.

Charlotte Villiers would have seen me with him instead of with you, and she would have told everyone in town."

"Why is this so important to you? Why let the gossips bother you?"

Libby turned away, staring at a light across the river. "Because someday, you're going to leave and I'm going to have to live here. And I don't want to be known as the poor fool who slept with Trey Marbury."

Trey reached out and found her hand, then drew it up and out of the water. He laced his fingers through hers, then kissed the back of her hand; his lips were warm on her cool, damp skin. "I came here the first night I was in town," he admitted. "I remembered this place from that night we spent together before I left for college. I wanted to see if it was still the same."

"That night is in the past," Libby said, reluctant to talk about painful memories. "We were different people back then. We were just kids."

"Sometimes it seems like it was yesterday. And then, when I came here again and I saw you, it took me back to that time."

"You saw me?" Libby asked.

He nodded. "You were swimming. You stood right over there and took your clothes off and I thought I'd stepped into a dream. God, you were so beautiful—*are* so beautiful. I didn't realize it was you at first. Then you turned and the moon lit up your face, and I was that kid again."

"Do you ever think about that night?" Libby asked, her voice trembling slightly.

"Yeah, I do," he admitted. "A lot. I was pretty confused and you made me feel better."

"The sex?"

"I know I wasn't that great, but—"

"You were," Libby said, reaching up to smooth her hand over his cheek. "I wouldn't have changed a thing."

He bent his head and looked into her eyes. "You know, that was my first time, don't you?"

Libby bit back a gasp. "But I thought—"

He chuckled softly. "Yeah, the old expectations again. I kissed a lot of girls and we did a lot of other things. And there was a lot of locker-room talk and speculation. But the truth of the matter is, I was scared. I had a way out of this town—a way to get out from under my father's thumb—and I didn't want to do anything to mess it up."

"Then why did you do it with me?"

"Because it felt right. I honestly thought you cared about me."

"I did," Libby said. "But then you know that, don't you." She didn't want to make him feel guilty for the past, for all the hurt his desertion had caused. So much of who he was had been tied up with his family that it was no wonder he'd walked away and never looked back. And the letter she'd written him must have seemed like even more pressure.

"You were my first, Libby. And I don't think I've ever forgotten that. Just being with you, talking to you that night. You seemed to understand what I was going through. I never thanked you, but in a way, you kind of made me the man I am today."

She brushed her fingers across his lips and Trey kissed her fingertips. Though she couldn't see the subtleties of his expression, she heard the emotion in his voice. "I never really got over that night, either," she murmured. She leaned forward and kissed him, drawing her tongue along the crease of his lips.

For a long time they explored each other's mouths, their hands and lips the only point of contact. The cooling water swirled around them, gliding over naked skin and heightening sensation.

Trey slipped his hands around her waist and pulled her close, their bodies meeting beneath the water. He picked her up and pressed his lips to the base of her throat. "Neither one of us knows what's going to happen here," he whispered. "But when we're together, it feels good. Why should we deny that?"

Libby furrowed her fingers through his wet hair. "Just because it feels good, doesn't always mean it's a good idea."

He smoothed his hands along her thighs and gently drew her legs up around his waist. Libby held her breath, trying to slow the furious pounding of her heart. They were so close. If she just sank down slightly, he'd be inside of her.

"I like kissing you, Lib. And I like touching you. If you don't want me to do that, you're going to have to tell me to stop."

"I have," Libby teased. "You don't listen."

"All right," Trey said. "Tell me once more. Tell me not to touch you."

Libby opened her mouth, but Trey quickly kissed her. When he drew back, she shook her head. "That's not fair."

"What's not fair is this body of yours." He shifted slightly and Libby felt his hard shaft probe at her entrance. And then, she moved and he was inside her, the contact taking them both by surprise.

A low moan slipped from his throat as she let herself sink down on top of him. Libby froze, trying not to move; their bodies were nearly weightless in the water. She sensed he was dangerously close to losing control, but it felt so good to have him buried deep inside of her.

"Oh, God, Libby," he said, the words tight in his throat. "Don't move."

Libby shifted again, drawing herself upward, the tip of his shaft teasing at her entrance. "I won't," she murmured, kissing him again. She sank down again, tipping her head back and enjoying the sensation.

He sucked in a sharp breath. "If you keep this up, I'm not going to want to stop." Slowly, he lifted her higher until the contact was completely broken. And then, he let his tightly held breath escape. Furrowing his fingers through her wet hair, Trey dragged her into another kiss, seducing her with his tongue and his lips. And when she was breathless with desire, Trey gazed down into her eyes. "The second time we make love is not going to be in a river," he said.

"Where then?" Libby asked, her fingers drifting below the surface. She ran her fingers along the length of his shaft.

He moaned softly and then grabbed her wrist. "Let's do what I said before and get out of town," he said, his lips warm against her ear. "Let's make this about us, instead of everyone else in Belfort. I want to spend days in bed with you, Lib, and we can't do that here."

"Where?" she asked. "And when?"

Trey chuckled. "Anywhere and as soon as possible. You just let me know and I'll be there."

"I have to go to New Orleans tomorrow on business. My flight leaves at one tomorrow afternoon, Delta 762. Meet me at the airport in Charleston and we'll go together. We can stay a few extra days."

He grinned, then kissed her again, picked her up and carried her out of the water. "All right. I'll meet you there."

Libby stared into his eyes, her fingers smoothing over the planes and angles of his face. Maybe it was best that he couldn't really see her, couldn't see the indecision in her gaze. "Sometimes, I wonder if this has all happened too fast. Look at me. I'm swimming naked in a river with a man I barely know. A few weeks ago, the most excitement I had in my life was when I found an organic bug spray for my roses."

"Believe me, sweetheart. I can guarantee I'll be a lot more exciting than bug spray."

"Show me then," Libby murmured, nuzzling her face. "Touch me."

Trey growled playfully, then picked her up and tossed her into the water. He swam after her and then pulled her beneath the surface, kissing her as they sank.

They played in the water for a long time—touching and kissing, talking and teasing, bringing each other to the edge of pleasure and then dancing away. Libby could have spent the entire night in the river with him, simply to be near him.

Though they both wanted to make love, they'd reached an unspoken agreement. They walked from the water, hand in hand, and dressed each other—his hands smoothing over her body, her fingers caressing him. And when he left her at the door, he left her wanting the feel of his hands, still warm on her body, and the taste of his tongue, still damp on her lips. She thought about sneaking out and crawling into his bed, but Libby was willing to wait, knowing that when they were together again, it would be the realization of every fantasy she'd ever had about Trey.

It would happen, it would be perfect—and it would change everything between them.

6

"COME ON, BEAU, let's go." Trey opened the driver's side door to the Jeep and waited while the dog jumped inside. Then he tossed his bag on the back seat.

Though it was just past ten, he still had to put gas in the Jeep, drop Beau at the kennel outside Belfort and pick up his ticket before he met Libby at the gate. They had decided to drive separately, and she had left early that morning with Sarah to do some work at the studio before leaving for the airport.

He and Libby had barely been able to walk away from each other the night before. He'd wanted to carry her up to her bed and make love to her right then. But he wanted Libby free of inhibitions and worries, not watching the clock and waiting for dawn. And the only way to have that was to get out of Belfort.

He slid in behind the wheel and backed out of the drive. But he'd barely turned onto Charles Street when his cell phone rang. He'd given Libby the number but as he picked it up and glanced at the caller ID, Trey recognized the Chicago area code.

"Hello, Mark," he said after switching on the phone.

"When the hell are you coming back to Chicago?"

"I told you I'd be gone for a few months. It's been three weeks."

"Seems like three years. I can't work with Dave. He just doesn't understand what I need from him."

Trey glanced over his shoulder as he turned onto River Street. "Dave Sorenson is my best architect, Mark, and I trust him. You can, too. He's up to speed on all the projects and he knows if there's a problem, he can call me."

"Well, there's a problem. The Elton Place project is about to fall through because Dave can't seem to convince the client to change the site plan."

"I'll call him later today," Trey said. "We'll work it out."

"You need to get back here."

"Don't worry. I'm coming back. If the Elton project goes south, I'll drive back for a few days next week and get it straightened out."

"You *are* coming back for good, aren't you?" Mark asked. "Just tell me that you are."

"Yeah," Trey murmured. "Yeah, I'm coming back."

Even as he said the words, Trey couldn't help but wonder if they were a lie. Chicago seemed like a world apart, a place that had been easy to forget now that he'd settled into the lazy rhythms of Belfort.

He'd come back to Belfort to deal with his father's estate and to come to terms with his death, yet he'd done very little to sort out those feelings. Instead, he'd thrown himself into an affair with Libby Parrish. Was his single-minded pursuit of her just a way to avoid dealing with the guilt? Or was he truly falling in love with Libby?

Before Clayton Marbury had died, Trey hadn't seen him for almost three years. And before that, it had been even longer. After the shoulder injury in college had knocked him out of football for good, his father's disappointment had infused every conversation and argument they'd had. Trey refused to return to Belfort but he occasionally joined his parents for Christmas at their cabin in the Ozarks. And his mother came to visit him twice a year in Chicago. He had waited for his father to make the first move and accompany her north. That had never happened, and he'd died still estranged from his only child.

As Trey turned onto Center Street, he brushed aside those thoughts, choosing to replace them with the problems at work. He grabbed up his cell phone and punched in the two-digit code for his office number. A few seconds later, the receptionist answered the phone. "Hi there, Elise, it's Trey. Can you put me through to Dave?"

He waited, listening to the canned music over the line. But when he glanced in the rearview mirror, Trey noticed a police car following hard on his back bumper. Almost immediately, the cop turned on his lights. With a soft curse, Trey glanced at the speedometer and realized he'd been going at least ten miles per hour over the limit. He quickly switched off the phone, tossed it on the seat next to Beau and pulled over to the curb.

Trey watched as the officer, a burly man with dark hair and reflecting glasses, lumbered up to the Jeep. When he stood beside the Jeep, Trey forced a smile. "Mornin'."

"License and registration please," the cop ordered.

"Can I ask why you stopped me?"

"License and registration," he repeated.

Trey reached over, flipped open the glove compartment and retrieved his registration, and then grabbed his wallet from the back pocket of his pants. The officer examined both carefully, shoving the sunglasses up on his forehead as he did. Trey thought he recognized the man, but he couldn't put a name to the imposing figure in blue.

"Chicago, Illinois," the officer said. "That where you're livin' these days? Tell me, Mr. Marbury, do they ride around all day talkin' on them little telephones where you come from? 'Cause here, we pay more attention to our drivin'."

"I'm sorry, I didn't realize there was a law against—"

"Well, there is here in Belfort. Passed it just last year."

Trey groaned inwardly. "I didn't realize that."

"I'm afraid I'm going to have to take you into the station."

"Now? Can't you just write me a ticket and I'll pay the fine?"

The cop slowly shook his head. "Seein' as you're from out of state, I need to check for any outstandin' warrants."

Trey smiled and tried to remain calm. A simple infraction now looked like it would take up more time than he had to spare. Libby was waiting and they were finally going to have some time to themselves. He needed to get to the airport! "Technically, I'm not from out of state. I grew up here. My dad was—"

"I know who you are. Now, if you'll just step out of the car, Mr. Marbury. I don't want to have to cuff you."

Trey pushed open the door. This was ridiculous! "If I'm riding down to your station in your car, what am I supposed to do with my dog?"

"Well, bring 'im with," the officer said as if the answer were self-evident. "Can't leave him in the car alone, can you? Not in this heat."

Cursing beneath his breath, Trey waited for Beau to jump out of the Jeep, then locked the door and followed the officer to his squad car. "Officer, I'd—"

"It's not officer," the man grumbled. "It's chief. I'm the chief of police here in Belfort, so you can call me Chief Talbert."

"Bobby Ray Talbert?" Suddenly the face and the hulking body were familiar. Bobby Ray had played on Trey's offensive line at Belfort High. "Geez, Bobby Ray, why didn't you say it was you? How are you? Hell, I didn't realize you were in law enforcement."

"That's Chief Talbert to you," he muttered.

Trey smiled. "Right. Chief. Well, this doesn't have to be complicated. I'm not a criminal. I'm on my way to the airport and I'd be happy to sign any papers and pay any fines right up front. And I can assure you that I don't have any outstanding warrants. I'm an architect in Chicago."

"We get plenty of northerners down here runnin' drugs up from Florida," he said. "It's my job to check these things out."

Why was everyone in Belfort determined to do his or her civic duty? Trey rode the three blocks to the police station in the back of Bobby Ray's cruiser. Beau stretched out on the seat beside him and when they got to the station, Bobby Ray ushered Trey inside. Beau, who had committed no crime, was allowed to lie on a sofa while Trey got a cold metal bench in a holding room.

He glanced at his watch and mentally calculated how long it would take him to get to Charleston. If he could get out and on his way within the next hour, he'd still be able to make his flight. But as the minutes ticked by, Trey realized that the police in Belfort moved as slowly as the rest of the folks in town.

After an hour, Trey stood up and asked to use the phone, but the female officer at the desk ordered him to sit down and wait. He considered calling a lawyer, but he'd have to use his one phone call to get hold of Libby at the airport.

Sometime before one, after nearly three hours of waiting, Trey decided he'd had enough. He demanded to see the officer in charge or he'd be forced to call a lawyer. A few minutes later, Bobby Ray strolled in and sat down on the bench beside him. He handed him two tickets. "There's one there for the cell phone violation and one for speeding. You were clocked going ten miles per hour over the limit. I also have you for an unlicensed dog and a rolling stop when you turned onto Center Street, but I'm goin' to let you slide on those."

"Thank you," Trey said, pushing to his feet. "I'll just take care of these and be on my way."

"Not so fast," Bobby Ray said. "There's something else. I got a complaint about you the other day and I just wanted to let you know, I'll be keeping an eye on you, Trey Marbury."

"A complaint?" Trey asked.

"Here in Belfort we have an old law on the books that prohibits fornication between two unmarried people. I understand you've been chasing Lisbeth Parrish around town."

"Great. Now you're going to get involved in our personal lives, too? Join the crowd."

"I take a particular interest in Lisbeth. She's a fine, upstandin' citizen and a local celebrity. Plus, she's a damn fine cook. So you can see, I wouldn't look fondly on you takin' advantage of her. So watch yourself, boy, or you're going to end up back in this cell and it'll take a whole lot more than a couple hundred bucks to get you out." With that, Bobby Ray got up. "You can leave now. Y'all have a pleasant day."

Trey was forced to walk back to his Jeep, Beau trotting at his side. By the time he'd finished paying the fines and buying a Belfort license for his dog, it was well past one. He had no idea where Libby was staying in New Orleans, so when he got home, he called information for Sarah Cantrell's number.

"Unlisted," he muttered as he threw the phone onto the floor. "This is just great."

The only saving grace of getting arrested and missing his flight was that now he'd probably have the entire weekend to figure out just how he was going to explain this to Libby.

"You were great," Sarah said. "I don't know why you get so nervous before these things. You're always very entertaining. That story about the grits had them rolling in the aisles."

"It did go well," Libby said. "But they didn't laugh at my gumbo joke. And I missed a whole section when I was talking about low-country cuisine."

"Well, we sold over two hundred cookbooks and

we took a bunch of orders for the new DVD. I'd call this weekend a great success."

"Yeah," Libby murmured. "Great."

Sarah shook her head as she reached for her luggage on the carousel. "You've been moping around all weekend. Would you like to tell me what's wrong?"

"Nothing's wrong. I'm just tired and I want to get home." She grabbed her bag, but it slipped in her hand and landed on her foot. Libby cursed and kicked the bag, tears welling up in her eyes. "God, I hate my luggage!"

Sarah frowned, shaking her head. "You know, this mood of yours probably has nothing to do with your luggage. I'd venture to guess that this has something to do with Trey Marbury, seeing as how you haven't mentioned him all weekend."

"I don't ever want to hear his name again," Libby muttered. "If you say it, I'll fire you."

"You can't fire me because I don't really work for you," Sarah said. "I own the production company that produces your show. Technically, you work for me."

"Well, then, you should fire me for being such an idiot."

"I generally think you're pretty smart, Lib."

Libby shook her head and she dragged her suitcase toward the door to the parking lot. "Not when it comes to men. I invited Trey to come with me this weekend. He was supposed to meet me at the airport on Friday and we were going to have a nice romantic weekend away from Belfort. We were going to have a wonderful time and I was really looking forward to it."

"What happened?"

"He stood me up. He never showed up at the airport, he didn't call. He just left me waiting there feeling like the biggest fool in the world. The same way he left me waiting twelve years ago."

Sarah patted Libby on the back. "I'm sorry. You should have told me."

"At first, I was humiliated," Libby continued, relieved to finally unburden herself. "I mean, I waited until the last minute to get on the plane. And then I got angry. I really was hoping that this weekend would..." She shook her head. "I hoped it might make things clear between us."

"He probably has a good explanation," Sarah said as they got into the elevator in the parking ramp. "Maybe something came up, a family emergency or something to do with his business. Did you check your machine?"

"I can never remember the code," Libby said.

"And he didn't leave a message at the hotel?"

"I don't think he knew where I was staying."

"Nice planning there, Lib. You invite the man away for a romantic weekend and you don't bother to tell him where you're going?"

"I don't want to talk about this," Libby said, her nerves frayed and her patience waning. She rubbed at a knot of tension in her temples. "This probably happened for a reason. We're not supposed to be together. It's...fate. Maybe I'm glad he didn't show. It would have made things more complicated and I don't need that in my life right now. The truth is, the closer we get to actually doing it, the more scared I become."

"Scared of what?"

"What if making love to Trey changes everything?

What if I fall in love with him again? I'm not sure I'd be able to watch him leave."

"I've watched you over the past few weeks and I think you're already in love with the guy."

"I am not!" Libby cried, picking up her pace when she saw Sarah's car. She waited for her friend to unlock the trunk and then threw her bags inside. "What we have is just a bad case of lust, not love."

"Right now, I don't think you can tell the difference," Sarah said.

They drove back to the station in silence. Libby tried to stop thinking about Trey, but she kept trying to rationalize what had happened. Maybe Sarah was right. Maybe he had a good excuse. But in the end, did it really make a difference?

When they got to the station, Libby put her bags in her car, then turned to say goodbye to Sarah, anxious to get home and find Trey.

"Are you going to be all right?" Sarah asked.

Libby nodded. "Sure. Hey, whatever it is, I can handle it. I'm in complete control. Well, maybe not complete, but—"

"Don't go home, then," Sarah said. "Let's get some dinner. We'll drive back together and stop to eat at that seafood place we like. You can pick up your car when we come in for the lighting design tomorrow."

The receptionist greeted them as they walked inside and then waved a sheaf of pink message slips in their direction. "I have some messages for you, Miss Parrish. This guy has been calling all weekend. He says you know him and that he was supposed to go to New Orleans with you. He asked where you were staying. I think he might have been calling for

Dewey, you know, that crazy fan who's always following you around. I recognize Dewey's voice so he never gets through anymore but—"

"Trey Marbury?" Libby asked.

"Yeah, that was his name. Do you know him?"

Libby nodded. She picked up the stack of messages and flipped through them. "Did he say anything?"

"No, just that you should call him. Oh, then the last time he called, he mentioned something about leaving town and he left his cell phone number."

"What?"

"He said he'd explain in his letter."

"What letter?"

The receptionist shrugged. "I don't know. Maybe he sent it to your house."

"Come on," Sarah said, pulling her toward the door. "I'll drive you home now."

"I can drive," Libby said as they went out. "I'm fine. Hey, I always knew he'd leave sooner or later. It's better that it was sooner, before I got too attached."

Sarah walked Libby back out to the parking lot, then wrapped her arms around Libby and gave her a hug. "I've got a few things to do here, then I'm headed home. Why don't you and I rent a movie tonight and eat two or three of those pies you keep in the freezer? We'll have a girl's night."

Libby shrugged. "I'm really tired. I think I'm just going to take a shower and go to bed early. But I'll talk to you tomorrow, all right?"

Sarah waved as Libby drove out of the parking lot and headed for the highway. "Maybe this is for the best," she repeated as she fixed her gaze on the road. "I was falling in love with him."

But admitting her feelings didn't seem to mitigate the pain and regret. Would it take her another twelve years to get over Trey Marbury? Or would she spend the rest of her life wondering what might have been?

THERE HAD STILL been no relief from the heat wave after another week and a half. Every window in Libby's house had been thrown open to catch even the slightest breeze. People on the street talked about the weather forecast in great detail, praying for rain. Libby had taken to wearing the lightest cotton dress she could find and forgoing underwear if she wasn't planning to leave the house.

The only time she had a moment's relief was when she stood in front of the refrigerator or the air conditioner that rumbled in her bedroom window. Beyond that, she tried to stay still as she could and take a cooling shower whenever the heat became especially unbearable.

Libby peered out the screen door at the house across the street. It was Thursday afternoon and the bridge club was in full swing in the Throckmortons' front parlor. No doubt, the subject of today's conversation would be Trey Marbury's hasty exit from Belfort.

The breeze teased at her hair and she stepped out onto the front veranda to enjoy it while it lasted. Her gaze drifted over to the house next door. Contractors had been hard at work there, and she'd heard through the grapevine that the guys in charge regularly spoke to Trey. But she hadn't heard a word since he'd left.

Libby sat down in one of the wicker rockers and pulled out the letter Trey had left in her mailbox.

She'd taken to carrying it in her pocket so she could read it whenever she felt the need. Libby had hoped that she might find something in his words that would tell her she'd made the right decision, that putting Trey firmly in her past was the only course of action.

She slipped the letter out of the envelope and unfolded it, then slowly read the words again.

Dear Libby,
I'm not sure I can explain the events that conspired to keep me from making our flight and it probably doesn't make a difference. If you're angry with me, then my explanations won't matter. Maybe missing that plane was a good thing. It gave me some time to think and I realized that I've been pushing you toward something I'm not sure you're ready for. Now, I have to leave and I'm hoping this will give you time to decide what you really want. I'll be back soon. But I do know that we're going to have to either finish this once and for all—or start planning a future together. I'm sorry if I messed up your life here and if my return has caused you more pain than our time together was worth. But I didn't want to walk away again without telling you that you have and always will own a part of my heart.
Take care, Trey
P.S. If you want to talk, you have my number.

Libby stared at the note for a long time, the words blurring in front of her eyes. Her anger at Trey had dissolved over the past ten days and now she felt only a dull ache in the vicinity of her heart. She missed him. But Libby had to admit the distance had given her perspective. She'd come to realize just how deep her feelings were for Trey.

It wasn't about lust and it wasn't about control anymore. She wanted to surrender to him, completely and utterly, and forget about the repercussions. She couldn't be happy unless she let herself love him—even if it was for just a little while.

She reread the text, but as her gaze scanned each line, Libby realized that something had been bothering her about the letter, something nagging at her mind. And it had nothing to do with the sentiments expressed. She walked back inside the house, heading directly to the kitchen.

Trey's first note was still in the drawer beneath the microwave. She'd been afraid to take it out, afraid that the erotic words might bring back feelings she wasn't prepared to deal with. But as she laid the two side by side on the table, the problem became clear.

"Oh, God," she murmured, her eyes darting back and forth between the two letters. The handwriting on the first looked nothing like the handwriting on the second! So if Trey had written and signed the second, then who had sent her the first?

"Carlisle?" Libby murmured. She moaned and then covered her eyes. But she'd mentioned the letter to Trey that night before she'd tied him up on his veranda. And he hadn't questioned her about it. "What man would ask questions in a situation like that?" she reasoned. "He wasn't thinking with his head, he was thinking with his…"

Her cheeks warmed and she drew a deep breath, trying to make sense of her chaotic thoughts. Outside, a dog barked; the sound grated on her nerves. With a soft curse, she snatched up the letters and walked to the back door. At the same moment, Beau bounded up on the veranda. Libby screamed in surprise and then realized if Beau was home, so was Trey.

She pressed her palm to her damp forehead, then frantically combed her hair with her fingers. Trey was nowhere to be seen, but she knew he wouldn't be far behind. She needed a shower and a dress that didn't look like she'd slept in it.

Libby raced through the house to the stairs, but she was only halfway up when a knock sounded on the back door. She stopped in her tracks.

"Libby?"

She drew in a quick breath at the sound of his voice. Her heart began to race and for a moment, she forgot to breathe. She turned for the kitchen and then decided that she couldn't face him looking like a wreck. In the end, Libby just sat down on the stairs, too confused to move.

The screen door creaked and she heard footsteps echo through the house. "Libby?" She tried to stand, but her knees were weak. She wrapped her fingers around the balusters and waited. A few seconds later, Trey wandered into the entry hall.

"Libby?"

"Hi," she murmured.

He circled the newel post and sat down next to her. "I'm back," he said, staring at her with a perplexed expression.

"Yes, you are."

"I wasn't sure whether I should come over," Trey said.

"It's all right. I would have brought Beau back."

"That's not what I meant. I wasn't sure that you'd want to talk to me. You didn't call."

"I thought it would be good to give it some time," Libby said. "You were right. We needed a chance to take a breath."

He reached out and took her hand, weaving his fingers through hers. In truth, she wanted him to pull her into his arms and kiss her senseless, to erase every last doubt from her mind. His absence had only made her realize that her life seemed empty without him in it.

He stroked her face, his gaze moving between her eyes and her lips. "I missed you, Lib. I drove all night to get back here." He brushed his mouth across hers, his tongue tracing the crease of her lips.

Libby wrapped her arms around his neck and lost herself in the taste of him. She lay back on the stairs and he stretched out over her, deepening the kiss until desire overwhelmed her. When he drew back, he smiled at her, smoothing his fingers along her cheek. "God, I almost forgot how beautiful you are." He pushed to his feet and pulled her up along with him. "Come on," he said, pulling her up the stairs.

When they reached her bedroom, he pulled her down on the bed and slowly began to undress her. "Wait," Libby said, shaking her head.

"Wait?"

"I need to know about this," she said, holding out the letter she still clutched in her fingers.

He sat up. "I figured I should at least say goodbye," he murmured. "I tried to call you, Lib, but I couldn't find you. And then Mark called from work and I had to go back."

"And this," she said, holding out the other letter.

He frowned. "What's that?"

"I got it in my mailbox the day after you came to me, the night of the storm. I thought it was from you, but the handwriting doesn't match."

Trey scanned the note. "Wait here," he said, crawling off the bed. He hurried downstairs and Libby heard the screen door slam behind him. She lay back on the bed and tried to slow her pulse. Had she known of his return, she might have been able to steel herself against these feelings. But she felt as if she'd been ambushed by her own desire.

A minute later, Trey rejoined her upstairs, handing her a letter as he sat down. "Whoever wrote that one, wrote this one, too. The handwriting is the same."

Libby scanned the contents of third letter, her eyes widening as she read. "You thought I wrote this? That's why you came to me that night?"

"And this is why you came to me a few nights later," he said. Trey chuckled. "It seems someone is playing a little game with us."

"Who?"

"Does it really matter?" Trey asked, nuzzling her neck.

"Of course it does."

"Why? Letters or no letters, I think what happened between us would have happened anyway. We had unfinished business, Libby. Maybe that's why I decided to stay here in Belfort or why you automatically thought that the letter was from me."

"And now it's finished?" Libby murmured.

"Not by a long shot." His gaze searched her face. "As far as I'm concerned, it's just getting started."

Libby drew a ragged breath. "But sooner or later, you're going to leave again. And I'm going to have to get used to life without you next door. Without you in my bed."

He opened his mouth and then snapped it shut again. "What do you want from me, Libby?"

She bit her bottom lip to keep from answering truthfully. What she really wanted was for them to live happily ever after. She wanted to grow old with him in Belfort, raising a bunch of kids and spending their lives madly in love with each other. But Libby knew that the chances of those wishes actually coming true were slim to none. "I want time," she said. "Time to figure out what this all means and what I should do about it. I thought I knew what I was doing, but I didn't."

He furrowed his hand through the hair at her nape and pulled her closer, pressing a kiss on her forehead. He lingered there for a moment and Libby prayed that he wouldn't wander down to her lips.

"Then take the time," he murmured. "When I make love to you, Libby, I want you there, body and soul." He crawled off the bed and handed her the letters, then smiled down at her. "I'll see ya, Lib."

"See ya, Trey," she said.

Libby drew a ragged breath and sank back into the pillows, throwing her arm over her eyes. She'd bought herself some time, but what good was it going to do? The simple fact was, she wanted Trey. As long as he was living next door, she'd want to talk to him and touch him, kiss him and share her body with him.

Libby crawled off the bed, grabbing up the three letters. "I am such a coward," she muttered. She'd seduced him when she was seventeen. She was a grown woman now and she was more insecure than she had been back then.

"It's nice to know that I've actually regressed in my sex life," Libby muttered.

7

THE OFFICE WAS located in a small brick building on River Street. Trey had called his father's secretary and asked her to meet him there at noon with the keys. Though he'd been putting off going through his father's business effects, Trey figured it was something that had to be done sooner or later. The building would have to be put up for sale before he could think about heading home.

"No one's been here for months," Eloise said as she unlocked the office door. "I think your father kept the office because of me. You know, he paid me my full salary, even though all I really did was collect rent and deposit the money in the bank account. The tenants could have mailed the money directly to him, but he was very generous that way."

"I've heard that about him," Trey murmured.

Once he walked inside, Trey wasn't sure whether he really wanted to be there. As a kid, he used to spend Saturday mornings at the office with his father, anxious to please and starved for the attention. But sometime after he had reached the age of twelve, Trey had begun to rebel, chaffing at the expectations his father had of him.

Football became the focus of his life from the time

he'd entered high school and it was something that was all his—until his father intruded on that as well. Trey's mother always used to tell him that Clayton Marbury's meddling was the way he showed his love. But it never felt like love to Trey. It felt like punishment.

"I've boxed up all the files," Eloise said. "But I didn't touch anything in your father's office. I thought that was for the family to do."

"Thanks," Trey said.

"There are some extra boxes in the corner." Eloise patted him on the shoulder. "I'm sorry about your father, Trey. He was a good man."

"Thanks," Trey repeated, now numb to the expressions of sympathy.

She handed him the key and then left him alone with the task and his thoughts. Trey drew a deep breath and slowly walked through the reception area toward his father's office. He'd thought about hiring someone to do this job, but then realized it might help to deal with the memories straight on. That's why he'd taken time from work to come back home, so that he could get everything clear in his head.

The blinds were pulled and the interior of the office was warm and stuffy. Trey crossed to the huge windows and threw them open to the light and the fresh air. This had been his father's entire life, the work that he'd loved, the hub of his little empire. At least Trey could understand that passion. He felt the same way about his own work.

He took in the space—from the abundance of natural light, to the high ceilings, to the vintage details. The office would be perfect for an architect, with plenty of wall space for sketches and blueprints. But then, he wasn't going to consider staying in Belfort unless he had a reason to stay. And right now, his only reason was keeping her distance.

Trey sat down in the huge leather chair and tipped his head back, closing his eyes and letting more memories flood his brain. He'd never really taken the time to pinpoint when it had all gone so bad with his father, when they'd stopped talking to each other and retreated into anger. But he did remember happy times as a boy—tossing the football around on a Sunday afternoon, driving to Atlanta for a baseball game, fishing off a pier in the river.

"Hey, there."

Trey opened his eyes to find Libby standing in the doorway. He couldn't help but smile at the sight of her. She wore a pretty flowered dress and her hair was pulled up in a haphazard ponytail, strands of blond caressing her cheeks. They hadn't spoken in three days and he'd begun to wonder if he'd ever see her again. "Hey, Lib."

"I saw you come in here," she said. "I thought you might want some company."

"How is it you know exactly how I'm feeling? My own father, whom I lived with for years, never had a clue what was going on in my head." Though he'd decided to give her space, that didn't mean that he'd stopped thinking about her. If anything, his attraction to her had intensified. There was just something about Libby. She understood him like no one else ever had.

"I guess I'm just really smart," she said with a coy smile.

"Yes, you are," Trey replied. "And very beautiful, too."

She crossed the room and circled the desk. "So this is your dad's office," she murmured, taking in all the details. "Headquarters of the evil empire?" Libby smiled ruefully. "We used to drive past here when I was a kid and my father always had something nasty to say. He usually put a curse on the place. You're lucky he didn't know any real voodoo."

Trey chuckled softly and he reached out and captured her hand. He pressed a kiss to her fingertips. "That feud. I don't even know when it started. My parents used to talk about it all the time, but I never paid attention."

"The Throckmortons know all the details," Libby offered. "If you're really interested I'm sure they'd be happy to fill you in. It had to do with one of my relatives getting shot in the butt by one of your relatives."

He pulled her down on his lap and grinned. As long as she was here, he wasn't going to let the opportunity slip by. "I think you and I have pretty much put an end to the hostilities. Why don't we declare an official ceasefire right now?"

She stared into his eyes, then brushed a quick kiss over his lips. "Deal," she said.

Touching her again felt good, Trey mused, her silken skin, her delicate fingers. She'd driven him wild with those hands, with that mouth, with her body. He wondered how he'd ever be able to touch another woman again without thinking about what he'd shared with Libby. And in that instant, he realized he didn't want any other women.

"So, are we kissing again?" he asked, pressing his lips to her bare shoulder. "Because if we aren't, I'd like to know so I don't make an ass of myself."

Libby pushed off his lap and wandered over to the shelves behind the desk, refusing to answer his question. She picked up a photo of Trey in his football uniform. "You used to be such a babe," she teased.

"Right," he muttered, laughing as he spoke. "That's all padding. I was a pretty skinny guy."

"You've filled out nicely. I was so in love with you back then, skinny legs and all."

Trey spun around in the chair and then reached up to rest his hands on her waist. He leaned forward and pressed his forehead against her belly. "I'm glad you're here. I miss you, Lib. I'm not sure why this is so difficult, but it's easier now that you're here with me."

Libby gently ran her fingers through his hair, the action calming him. "You and your father had a lot of issues and you were never able to get past them. Maybe you regret that you didn't try hard enough."

"I didn't try at all," Trey admitted. "And I should have. God, Libby, I don't want to spend the rest of my life keeping that resentment all bottled up inside me. For a long time, I hated him. And then, I just felt sorry for him. And now I realize that, despite everything, he was still my father and he was just looking for a way to love me."

"I think your father wanted you to grow up to be a good man. And he was trying his hardest to make sure that happened. He just didn't know how to do it the right way." She bent down and kissed the top of his head. "But he succeeded because he did raise a good man."

He looked up at her, emotions welling up inside of him. "So you were in love with me?"

"I was a very silly girl with some very strange romantic ideas," she said, brushing a lock of hair off his forehead. "But I've grown up now."

Trey wondered what it would take to get Libby to love him again. Because he wanted to tell her exactly how he felt, wanted to say those words to her before it was too late.

"I should get some boxes," she murmured. Libby slipped out of his grasp and went outside to the reception area. When she returned, she began packing away the items on the shelves behind the desk, then paused when she came upon a large book. She laid it on the credenza and opened it. "Look at this," she said.

"What is that? An atlas?"

She shook her head. "It's a scrapbook."

Trey stood behind her, his chin resting on her shoulder, his arms wrapped around her waist. Libby flipped through the pages, each of them covered with newspaper clippings. His father had saved every mention of Trey in the newspapers, from the time he'd played in his first junior varsity game to all the articles about his shoulder injury at Tech. "I can't believe he kept all this stuff."

"It's obvious he was very proud of you," Libby said. "If he wasn't, he'd never have kept a book like this."

Trey turned her around in his arms, his gaze fixed on her beautiful face. How was he supposed to stop himself from kissing her or touching her? Over the past weeks, he'd almost taken the opportunities for granted, but now... "Oh, hell," he muttered.

He quickly cupped her face in his hands, searching her wide green eyes for a clue to her feelings. Then he bent close and kissed her, softly and gently, lingering over her lips, tracing a line with his tongue. "If you don't want me to kiss you, then you'd better tell me to stop," he murmured against her mouth.

"Don't stop," Libby said, her palms smoothing over his face.

"Why was it we decided we shouldn't be together? I forget."

"I needed time to think about all this."

"And have you thought about it?" Trey asked. "Because it's all I've been thinking about, Libby. And I just want to stop thinking and start feeling again."

She shook her head. "Trey, I—"

He pressed a finger to her lips and forced a smile. "I'll try not to kiss you. But, hey, you're welcome to kiss me anytime you want."

"I'll keep that in mind."

As Trey helped Libby pack up the rest of the books, he watched her move around the room. How the hell had he walked away from her that first time? He'd been too young and too stupid to realize what she'd offered him. And now that he'd had a second chance at it, he'd managed to screw it up somehow.

He wanted Libby to want him the way that he wanted her, with a need that bordered on irrational. He didn't want to have to hold back, to restrain his desire and wait for her to kiss him. He wanted her in his arms when he fell asleep at night and when he woke up in the morning, and he wasn't going to settle for anything less.

They worked through most of the afternoon, and for the first time, Trey had a chance to see another side of Libby. She was sweet and funny and open, and organized to a fault. They talked more about his childhood and his problems with his father and by the time they finished packing up the office, Trey felt as if he'd worked through some of his guilt.

He'd also come to realize that he was in love with Libby Parrish. Trey had never really understood what his married friends saw in a lifelong commitment to one woman. But after spending the afternoon with Libby, he could visualize a life with her, with a woman who understood his deepest fears and insecurities. But his experiences with women in the past had left him completely unprepared to make a future happen with Libby.

"That's it, then," Trey said, staring at the stacks of boxes.

"What are you going to do with all this?" Libby asked.

"Put it in storage, I guess. Until all the properties are sold, I suppose we'll have to keep it. The personal stuff I'll send to my mother."

"Well, I should go then," she said. "I've got some work to do at home."

Trey reached out and took her hand, lacing his fingers through hers. He drew her fingers up to his mouth and placed a kiss on her wrist. "Thanks for your help. I owe you dinner. Or a cake, or something."

"No problem," Libby said, smiling winsomely. She took a deep breath and pulled her hand away to rub her palms on her skirt. "Well, I'll see you, then."

"Right," Trey said, fighting an urge to pull her into his arms again. "I'll see you."

He watched her walk to her car from the office window. A rumble of thunder rolled in the distance and the sky was growing dark with clouds. The breeze freshened and suddenly shifted direction. Trey closed the window, then took one last look around the office. He'd put some things to rest today. He'd be able to leave his problems with his father in the past and move on with his life—a life that he hoped might include Libby Parrish.

As he jogged down the steps and walked outside, the wind began to buffet the trees along River Street. He ran to his Jeep and hopped inside, then pulled out into traffic. A moment later, the first raindrops splattered on the windshield.

Trey thought about the last time it had rained. He'd spent that night in Libby's bed, sneaking away in the early morning light. He flipped on the wipers as he turned onto Hamilton Street. Wind-whipped leaves swirled on the pavement and lightning flashed overhead as images of that night whirled in his brain.

He pulled into the driveway a few minutes later and drove to the old carriage house that served as a garage. A storm like this often brought hail, so he pulled the Jeep inside and ran for the house. At the last minute, he decided to check on Libby, to find out if she'd put her car inside. He knew it was a feeble excuse, but Trey didn't care.

As he cut through the azalea bushes, he saw Libby standing in the middle of the back lawn, her face turned up to the sky, her arms outspread. Her cotton dress was soaked and clung to her body as the rain dripped off her fingertips. Trey watched her for a long moment, stunned by her beauty, and then slowly started toward her.

Perhaps she sensed his presence or perhaps she'd had enough of the cooling rain. But when she opened her eyes, she looked directly into his gaze. He froze and they watched each other for a long time, both of them weighing the consequences of what they were about to do. And then, as if the rain had washed away the last traces of indecision, they walked into each other's arms.

Trey tipped her damp face up to his, covering her mouth and drinking in the taste of her. Their kiss turned frantic and he moved from her mouth to her cheeks and her eyes and her forehead, the rain cool on his lips, her skin warm.

They didn't have to speak, to verbalize what they both felt; it was there in every breath, in every sigh. They needed each other and, suddenly, all the rest of it didn't matter.

Trey scooped her up into his arms and carried her across the lawn. When they reached the shelter of the veranda, he set her on her feet again and kissed her, this time whispering her name over and over again. He would have been satisfied to leave her there, knowing that this might be all she wanted. But Libby took his hand and drew him inside, letting the screen door slam behind them.

They slowly walked up the stairs to her bedroom, the rain pounding on the roof and hissing on the hot pavement outside. The thunder of the storm obliterated all thoughts of the outside world. He'd been waiting twelve years for this, searching for a woman like Libby and never finding her.

And now, as they walked toward her bedroom, Trey realized that there was no other woman for him. There never had been. From the first moment he'd touched her, he'd fallen in love with Libby and now that he'd found her again, he had every intention of spending the rest of his life with her.

His hands skimmed over her body and Libby tipped her head back as Trey kissed her neck. Why had she even bothered to deny this need? Now that she'd given up the fight, Libby could only feel relief. She would take her pleasure from Trey and count herself lucky that they'd managed to find each other again. She'd worry about the rest later.

Her dress and hair dripped water around her feet. Trey moved lower and then cupped her breast. His warm mouth fixed over her nipple, the nub pushing against the wet fabric, a wave of sensation racing through her. Libby moaned, furrowing her fingers through his hair.

Frustrated by the barriers between them, she pushed him away and reached down for the hem of her dress. She yanked it over her head. At the same time, Trey shrugged out of his shirt, tossing it aside. Libby reached for the button on his shorts, but he caught her wrists.

"Before this goes any further, I have to run back to my house. I forgot something there."

Libby pressed her face into his chest, the light dusting of hair tickling her nose. "You don't have to," she said.

"Lib, we can't—"

"No." She smiled up at him. "The last time I was in Charleston, I took care of that. Although Harley and Flora Simpson might be angry, I took my condom business elsewhere. I thought it best to be discreet."

He wrapped his arms around her waist, pulling her body against his. "Good girl. This is Belfort, after all, and we wouldn't want to start any gossip." With a low chuckle, he steered her toward the bed. Trey stared into her eyes, gently brushing the damp strands of hair from her forehead and temples. "Are you sure you want this?" he asked.

Libby smiled. "I haven't ever stopped wanting it." She hooked her fingers around her panties, then slowly slid them over her hips and along her legs before kicking them aside. Then she reached over to Trey and stripped off his shorts and boxers, allowing her hand to brush against his growing erection.

His breath caught in his throat as she walked to the bedside table and retrieved the box of condoms. Libby handed them to him and he tossed them on the bed, then tumbled them both onto the four-poster.

She expected him to seduce her quickly, but Trey had other ideas. He roamed over her body, his lips exploring sensitive spots, his hands running along her limbs and torso. Libby closed her eyes and gave herself over to experience, letting him have his way with her, surrendering completely to the experience.

He pressed a kiss against her instep, then slowly worked his way upward. But this time, Trey stopped, his mouth trailing along her inner thigh. Libby held her breath and in a heartbeat he was there, his tongue parting her and finding the sensitive heart of her desire.

He teased and tasted, drawing her along with him until Libby's fingers were twisted in the sheets and her body arched against him. "Trey," she murmured, his name on her lips the only link left to reality. His tongue slipped inside of her and Libby cried out, a wave of pleasure washing over her. She felt herself teetering on the edge, but then, as if he could sense her excitement, Trey brought her back down.

He braced himself, levering up from the bed. "I want to feel you come. I want to be inside you when that happens." Trey reached over her to retrieve the box of condoms, then tore open one of the foil packages and handed it to Libby.

But Libby set the condom aside and began her own exploration of his body. Her lips found familiar spots on his neck and his chest, then teased at his shaft before moving on. His body was perfect, lean and hard, his skin smooth.

Everything that had happened between them, from that very first argument in her rose garden, had led to this. Somehow, time had collapsed and she was here with the boy she'd loved all those years ago. But he wasn't a boy anymore. He was a man who knew what he wanted and right now, he wanted her.

Libby picked up the condom and slipped it out of its package. Trey braced his arms behind him and watched as she drew it over his shaft. He held his breath and tipped his head back, a lazy smile curling his lips.

"What do you want?" Libby asked, letting her fingers drift along his rigid desire.

"I want you," Trey replied.

Libby pressed her hand against his chest and pushed him back into the pillows, then straddled his hips. She moved against him, his shaft pressed against her moist entrance. And then he was inside her, penetrating just slightly at first. Libby arched her back as she slowly sank down on top of him, burying him to the hilt.

He grabbed her waist and held her still for a moment. Libby remembered the first time they'd done this, how clumsy and awkward and unnerving it had been. But now, it seemed like the most natural thing in the world, to share this intimacy with Trey, to invite him inside her body.

"Slow," he murmured, loosening his grip on her waist.

Libby smiled and pushed up on her knees, then slid back down over him. "That slow?"

Trey growled. "You're bent on torturing me, aren't you?"

She moved again, this time sinking deeper. "I believe I am."

Trey reached between them and touched her, gently rubbing his thumb against her sex. "Then I'll have to return the favor."

Libby smiled, drawn into his little challenge and determined to emerge victorious. But as she moved above him, the tension inside her began to build and her thoughts became more focused on the waves of pleasure coursing through her body, centered on the touch of his fingers where they were connected.

He brought her close again, only this time she picked up her pace, leaning over him and kissing him deeply. Her hair fell around her face and his breath came in shallow gasps as their lazy lovemaking began to take on an unrestrained edge.

Trey murmured softly against her lips, urging her forward. And then, suddenly Libby was there, her body tensed and her nerves tingling. She gasped as the first spasm hit her, then cried out as exquisite sensations overwhelmed her body. She kept moving, driving him deeper until his hands clamped down on her hips and he found his release. The pleasure seemed to go on forever, her limbs going numb, her nerve endings alive.

And when it was over, she began to move again, very slowly, drawing the last shudder out of him. He groaned and then rolled her over beneath him, their bodies still joined. "I'm not even going to ask how you got so good at that."

"What I lack in experience, I make up for in enthusiasm," Libby teased. "That, and I read a lot of books."

They lay in bed for a long time, wrapped in each other's arms and listening to the storm outside. And when they were ready, they made love again, Trey stirring her desire and possessing her body like no man ever had.

As Libby stared up into his eyes, his hips nestled between her legs, she realized that she could spend a lifetime caught up in this passion. Now that she had him in her bed, she never wanted to let him go.

But deep in the most secret corner of her heart, she knew there'd come a time when her bed would be empty and her body unfulfilled. When that time came, Libby vowed to remember this moment, with him moving inside her, his handsome face suffused with pleasure. That would be what she'd live with and Libby was satisfied it would be enough.

A COOL BREEZE WAFTED through the room, the curtains billowing out from the windows. Trey opened his eyes to the early morning light, then snuggled up against the slender body beside him bed. He sighed softly, nuzzling his face into the curve of Libby's neck.

The rain had continued for most of the night, finally breaking the heat wave that had oppressed the area for weeks. The air smelled fresh and green, and the birds sang more vigorously in the live oaks.

He reached up and smoothed a strand of hair off her forehead. They'd been awake until just before dawn, talking and making love, then talking some more, all the years apart providing fuel for their conversation. He'd anticipated that when it finally happened between him and Libby, it would be like his wildest fantasy. And now that it had happened, he'd been proven wrong. Making love to Libby had been so much more than a fantasy.

It hadn't just been about pleasure, although the sex had been incredible. He'd made love to this woman for only the second time in his life, and it had felt totally and perfectly right. They belonged together—he knew it as he moved inside her, as he watched her pleasure increase and as she shuddered in his arms.

Trey found the symmetry of their relationship almost poetic. He'd never believed in love at first sight, but that's what had happened with Libby. It had just taken them a little time to find each other again. And now that they had, he didn't plan ever to let her go.

"Hey, Lib," he murmured, brushing a kiss across her lips.

"Umm?"

"Are you awake?"

She slowly opened her eyes. "I am now." Yawning, she drew her hand over her eyes. "What time is it?"

"I don't know. Probably close to eight. Maybe even nine. I thought maybe I'd go out and get us some breakfast."

She wrapped her arms around his waist and nestled into his body. "No, don't leave. I'll make breakfast. Or lunch. Or we'll have pie. I have apple pie in the freezer."

"All right. Pie sounds good. Can we eat that in bed? Now that I've got you here, I don't want to let you leave."

Libby sat up and brushed her hair out of her eyes, tugging the sheet up around her naked body. "I have to go to Charleston today. We're going to do a test taping of the show. We have to see how the new set and lighting look before we start taping next week."

Trey groaned. "You have to go?"

"I do," Libby said, leaning over and kissing him softly. "But I'll be home by seven or eight. We could have a late dinner."

"Then you're thinking you might want to see me again?" Trey asked. "This isn't just a one-night stand?"

She shrugged, then smiled coyly. "Yeah. Maybe we could try this again."

"And you're not worried about the gossips anymore?"

She giggled and then rolled on top of him. "Not so much. I'm doing exactly what I want to do and if they want to waste their time speculating about it, they can. They'll never really know how good it was anyway." She wriggled against him and Trey felt himself growing hard again. "After you make love to me again, maybe we should go out for breakfast."

Trey rolled her beneath him and gazed down into

her eyes. "I think we might want to wait on that, Lib. At least until you've had a chance to talk to the chief of police."

"Bobby Ray Talbert? Why would I want to talk to him?"

"He's the reason I didn't get on that plane to New Orleans."

She frowned. "What?"

"He hauled me into the police station on some trumped-up charges and then he told me if I continued seeing you that he'd arrest me again. I don't think he cares for me too much. He seems to have a crush on you."

"Bobby Ray Talbert asks me out twice a year," Libby explained. "Fourth of July and New Year's Eve."

"Maybe you should go out with him," Trey teased, "so I don't end up in jail."

"What you did to me should be against the law. It felt too good to be legal."

"According to Chief Talbert, it is against the law here in Belfort. Unless we're married, of course. Then it would be perfectly legal." He paused. "Maybe we should get married."

He kept his tone light and teasing, as if he were merely joking. But in truth, Trey wanted to see her reaction, to test her feelings for him. Had she ever considered a future with him? Was marriage completely out of the realm of possibility?

Her brow furrowed into a frown, then she laughed. "Right. With you in Chicago and me in Belfort? Trey, you don't have to make me any promises. And you don't have to feel as if you owe me anything. I know you're going to leave sooner or later, and I'm all right with that. We'll enjoy the time we have together and that will be enough."

Trey stretched out beside her, his arm braced against the pillow. "What if it's not enough for me?"

She fixed her gaze on his, as if trying to read the sudden shift in his mood. "What are you saying?"

Trey saw a flash of panic in her eyes and he chuckled softly. "Nothing. It's just...I'm going to miss you when I leave."

She brushed a kiss across his lips. "I'll miss you, too." Libby tossed aside the sheet and crawled out of bed, then grabbed her robe from the chair near the window. "So what do you want for breakfast? I can make waffles or pancakes. Eggs and grits. We can have biscuits and gravy."

Trey grabbed her hand as she passed the bed, yanking her down on top of him. "Right now, I'd settle for a few more minutes of you."

But as he kissed her again, Trey knew it was a lie. A few more hours, a few more days, would never be enough. He wasn't about to settle for less than a lifetime.

8

LIBBY MOANED SOFTLY as she opened her eyes. The sun had come up long ago but for the fifth morning in a row, she and Trey had decided to sleep late. There didn't seem to be enough hours in the night for them. She rolled over and snuggled against Trey's body, slipping her arm around his waist.

They'd fallen into a routine of sorts. By day, Trey spent his time overseeing the renovations next door, stopping by to share lunch with her if she wasn't at the station in Charleston. Later in the evening, they'd have dinner, the meal filled with conversation and good food, laughter and wine, as they recounted the events of the day. But they usually found one excuse or another to turn in early and then their night would begin, a long night of lovemaking.

Nestled in the curve of his arm, Libby kissed his shoulder. She'd grown accustomed to having him in her bed, his hair dark against her pillow, his limbs draped possessively over her body. It felt…right.

Libby knew it would be foolish to allow herself to depend on him. Trey had a career and a life in Chicago. When it was time for him to leave, she'd be devastated. But her affair with Trey had been exactly what she needed, a reminder that her life was there to be lived if only she was willing to take a few risks.

There would be other men, she told herself. Maybe not as wonderful or exciting as Trey. Though he was her first love, she had to believe he wouldn't be her last. She looked at his face, the features so familiar to her now, and a wave of emotion washed over her.

Tucked away, deep in her heart, a tiny glimmer of hope had begun to grow. Maybe there was a chance for them, slim as it might be. She didn't want to believe it, but she couldn't help herself. Libby had always been too romantic for her own good.

She pushed the thoughts out of her mind and carefully slipped out of bed. After grabbing her robe, she wrapped it around her naked body and then curled up in the chintz chair by the window. Beau had taken to sleeping in the chair, enjoying the benefits of a second home and a lenient hostess. But he was stretched out in front of the door and barely lifted his head to greet her.

Libby tucked her feet beneath her and watched as Trey slept, memorizing each feature of his handsome face. Some day, she'd want to remember the tiny scar on his chin or his impossibly thick lashes or his sculpted mouth. Someday, that would be all she had left, an image of him she kept locked away in her mind.

Trey stirred, then reached out to the empty spot beside him. When he didn't find her there, he sat up, rubbing the sleep out of his eyes. "Hey," he said.

Libby smiled at him. He looked so boyishly handsome in the morning, his hair all mussed, his eyes half-hooded. "Hey, yourself."

"What are you doing up?"

Libby shrugged. "Just watching you sleep."

He reached out his arm toward her and crooked his finger. Libby pushed out of the chair and crawled back into bed beside him. He pulled her up against his body, tucking her backside in the curve of his lap. "God, I love waking up with you."

"That's because I always make you breakfast," Libby murmured, slowly stroking his arm.

He rested his chin on her shoulder. "That's not true. And to prove it, I'll make you breakfast this morning. What are you hungry for?"

"Can you even cook?" Libby asked.

"No, not very well. I can make toaster waffles and I'm pretty good with cereal. I once tried French toast, but that was a disaster. I figure if I make an effort, you might offer to help."

"Do you want eggs and bacon or pancakes?"

"Yes, please," Trey said. "And I'd really love some of those biscuits you make. Maybe with some honey?"

Libby kissed his arm and then sat up, resting her chin on her knees. "I think we used all the honey last night. I'm going to have to wash the sheets, they're so sticky."

The doorbell rang and Libby groaned. Beau jumped up and barked, but Trey called him over and ordered him to lie down beside the bed. "Who'd be ringing the bell at this hour?" she muttered.

"It's probably Carlisle. I don't know why he has to hand-deliver your mail." Trey sat up and tossed the sheet aside. "Let me go down. I'll get rid of him."

Libby yanked him back onto the bed. "Don't you dare. I suspect he might have been the one to complain about you to Bobby Ray Talbert. I don't need him running over and telling the chief of police that you and I have been fornicating."

"Is that what we were doing?" Trey teased. "Can we do it again?"

Libby slapped at his hand as she slipped out of bed. "No, not now." She adjusted the belt on her robe. "I'll be back in a second."

The doorbell rang again and Libby raced down the stairs and pulled the front door open. But Carlisle wasn't waiting on the porch with a package. Instead, Libby found Bobby Ray Talbert waiting, his hat clutched in his hands. His face was flushed and he shifted nervously, back and forth, from one foot to the other.

"Mornin'," he finally said in a strangled voice. "I—I mean, mornin', Miss Lisbeth."

Bobby Ray always turned into a blithering wreck whenever she was within ten feet. "Good morning, Chief Talbert."

He laughed uneasily, his gaze dropping to his feet. "You can call me Bobby Ray," he murmured.

Bobby Ray usually preferred to approach her at the grocery store or the post office. He'd never once been brave enough to climb the front steps of her porch. "What can I do for you, Bobby Ray?"

"I was just over next door, lookin' for Trey Marbury. He's not home. You wouldn't know where he was, would you?"

"Now why would you think I'd know?"

Bobby Ray shrugged. "There—well, I'm not one to take gossip seriously—but, you know, there have been rumors floatin' 'round town."

"I'm surprised you're listening to gossip, Bobby Ray. Don't you law enforcement officers usually focus on facts?"

"Well, yeah...most times. But there are cases when a—a rumor might be just as helpful." He turned his hat over in his hand and idly brushed a speck of lint from the crown. "Would you mind if I came in? There's a few matters I'd like to discuss with you. Maybe you and me could have a glass of lemonade?"

Libby glanced over her shoulder. Could she really refuse the chief of police? If she did, Bobby Ray was bound to get suspicious and he was a stickler for the law. The last thing she wanted was for him to haul Trey out of her bed and charge him with fornication.

"All right," she said. "But I'm not dressed. Maybe you could walk around back and I'll join you there in a few minutes with a cool drink."

He nodded, a wide smile breaking across his face. "Well, fine then. It's a date." His smile faded. "I—I mean, not a date date. Not that I wouldn't mind a date...date. It's just that lemonade isn't...well, that's not what I meant."

"I understand, Bobby Ray. And I'll meet you out back in a few minutes."

"Take your time," he said, backing toward the steps.

Libby waited until she heard his footsteps on the side veranda. Then she raced back up the stairs, nearly tripping as she rounded the landing. She found Trey still lying naked in bed, his arm thrown over his eyes, the sheet tossed aside. "You have to get up," she whispered. She crawled over the bed and shook him hard. "Trey, get up."

Trey moaned, then rolled over on his stomach. "Did you get rid of Carlisle?"

"It wasn't Carlisle. It's Bobby Ray Talbert. He's waiting on the back veranda. I'm supposed to bring him lemonade."

"Good," Trey said. "I love your lemonade. I could use a glass of something cool. You think he wants to join us for breakfast? Maybe he could cook."

"You have to leave," Libby whispered. "And take Beau with you."

"Come on, Lib. I thought we'd spend the day together. I don't have any contractors at the house. I've got the entire day free." He grabbed her waist and pulled her back into the bed. "I'll do very nasty things to you if you let me stay."

"You can't! The chief of police is downstairs. Now get dressed and then wait a few minutes and sneak down the stairs. Go out the front door. I'll keep Bobby Ray on the back veranda until you're gone."

"Damn it, Libby, I'm not going to sneak out. Why don't you just tell Bobby Ray and Carlisle and the rest of the folks in town to mind their own business?"

"This is neither the time nor the place to argue about privacy issues."

"This is the perfect time," Trey teased.

"And what am I supposed to say? 'For anyone who cares, I am sleeping with Trey Marbury. He does unspeakable things to me in bed and I actually enjoy them!' After my announcement, I could answer questions, kind of like a press conference. Then they can slap the cuffs on you and lead you into jail."

"Maybe I should tell everyone that I'm the guy

who has every intention of making an honest woman out of Lisbeth Parrish."

"Don't be silly," Libby said.

"I'm dead serious," Trey countered.

"And what is that supposed to mean? Are you planning to marry me?"

"I don't know. Would you consider marrying me?"

Libby looked around for her dress on the floor and waved it at him. "This conversation is getting more ridiculous by the minute."

"Answer me, Libby. I want to know where you see this relationship going."

"I'm supposed to be asking the questions like that and you're supposed to be evading the answers." She untied the belt to her robe and let it drop to the floor. Then she shrugged into her dress and ran her fingers through her hair.

"Damn it, Libby, I'm tired of you dancing around the issue. I want to know where the hell I stand. Is this just about sex? Or is there something more here?"

"Gee, it's funny you should ask that. Because that's what I was asking myself twelve years ago. Was that first time, down at the river, just about sex?"

"Of course it wasn't."

"Well, you had a funny way of showing it." She picked up his shirt and tossed it at him.

"Me? I'm the one who wrote you six letters. And you never answered one."

"You're lying."

"Why would I lie about something like that? Libby, I thought our night together was incredible. When I got to Atlanta, I couldn't think about anything else. And when you didn't write back, I thought you didn't care so I stopped writing. I didn't come home because I didn't want to run into you. Seeing you again would have been too painful."

"I wrote you a letter. You're the one who never wrote to me. Don't lie to me, Trey."

"I'm not. I never got a letter from you, Lib. If I had, I would have come home the very next weekend. I wanted to see you again."

Libby shook her head, pressing her fingers to her temples. "We don't have time to figure this out right now. Just get dressed. I'll come over later and we'll talk."

Trey reluctantly crawled out of bed and picked up his jeans from the floor. He pulled them on without bothering to put on his boxers. "You know, Bobby Ray Talbert does not have jurisdiction over our love life."

"We have no love life," Libby said. "We have a sex life. That's normally not a permanent situation. We don't have to burden the people of Belfort with the incredible details of what goes on in my bedroom."

Trey grinning. "You think it's incredible?"

"You're missing the point. I just need you to stay on your side of the bushes until things cool down with Bobby Ray."

"Hell, nobody enforces those laws anymore. I'd like to see him arrest me."

"Just go home," Libby insisted.

"How am I going to be able to sleep without you?"

"Try. Close your eyes and it'll come to you."

"I'll come to you tonight, after Bobby Ray is tucked safely into bed," Trey said.

"No!"

"Then you come to me."

"No!"

She hurried out of the room and back down the stairs. Peeking through the kitchen window, she checked on Bobby Ray, then grabbed a pitcher of lemonade from the refrigerator and a pair of glasses from the cupboard. Libby pushed the screen door open with her backside and hurried over to the pair of wicker chairs.

"It looks like it's going to be another hot day," she murmured as she filled his glass.

"Folks 'round town get a little testy with this heat," Bobby Ray commented. "Yesterday, I warned Eudora Throckmorton about crossin' in the middle of the block and she hit me with her purse. I could have arrested her. That's a 243, assaulting a police officer. I let her go with a warning."

"That was very kind of you," Libby said. "Now, why don't you tell me why you stopped by? Did I do something wrong?"

"I hope not," Bobby Ray said. "Let's call this a preventative visit. I understand that Trey Marbury is a handsome, sophisticated city boy now and some women in this town might find that type attractive. I've heard the rumors."

Libby stifled a groan as she raked her hands through her tousled hair. She found a sticky spot at the nape of her neck and winced. How had she managed to get honey back there? "You know how the gossips are here in town. They'll say just about anything to make a story more interesting."

"I'm not going to let him run around stirrin' things up."

"Stirring things up?"

"Yeah. Stirrin' women up. We have an ordinance in Belfort prohibitin' fornication between two unmarried people. Granted, the ordinance was passed in 1889, when some hookers from Charleston showed up at one of the local taverns. But still, a law is a law, and I intend to enforce that law." He paused. "If you know what I mean."

"Do you really think that law is fair?"

He stared at her for a long moment. "It's there to protect the citizens of Belfort—and that includes you." He guzzled down the rest of his lemonade, wiped his lips with the back of his hand, and pushed to his feet.

"And what if two unmarried people are in love?" Libby asked.

Bobby Ray blinked in surprise. "In love? Are you in love with Trey Marbury?"

"No!" Libby said, shaking her head. "I was just posing a hypothetical." She cleared her throat. "That's a 'what if' situation."

"Right," Bobby Ray murmured, nodding his head. "Well, I don't think the ordinance says anything about love bein' an exception to the rule. I'd still have to make an arrest." He adjusted his hat, then pulled out his sunglasses and slipped them on. "There are people in this town who care about you, Miss Lisbeth. You live here and he don't. I'm gonna do what I can to make sure you don't get hurt. That's my job." He gave her a quick nod. "Have a nice day, now, ya hear?"

With that, Bobby Ray strode across the veranda and disappeared around the corner of the house. Libby sat back in her chair and released a shaky breath. This was crazy! It wasn't just the gossips anymore; now law enforcement was poking into her personal life. Libby pushed out of her chair, cursing softly as she walked back inside the house.

Was sex with Trey worth getting tossed in jail? She moaned, then raked her fingers through her hair. "Yes," she murmured. "Absolutely."

But it wasn't just about sex anymore. And her question to Bobby Ray hadn't been purely hypothetical. What if she was in love with Trey? Libby wandered through the house, then climbed the stairs, mulling over the possibility. She'd tried so hard to keep herself from falling in love, but when it came right down to it, she'd probably fallen in love with him that day in the rose garden. Or maybe she'd never fallen out of love.

But love meant total surrender, tossing aside all her fears and risking her heart. It also meant a wedding and a long happily-ever-after. When she reached the second floor, she turned toward her bedroom, then changed her mind and walked to the attic door.

The stairs were dusty and steep. Libby crossed to the windows and threw them open to let the stifling heat escape. She used to play in the attic as a child, dressing up in the old clothes that had been packed away in the boxes. She pulled an old sheet from the top of a cedar chest and lifted the lid. Inside, carefully packed with tissue paper, was her great-grandmother's wedding dress. When she'd been little, she'd decided that one day she'd walk down the aisle wearing that dress.

Libby carefully withdrew the dress and held it up in front of her. But as she pulled the skirt from the chest, a small stack of letters scattered on the floor. Frowning, Libby gathered them up, draped the dress over her arm and headed for the stairs.

When she reached her bedroom, she carefully laid the dress across the bed and then sat down at the foot to examine the envelopes. There were five or six smaller letters addressed to her with no return address. But it was the larger envelope that caught her eye. She gasped as she recognized the handwriting as her own.

"Oh, my God," she murmured, her gaze skimming along the address. She drew her thumb over the stamp, then stared at the words printed below. "Insufficient postage."

She shuffled through the rest of the envelopes, six letters written by Trey and addressed to her. They'd been opened. And her letter to Trey had been returned by the post office. A single first-class stamp hadn't covered her ten-page missive.

The only way they could have ended up in the attic was if her mother had placed them there. If her father had found the letters, she would have been punished immediately. No, this was definitely the work of her mother.

Libby clutched the letters to her chest and drew a ragged breath. This changed everything. Trey hadn't deserted her all those years ago. Maybe he had even loved her. She'd been so quick to accuse him of lying earlier that morning.

The new revelations spun around in her head. If he cared about her back then, maybe she did have a chance at a future with Trey. Maybe he'd been the right man all along. The *only* man for her.

TREY STROLLED OUT to the back veranda, stretching his arms above his head to work the kinks out of his neck. He'd been refinishing floors all day long and his arms ached from fighting the floor sander for eight straight hours.

He brushed the dust out of his hair and then bent down to give Beau a pat on his head. The dog was curled up on the veranda, choosing the quiet spot over the noise of the sander.

He glanced over at Libby's house and saw the kitchen light was still on. Trey wandered across the yard and stepped around the bushes, anxious to see her. He found her sitting in one of the wicker chairs on the veranda, the light from the back door illuminating her profile.

He stepped closer. "So, are we safe?" Trey whispered. Libby jumped slightly, as if he'd startled her. It was then he saw the tears glittering in her eyes. "Hey, what is it?"

He crossed the distance between them in short order, taking the steps two at a time. Trey bent down in front of her, capturing her hands between his. "Libby, tell me. You're crying."

Libby brushed the tears away and shook her head. "No, I'm not."

"Come on, don't worry about Bobby Ray Talbert. I'm not going to let him arrest us."

"That's not what I'm upset about. I—I was just looking at these letters," she said. She handed him a small stack of envelopes and he stared at them, confused. "Do you remember those?" Libby asked.

Trey examined them closely in the light filtering out from the kitchen, immediately recognizing the handwriting and the return address. "I wrote these to you from college. I thought you said you never got them."

"I didn't. My mother must have kept them from me. And here's the one I wrote to you. It was ten pages long. See, I didn't know to put enough postage on it, so it came back and she kept it."

"Why are you crying?"

"Because we lost so many years," Libby said.

"No," Trey said, shaking his head. "No, you can't think of it that way. Libby, if I *had* gotten this letter, I might have come back to Belfort and we might have tried to see each other. But sooner or later, our parents would have found out and forced us apart. Back then, we weren't strong enough to fight them and we probably would have gone our separate ways. We came back together at exactly the right time for both of us." He drew her into his embrace and stood, pulling her up along with him. "I don't regret what happened back then. I'm falling in love with you, Lib. Right now."

"I think I'm falling in love with you, too," she murmured.

He hadn't expected to say the words, but they'd just come out. And now that they had, Trey knew there was absolute truth in them. He stepped back and looked down into Libby's face. Her tears had turned to a tiny smile. Trey chuckled. "I think that was a pretty important moment there."

"I guess it was," Libby said.

"So what does this mean?"

She pressed her nose into his chest and shrugged. "I'm not sure. I've only been in love once in my life. I'm not sure how it's supposed to feel."

"Whoever he was, I'm glad he wasn't able to see what a great woman he had."

Libby took the letters from his hand and held up the thick envelope. "Read this," she said. "Then you'll understand." She took his letters and pressed them against her heart. "I'm going to keep these. They were beautiful letters, Trey."

"So where do we go from here?" He kissed her forehead, inhaling the scent of her hair. God, he hated not being able to touch her the way he wanted, not being able to crawl into bed next to her and hold her all night long.

"You're going to have to go back to Chicago soon. Let's see where we are then."

"Are you going to tell your parents about us?"

She shook her head. "Not right now. We don't need to figure out the rest of our lives right this minute, Trey. Let's just see where this goes."

Though she'd said the words, Trey sensed that she wasn't really sure about her feelings yet. She still kept something in reserve, a piece of her heart that she refused to offer. And until he had captured every ounce of her love, Trey couldn't count on a future with Libby. "I'll never hurt you. I promise."

She smiled. "I think I finally believe that."

Trey nodded and pulled her into another hug. "All right. That's a start." He furrowed his hands through her hair, then tipped her face up to his. "Come on. Let's go take a shower and then crawl into bed and make love all night long."

"We shouldn't," Libby said. "The last thing we need is Bobby Ray throwing us both in jail. I need to find out if he really plans to enforce this law before we actually commit another crime."

"I'll get up early and leave before Bobby Ray gets

up. Or you can come to my place and I'll send you home before sunrise." He paused as he saw the pained expression on her face. Guilt cut through him. He was pushing her too hard and she was backing away again. "All right, I'll go home and sleep with Beau. But he doesn't smell nearly as good as you do and he has hairy legs."

Libby giggled, then pushed up on her toes and kissed him again. "We could take a swim before we go to bed," she suggested. "Fornicating might be against the law, but skinny-dipping isn't."

"I think I'd like that." Trey tossed the letters onto the chair, then took her hand and pulled her down the steps. But she stopped him in the middle of the lawn and threw her arms around his neck.

"It's all too complicated," she said. "We should just sleep together and force the issue. Make Bobby Ray arrest us and throw us in jail."

Trey knew that her desire for him had overwhelmed her common sense and she'd probably regret her actions in the end. "We'll figure it out as we go along," he said, scooping her up off her feet and carrying her across the lawn. "You know, we still don't know who sent those two other letters."

Libby smiled. "I really don't care. As you said, they brought us together—that's all that matters."

When they reached the river, they quickly tore off each other's clothes and waded into the water. And later, after he'd kissed Libby good-night at her back door, Trey sat in his kitchen and read the letter she'd written him twelve years ago. His mind wandered back to the words she'd voiced earlier that evening, that she'd loved only one other man. After reading her letter, he realized he was that man. But he was a boy back then, still finding his way and wondering what life held for him.

Now he knew. He wanted to marry Libby Parrish. He wanted to make a life with her and start a family, to create something special. He wanted to be a devoted husband and a good father, and he was willing to do whatever it took to make that happen.

He just hoped that Libby would forgive him for his methods, because he didn't want to wait another second for their life together to begin.

THE DOORBELL RANG just as Libby finished mixing a piecrust. She'd found a new recipe for a Black Bottom pie she wanted to test and include in the new cookbook. She grabbed a dish towel and wiped her hands, then turned to see Sarah rushing into the kitchen. Her friend was waving a copy of the newspaper in her hand.

"Did you see this?" she asked. "It's yesterday's paper."

"I saw it," Libby said. "I haven't read it. Other than obituaries and softball scores, there's never much in the *Belfort Bugle*."

"There is in this issue, and everyone in town is talking about it."

"Oh, no," Libby said. "Don't tell me they've started printing gossip in the paper now. Trey and I have been very careful since Bobby Ray paid me a visit last week. I have to say, the sneaking around makes it even more exciting. By day, we pretend we don't know each other and by night...well, it makes things very intense."

"You're not going to have to pretend anymore. Item number five under new business for the city council agenda. Discussion of the repeal of ordinance 321.7."

Libby frowned. "Fornication?"

"Fornication," Sarah repeated. "And guess who brought the matter before the city council."

"Trey Marbury?"

Sarah nodded. "I drove past city hall and there's already a line. The Ladies' Auxiliary from the Baptist Church is selling lemonade and cookies outside and there are pickets on the sidewalk. This is the most exciting thing to happen in Belfort since Kitty Foster left a naked mannequin in the window of her dress shop."

Libby tossed the dish towel on the counter and smoothed her hands over the front of her dress. "I guess we'd better get down there."

By the time they reached city hall, the spectators had already begun filing inside. Libby stood on her toes as they entered the meeting room, trying to see over the crowd. She saw Trey standing near the front. He looked so different from the sleepy, tousled-haired man she'd sent from her bed that morning. His hair was neatly combed and he'd shaved. He wore his business suit and a silk tie, a stark contrast from his usual baggy shorts and bare chest.

She pushed through the crowd, worked her way to the front of the room and then tapped him on the shoulder. "What are you doing?" she whispered.

"Hey there, Lib. I'm glad you're here. I can use all the support I can get."

"Why should I support this? My personal life is about to become public debate."

Trey reached out and grabbed her hand, lacing his fingers through hers and then pulling her into a quiet alcove near the fire exit. "I figured if they wanted us to play by their silly rules, then we'd just have to change the rules." He bent close to kiss her, but Libby shook her head.

"This is not some game," she said. "This is my life we're talking about. The minute you stand up and oppose this ordinance, everyone is going to know why."

"Come on, Libby, they already know. This whole town has known our business since the day I moved back. I want to be able to enjoy our time together, don't you?"

He idly stroked her arm and for a moment, the sensation distracted her. She swallowed hard. "And the only way you can enjoy it is if we can fornicate freely in Belfort?"

His lips curled into a devilish smile. "Well…yeah. Maybe. If I want to spend the night with you, I shouldn't have to sneak out of your bed before dawn. Hell, last night, Bobby Ray was parked in front of my house until 11:00 p.m. And he was there again this morning at six. He's determined to catch me and one of these days I'm going to oversleep."

"Please," Libby said. "Just drop this, Trey. Come home with me and we'll figure out another way. We can always fornicate out of town if we have to."

Trey shook his head. "I'm not leaving, Libby. I'm here for a reason. This law should have been off the books years ago."

"This is ridiculous! I can't support you on this."

She spun on her heel and walked to the back of the

room where Sarah had saved her a seat. "He's determined to go through with this."

"Trey looks really good in a suit," Sarah murmured, leaning closer. "I mean, he has the whole rugged carpenter thing going for him, but that suit makes him look completely yummy."

Libby rolled her eyes and sighed.

A gavel sounded and the crowd in the room quieted. "This meeting of the Belfort city council will come to order." Sam Harrington, president of the council, surveyed the room and then whispered something to the other four members; they all nodded. "Due to the size of the crowd, we're going to get right to the matter at hand so you can all get home for lunch. I'd assume most of you are here about ordinance 321.7, prohibiting fornication between unmarried individuals. Mr. Marbury, present your case."

Trey cleared his throat as he walked to the front of the room. "Council members, most of you know me. I spent the first eighteen years of my life in Belfort and I recently bought property here, so I feel I have a right to oppose this ordinance on the grounds that it infringes on personal privacy as guaranteed by the Constitution."

An elderly man stood up. "There's nothin' in the Constitution that gives single folks the right to mess around! I didn't have that freedom when I was young, why should you?"

The rest of the crowd began to shout and Sam Harrington pounded on his gavel until the room was silent again. "Reverend Arledge, let's hear your views on this."

The Baptist minister stood up. "Repealing this ordinance is a test of the moral foundations of our town. What kind of message are we sending to our youth if we say that premarital or extramarital sex is acceptable? I would strongly urge the council members to uphold this law."

"How long has it been since this law was enforced?" Trey challenged. "We all know that there's illegal sex going on in town. Either fully enforce the ordinance or take it off the books. But be prepared to have a jail full of fornicators."

"Chief Talbert, when was the last time the police made an arrest under this ordinance?" Sam Harrington asked.

Bobby Ray stood up. "That would have been in 1923, sir," the chief answered.

"Miss Eulalie. You have something to add?"

The elderly woman stood up, her handbag tucked neatly beneath her arm. "Although I'm a God-fearin' Baptist, I agree with Mr. Marbury. This is a constitutional issue. I'm not sure I want Bobby Ray Talbert standin' in my bedroom every night."

The crowd broke into peals of laughter and Libby couldn't help but grin. The thought of Miss Eulalie even having a sex life was too outrageous to ignore. Or perhaps it was the image of Bobby Ray and Miss Eulalie engaged in compromising behavior in her bedroom that people found so amusing. Sam banged his gavel to restore order.

"She's just interested in the additional gossip," Sarah whispered. "More illicit sex means more to talk about with the bridge club ladies."

"I have a question to pose to Mr. Marbury." Bobby Ray Talbert turned to the crowd. "If he's talkin' about premarital sex, as an officer of the law, I don't have a problem with that—as long as he takes the marital part just as serious as he takes the sex part."

"There's a good point!" Carlisle Whitby cried. "Let's see him answer that."

"Yes," Reverend Arledge said, jumping back to his feet. "I'd like to know if Mr. Marbury has considered marriage as an answer to his...problem."

"Mr. Marbury?" Sam and the council turned their attention back to Trey. "Has that thought ever crossed your mind?"

Trey turned around to look at the crowd, his gaze finding Libby's and holding it. "It has. I'm not sure she'd accept my proposal. She still has doubts about my feelings for her."

"That's easy for him to say," Wiley Boone shouted. "But can he prove his intentions are honorable?"

Trey reached into his jacket pocket and withdrew a small velvet-covered box. He slowly opened the box and held it out to the crowd. They all—Libby included—gasped at the sight of the large diamond ring inside. "I'm still hopeful she'll come around. That's why I bought this ring."

The entire crowd turned around to stare at Libby. She felt her face flame with embarrassment. Everyone was waiting for her to say something! But what was she supposed to say? Was Trey actually proposing to her? In front of all these people?

She glanced over at Sarah to find tears gleaming in her best friend's eyes. Libby drew a steadying breath and then slowly stood up. "I—I have a question for Mr. Marbury. I'd like to know his views on long-distance marriages. After all, he does live and work in Chicago. Would he expect this...potential wife to follow him or would he consider staying in Belfort?"

The crowd turned their attention back to Trey. A tiny grin quirked at the corners of his mouth. "I think I could be persuaded to stay in Belfort. I have a nice house here, and this is where I grew up. The woman I love lives here. Why would I want to leave?"

The meeting room fell silent as everyone waited for Libby's response. Sam Harrington cleared his throat. "I think we've gotten a bit off topic here." The crowd didn't agree as they simultaneously shushed him. He rolled his eyes and then nodded to Libby. "Do you have a response to that, Miss Parrish? If not, we need to get back to the agenda."

Libby swallowed hard, her heart hammering in her chest. "I—I don't have a response because I wasn't asked a question."

"Mr. Marbury, do you have a—"

"Oh, for goodness sake, Sam," Eulalie Throckmorton scolded. "Can't you just hold your tongue and stay out of this?"

"Sorry, Miss Eulalie," Sam muttered. "Please, continue."

"I do have a question," Trey said, "but I don't want to ask it until I can be sure of the answer." He slowly circled the crowd as he moved down the center aisle of the meeting room, his eyes fixed on Libby, the ring clutched in his hand.

"You're going to have to ask the question, before I can give you an answer," Libby said, stumbling over a few spectators to get to the aisle.

When they finally stood in front of each other, Trey

reached over and caressed her face with his hand. She closed her eyes at his touch, the crowd fading away right along with her doubts. "You really want me to do this here?" he murmured.

"I think you should finish what you started," Libby replied, her eyes skimming over his handsome features.

Trey chuckled softly. "All right, here it comes." He dropped down to one knee and grabbed her hand. Then he cleared his throat and spoke in a voice that carried throughout the meeting room. "Libby Parrish, I've been in love with you for years. I didn't realize it until I came back to Belfort. And now that I have, there is no way I ever want to leave you again. If you agree to marry me, I promise to spend the rest of my life loving you, and that alone will make me the happiest man in the world. Will you marry me, Libby?" He let go of her hand, took the ring from the box and then held it out to her as he waited for her reply.

She didn't even have to think before she replied. Emotion welled up inside of her as she realized she couldn't imagine her life without Trey in it. "Yes," Libby murmured, her eyes filling with tears of happiness. "Yes, Trey Marbury, I will marry you."

He slipped the ring on her finger, then stood and drew her into his arms. He kissed her, so passionately that he stole Libby's breath away. The townsfolk in the meeting room leapt to their feet and began to clap and shout and whistle their approval. Trey wrapped his hands around her waist, then picked her up and spun her around. Libby held fast to his shoulders as she looked down into his eyes.

"You'd really stay in Belfort for me?" she asked.

"Sweetheart, there never was a choice. From the moment I saw you again, I knew this is where I belong. In your life, in your arms, in your bed. And in your heart."

9

"I CAN'T BELIEVE he did this. Of all the underhanded, rotten things Bobby Ray Talbert could have done on my wedding day, this has got to take the cake."

"Are you sure he actually arrested Trey?" Sarah asked as she pulled up in front of the police station.

"Trey called me on his cell phone from the back of Bobby Ray's police cruiser. He told me to bring money for bail, so I assume he's been arrested." Libby shoved open the car door and struggled to climb out of the front seat, her great-grandmother's wedding gown tangling around her legs. She held up the skirt, then brushed the lace-edged veil out of her eyes. "I swear, Bobby Ray will live to regret the day he messed with my happily-ever-after."

"Libby, just calm down. Bobby Ray is still chief of police in Belfort. Sassing him might just put you in a cell right next to your bridegroom's."

Sarah opened the lobby doors of the police station for Libby and then pushed the train of her gown inside as she followed her. "You know, Bobby Ray did have a teensy little crush on you. Maybe he's jealous that Trey is walking down the aisle with you instead of him."

Libby turned on Sarah, her anger at Bobby Ray

bubbling over. "I love Trey and he is the only man for me and what Bobby Ray thinks about our relationship doesn't matter. If I don't marry him today, I'll marry him tomorrow! And I'll send Bobby Ray the bill for twenty pounds of crab claws."

When they got inside, Sarah grabbed Libby's hands and pulled her to a stop. She reached up and gently straightened her veil, then forced a smile. "You look beautiful."

The anger dissolved from Libby's face. "So do you. I'm so glad you're my maid of honor. I couldn't have planned this wedding without you."

"As your maid of honor, I'm going to give you one piece of advice. When all else fails, cry. Tears can be a very persuasive strategy when dealing with men like Bobby Ray," she said.

Libby nodded, then turned and walked through another set of doors into the reception area of the police station. The officer on duty gasped in surprise when he saw her approach in her wedding gown.

"Can I help you?"

"I want to see Chief Talbert. Tell him Libby Parrish is here to fetch her bridegroom." She tapped her foot impatiently, then glanced back at Sarah who waited on the other side of the doors.

"So, you gettin' married or are you married already?" the desk officer asked.

Libby sent him a withering look. Then she picked up her skirts and walked past the desk toward the offices. "Bobby Ray Talbert, get out here!"

"Miss, you can't go—"

A few seconds after that, Bobby Ray lumbered out of his office, a powdered sugar doughnut clutched in his fist. A few seconds later, Wiley Boone and Carlisle Whitby appeared in the door behind him.

Libby stared at the trio in disbelief, her hands hitched on her waist. "I can't believe this," she muttered. "Did you three conspire to ruin my wedding day, or was this all Bobby Ray's idea? I want to see Trey right now." She brushed past the trio to the heavy iron door that served as the entrance to the holding cells. When she pulled on it, it refused to open. She glared at Bobby Ray, who hurried over to unlock it. "You have no right to hold him."

He frowned, his face turning red. "I'm the police chief in this town and I can pretty much do what I want."

"What's his bail?"

"Well, that hasn't been determined yet."

"I want to see him," Libby said. "Right now."

Bobby Ray opened the door and allowed her to pass, then followed her back to the cells. When Libby glanced over her shoulder, she saw that Carlisle and Wiley had tagged along after the police chief. Libby found Trey sitting in the first cell, dressed in his tuxedo.

He stood the moment he saw her, a slow grin replacing his pensive expression. "God, Lib, you look beautiful."

She paused and smiled. "Thank you." Reaching through the bars, she cupped his face in her hands and pressed a kiss to his lips. Then she turned on Bobby Ray. "Unlock this cell. I want to give my fiancé a proper kiss."

Bobby Ray did as he was told and Libby rushed inside the cell and threw her arms around Trey's neck. "I'm going to kill Bobby Ray," she murmured as Trey covered her mouth with his.

"Not if I get to him first."

Libby glanced over her shoulder. "What's his crime?"

"Well, I haven't really charged him yet. As soon as I locked him up, he refused to answer any of my questions."

"You have to charge me or let me go," Trey said. "Our wedding is supposed to start in a half hour and considering all the work Libby has put into this, I wouldn't want to mess it up if I were you."

"He don't have to do anything," Wiley piped up. "He's the police in this town."

"If you're arresting Trey for fornication, then you're going to have to arrest me, too," Libby said. "Because the last time I checked, it's really hard to fornicate all by yourself." Libby stepped out of Trey's embrace and held out her hands. "Maybe you'd better cuff me," she said.

Bobby Ray's face flushed beet red. "I—I just brought him in 'cause I wanted to have a little talk. Then Wiley and Carlisle here started eggin' me on and it turned into a big old mess."

"What did you want to talk to Trey about?" Libby asked.

Bobby Ray shrugged, his gaze fixed on his footwear. "I wanted him to know that if he ain't good to you, then I'm goin' to make his life a pure kind of hell. You're just about the sweetest girl I ever knew and I don't want to see you gettin' hurt, that's all."

Libby opened her mouth to chastise Bobby Ray, then snapped it shut. The man had such a look of dismay on his face that she felt sorry for him. She'd never realized that Bobby Ray's feelings ran so deep. "This wedding is what I want, Bobby Ray," she murmured, placing her hand on his arm. "I love Trey. I fell in love with him when I was seventeen, while you were chasing Mary Beth Warniman around town. And I want to marry him—preferably today."

"You goin' to treat her right?" Bobby Ray asked Trey.

"I am," Trey said. "And if I don't, you're welcome to throw me in jail."

Libby sent Trey a silencing glare. "Bobby Ray, if you let Trey out of this cell right now, then I'd be prepared to offer you a guest spot on my cooking show. You'll be more famous than the governor. You can make any recipe you'd like." Libby paused, waiting for her offer to be fully appreciated. "I understand you make a mean shrimp boil. We've never done a shrimp boil on my show."

"I'm told I make a good she-crab soup, too," Bobby Ray said.

"We'll make whatever menu you'd like," Libby said. "And I want to tell you that I have a lot of nice single women who watch my show who'd be very interested in a man who knows his way around a kitchen. Why, I bet you'll get stacks of fan mail. Especially if you wear that uniform."

"I'm known for my ribs," Carlisle said. "I'm sure your viewers would be interested in my secret sauce."

Wiley frowned. "I can't hardly boil an egg," he muttered.

"It's either Trey or the shrimp boil," Libby said. "Take your pick."

"Leave him in jail," Wiley said.

"I'd take the shrimp boil," Trey suggested.

Bobby Ray glanced back and forth between Libby and Trey. "All right," he replied. "I'm thinkin' that would be the best way to go."

Libby pushed up on her toes and gave Bobby Ray a kiss on his cheek. "Good choice. Now, can we please leave? We've got a wedding to attend."

Bobby Ray stepped aside, pulling the cell door open as he did. "I'm sorry I put you in jail. I just wanted to make sure Miss Lisbeth would be happy."

Trey clapped the police chief on the shoulder. "That's all right, Bobby Ray. I suppose that's all part of your job protecting the citizens of Belfort."

The chief nodded. Trey grabbed Libby's hand and hurried her out to the street. Sarah was waiting in the car, the engine running. "I'm sorry about this," Libby said to Trey. "I wanted our wedding day to be perfect."

Trey pulled her to a stop and gave her a kiss. "Sweetheart, someday we'll tell our grandchildren about the day the police chief threw their grandfather in jail for trying to marry their grandmother. It may rival that story about Lucius Marbury shooting Edmond Parrish in the behind."

Libby pressed her finger to her lips. "Don't you dare bring up that silly feud around my father. I had enough trouble getting him to come to this wedding. I don't want anything else to go wrong today."

"Your wish is my command," Trey said, staring down into her eyes, a devilish grin quirking his lips. "I love you, Libby."

Libby looked up at Trey, then threw her arms

around his neck and kissed him. "And I love you, despite your criminal tendencies."

"Sometimes, I wonder at the luck that brought us together."

"It wasn't luck," she said and smiled coyly. "I know who wrote those letters."

"You do?"

"I found the exact same handwriting on one of our RSVP cards. And you'll never believe who it was."

"Are you going to tell me?"

Libby shook her head. "I have to save a few secrets for the wedding night."

With a playful growl, Trey picked her up and spun her around, her veil floating in the warm summer breeze. "Then let's get married, Libby Parrish. Before I manage to break another one of Belfort's laws."

"That's a fine idea, Trey Marbury." Libby placed her hands on his cheeks and gave him a long kiss. "The sooner I marry you, the sooner this town can start talking about someone else."

Epilogue

"WHAT IS GOING ON across the street?" Charlotte Villiers asked.

Eulalie Throckmorton stepped over to the front parlor window and looked out at the trucks parked in front of Libby Parrish's house. "I'd expect they're here to pick up the tent. Don't you know? The wedding was last weekend. Trey Marbury and Libby Parrish tied the knot. Engaged and married all in one month. She claims it wasn't a shotgun wedding, but I can't help but have my suspicions."

"I don't understand why they had it outside," Charlotte said. "Especially with this heat." She fanned herself with her hand and then took a sip of her iced tea.

"It was a very small wedding," Eudora explained. "Lalie and I were invited, since we were responsible for getting them together—although I don't believe they're aware of that fact. We plan to tell them on their first anniversary."

"I heard her father refused to come," Charlotte said.

"At first he wasn't happy at the prospect of a Marbury in the family," Eudora explained. "But Lisbeth's mama convinced him. She had a change of heart about the Marburys. Carolyn Parrish and Helene

Marbury are lookin' forward to the grandbabies, the first generation of Marburys and Parrishes who won't be at each other's throats."

"How is it that you got them together?" Charlotte asked.

"Well," Eulalie said, "it was all my idea. We started with a letter. A very erotic letter, mind you. And that got the ball rollin'."

Eudora sat down on the chair opposite Charlotte. "Oh, but tell her about the research, Lalie. We went to that adult bookstore on the interstate south of Walterboro. My goodness, that was an experience. We picked up several interestin' items."

Charlotte gasped, pressing her fingertips to her lips. "You've been to an adult bookstore? Do tell. I've always been curious as to what kind of books they would carry. I suppose a lot of D.H. Lawrence."

Eudora frowned, considering the comment for a moment. "I can't say that we saw any books," she replied. "They had a lovely selection of magazines, though. And the novelty items were quite interesting. But we were mainly there for the videos. We really needed to see what was new in the world of sex."

Eudora carefully refilled Charlotte's glass and tucked a fresh sprig of mint on the rim. "Things haven't changed much," she said. "The young people still enjoy the basics. Although, there did seem to be more of an emphasis on costumes. And we did notice that sex in public places was encouraged in these films. And it wasn't always just two people, if you know what I mean."

"There were animals?" Charlotte asked.

"Well, I suppose there may have been a few films

that featured horses," Eulalie said. "But I'm speakin' of other individuals. I believe they call them corgis."

"No, dear, that's the dog," Eudora said. "It's orgies. With an *O*."

Charlotte lowered her voice. "Speakin' of sex in public places, I remember when I saw Libby Parrish and Trey Marbury in the ladies' room at Tarrington's. I do believe they were about to have sex when I walked in."

"That was our first outside confirmation our plans had borne fruit," Eudora said. "I am surprised at how successful we were. I think we should try this again."

Eulalie shook her head. "Oh, I don't know, Dora. It was an interesting experiment, but perhaps we should stick to the more traditional methods of matchmaking. I'm not sure I could watch any more of those movies. The plots are just so silly."

"I don't think people really watch them for the stories," Eudora said. "With all that groanin', you can barely hear the dialogue anyway."

"Is that right?" Charlotte said with interest.

"We still have them," Eulalie said. "We wanted to throw them away, but Dora was afraid the garbage men would see them and think poorly of us." She took a sip of her tea. "Would you like to see them, Charlotte? The ladies won't be here for bridge club for at least fifteen minutes."

"Oh, I couldn't," Charlotte said. "Although, I must admit I am curious. You know, before my Harold passed, he was the only man I'd ever seen naked. I've always wondered whether he was...representative of the average male anatomy."

"I'm not sure you can gauge that from these films. It seems that rather than talented actors, they prefer to hire men who are extremely well-endowed," Eudora said. "I could get one of them up on the video player in Papa's study. Do you think the other ladies might be interested in watchin'? Believe me, when I first saw it, I have to admit to gettin' a bit hot and bothered by it all."

Eulalie took one last glance through the curtains and sighed. "You know, Dora, we do have one problem. Now that they're married, they won't provide any titillatin' new gossip. Perhaps that's reason enough to find ourselves another couple to turn our efforts toward."

"I'm sure the ladies of the bridge club would like to get involved," Charlotte said. "We could make it a club venture."

"It could be considered a community project," Eudora offered. "After all, Libby and Trey are gettin' married and they'll be startin' a family here in Belfort. And isn't that good for our community?"

The three ladies picked up their iced teas and walked back to the study, chatting about their newest project. For the first time in years, Belfort had become a most interesting place to live. And Eulalie and Eudora Throckmorton were determined to keep things that way for a long time to come.

FIONA HOOD-STEWART
The Journey Home

Spanning the heather-covered hills of Scotland, the exotic glamour of Buenos Aires and the sultry heat of Miami. *The Journey Home* is a story of power, money, loyalty… and old buried secrets that refuse to die.

AVAILABLE NOVEMBER

AVAILABLE FROM BIG W, KMART, TARGET, BORDERS NEWSAGENCIES AND SELECTED BOOKSTORES.

Shop online at **www.eHarlequin.com.au**
or call **1300 659 500** (AU), **09 837 1553** (NZ) for home delivery

In-store 1st Nov

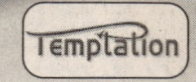

(Temptation)

Available Next Month

The Best Man In Texas
Kristine Rolofson

Wilde For You
Dawn Atkins

Seduce Me
Jill Shalvis

Wickedly Hot
Leslie Kelly

Not Exactly Pregnant
Charlotte Maclay

The Rancher Gets Hitched
Cathie Linz

AVAILABLE FROM

Target • K-Mart • Big W • Borders • selected supermarkets
• bookstores • newsagents

OR

Call Harlequin Mills & Boon on 1300 659 500 to order
for the cost of a local call. NZ customers call (09) 837 1553.

Shop on-line at www.eHarlequin.com.au

sexy, sassy and seductive

Harlequin Mills & Boon

Temptation

6 Brand New Stories Each Month

BOM01

Join The Book Of The Month Club today!

Harlequin's Book Of The Month Club offers you the convenience of receiving your favourite books delivered direct to your door at fantastic prices. Not only do you save money, but you also save your valuable time - don't waste it searching for a parking spot again!

Each month, our editorial staff select the Book Of The Month. Once you join, you will be sent our selection automatically each month - with no postage and handling charge! You will receive great editorial from our best-selling authors, meaning fantastic variety for you. If you prefer, you can return any month's selection, without missing out on any future selections.

A totally flexible way of buying the best stories every month - before they are available in the stores!

What more could you ask for?

- ☑ Free postage!
- ☑ Best-selling authors!
- ☑ Variety every month!
- ☑ Direct to your door!
- ☑ Great editorial!
- ☑ Value for money!

If you would like to sign up or if you have any questions, please call our friendly customer service team on:

Aust: 1300 659 500   NZ: 09 837 1553

Due to the nature of the program, prices vary each month. Members may return any selection if preferred and may cancel at any time. Harlequin Enterprises reserves the right to refuse any application, and prices and product may change. Harlequin Enterprises reserves the right to change any aspect of this promotion. This offer is open to Australian and New Zealand residents over 18 years of age.
Harlequin Enterprises (Australia) Pty Ltd ABN 47 001 180 918

One Christmas Night

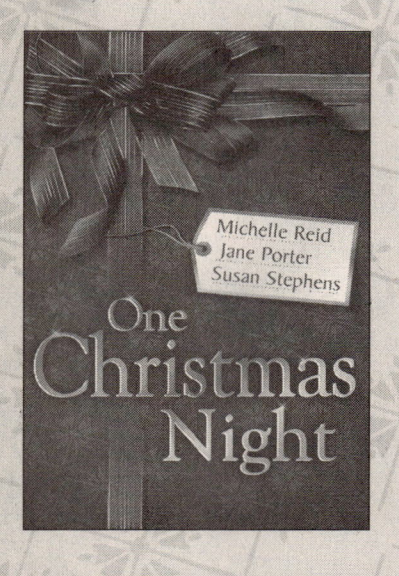

Includes 3 brand new sexy Christmas stories from bestselling authors Michelle Reid, Jane Porter and Susan Stephens.

A Sicilian Marriage
Michelle Reid

The Italian's Blackmailed Bride
Jane Porter

The Sultan's Seduction
Susan Stephens

AVAILABLE NOVEMBER

AVAILABLE FROM BIG W, KMART, TARGET, BORDERS NEWSAGENCIES AND SELECTED BOOKSTORES.
Shop online at **www.eHarlequin.com.au**
or call **1300 659 500** (AU), **09 837 1553** (NZ) for home delivery

ONC1004